Praise for The House War series:

"In a richly woven world, and with a cast of characters that ranges from traumatized street kids to the wealthy heads of the most prominent houses in Averlaan (sic), West pulls no punches as she hooks readers in with her bold and descriptive narrative."   —*Quill & Quire*

"This is a compelling story with riveting and finely wrought characters that will keep you up well into the night. This story will go down as one of the best novels in its genre, propelling West into the ranks of Robin Hobb and George R.R. Martin. It's simply a great read, don't miss it."   —*themaineedge.com*

"West is growing into a superb storyteller as demonstrated by this best effort to date with a fully realized world populated by a diverse range of nicely developed characters and a compelling storyline that hooks readers in from the start."   —*monstersandcritics.com*

"I am glad I read it. It is out of the ordinary for a fantasy tale, and is a *Hamlet* rather than a *Henry V*."
    —*Grasping for the Wind*

"Michelle West tells a wonderful tale…. I really like the way West draws the characters, making them, even the children, memorable. A lot of untold riches are implied here, and I'm waiting eagerly for sequels."
    —*Phildelphia Center City Weekly Press*

"This is a fantastic epic fantasy filled with intrigue and mystery that fans of Kate Elliot will appreciate…a vivid world that readers will believe exists with them in it."
    —*Alternative Worlds*

CITY OF NIGHT

A *House War* Novel

MICHELLE WEST

DAW BOOKS, INC.

DONALD A. WOLLHEIM, FOUNDER

375 Hudson Street, New York, NY 10014

ELIZABETH R. WOLLHEIM
SHEILA E. GILBERT
PUBLISHERS

http://www.dawbooks.com

First Paperback Printing, January 2011

1 2 3 4 5 6 7 8 9 10

DAW TRADEMARK REGISTERED
U.S. PAT. AND TM. OFF. AND FOREIGN COUNTRIES
—MARCA REGISTRADA
HECHO EN U.S.A.

PRINTED IN THE U.S.A.

This is for Gordon and Katri West.

Even if I could choose my in-laws, I don't think I would have had the temerity or self-confidence to ask them to consider being mine; they came with Thomas, for which I will be eternally grateful.

Acknowledgments

The care and feeding of a writer—or at least of this one—is often a thankless job. To ameliorate that in some small way, because I am enormously grateful for those in my life who do, I'd like to thank them.

I have a small house and a large extended family, and one of my youngest son's friends told his mother "so *many people* live there!" While this is not actually true, it might as well be. My mother and father, Ken and Tami Sagara, my husband, Thomas West, my two sons, Ross and Daniel, hold the fort. They shop, clean, and eat around me when I'm writing, which means I *can* write. They also listen to me fret and complain, but I'd probably do that anyway. Thomas first-reads as well.

My extended family: John & Kristen Chew and their two sons, Jamie and Liam, bring the world to the writer when the writer is being a deadline-obsessed hermit. They frequently accompany my brother and his wife, and there's something comforting about the sound of the Wii in the living room, because it means someone's having fun.

My *very* extended family: Terry Pearson, who reads everything in the roughest possible form any person but me will ever see it in, and the denizens of both the Michelle West Yahoo group and my livejournal, who patiently endure the long gaps in my on-line participation. I know that some writers need to interact and be social; it energizes them. It energizes me, too—but on occasion it's the type of energy that makes it harder for me to sit still in front of a keyboard, and when I realize that's happening, I do shut down a bit.

When the book is finished, I send it to my editor, Sheila Gilbert. It really is like sending a child to their cousin's after all these years; inasmuch as a business that weds creativity can be, DAW is part of my family. I felt that way seeing Sheila, Marsha, and Betsy (Wollheim) at the Worldcon in Montreal, and I felt that way about those who couldn't make it, like Debra Euler. I also want to mention Joshua Starr, who is the very helpful person who answers the phone when I call these days. It is a blessing to be able to send the book that I worked on for over a year to them.

Prologue

11th of Wittan 409 AA
Averalaan

WATER LAPPED AGAINST THE curved sides of the ships that lined the docks in the harbor over-seen by the Port Authority. This gentle but persistent slap of sea against bow wasn't always silent—but at the height of day in the Summer, other noises, louder and more insistent, held sway.

Cursing, some genial, some jovial, but most ill-tempered, issued forth in a dozen different languages from the mouths of sailors as they lowered gangplanks into crowds and maneuvered cargo hoisted by nets or hooks from the hidden, but cavernous, ships' holds. Men in clothing fine enough to distinguish them from these sailors were little better in their choice of words, and these, too, arms free of burden, came streaming down the planks, anxious for solid ground beneath their feet.

The breeze that came from the sea was strong enough to kick flags from their limp positions at the top of masts, and these flags, higher by far than the roofs of the tallest buildings found in the Free Towns, made the port look like an odd, floating city, or perhaps a small empire, for each ship was rumored to be its own small nation, and laws on the deck were the captain's laws. Three ships east, flag flying high, was the full sun against an azure that suggested sky; beside it, in purple and gray, a merchant ship declared its allegiance. The ships themselves differed in size and style, just as manors might; they shared the long, long stretch of dock because there was no other way to deliver their goods to the largest city in the Empire.

Only in port were the men governed by the laws of the Empire of Essalieyan, and the Port Authority had volumes of just such laws for visitors and those new to the City itself to peruse. A reminder, or a warning, they sat behind the harried clerks who looked at manifests, ordered checks of cargoes and containers, and made notes for the purposes of the magisterial guards whose duty it was to protect the interests of the Kings—or more likely their taxes—on this side of the water.

These clerks could be heard speaking in any number of languages, and the words that came most frequently to the lips of tired sailors never crossed theirs. They could be curt, they could be cutting, and they could—with ease—see through a person as if they had ceased to exist at all. But no one who wore the colors of the Port Authority—an austere teal with a hint of silver—was both crude and employed; they dispensed law in the fiefdom of the Port Authority as if they were nobles. Harried, overworked nobles in this season.

They could also offer answers to a person who asked when a ship was expected to dock.

It was from one such man that the pale boy with the very unusual hair had received such information, and he had come every day to the port at dawn, finding—somehow—a space in which to stand and observe that did not often put him in the way of busy, or grouchy, men.

Terrick Dumarr was the name of the clerk who had been called to dispense the information. He was, as clerks went, an imposing figure: Six feet, four inches in height, and some very large number of inches around, none of which were fat. He was a far cry from young, but he had weathered age with the spare grace that would not be out of place in the Commanders of the

Kings' armies; nor would he have looked out of place had he been standing by the far wall in chain mail with a sword at his side.

He was not, however, relegated to the far wall, much as he might have wished otherwise. He, like the other men and women, had responsibilities that could somehow be reduced to the sheaf of papers that littered the three desks behind his broad back. But if he was expected to work, he was also expected to eat, and he waited for the sonorous horns to sound out the hour.

He glanced around the large room. Support beams were placed throughout its length, but no walls divided the room, the exception being a single very thin wall, with its obvious windows, that served to separate the employees of the Port Authority from men so impatient or temperamental that they might consider violence at the receipt of news little to their liking.

Instead, small fences with velvet ropes that had both faded and frayed over time were erected throughout, an obstacle course for those who had business with the Authority. Some of these, well-dressed and reprehensibly well spoken, would journey, manifests signed and sealed, from the Port Authority to its sister in suffering, the Merchant Authority, where most of the commerce in the Empire was controlled.

But it was not these men, in various poses of irritation, boredom, or exhaustion, that demanded Terrick's attention; it was the boy.

Three days, Terrick thought, as he caught sight of the boy's hair; the rest of the boy, who was not yet of any notable size, could be lost in the crowd, but his hair, its pale locks rising in a spiral, could not. He was perhaps fourteen, if Terrick judged correctly, perhaps younger, and it was clear that the worn pack he carried upon his shoulders—at all times—contained the whole of his previous life, whatever that had been.

But he was quiet, this one, and when he had chosen to address the first clerk he could see, he had spoken in Rendish. The clerk—Barriston—was barely up to the task of identifying the language, but had he been unable to distinguish it at all, he would have been employed elsewhere, which would have been a blessing.

Instead, with his small scrap of knowledge a bandage over the gaping wound of his ignorance, he had bid the boy remain, and he had come to the area in which the Port Authority's employees took a moment of rest. "Terrick," he'd said, tapping the man smartly on the shoulder, "I have one of your barbarians outside."

Terrick, prevented from strangling Barriston by the necessity of both eating and breathing—the Authority guards frowned on what the Empire would have considered murder—had merely nodded. In any other circumstance he would have taken his time, but whoever the visitor was, he'd spoken to Barriston for long enough.

"He's young," Barriston felt the need to add, "and if he were Imperial, I'd give him the lecture on running away to join the merchant ships." Meaning, of course, that it was up to Terrick to deliver that lecture—in the appropriate language.

But when Terrick emerged from the relative privacy of the back offices to the wide and open crowd that comprised the Authority in its busiest season, he stopped walking, and received, as a reward for this moment of surprise, a back full of Barriston, scurrying head down to his wicket. Terrick mumbled something which Barriston heard as an apology; the large man didn't bother to correct this. Instead, he looked at the boy, his wide, gray eyes unblinking. Almost self-consciously, he straightened his back, lifting his shoulders and assuming every single inch of the height so many Imperial citizens found so interesting.

Barriston regained his place behind his own wicket. The boy was then directed to Terrick, who pulled a stool up to one of the wickets that had been closed—for the half hour—for lunch. It had taken the boy five minutes to reach Terrick, and during that time, Terrick had watched in silence, evaluating.

The boy wore an old cloak that trailed a few inches off the ground; it was sturdy, the color faded to a serviceable gray. His boots were a shade of brown that suggested both age and dust, but they were whole, although the laces were knotted in places, suggesting wear. He also wore a short sword, which he never touched; it hung on his left side, implying that he was right-handed. He was young for its weight, by Imperial standards—Terrick thought him fourteen, with a margin for error of two years on either side. There was nothing about the boy to suggest affluence, and indeed his weight suggested its opposite—but all of these things paled into insignificance beside the fact of his hair.

It was so pale a platinum as to be white, and it had been pulled from face and neck, greased, and twined around hidden wire. A spiral. It was dusty, yes, as the boy was—but it was unmistakable.

The boy was not injured; he didn't limp; nor did he cringe when people attempted to cut ahead of him in their impatience. He chose merely to turn sideways and slip out of their way, ignoring their glares or their angry words; he never chose to confront.

And when he stopped, at last, in front of Terrick's wicket, the gray circles under his eyes seemed to occupy half of his face. Terrick nodded at the boy, and the boy grunted back.

"I've come," the boy said in Rendish, "for the *Ice Wolf*. I was told you would know when it was due in port." He paused, and then added, "Or if."

Terrick nodded, and reached for the paper beside his elbow, as if it contained information that he didn't readily have. He leafed through the paper, the Essalieyanese words blurring until they were odd scratches, as they had once been in his youth. "It's due in three days, but those are sailing days; it may be delayed by a day or two."

"Which dock?"

"Seven," he replied.

"Three days."

Terrick nodded. He felt, rather than saw, Barriston's harried glare. He even opened his mouth to begin the lecture one generally offered the young, but his jaw snapped shut before the words escaped. The boy wasn't running. "Three days," he said quietly. He did not ask the boy where he was staying. It didn't matter. He would be back, and Terrick guessed that he would wait by the docks, or as close as was safe, until the *Ice Wolf* made port, cast rope, and laid down gangplank.

Nor was he wrong. For each of two days, the boy had come; he was on the docks before the sun touched the horizon, and he lingered until the moon could be seen, bright and clear, in the humidity of the Averalaan summer.

On the third day, seeing him in the crowd, Terrick lifted his head; when the horns lowed the start of lunch, Terrick left his wicket, but instead of retreating to the relative quiet of the desks that lined the back wall, he braved the crowd. Not that the crowd was ever that thick when he chose to risk it; like the sea over which the Port Authority played Baron, it parted when he dove in.

The boy looked up as he approached.

"Come eat with me," he said, surprising them both. "I've food, and there's not as many of these damn people in the back. I'd be glad of the company."

The boy's eyes narrowed slightly; he had some pride left in him. But he was not suspicious, and in the end, he nodded and followed where Terrick led.

Terrick did, in fact, have extra food. A whole loaf, thick smoked meat, a round, soft cheese in the thin cotton cloth that gave it shape, and cherries. He had wine, but offered the boy water instead. He nodded at a chair, which the boy pulled toward the desk.

"Boy," he said, while he tore the loaf in two roughly equal halves, "why are you looking for the *Ice Wolf*? You're far from home, if you think you belong on its decks." He paused, ripping the two halves in half, and added, "I'm called Terrick in these parts."

"I'm called Angel," the boy replied.

Not a Rendish name. Not even close. Terrick recognized it as an Imperial word, although he couldn't recall what it meant. "Angel?"

"My mother chose it; my father accepted it. I was born in the Empire," he added. It wasn't a precise description, because the Empire was very, very large. But Terrick understood that it meant the boy was not born in the North, and nodded.

"A wise man doesn't stand between a mother and her son," Terrick replied.

A glimmer of a smile touched the boy's lips. It was there and gone again, and Terrick, with decades of life and observation behind him, knew that the boy's father was dead. And likely the mother as well.

But the boy surprised him. "My father used to say that."

"Wise man," Terrick replied, with a wry smile. His glance strayed to the boy's hair. And away. Years of working at the Port Authority had taught him how to talk, how to listen, and how to ask questions in a variety of tones—but there was no easy way to ask the question that hovered behind his lips. No way of knowing whether or not it would give offense. In the North, it would. But the boy was not born to the snow and the brief, brief summer.

"Do you speak Weston?"

Angel nodded. His mouth was dusted with bread crumbs, and he chewed slowly and methodically. When he spoke again, he abandoned Rendish, and instead adopted the informal and slightly accented Common that came from the West. "I heard what the other man said," he told Terrick softly. "Barbarian."

"Why did you not ask your question in the Imperial tongue?"

Angel shrugged. "I don't know," he said, swallowing. "Someone told me the Port Authority would have men who could speak my father's tongue, and I wanted to see if it was true." He took a long drink of water, and then said, "And it was. Are you from the North?"

"I was born there," Terrick replied casually. As if being born in the North was not significant. As if living in a city with more people in its sprawling walls than were contained in some small nations was, as it seemed to be for so many who lived here, a matter of accidental choice, a simple whim.

But the boy looked up at Terrick. "And you live here?" As if he understood the significance. As if he could.

"Your father did," Terrick pointed out.

"You were born in Arrend?" The boy pressed.

Terrick chose to take a long drink of wine; he drained the cup. Filled it again, noting the boy's serious expression, his dark eyes so at odds with his hair and the paleness of his skin. *Winter skin,* Terrick thought. Terrick's was as ruddy as an Imperial.

"Aye," he said heavily. He considered filling his glass again and managed—barely—to think better of it. Drink on an empty stomach, even at his obvious size, was ill advised, and he had lost the appetite for food.

The boy, this Angel, had not, but ate slowly.

"Do you know why your father left?"

Angel shrugged, but it was not a casual motion; it was forced. "He didn't like to talk about it," he said at last, after an audible swallow. He lifted his water glass, and took his time drinking, as if to hide behind it.

"He wouldn't," Terrick replied. "No more do I."

"I didn't ask," the boy began.

"No," Terrick said, lifting a hand. "It's why you're still alive. But if you've sense enough not to ask, you've got the wits you were born with. Why are you here, boy?"

"For the *Ice Wolf.*"

"Yes, I understand that much. But your father—" He hesitated, and then seeing the hair that the glass couldn't obscure, surrendered. Surrendering with grace was not a skill that Terrick had seen a need for in his youth, and he had mastered it in his later years with difficulty and reluctance. "Your hair, boy," he said, keeping his tone even and quiet. "It marks you. It's a statement."

Angel nodded, but he grimaced.

It took Terrick a moment to understand what it meant, and surprise kept him from comment. "There are men who would kill to be allowed that style," he said instead. "Even if it sets them apart. The inconvenience would not be an issue." He spoke stiffly, and more significantly, in Weston.

"They probably didn't grow up in the Free Towns," Angel replied. But after a pause, he added, "I didn't wear my hair like this when I was growing up."

"No, you wouldn't. It's not for children."

"That's what he said," the boy replied. "My father," he added, as if his meaning were not plain.

"Did he style his hair that way?" Terrick asked, striving for casual.

"No." The boy looked up as he answered, his eyes the color that steel would be if it were blue. They saw everything in a moment, those winter eyes; they saw the surprise that Terrick could not keep from his face, if only for a second. "You knew him." It wasn't a question.

"Aye," Terrick replied. "I knew him. And if I had to guess, this fool errand was undertaken on his behalf. He's dead," Terrick added quietly. "Don't look so surprised, boy—if he were alive, you wouldn't be here.

"But he didn't send you to kin. He didn't send you to keep you from starving. If he asked you to make this journey, he wanted—"

"He sent me," Angel said, his soft voice breaking the flow of Terrick's accented Weston, "to speak with Weyrdon."

Smoothing the accent out of his voice, and freeing it, in the process, of any signs of agitation, Terrick said quietly, "Think on it, boy. Think again. Reconsider."

"Why? Do you think he'll try to kill me?"

"There is every possibility he will do just that."

"Why?"

"Does it matter? The *Ice Wolf* is his ship, and if you're on it, you're his."

The boy's face, carefully neutral, gave little away, but he didn't seem surprised. Nor did he seem afraid. He was set on this course of action, and while it was admirable—after all, the death of kin was at the foundation of many great men—Terrick found that he was not yet ready to acquiesce.

He should have been, of course. Perhaps the Empire did, in the end, change more than just complexion.

"Take your hair down," Terrick told Angel. "If you're determined to do this, take your hair down."

Angel refused without opening his mouth. Or rather, without speaking; he had continued to eat while Terrick spoke. Only when he had finished did he speak again.

"If you knew my father," he said, with a dignity beyond his years, "you would understand why I can't."

"The man I knew would have cut off his own hand before he let his hair down. You said he did just that. Clearly, time makes its changes." He did not attempt to tell the boy that he might be mistaken, that the boy's father and the man that he knew might not be the same. Had he believed it—had there been the possibility of belief—he would have.

"The right to bear a sword," Angel replied, "isn't an obligation to use it; it isn't even an obligation to carry it all the time."

"It depends," Terrick replied, "on your duties and your responsibilities. Boy—"

"He was asked to leave," Angel said.

Silence. Terrick was not a man who was uncomfortable with silence, and he often privately despised those men and women who were—they filled it with useless noise and inane babble simply because they were afraid of what might be noticed if the words ran dry. But some silences were merely a lid over words. This, he now removed.

"I think," he said slowly, "that you do not understand Weyrdon—or any of the clans—if you can say that. It's possible your father chose, for your mother's sake, not to explain too much. But Weyrdon does not ask men to leave. If he feels that there is reason for them to do so, he kills them.

"Not all men serve the clans; not all men are born to them. Some that are not are elevated to their ranks. They're not Northern ranks," he added. "They're simpler, cleaner, and more absolute. Take your Barons," he continued. "They serve the Kings, but they rule their own lands. They cannot secede; secession is called rebellion here and it is a matter for war."

"He wasn't a Baron," Angel said, and this time, his eyes rounded in surprise. The red flush that spoke of anger, so obvious in the pale-skinned, colored his cheeks.

"No. It is not an exact analogy. But to leave is to be forsworn. Your life is forfeit, because without the fealty of your sworn oath, your life is meaningless."

"You're here."

"I was not Weyrdon's," Terrick replied.

"You didn't serve the clans?"

Terrick was silent for a long moment. At his back the horn began to blow; lunch—and this unexpected conversation—was drawing to a close. "No," he said, as he rose. "Lunch is over," he added. "And if we're lucky, the *Ice Wolf* won't dock before—"

"Before?"

Terrick met the boy's steady gaze, seeing both his evident youth and a hint of the steel that would serve him should he survive to be, in truth, a man. Without preamble, for the horn sounded a second time, and the wicket had to be filled before the end of the third, he said, "I served Garroc."

"That's—that was my father's name."

"Yes," Terrick replied heavily. He rose. "Leave the cups," he said, not looking over his shoulder, "and meet me here when my shift ends."

Terrick watched the docks. The ships' masts loomed, flags flying, over the surly crowds. The Port Authority boasted both large windows and tall ceilings, and he could also observe through the open doors—unless there was sudden summer rain, a distinct possibility in this humidity, they were not closed while the docks were in use. Over the heads of the people pushing past each other in their rush to stand in line—something Terrick was certain he would never understand, no matter how many years he spent in the City—he could see which ships had approached, and which had been given permission to cast ropes and lower planks.

The *Ice Wolf* was not among them.

Although he seldom concentrated on future work when so much work was demanded right now, he kept an ear out. The younger members of the Order of Knowledge watched the seaway; the merchant ships owned by The Ten—as well as those owned by Houses less distinguished by history and political power, but not by money—often employed a ship's mage, and they made their reports and asked their permissions when they were miles from shore. These reports were often taken to the Portmaster or his harried attendants, and he stopped one such young woman to ask about the *Ice Wolf*.

The *Ice Wolf*, of course, carried no mage—had there been one foolish enough to set foot on its decks, they might preserve the body—but the mages in the port's tower often called out the names of the ships that were approaching. No considerations were to be made for these ships, but the warning was appreciated nonetheless.

He asked the girl to keep an ear out for any mention of the *Ice Wolf*, and although she was surprised, she nodded and offered a brief half smile as the Portmaster bellowed her name.

But while he listened, he also kept an eye on the boy. He could see none of the father in the son, except for the coloring of his skin; even Garroc's hair had been a bronze that tinted gold in the sun's light. Garroc had been large, and Angel, at fourteen, was of medium height; neither too short nor too tall. He was slender, although Terrick's practiced eye could see the definition of muscle in his exposed lower arms and his wrists. He carried only an Essalieyanese short sword. A long sword would have been beyond his reach.

But he did not carry his father's ax. And he did not carry his father's name.

The Imperial notion of beauty was absent, as were the things that compensated for its lack: he obviously owned neither land nor title. He was not ugly; he could, if it weren't for the utter stillness of his presence and the existence of his hair, have been one of a hundred boys his age. But he had once again taken up position on the docks from which he might watch ships come into port, and he managed, with economy of movement, to avoid the men who might have cursed him for standing in the way. He waited, this boy.

Terrick, better than most, knew both the cost and the value of waiting.

Had he not waited the better part of two decades, trapped by the Port Authority wicket and old vows that had, as the years passed, become increasingly foreign? It was almost done, the waiting. One way or the other, it was almost done.

And what would he do, when it was?

When the sun began to sink, the boy entered the Authority building. The Authority building did not face west; the whole of its bank of windows, and its tall, wide doors, were oriented to the east, where the docks, and beyond them, the sea, lay. But the lengthening of shadows and the slow darkening of bold azure were enough of a sign—that and the thinning of the crowds. As people ceased their endless surge from ship to land, the wickets slowly closed, and the clerks began to make headway into the paperwork that any ship docking produced; they would work well into lamplight hours before they stumbled back to their respective homes. At the height of Summer, the working day was long, but it was not the length of the day that had wearied Terrick.

It was the uncertainty caused by a young boy. That boy allowed himself to be ushered toward the doors, but Terrick shouted a quick Weston request, and the guards, sweltering beneath the weight of chain hauberk and its underpadding, let him slip free of their subtle net. He slid between them with easy grace and approached Terrick.

"I'll be an hour or two," Terrick told the boy. "But there's dinner at the end of it, if you've nowhere else to be."

*   *   *

Angel waited in silence. One or two of the dozen guards the Port Authority employed gave him an odd look, but they held their peace. Terrick's barked order—or request—had carried the weight of the Authority, and as the guards and the rest of the clerks took down the frail, velvet barriers that somehow managed to keep frustrated men and women in narrow, straight lines, Angel stood beside the walls nearest the now closed doors, watching. Lamps were lit, and in the ceiling beams closest to the back room in which he and Terrick had shared lunch, magelights began to glow brightly; unlike simple lamplight, they did not flicker or dim.

The floors here were stone, and at that, a marbled stone that, when mopped and dried, reflected light as if it were glass. In the day, Angel hadn't noticed, because in the day, the floors were anything but clean; too much dirt, too much dust, and far too many people all but hid them from view.

Empty, the Authority now seemed like a vast barn, and the distance from door to wicket seemed to grow as he watched people leave. In ones and twos, the younger runners dressed in the two-tone teal and silver that graced all of the men and women—even the guards— made their way to the doors and let themselves out, nodding to Angel, some with obvious curiosity. He nodded in reply, but said nothing; nothing was safest.

Least said, his mother had once told him. He couldn't remember the rest. Found that he didn't want to, here. His mother would have hated this noisy building, with its angry visitors and its tired clerks. She would have hated the language, although her own could be colorful when the need for it arose. And she would, he knew, have feared Terrick, because she had always been uneasy with her husband's kin.

In all of Angel's early life, he had seen evidence of his father's people only three times, and twice, it had ended in a death. It hadn't been his father's death—but it could have been, and his mother knew it.

It was the only time that his mother, when urged to

silence by her husband, had actually obeyed. But she didn't trust the Rendish.

The third time, there had been no drawn sword. His father had not left the fields upon sighting the visitor, nor had he instructed his wife and child to go—and stay—indoors. He had looked up—he always did, and usually before his wife had even heard the distant movement of horses or men on foot—but he had again bent his back to his work, and he did not leave it until the man was almost upon the house.

That man, pale-haired and only slightly shorter than his father, had approached his father in the flats of fields that were not yet sown, and he had waited in silence for his father's acknowledgment. If his mother was the talkative one, if his mother was the hospitable one, his father was rarely rude, and Angel, working by his father's side to dig and turn the earth that would grow vegetables for their own use, had been surprised at how long it took his father to finish.

But he had risen, wiping his hands on the heavy tunic he wore in the planting season, and he had straightened his shoulders. He hadn't said a word.

Neither had the man. But the man's hair, rising above his head in an almost unnatural spiral, marked him clearly as Northern. As clearly as his father's hair sometimes did, it was almost identical. They had exchanged a glance, and then, as if that glance were words, they had walked together toward the copse of trees that served as a windbreak. Angel wanted to follow. He started to, but his mother called him back, and when he obeyed with reluctance, she caught both his shoulders, one in either hand, and gripped them tightly enough to cause pain.

But she hadn't said a word.

His father, from a distance, spoke with the stranger for maybe two hours by the fall of sun; he did not invite the man into his home, and he did not introduce him to his wife or his son.

The man, however, had walked toward them both,

stopping far enough away that Angel's mother could see he meant no harm.

"You are Garroc's son?" he asked, in Rendish.

With his mother's hands curved like claws across the ridge of either collarbone, Angel had contented himself with a voiceless nod.

The man had said nothing else. Instead, he had nodded once to Angel's father, a brisk nod, and he had retraced his steps, leaving the field and all sight of the farm. His father had waited until the man had vanished from sight, and then, in silence, he had picked up his hoe, motioning for Angel to do the same.

He had not explained the stranger's visit, and Angel knew better than to ask. But it had been hard, then.

He glanced at the magelights. There were magelights in the Free Towns, but only in the Town Hall and the mayor's residence; they were rare, there. Everything was. Here? They seemed to be everywhere; on long poles that, evenly spaced, were spread across the City, street by street, no matter how poor the buildings seemed to be; on similar poles that ran the length of the docks; in the windows of merchant shops in the Common—everywhere. Magic, it seemed, was common, so ordinary that the citizens of Averalaan didn't even pause in wonder at the evidence of it.

Was it any wonder that it was in this city that the *Ice Wolf* docked?

Terrick was the last to leave the back rooms. This was not always the case, but tonight he worked more slowly, forcing himself to be methodical. He checked manifests against ships, and signatures against signatures, setting aside one bill as suspect. In the quiet of the Port Authority building, he could work without interruption, and in truth, he often looked forward to the end of day, when the streets were dark and the long, long stretch of building at last fell silent. One or two guards would weather the night hours, but they knew all of the clerks, as well as the runners and the portly man who served as Portmaster in any season that wasn't the rainy one. They would not disturb him unless an emergency arose.

Nor, he thought, grudging it, would the boy. Glancing out of the door, he saw Angel standing quietly beneath the magelights. He was not sitting, and he had not chosen to lean against the wall; he did not fidget, and his expression was carefully schooled.

Can you use that sword, boy?

He shook his head. The wrong weapon, the wrong man. But still, the boy waited. Just as Garroc would have waited, in his position. Aye, Terrick thought heavily. Garroc's son. He signed off on the paperwork, tidying it into a meticulous pile in the center of his desk. Then he rose, removing his key ring, and made his way past the thin wicket wall and into the building itself.

Angel looked up when Terrick entered the room, and Terrick nodded. Together, they approached the front doors by which the two guards were stationed.

"Late night for you, eh, Terrick?" one said.

Terrick shrugged and grimaced. "And an early morning, come tomorrow."

"Trouble?"

"Not worse than usual."

The guard snorted and grinned broadly. "I've seen your definition of 'not worse.'"

Angel did not know the way to Terrick's home, and Terrick had intended to lead him there; at the end of any day in which ships docked continually, only the very young had energy for much else. That Angel was among the very young was not in question, but in a city the size of Averalaan, strangers with no coin to spend often found very little to occupy their time. Or at least very little that the magisterial guards did not frown on.

But Angel was clearly used to walking, from somewhere to the port, and from the port to somewhere. He started to walk, as if the path were so familiar it guided his steps, and Terrick, curious, fell in. He did not ask the boy where he went; he was content—and this surprised him—to follow.

Garroc's son followed the harbor's line until it reached the seawall. It was not a short walk, and further, was not in the direction of Terrick's home and much-desired dinner, but as they climbed the stairs along the seawall, Terrick understood the purpose of this odd pilgrimage.

In the moonlight and the starlight of the humid night, the walls curved out in a demicircle, and in its center, a lone statue stood. Or towered. Terrick stopped walking for a moment, to see what Angel would do: Angel continued to walk.

Night, Terrick thought. Night was the time that the people of Averalaan chose to approach this statue, this solitary edifice. It was superstition, and at that, a superstition that was entirely Weston at heart, which prevented sensible people from arriving in the daylight hours. Terrick knew this; he had come, himself, during the day. In the day, one could clearly see the towering figure of a man, carved from ancient stone that the salt winds had not managed to weather or destroy. Nor had the seagulls and the other birds that chose his shoulders as perches, unaware of the gravity and the import of his ancient legend.

He joined Angel at the foot of the statue; Angel looked up at the forbidding profile of a man in his prime. "Moorelas," Terrick said softly.

Angel nodded.

"Why do you come here?"

"Everyone knows his story," Angel replied. It was not the answer Terrick expected, but so little about this boy could be expected. "Everyone knows it. Priests, merchants, guards, children. It doesn't matter where you are, or where you go—you can see children skipping ropes and stone tosses, and you can hear them sing his name. Here. In the Free Towns. In any town in the Empire, I think.

"It's peaceful here, at night. It makes me feel like the world is a smaller place."

Terrick nodded, although in truth, Moorelas' Sanctum, as this statue was inaccurately called, had never quelled the onset of brief and desperate desires for home. "He is known, by a slightly different name, in the North."

"Oh?"

"Morr Aston."

"Do they talk about where he fell?"

"In the City of the Dark League, in the time of gods. He injured the god whose name we do not speak, but in the end, he was betrayed by his companions, and he perished before the god could be killed." Terrick looked up at the hope of the mortal world, if such a thing could truly exist in the time when gods walked the planes. "Why do you not visit in the day?" He expected the common lore to answer him: Moorelas' shadow was considered, by many, a harbinger of doom. And, Terrick supposed, it was a safe and tidy harbinger, as it could be so easily avoided.

Angel said, quietly, "I have. But I watch the docks during the days."

Terrick, slightly humbled, and not of a mind to share this, said gruffly, "Dinner."

Home was a set of rooms above one of the smithies in the Common. It suited Terrick in the rainy season; in the humidity of the summer months it was barely tolerable—but when he had first arrived on these foreign shores, the habits of his youth had not yet been shrugged off, and in the smithy, there was continuous warmth. In his youth, the village smith would have occupied the building, making rooms available for his sons and their wives—but in Averalaan, while smithing was an honorable trade, it was one of dozens. And the sons of this particular smith were not of a mind to make their father's space their home.

It was strange to Terrick.

More so, The Ten, with their disavowal of blood ties. But what could one expect of the City ruled by men who chose wives to bear children for their own fathers? Terrick had chosen his course, and he intended to stay the distance. He had learned.

He glanced at the boy by his side. "Is this the first time you've visited Averalaan?"

Angel nodded. In Rendish, he said, "It's very large."

Terrick chuckled. "Aye, it's that." But he fell silent again; it was seldom that he had company on his trek to the Common from the busy port docks. The Common at night was silent; magelights, well below the heights of the trees for which the Common was famed, were glowing brightly in the humid air. The sky was cloudless, the stars clear. The face of the bright moon was edging to fullness, but it was the dark moon he sought for a moment.

Years, he thought. Years he'd been here, and the moons and the stars were the same. The stalls, boarded over, and patrolled frequently even after sunset, were also the same, and if the men and women who occupied them had weathered those years, so had he. He had not lifted an ax since he had set his own aside. His hands ached a moment, remembering the ghost of her weight.

"Here," he said, more sharply than he had intended.

Angel heard the shortening of the syllable without apparently understanding it; he followed where Terrick led. The door that led to his room was to one side of the smithy, and the stairs that door opened into were narrow and steep, and framed by a wall to either side.

"You live above the smith?" was the question that drifted up Terrick's back. There was, in his tone, a mild surprise, and given how carefully neutral the boy had forced himself to be thus far, it caused Terrick to smile. But it was a pained smile, an echo of the smile he might have offered his younger self; he certainly would not have cared to offer that younger man anything as sensible as advice.

Thinking this, he made his way into the kitchen. The windows that fronted the Common were open to the moon's full light, which silvered everything it touched. In this half-darkness, he made his way to the lamp.

"I live in the dark," he told Angel.

"You don't have a magelight?"

"Gods, no. They're expensive."

"They seem to be all over the place."

"Aye, they seem to," Terrick said, struggling to light the lamp's oil. "But it's just light, and the lamp does me fine. There's a seat by the table you can take if you've a mind to sit; you've been standing all day. It won't take a minute to get food, but it's not fancy; I don't cook much in this weather, and I don't get many visitors," he added.

The boy surprised him. "Do any of the ones you get try to kill you?"

He ceased his fumbling with the lamp, although he did not turn back to the boy. In the darkness there was a quiet that light—any light—seemed to break. He schooled his expression—such a Weston phrase, that, and it now came naturally to him—even though the boy couldn't see it. Then he forced his hands to continue their work.

"That's an odd question to ask of a man who works as a clerk for the Portmaster," he said at last, choosing the words with care, but delivering them as if they were unimportant.

"It's not to a clerk that I ask it," Angel replied gravely.

"And did your father have visitors who were fool enough to try to kill him?" And did one of them succeed, boy, is that why you're here? The lamp flared to life, flickering as he opened the valve to allow more oil to burn. He lifted it and turned to catch the boy's wary expression. His own, he knew, gave nothing away.

"Twice," he replied. "My father sent us into the house; my mother closed the shutters."

"But your father came back."

Angel nodded.

"Did you see his enemies?"

"Not alive."

"And dead?"

"When my father was digging a grave."

"Did you notice anything unusual about them?"

"They were marked," he said. "Tattoos, I think."

"Their hair?"

Angel nodded. "Like my father's. But not the same."

He paused and then said bluntly, "Why did they try to kill him?"

Terrick snorted. "I don't know."

"But you're not surprised."

"No. I would have expected Weyrdon—" he lifted a hand. "Do you understand how far away from home your father was?"

"He was at home," Angel replied.

"Aye, perhaps he was. But he left Weyrdon, and none of us—not one—understood his purpose."

"Maybe he loved my mother enough to stay." A hint of steel in those words. A hint of defiance.

Terrick could have explained to the boy why everything he had just said was wrong; he opened his mouth to do just that, shutting it on the edge of the words. Did it matter, in the end? They were dead, Garroc and this wife, and all they had left behind stood before Terrick in a lamplit room.

Terrick shook his head. "I forget myself," he said. "We both have to eat; we can talk when there's food ready."

"There was a third visitor," Angel said, when food was on the table between them and bread broken. It was warm and humid in the confines of the small room, and the lamp cast shadows that reminded Terrick of large and open fires in a much colder clime, beneath the early night sky.

Terrick ate. He said nothing, waiting for the boy to offer more, but when it became clear that the boy wouldn't shoulder the conversation himself, Terrick at last set aside the caution and isolation of almost a decade. That he did it quietly, and with a minimum of fuss, did not lessen the fact.

"Tell me," he said, "about this third visitor."

Angel shrugged. "My father didn't send us away," he said at last. "I don't think he was surprised to see the man, but I don't think he was happy either. He didn't invite him into the house, he didn't offer to feed him—and my mother didn't either. They always did that," he added softly. "They fed everyone who stumbled across the field. If they didn't crush anything while they were doing it." He stopped eating for a moment, his eyes vacantly staring at the contained fire on the table. After a moment, his gaze became focused, and he pulled it away, glancing at Terrick.

"He was of Weyrdon, I think."

"You're not certain."

After a moment, the boy said, "He was of Weyrdon." Terrick nodded. "Your father spoke with him?"

"And he walked away," Angel replied, tearing bread into smaller chunks almost absently.

"The stranger said nothing to you?"

"He asked if I were Garroc's son."

"Nothing more?"

"Nothing. He nodded, and he left."

"How long ago was that?" Terrick was sifting through manifests and shipping schedules, the paper in his mind almost as readily accessible as the actual paper in his hands would have been. "Three years?"

The boy was surprised enough that he let it show. But he was careful enough to hold his words for a moment, and when he did speak, surprise had given way to the beginnings of suspicion.

Garroc, Terrick thought heavily, *he is your son.*

"It was three years ago. Why do you ask?"

"Meaning, how do I know?" Terrick smiled grimly. "One of the men left the *Ice Wolf.*"

"They all leave the ship."

"He left and did not return. I did not see him return to the port until the *Ice Wolf* had sailed north and back again, carrying a different cargo. He was not," Terrick added, "a man that could easily be missed in a crowd."

"Not by you, you mean."

"Not," Terrick said heavily, "by anyone. He is not a young man, and it was never his intent to remain in the Empire; it would have been beneath his dignity to absorb or reflect Imperial customs."

"My mother said Arrend is part of the Empire."

"And your father?"

"He . . . didn't agree."

"In this, trust your father. We make no war upon the Empire or its subjects," Terrick added, "but we pay no tribute to foreign kings. Make of that what you will." He paused and then added, "I mean no insult by this, Angel, but if you go to the *Ice Wolf*, you keep your mother's opinion to yourself."

If Angel had, in his caution and his reticence, proved himself to be Garroc's son, he proved himself to be more, or different, now. He nodded, his expression thoughtful, the passing insult ignored. Terrick himself, at the boy's age, would have been angry at the implication that he was fool enough to insult Weyrdon, or ignorant enough; Garroc would have been enraged. But the boy? Neither.

"Did you recognize him, when he left the ship?"

Terrick nodded.

"And you thought he might try to kill my father?"

"In truth, boy, while I thought of your father, I thought it highly unlikely that he would be able to find him. As I said, it's not his way to bend to foreign customs, and he was unlikely to find much help."

"He did find him."

"Yes, and it surprises me."

"And it doesn't, as well?"

Keen-eyed boy. Garroc's son. But for the first time, Terrick found himself wondering about the mother. Some of the mother—besides just the name—was in the boy, and if it wasn't the harsh cold of the North, if it wasn't the steel and the ice, it was as strong in its own way.

Were you happy, Garroc? Terrick thought, for the first time. As if it might have meaning.

"And it doesn't, as well. Where did you live?"

"In Evanston." He waited a moment, watching Terrick's face for some sign of recognition. When it failed to appear, he grimaced—and looked, for a moment, young. "Evanston is one of the Free Towns."

"The Free Towns? To the west of the Empire?"

"Between the Empire and the Western Kingdoms, yes."

"A good distance to travel." Again, he began to sift documents contained only by memory, this time leaving the familiar manifests and Port Authority papers for her maps. The maps with which he was familiar were only accurate along the coasts—which, given they were Port Authority maps, was to be expected—but the scale and distances for the much less detailed landlocked country were good; they would not account for roads or difficult terrain, but they would give him a rough estimate of distance.

"He made his way there directly," Terrick said. "And if possible, he traveled by horse or carriage for some part of the journey; he made good time both there and back. He was not known as a horseman of any quality," he added.

Angel nodded absently. "So you think he knew where to find my father."

"It looks that way."

"But the others found him, too."

"They did not leave that ship," Terrick replied heavily. "They may have left other ships from the North, but they did not stop by the Port Authority. We have some custom with the Northerners; it is why I was employed." In truth, his preference would have been to stand as a guard in the busy building, although the guards saw little battle. Even tired and angry people were aware in some corner of their minds that they depended on the goodwill of the Imperial Port Authority for their living.

"But not why you chose to take the job?"

"No." Terrick found that even the pretense of eating was beyond him, and rose, turning away from both light and visitor so that he might look out into the summer streets. At night, they were their own landscape, as different from day as North from South. He took a breath of humid, hot air, and expelled it from his lungs with a keen distaste. The homesickness that had characterized his beginnings here was strong, tonight. It could be laid at the feet of this boy, if he were of a mind to assign blame.

But he was practical; blame served nothing now.

"They did not pass through the Authority and I cannot therefore track their journey. They could have been months tracking him down; they could have been years. Garroc came for the Kings' Challenge," he continued. "As an entrant, he was not invisible."

"Wait—are you saying my *father* was in the Kings' Challenge?"

At that, Terrick turned, a half smile on his lips. "Had he taken the challenge some five years earlier, I believe he would have won. It is often a Northerner who wins the wreath," he added, "But if he did not win—and he did not—he was noted, and in the end, he chose to accept employment in House Kalakar." So much effort, to say the words.

"He served The Kalakar," Angel said, ignoring that effort without apparent awareness.

Stiffly, holding onto his anger with as much care as he had ever held anything, Terrick said, "No."

"He did," Angel answered quietly.

"No. He was employed—"

"He was a House Guard," the boy replied, his face shading, in the lamplight, to a definite red. Protecting, Terrick saw, his father's memory. Defending his dignity and his honor.

Unaware that in so doing, he was destroying Terrick's ability to do the same. "He could not take another master," Terrick all but shouted. "He served Weyrdon!"

The boy fell silent, and Terrick thought the matter resolved. But the boy was, in his fashion, still Garroc's son. "You can serve The Kalakar and serve the Kings at the same time. They rule," he added, "but they don't demand the deaths of those who choose to pledge allegiance to the Houses who also serve."

"You do not understand the clans. You do not understand Weyrdon."

"No," Angel replied, the heat slow to leave his cheeks. "But neither do you."

The silence that followed the boy's flat statement was as cold a silence as any that Terrick remembered from his youth. And in his youth, as in the occasional winter that crept in beneath the cover of the cold rainy seasons in the Empire, cold could kill. It was not, however, the only thing, and Terrick laid his palms flat against the surface of a crumb-dusted tablecloth to indicate that he had not—yet—reached for a weapon.

The courtesy—if such a thing was indeed within the purview of the Southern sense of polite behavior—was lost on the boy; he had made his comment as an observation, no more; he had no reason to understand how much of an attack it was.

Had he been, in truth, Rendish, he might well be dead, the courtesy owed guests one had offered the hospitality of the hearth notwithstanding. But he would not have offered anyone but Garroc's son this opening—and the child was Garroc's son. If the boy did not understand his birthright, if he did not understand his father's senseless betrayal of their entire life, it was not, in the end, his fault.

"Be careful what you say, boy."

Angel, eating slowly and methodically—as he had done at a lunch that now seemed in the distant past—swallowed. "It wasn't meant as an insult," he said carefully. "But you don't. You don't understand my father's role. You don't understand why he left, or for what reason."

"And you do?"

Angel said nothing. But it was a nothing that held no fear, no timidity. He was not bold, this boy; he did not try to stake out space by size or temper; he did not care, in fact, to cut out a place he might stand in and call his own. This, at least, Terrick had seen clearly when he'd watched the boy on the docks and in the Port Authority. But if he did not seek his safety in this most obvious of gambits, he did not relinquish whatever it was that made him Garroc's son.

Terrick waited.

After a long pause, the wait was rewarded.

"No," Angel said quietly. "I don't. I understand what he believed," he added, and for just a moment, the boy's loss was fresh, and his eyes, wide, were shadowed by it: death, and mourning that had not yet run its course. "But, Terrick, he was asked to leave."

"By who?"

"Who else could ask?" The boy now placed his hands, palm down, upon the tabletop, just as Terrick had done, but without the obvious anger to make of that gesture a statement. "He loved my mother," Angel said quietly, as if he now picked up the threads of an entirely different discussion; as if the discussion he was continuing could have the same import as the one he had—at least for now—abandoned. "And he understood the farm. He worked with the mayor, even if he didn't like him much. He taught some of us."

"Taught?"

"How to use a sword," Angel said. "How to kill a man." He looked away, his profile caught and heightened by the lamp's light. "It saved us, in the end, but it didn't save him."

"They came back to kill him," Terrick said heavily.

"They? Oh, the Northerners." As if he weren't one. "No. Not them. There are many things, my father used to say, that will kill a man. Most of those don't even know that they're killing us. The cold," he added softly. "Water. Fire. Time. Other things."

"He said that, did he?"

"All the time," Angel said, his voice uninflected. "But when he taught us to use the sword? He said, in the end, that you fight the things that *can* be fought. You fight those things as if they were everything—anything—in the world that could kill you, or that had harmed you, or your family."

Terrick nodded. "That, at least, I can believe. I can almost hear him."

"He also said that stupidity and anger aren't the same," the boy added, with a wince. "He had a lot to say about stupidity. Most of it ours."

"Why did he teach you?"

"He thought we should know. My mother—many of our mothers—didn't approve, but . . . he thought it was something we should know." He stopped for another moment. "When the rains come late," he said at last, "the Free Towns have problems with raiders. They cause merchants problems as well, on the routes through the Towns; if it's bad enough, the Kingdoms or the Empire will send men, quietly."

"And the rains came late."

"For three years," Angel replied. "He taught us. We learned. He wasn't the only one to die."

"And your mother?"

"My mother, as well. And Emily, and David—" He paused. Shook his head. "They were children. From another farm."

"And so you came here."

"Yes."

"To meet the *Ice Wolf*."

"Yes."

"What do you hope to learn, Angel?"

"Why."

"Why?"

"Why my father was asked to leave. Why he chose to live in the Empire. What he wanted, from Weyrdon, and what Weyrdon wanted from him."

"And then?"

Angel shrugged. "I don't know. It depends on his answer." He added, quietly, "My father wanted me to do this."

Terrick nodded. This, at least, did not surprise him. "And you?"

"Me?"

"What do you want?"

Silence again, a different silence. Terrick bowed his head. The boy had come this far to fulfill a duty that he, as a son, could not ignore. But that duty consumed all thought; it was the only future Angel could see. Beyond that? He had not considered.

"Will you tell me, in the end, what Weyrdon says if you survive?" He kept all hope and all desire from the words; only the fact that he had asked at all exposed them. But to a man from Arrend, it would have exposed everything. And perhaps, in some fashion, blood ran true, no matter where the child had been raised. The boy met his gaze, and held it, searching for something. What, at his age, and with his life, he might search for, Terrick could not be certain.

Nor could he be certain what, in the end, was found—but something was.

"If I survive," Angel nodded bleakly. "I give you my word, Terrick. If I survive, I will tell you what I know." He paused and tore a piece of bread into something that could comfortably fit in his mouth. "The bread here is so hard," he added, speaking as if to himself. Sounding, for a moment, much younger than he looked.

Then he drew breath. "I will tell you what I know, and I hope it makes more sense to you than it does—than it ever did—to me."

And after that, silence for a long stretch of time. Terrick let the oil burn; it was costly, but as he seldom entertained guests of any significance, he could afford the hospitality. There was never any question about Angel's significance. Boy or no, he was the son of the man that Terrick had served for much of his adult life. He watched the boy eat in silence, and found the silence difficult.

But words presented a different difficulty. Were the boy Garroc, they might have spoken, or they might have passed the night in companionable silence; were he Garroc, they might have argued, raising voices as if they were blunt weapons, and words as if they were edged. Garroc and Terrick had seldom come to blows—but not never.

Service and servility were only conflated in the confusing and complicated cultural grayness of the South, and nowhere more so than in Averalaan.

But against this boy? Terrick could not raise voice; could not even imagine raising hand. They had fought no wars together, survived no conflicts, tested no loyalties; nor had they felt the keen and biting edge of an oath's many restrictions, circling different sides of it, seeking the advantage of terrain. Seeking, perhaps, the truth that lay at the heart of all great oaths; that gave them the power to bind a life, year after year, to the Port Authority.

Terrick found himself mulling over words as if they were the sodden leaves that blanketed the Common at the start of the rainy season. They were thin and flat and limp, and they had no resonant power, not yet; power, with words, was something both given and taken—and how could one do either, when one did not have the measure, in the end, of the man?

Or of the boy.

Angel's hair, so pale it was almost white, rose above his face and his porcelain forehead like a crown. Like, in truth, a crown that fit poorly and might topple at even the slightest of turbulence. Garroc had done this, he thought. Garroc had taught the boy how to plait his hair, how to wire it, how to mimic adulthood.

But—and this from the vantage of years—was that not what they all did? Was it not how they all learned? By mimicking adults and adult behavior until the mimicry and the fact could no longer be easily separated?

No, it wasn't his age that made Terrick uncomfortable, for he had been such a boy, and seen many more such boys when boyhood had passed—thankfully— beyond his grasp. Not to one of those boys would he offer this embarrassing and tongue-tied silence. And why?

Because those boys were not foreigners.

This one was.

Angel could speak Rendish, and could even speak it well; he could openly declare his allegiance by styling his hair in that particular design. He could wear a weapon as if it were not a hoe, not a farmer's tool. But all of this was superficial; what the boy was, beneath these things, was hidden. Terrick—and Garroc before him—had never trusted the superficial to tell them what they needed to know; they read a man's intent by more than the color or style of his hair or the clan-marks, more common, that he wore across his skin.

But the boy's caution, while commendable, gave little away; were it not for the quiet comment he had made about, of all things, bread, he might have lied about his age, either raising or lowering the number. He stood on the threshold, this one, or perhaps on the fence; one way or the other, he would have to jump off.

And he would do that, tomorrow, regardless of whether or not he understood the decision.

"Angel," Terrick said quietly, when the boy had stopped eating for long enough that he might indeed be finished.

Angel met Terrick's gaze and held it, an acknowledgment that younger children often failed to offer. In the face of that steady gaze, Terrick momentarily lost the words, for there was, in the lines of the boy's chin and cheekbones, something of Garroc—the Garroc that Terrick had met in the snow and cold of a distant youth.

Angel surprised him. "You've met Weyrdon, haven't you?"

"Yes."

"His son?"

Terrick shook his head. "While he lives, he is Weyrdon. When he dies, perhaps his son, after him. Perhaps his brother, or a cousin."

"But—the hair—" He lifted a hand self-consciously to touch his hair, as if aware that he wore the hair the way another might wear a hat—it was external, not yet of him, if it would ever be.

"It marks you as Weyrdon, yes."

"But not the man who commands all of Weyrdon."

"A man does not exist apart from those who serve him. He is Weyrdon, but those who serve him are also Weyrdon. Those who serve will never be confused with the man who leads—but they will be seen as an extension of that man, more valuable in all ways than even the sword he wields, although the sword might be older. Weyrdon is judged by the strength of those men, and judged, as well, by the strength of their oaths." He let the words settle around the boy, wondering if Angel understood.

Angel thought about this for a while. "In the Empire, the ruler of the House takes the name. So the ruler of Kalakar is *The* Kalakar, and all those who take the House Name are AKalakar."

"It is not of the South you must think," Terrick said, frowning.

Angel's lips creased in a smile that was startling, if brief. It was unfettered, for a moment, by oaths or worry; it made him look young—or rather, appear as the ideal of youth. There was no caution at all in the expression. "My father—" he began. The smile dimmed, fading into something that was grayer and darker. It was, Terrick thought, very like the smile that Garroc had offered him so many years ago. "My father would have said that."

"Then I will stand in his stead," Terrick replied gravely. "I cannot take his place, nor would I be fool enough to try. The South, once you reach the *Ice Wolf*, is not your concern."

Angel, reaching for a slender rind of cheese, said, "But it is. And it was my father's as well."

"Aye," Terrick replied. "Do not look to me for explanations; I little understood his choice, years ago—and I understand it no better now." *But now, boy,* he thought, *I fear its weight and its consequences.*

"Then tell me about Weyrdon. You met him."

Terrick nodded.

"Did you meet him before or after you met my father?"

And allowed himself a half smile. He could not see where the boy's conversation would lead, but he was willing to follow it to its natural conclusion. Garroc's son, indeed. "Many years after," Terrick replied.

Angel chewed thoughtfully on the rind, and Terrick almost rose to get more food. But the boy chose to speak as Terrick placed his hands on the table to push himself out of his chair, and the boy's voice pulled him back down again, as if it were gravity.

"You said you served Garroc."

"Yes."

"And my father served Weyrdon."

"Yes."

"Did you give him the oath that he gave Weyrdon?"

Silence. The pause of drawn breath and gathered words. All of these words, Terrick rejected. "No," he said quietly. Just that.

"So you were friends?"

"We were."

"But he wasn't your lord?"

Terrick lifted both hands to his face and pressed his fingers against his closed lids. "He was," he replied at last, as he lowered his hands.

"I don't understand."

"No. You don't."

"But I need to."

"Yes."

"Can you explain it to me before the *Ice Wolf* reaches port?"

"No." He lifted a hand as Angel's mouth parted. "I can try," he said heavily. "But I fear it will make little sense to you."

"Little is better than none."

"That would be your mother speaking."

Angel's face showed a hint of surprise; it was a subtle shift of brow, a slight widening of the eyes. "It was something she used to say." His voice was quiet, almost gentle. "How did you know?"

"Because Garroc would never have said it. We hold the opposite to be true: A little knowledge is a dangerous thing. It is like the ice above water that looks solid, but is too thin to support a man's weight; you break the surface and the water takes you. Better never to trust that ice in warmer weather." He frowned. "You will excuse me if I attempt to salvage my reputation."

"Pardon?"

"I am your host, and I have invited you into my home for a meal. You are still hungry. I have therefore failed, and unless I wish to brave the fury of my ancestors' hearth spirits, I must make amends." He glared at the boy, and added, "I am getting more food."

He was rewarded by a flush that, in the dim light, would have been hidden by a darker complexion. But he was also rewarded by a rueful smile.

Terrick took his time gathering both food and wine. The lamplight wasn't necessary to the work, and he worked slowly and methodically, as was his wont. He was at home here, in a way that he could not have foreseen in his youth.

"Garroc was older than you are now when we first met," Terrick said quietly, feeling the boy's attention at his back. "He was not yet at his full height, but he was strong and quick—quick to think, quick to speak, but still cautious in action. We had, in our village, some problem with raiders from farther north, and we had seen fighting, and death.

"We did not like each other much when we were introduced; he came from a village some few miles through the snow, and I thought him proud and reckless. I distrusted him; he intended to fight in my village, and not, in the end, in his own. A way to minimize losses," he added. "His own. As he—and the men who came with him—were outsiders, it was a commonly held opinion—but we were desperate enough to accept aid. And he, although I did not appreciate it at the time, was desperate enough to offer." His hands had ceased their motions—what had he been doing? Cutting. He returned to the task, seeing snow and ice and the red spill of frozen blood that spoke of battle.

"We are often called a harsh people, for a harsh climate. There is truth in it; those raids were not the first time I had witnessed death, nor would they be the last. We do not—as the Southerners do—dream of peace. But we dream of strength, for there is safety in strength, if safety can be found at all.

"Leading men is not a simple task. Giving orders may appear simple to those who have never given them," he added, reaching for a plate, "but when you see the cost of those orders in the corpses of the men—and women—who followed them faithfully, you begin to understand the price paid by those who undertake the burden of leadership.

"It is not easy to be a good leader. It is very easy to be a bad one. Most of us, in the end, would become bad leaders," he added as he turned, carrying the plate back to the table. Angel was watching the fire, but listening to the words as he did. It was a small fire, and the words were Rendish, although throughout the meal they had wandered casually between their two tongues.

"Why?"

"Because it is impossible to be perfect, in this life. And when we make mistakes—and our mistakes are measured in the lives of those who are forced, by circumstance, to trust us—many of us will hide from the cost of our power, without surrendering that power itself." He frowned at Angel's expression. "In order to lead effectively, when we know men will die no matter what we do, we protect ourselves from pain by refusing to care or countenance death. We lay blame anywhere else. We hide from the truth of ourselves.

"Eventually, it is power that we are left with—but power unleashed from its moorings. We no longer remember why we took power in the first place, and the reasons we come up with to justify continuing to hold that power? They are all bad."

"My father never wanted power," Angel said quietly.

"No. But when we met, he had taken it anyway. I did not trust him, not then. But I learned," he added softly. "A few deaths, his men and our own, and I learned. He was younger then, and he burned, his eyes like dark fire. Things that angered or enraged me, he could accept as simple fact, as if it were snow or ice floe. He did not let his temper rule him—not when lives depended on it. And lives did," Terrick added.

"We are not afraid of tears, in the North. Grief does not unman us. The women are harsh," he added, "and often hide grief behind faces no warmer than stone. But we—we know how to grieve. He grieved for our dead as if they were his own, and he would not leave our bodies behind. The men, many older, followed him. I followed him. When we at last found the raiders, and destroyed them, Garroc and his men were no longer outsiders; they were ours. And we, in turn, were theirs. That was his gift, boy.

"I was by his side. He wielded an ax, then; they called him Stormfury, and—" Terrick laughed out loud at the memory, "he was embarrassed by it. Not even frostbite could redden his skin the way embarrassment did, and the old women loved to tease him."

"But why?"

"I don't know. Maybe it was their way of showing him that he had become—in so short a time—like a son. He would rather, he told me, face the raiders. He did not want our admiration, and he did not want our mute obedience. But he had at least the first, and if we were not mute, we listened more often than not, and it was his lead that we followed.

"And when he left the village, I asked his leave to accompany him to his home, or what was left of it, and he granted it." He paused, and then added, "I served Garroc, in the North. And when Garroc met Weyrdon, and I saw Garroc take Weyrdon's measure, I understood what would happen next." He wanted to stand.

He did not.

"Weyrdon was a man," he said quietly. "Older than either of us, but younger than I am now, he was unlike Garroc; in Weyrdon, with his honey eyes, it was said that Cartan walked the earth again—and in its fashion, Angel, it was true. I had seen Garroc, among the villagers, and I had left my home to follow him—but Garroc was to Weyrdon what the lamp is to the high sun.

"Garroc did not understand why men were willing to serve him. His humility was part of the reason they did, but he was not falsely modest, and as likely to issue a challenge at a perceived slight as any other man. He had had no desire to found a clan of his own, although he could have.

"But he understood, when he met Weyrdon, some part of what we saw in him."

"But you said Weyrdon wasn't like my father."

"He wasn't. What your father struggled to do, Weyr-don did as if it were simply a matter of breathing; he led. He walked among the dead, and he grieved for them, but their deaths—in our eyes—were ennobled by his grief and his gratitude. He came to the women to help wash the corpses of the fallen and clean them before they were placed on the funeral pyres.

"He could make himself heard—and felt—across the tented camps of a large army. His men did not worship him, but they revered him. He was like the warriors of legend," Terrick added. "And born to us in a time of need."

"There were wars?"

Terrick was silent.

"Terrick?"

But Terrick did not answer the question. Instead he said, watching the lamp fire and wishing that it were larger and louder, with a voice of crackling wood and timbre, "Garroc came to me after our campaign at the borders of Arrend. Five great clans were united behind Weyrdon's shield, and the eldest sons of many smaller clans bore spears in his vanguard.

"He told me he intended to offer his ax to Weyrdon. I knew," Terrick continued. "I knew, but I had avoided the knowledge for as long as I could. He was my lord," Terrick added, "in the Southern use of the word. I was his liege.

"He asked me to serve Weyrdon; he felt that Weyr-don would also honor my service. I refused."

"But why?"

"Garroc was the only man that I wished to serve."

"You thought that Weyrdon was worthy of his service."

"Yes. He was worthy of the service of any."

"But not yours." It wasn't a question. And it was. So many years, Terrick thought, since he had heard those words. So many years since he had refused to answer them. He might have refused now, without shame and without demur on the part of his guest.

Garroc's son.

"Perhaps," Terrick said quietly, "I felt I was not worthy to serve him."

Angel tilted his head to one side. He opened his mouth to speak—or possibly eat, as he seemed to never stop—but food didn't enter that mouth, and words did not leave it. Which was good; he was exercising some caution. Not even a guest called his host a liar with impunity.

Terrick rose, muttering about oil for the lamp. It was feeble, but he wanted to be free of the confines of the table. The boy would not press him for an answer, and he did not wish to surrender it. But the answer lay there in the silence, and the spaces between the words he had been willing to share.

Weyrdon was revered.

Garroc? No. Respected, yes, and followed. What he achieved, he achieved with struggle and work, and the dream of the achievement was always brighter, and more perfect, than the achievement itself.

Quick to anger, slow to awe, slower still to love. But the shadows he cast were the length of a man, no more and no less. He knew doubt and he knew despair, and he mastered them both with effort.

Terrick understood that man.

"So . . . he left you."

"No." Terrick shook himself with an effort that Garroc would also have understood. He returned to his chair, with oil. "I went with him. I was Garroc's man, and this was understood—Weyrdon was secure enough in his power that it was not seen as an insult to Weyrdon."

Angel was silent for a long moment. "And when he left Weyrdon?"

The silence was thicker and heavier now.

"You left with him."

"I could. I was not of Weyrdon." Terrick's breath was sharp. "Boy," he added, thickly, "I would have followed him into exile and I would have died at his side or his back."

"He would never have asked that of you."

Terrick's laugh was bitter and deep. "He asked it a hundred times."

Angel watched Terrick's face as his laughter faded; the bitterness remained. Terrick could mask his expression, but chose, at that moment, not to do so. He waited instead, wondering what the boy would say. Or if, in the end, he would say anything at all.

Angel's eyes were the color of winter sky in the lamplight when he at last shook his head. It was a slight motion, a contained one; he would speak, then.

"From what you've said, my father's departure from Weyrdon's side was a disgrace."

Silent, Terrick nodded.

"If he asked you to fight at his back, he meant you to face death—and facing it, risk dying. He would have asked that of you," the boy continued, after a pause, "because when he taught us to use these swords, he asked it of us, and we were younger and weaker. We didn't understand, then. We understood it later.

"But he would never have asked us to live in disgrace," Angel continued. "Possibly the children, or the old women, but I don't think so." Angel picked up a wedge of thick cheese. "He would never have asked it of you."

Terrick said nothing for a long moment. And then, rough-voiced, he said, "Boy, do you ever stop eating?"

Angel, half the wedge now in his mouth, laughed, and Terrick rose. "Sleep here," he said. "I'll wake you in the morning; I have to be down at the Port Authority by sunrise."

14th of Wittan, 409 AA
Averalaan

Terrick had learned to sleep in almost any weather, facing almost any threat. A warrior's trick—to take what was needed in the gaps of time that were offered. He had obviously fallen out of the habit, and it pained him;

it was not the only thing that he had lost with the passage of time, but it was telling.

The boy slept in the room, on the floor just beneath the open shutters, his face turned toward the bright moon. Her touch whitened his hair, and made his skin glow silver; the heat, at this time of year, was profound. As was so often the case with the young, sleep softened the edges of his expression, robbing him of years. Angel looked very much a boy.

But this boy, Terrick thought, in the silence of the early morning, had offered him some measure of peace. He would not have asked it—would not have dreamed that the asking would serve a purpose. Unasked for, he had offered Terrick truth: Garroc would not have asked any man to live a life of disgrace, bereft of honor or dignity. Not even Terrick.

That measure of peace, he had carried with him into the slowly unfolding, spare chaos that was the daily Common. Not all of the farmers or merchants had opened their stalls or parked their oddly designed wagons, but enough, used to the early morning routines of the City's varied workers, had; they charged a slightly higher price than they would charge in a few short hours, but Terrick, home after they had left for the day, paid their premium, purchasing bread, cheese, wine, and smoked meats before he returned to his home.

It was not unoccupied, for the moment.

Garroc's son. Terrick smiled briefly, and then drew breath.

"Boy," he said, in a harsh, Rendish bark. His smile grew as Angel startled out of sleep without completely evading its grip. "Do you intend to sleep all day?"

Given that the moons still ruled the sky, it was perhaps a less than generous question.

The mumbled apology that slid out of the boy's half-open mouth was entirely Rendish. The older man's grin broadened. For all the sleep he lacked, Terrick faced the morning as if it were a true dawn, and not another dismal, simple sunrise over a foreign city.

"I've prepared breakfast," he told Angel gruffly. "It's

not much—you've eaten more than five men my size, and I seldom have guests. But it's better than nothing; get up, wash your face and hands in the basin, and eat. But eat quickly," he added, glancing out the window. "We've little time before the sun crests the ocean, and I have a job I'd like to keep." This last, he said with a perfectly straight face. The boy nodded, rubbing his eyes with his knuckles. He didn't scoff, and by the lack of this, Terrick recognized, with a pang, the truth of his Imperial heritage. But Angel did rise, and he did clean up—inasmuch as a boy living out of a packsack could— and eat.

"Will the *Ice Wolf* be in port?"

"Waiting," Terrick replied. "If she's made harbor. If not, we've the day ahead of us."

Angel nodded, his glance straying to the dark streets of the Common.

"Nervous?" Terrick would not have asked a Rendish boy of Angel's age the question unless he wished to provoke.

Angel simply nodded. The grave glance he turned on Terrick was drawn, and tired.

Terrick's voice gentled as he spoke again. "You've been on the road, boy," he said as he pushed himself up and away from the table, the legs of the chair squeaking against the floorboards. "But you're almost there."

Angel nodded. He finished the last of the bread he had called so hard, and rose, pushing his empty chair silently across the floor.

"I don't know what to say to him," Angel told Terrick, as they traversed the empty streets. In half an hour, the farmers would be in the Common, and in an hour, the first of their customers would join them. Terrick would be installed on the stool in his wicket, listening to the complaints of tired men and women, and Angel would be waiting for the *Ice Wolf*. The Northerner knew which of the two would be the more difficult task, and he said nothing, waiting for Angel's words to play out.

"I don't know what to ask," he said softly. "I know I

had to come here. For my father's sake. For his name."
He glanced at Terrick and Terrick nodded. "But I don't
understand why my father couldn't come before he—
before. I don't know what I've got to say that my father
couldn't. Or didn't."

Above them, the leaves of the great trees stood like
anchored clouds, and the starlight, fading slowly, punc-
tuated the skies. Were it not for the heat and humidity
of the City in this season, the moment of quiet would
have made of the City a place where Terrick might feel
at home.

But Angel, unused to a city of this size, trudged by his
side, begrudging the South not one degree of its heat.
If sweat hadn't beaded on the boy's forehead, Terrick
would have wondered if he felt it at all. But . . . he didn't
complain.

He stopped walking for a moment, and Terrick grimaced; the Portmaster was Northern in temperament if
not in action, and he forgave dereliction of duty just as
coldly. He could not, it was true, attempt to have Terrick
executed, but his ability to exile Terrick from the small
fiefdom that was the Authority office had never been in
question. He said nothing, and after a moment, Angel
continued to walk.

"Do I offer him my sword?" he asked.

Take your hair down, boy, Terrick thought, but did
not speak; he had said it enough, and it was clear that
inasmuch as he could, Angel understood its significance.
"I am not the right person to ask."

"Because you never did?"

"That, too." He shrugged, walking a little more
quickly. "I don't understand what happened, between
your father and Weyrdon. But if the one Weyrdon
visitor you had was any indication . . . he was asked to
perform some duty in exile, and in secrecy. I don't know
what it was; I don't know if he succeeded or failed. Because I don't, I don't want to give you advice. If it's bad,
and you follow it, you'll pay. If it's good, and you don't
follow it, you'll feel like a fool. You are not," he added
quietly, "a fool. I do not know what you have to say to

Weyrdon, but you're cautious enough. You'll do fine," he added.

"You don't believe that."

Terrick grimaced. "Perhaps not. But I would like to believe it, and if your father talked to Weyrdon's man, and neither of them died—as you suggested—there's every chance that the belief is not unfounded."

Angel nodded, hesitant.

They walked in silence through streets that were waking to sound: footsteps, morning greetings, wheels that had seen too little oil in too long a time. In the Summer stillness, the sea breeze didn't push away the salt or the scents that gathered in the air. But the shade of night paled noticeably as they made their way toward the Port Authority. Terrick watched the skies, hazy with unshed heat, and he nodded to himself; he wouldn't be late.

As if that mattered.

He shrugged. Maybe it did. Maybe a lifetime of learned prudence—for he'd certainly little prudence in his youth—had become so ingrained it would ride his thoughts and actions forever. Maybe Weyrdon would see the boy and dismiss him for his Northernness.

And if he did? Terrick shook his head. He'd have his answer soon, for he could see, as the light strengthened, the distant sails of a familiar ship in the deepest part of the bay. He watched it in silence as he walked for a few minutes, and then he turned to Angel and lifted an arm.

"The *Ice Wolf*," Angel said, no question in the words.

Terrick nodded.

The boy straightened his shoulders, stiffening his spine; he gained a few inches as he did, although it neither added nor subtracted years. He asked no more questions, and his expression lost the nervous vulnerability that was so common in the unguarded faces of the young.

They walked to the Port Authority together, and when they reached the doors, Angel bowed to Terrick in a very Northern style. He wanted to tell the boy not to offer Weyrdon the same bow, but kept the words to himself. It was unlikely to offend anyone who was not seeking a reason to be offended, and if one were needed, Weyrdon would not have to look past the boy's spiraled hair.

"I'll wait here," Angel told Terrick, taking up a position not far from the Port Authority. He paused and then added, "Thank you."

Terrick nodded and turned toward the closed doors of the building. At this time, they wouldn't be locked, but they would be guarded; the guards were in the Authority building before anyone but the Portmaster.

A building such as this would never have existed in the villages or towns of Terrick's youth. Doors such as these would not have existed either, and as he opened them, he felt himself stepping across the threshold to another world—one which did not include Garroc's son. Or Garroc.

Inside the building the ropes were up, and the runners were leaving their first notes from the Portmaster at the various wickets. Today, Terrick's would be one of them, because the *Ice Wolf* was waiting the signal to approach the docks.

He made his way to the much more modest door that kept the visitors and the clerks on different sides of these wickets and opened it carefully, making his way to the wicket and the scrawled note. There was, of course, no manifest, and no hint of what lay in the *Ice Wolf*'s hold; they had requested permission to dock, and it had been granted. But Terrick's presence was required on the docks—if briefly—in order to obtain the manifests necessary to process the cargo. He had always wondered how the complicated processing of manifests—and the legal need for them—had been explained to the first Rendish ship to seek this port. He did not imagine it had been pleasant, and could not quite imagine that no blood had been shed in the process. But it had happened, and it hadn't happened on his watch.

He glanced at the windows, shuttered for the moment, and then rose, walking to his desk to retrieve the inkstand and well that he would refill many times before sunset's arrival heralded the end of another day.

Sunrise, on the other hand, had not yet begun this one, and until it did, he could not look past those closed shutters to see the back of the boy that Garroc had raised on foreign soil.

Angel thought of water: in the bay and across brow and arms and chest, salt of sea and salt of sweat, things that had to be endured. In the planting season, when the cold made sweat seem distant until the work began, and in the harvest, when the heat made the height of day a time to seek refuge in shade and stillness, Angel had endured. But he had had, at that time, a mother, a father, and a roof over his head.

Now, he had a ship in the distance. It was in no way home, although his father had come from its decks to Averalaan. He still couldn't think of his father—or his mother—without thinking of death and loss, and on the long road here, sheltered at sun's height by trees and the royal messenger service's standing stables, he had thought only of this moment.

But Terrick's question had taken root in thought, and he couldn't ignore it. If he survived, what happened then? What would Weyrdon ask of him, if he asked anything at all?

What had he asked of his father?

His father had never said. But his father, Angel thought, had died certain that, in the end, he had failed both his lord and his charge.

My father was not a failure. Angel's lips whitened slightly as he pressed them together, his neutral expression taking on a watchful, angry edge. He'd eaten, and he'd slept, and if he'd slept on the floor, there was still a roof over his head; he had the energy, now, for anger. He might not have it later, but it was better to spend it here, where it cost nothing.

He could hear his father telling him just that.

And he knew, as well, that he would never truly hear his father tell him anything again.

He waited while the sun edged up the horizon, watching the *Ice Wolf* as she sat in the bay. Watching, just as quietly, when she began to move. The Port Authority guards were more prominent on the stretch of dock that had gathered those men whose job it was to catch mooring ropes and secure them; Angel had watched them for three days. They were not the friendliest of men, but they reserved their curt words for people who were too stupid to get out of the way, and they stayed just as long as it took them to secure gangplanks, before drifting toward another dock and another incoming ship.

After they had left, men and women in the teal of the Port Authority would join their guards and they would meet the first few people to leave the ship; they would offer these strangers papers and ink—the latter usually carried by a younger person who was also dressed head to toe in teal—and the strangers would make some show of reading whatever it was they were expected to sign. Often it was a poor show, and in the cases of The Ten, most of the paperwork was dispensed with entirely.

But the papers, the ink, and the guards, adorned every single dock, regardless of the flags flown by the ships, and there were no exceptions made: The Port Authority had its laws and anyone who made port here was expected to follow them.

This much, Angel had observed over the long three days. It didn't surprise him to see three men emerge from the Port Authority building as its doors were at last pegged open. It surprised him slightly to see that one of these men was Terrick, but it shouldn't have— Terrick could speak Rendish, and he doubted that either of the other two who walked just in front of him could say the same.

The ship approached the dock, ropes were cast, caught, and looped around poles thick as old trees. Words were shouted—in Weston—from dock to ship; the words shouted back were Weston as well, but thickly accented, the syllables shorter and rougher.

Terrick said nothing; the crew on either side were clearly old hands, and the words might have been in a language birthed by the sea and all its demands, rather than by two different countries. When the gangplank was lowered, a single man stepped down the narrow and—to Angel's eye—wobbly incline, and he made his way to the flat of the dock at his own speed. He carried a staff; to call it a cane would be wrong in almost every particular—but had he carried a baby, Angel would have recognized him anyway, although he had only seen him once before.

He didn't know the man's name. His father had pointedly refused to even hear the question when Angel had asked it, and Terrick had also, obliquely, refused to surrender it.

The most senior member of the Port Authority now stepped forward, Terrick at his right; at his left, but lagging behind, a boy carrying an inkwell and a quill. The Northern man, his hair some sort of fierce crown over the pale honey of clear eyes, looked at both of these foreigners briefly, but it was Terrick who demanded his attention.

And it was to Terrick that he inclined his head.

Terrick raised a hand, an open hand, and held it in front of his chest, arm extended, for a moment. Angel thought it a salute of some kind, but he couldn't be certain; when his father had taught them the use of the sword, he hadn't bothered with gestures that had nothing to do with fighting.

But the Northern man inclined his head again, and raised the hand that held the staff, drawing the staff from the wooden planks as he did so. It was perfectly straight as he held it in the air, parallel to the dock, and he held it for longer than Terrick had held out his hand.

Angel could see Terrick's back, not his face. He wanted to move, then, to get closer, to change the vantage from which he watched, a mute witness. He could see the way Terrick's shoulders shifted, straightening his back.

He could see the Northerner's lips move, as the staff's end came to rest, once again, upon wood. But he could not hear the words the man said.

He wanted to.

And as if Terrick could hear that thought, Terrick himself turned to face Angel, unseen until that moment by any other on the dock. There was nothing at all in Terrick's face that could be called an expression; his lips, his eyes, the lines etched in his skin—they might be stone, for just a moment, a mask. Something to hide behind.

Angel understood.

He composed his own face in a similar fashion, although he felt he had nothing to hide. He then left the shortening shadows he stood in, and made his way down the dock.

Terrick turned back to the Northerner. Beyond the man's back, the Rendish sailors were busy; Angel could see them moving and hear—at a distance—the shouted Rendish curses they leveled at each other in their haste.

But he didn't watch them for long; the man was watching him, his gaze unblinking, his face as much a stone mask as Terrick's. A cold one, for a cold people and a land of ice and snow. It was hard to realize that his cold, clear gaze was gold—but it was merchant's gold, not wheat's gold.

Angel stilled for just a moment, and wondered bleakly if the man's eyes had always been gold, and he had failed to remember it, being caught by the strangeness of his hair, and the oddly veiled hostility with which he had been greeted.

No matter; they were clear now, and Angel knew that he gazed upon one of the god-born. He was not afraid of the god-born; indeed, as a younger child, he might have stood in awe of them, had he realized what they were.

But he couldn't afford awe today. He could afford only what he had been given, since the day his family had died: walking, one foot in front of the other, from Evanston to Averalaan, to this port and this dock.

By the time Angel reached the stranger, a second man had come down the planking, and this man carried pa-

pers that he handed to Terrick. Terrick took them and
made a show of leafing through them; the young assistant clerk stepped forward with his ink and his quill, as
the Portmaster proffered a different set of documents
to the second man. He in turn took them and made the
same show of leafing through them as Terrick had done
before he nodded briskly.

Angel waited in silence, as did the first stranger, the
man he had seen once before on his father's farm. The
Northerner waited in the same self-contained silence,
although his lips were compressed in a slight frown.
Clearly, the paperwork required by the Port Authority
was both foreign and beneath his notice.

But it was completed, and when it was, the Portmaster bowed and signaled an orderly retreat. Terrick, first
to arrive, was last to leave, and as he left, he briefly
touched Angel's shoulder. That was all.

Angel stood on the dock with the Northerner, the
sea lapping at wooden bow and round, thick pole. The
man with the pale spire and the long staff watched
him, as if waiting. Angel could play the waiting game
forever.

Forever was, in this case, five minutes, and Angel
knew this because, in his mind, he performed a simple
farm chore, putting everything but his body in motion.
Five minutes. He could mark time in longer ways, and in
shorter ones, but when he waited, he always chose some
way of keeping track of time; it was like keeping score.

The older man cleared his throat. "You are Garroc's
son," he said—in Weston. His eyes crinkled briefly, as if
the light on water had struck them unexpectedly.

Angel nodded. "And you are?" He also chose Weston,
as it came more naturally to him.

This caused a pale brow to rise, and one hand to
tighten on the staff. But Angel didn't move, and he
didn't speak again, and after a significant pause—feed
for the chickens entering the bucket—the stranger's lips
curved in a cold smile.

"I am Alaric," the old man said, in Rendish. "I advise
Weyrdon."

"I'm Angel," Angel replied, in the same tongue.

"Weyrdon is waiting for you."

Angel nodded, unsurprised. He shouldn't have been, but it didn't matter. In some way that defied logic, it made sense to him that his long trek from the ruin of the only home he had ever known would be significant enough that Weyrdon, in the remote North, would somehow know.

He approached the plank, but it was the old man's turn to play games. He did not move or step out of the way, and Angel knew better than to slide sideways around him. He didn't like the idea of wandering around on a ship trying to find Weyrdon, and he didn't think the welcome he would receive, without the permission of this grim stranger, would be worth the effort.

"Who do you serve," the man said at length.

Angel said nothing.

"Do you serve Weyrdon?"

And lifted his chin, meeting the old man's appraising glare. "I don't know," he said calmly. He could; the docks were Imperial, and he was still standing on them.

Again, the man's hand tightened on his staff.

A minute passed, two, five; the sailors were now standing loosely near the dockside of the ship, watching.

The old man offered Angel a second glimpse of his Winter smile. "A fair answer," he replied. "But not for one who styles himself of Weyrdon."

"I serve my father in this," Angel said softly. "And it was his request. If it offends, I apologize."

"But you will not change it?"

"No."

The old man surprised Angel, then. He laughed, and the expression shifted the lines of his face, robbing them of the dourness of age. "You are Garroc's son, indeed. Not as bold, not as aggressive—but it's in you, boy.

"We accept the mark as the honor paid to our dead, and we will allow you passage upon the *Ice Wolf*." He paused, and the lines of his face smoothed out once more. "But we accept it because you have lived in exile and understand it only as a mark of filial devotion.

Beyond this, no exception is granted. Come. Weyrdon is waiting."

Angel had never been on a ship before; he had sometimes taken rafts—of dubious durability—out on the rivers and the lake a few miles from the farm, but that was the extent of his knowledge. There, the water had been clear and warm; here it smelled and tasted of salt.

It was the salt that had surprised him the most when he had first made his way to the port; he could taste it on his lips, and feel it in the minute scrapes and cuts that he couldn't even remember getting. That and the smell of the City—all of it layered so densely it was hard to separate individual scents. He tried now.

Sweat, certainly, on these decks. The Northerners weren't clothed for the weather, as if heat were something to be disdained, a temporary inconvenience. They were bearded, but they did not—to Angel's eyes—look like barbarians or the savages that filled the colorful stories of traveling bards. They had scars, true, some visible across their arms and hands, some across their faces—but men had scars, his father had once told him; they were a type of writing.

He had seen the truth of it, even in Evanston, where many of the farmers had come from service to the Houses in the Imperial wars. He had seen missing limbs, had heard old war stories, or more common, the absence of war stories, the way the men turned a distant stare upon a random tree before they shook themselves, smiled, changed the subject. He had been young then; young enough to ask without a thought for their privacy or their pain. He had had no wooden sword, although he often picked up sticks, as young boys did, and the only time he had asked his father—who worked with wood in his spare time, because he disliked idle hands—to make him such a sword, he had seen the ice of the North in his father's eyes.

Swords are not toys.

His mother, tight-lipped, had commandeered the lecture, as she often did, but Angel didn't need to hear the rest of it to know that this was not a gift he could ask for again.

These men, these men were like the old soldiers—and the young—who came to the Free Towns; like and unlike. They wore their history across their bodies, each mark a story waiting to unfold—or more likely, a story shared only briefly by those who had been some part of its making. He was not a child now, and he did not ask.

Instead, he followed Alaric, past the men who stood, arms folded across their chests, eyes almost unblinking, as he passed.

But when he had almost reached the great, spiked wheel that stood beneath the mast at the height of the ship, one man stepped between Alaric's back and Angel. His hair was dark, which was unusual—a bear's brown, thick like winter fur.

"Boy," he said, using the Rendish word. "What news of Garroc?"

What he had not expected, Angel realized, was to hear his father's name spoken upon these decks. Not after speaking to Terrick, and not after listening to his father. The day his father had taught him to plait or wire his hair, there had been a lot of listening and very little questioning; his father had a look about him that discouraged curiosity when the cost of satisfying it was too high.

He almost didn't recognize the name, until the man spoke again, the syllables slower and more distinct, the name utterly clear. Angel gazed at this dark-haired stranger's scarred face, took in, at a glance, the fold of his arms as they rested to either side of his broad chest. His face was soaking—ocean spray or sweat, it was hard to tell—and his expression was completely neutral.

As if this were a test.

A test, and his father's name some way of passing it or failing it. He had been nervous since he had approached Alaric; he had spent his brief anger on the docks while waiting.

Or so he had thought; it flared, now, and it was sharp and cold in the summer heat. Of all games to play, of all the games he was willing to play, this was not one, and would never be one. He could hear his father's voice, the echoes of a life that was ended, urging him to be cautious, but he ignored it. Northern honor had had meaning to his father; Angel's honor, however, was of his own choosing.

Alaric paused and turned; Angel could see the fall of his robes shift. But he could not see the older man's face.

Nor had he need. "He died fighting raiders and defending his home."

The large man nodded. His expression did not shift or waver; his gaze was the unblinking gaze of a bird of prey. Or a vulture. Angel couldn't tell. But he had come here to honor his father, and he would not be afraid of his father's name. Not here. Especially not here.

Still, the man did not respond.

"He killed five," Angel added, the edge in the words unmistakable. A challenge. *Tell me,* he thought, his hand moving to rest inches above his father's short sword. *Tell me that he was a deserter. Tell me that he was a coward. Tell me that he was forsworn.*

But the man merely nodded again; his hands did not stray and he offered no response to the challenge that laced Angel's words, giving them a bright edge. They stood thus for minutes—and they were long minutes, although Angel could not force himself to think of farm chores as he usually did to mark time's passage.

But when the silence broke, it was the stranger who broke it. "You are his only son?"

Angel forced his hands to his sides. He couldn't quite relax, but the tone of the man's voice offered no cruelty, no mockery. Drawing breath before exhaling an inch or two, Angel replied. "I am. And it is to bring that word that I have come."

"Then deliver it." The man stepped out of his way. But he had not finished, not quite. "He was Cartanis' man, boy, and Cartanis knows his own."

Angel felt his throat constrict at the words—the unexpected kindness of a stranger. He would have swallowed the sudden tears that choked words and filmed his eyes, but he knew it wasn't necessary, here. What had his father said? *Men know how to grieve. In the North, men cry—but the women are harder and colder.* He had grimaced at his wife's back as he said this, and she had risen from her chores to glare at him.

"Do the women fight, in the North?" Angel had asked, when it had become clear that the glare was tinged with the usual affection.

"They fight in the South," his father had replied with a shrug, speaking of the Empire as if it were a foreign country, as he often did. "We all do what we must to protect the things we care about. Sometimes it isn't enough, but we're defined by how hard we try. Your mother wasn't raised to a sword, but she'd put a rake through a man's face to defend you."

Angel nodded, knowing it for truth. "But men cry?"

Garroc had nodded, lifting his head a moment at a passing breeze, an echo of spring in the growing heat. "Men cry."

"Why?"

And the silence that followed his question was the silence of old soldiers come from war who wish never to return to the truth of it. It was girded by a smile, by large hands ruffling Angel's hair—but it wasn't answered. Not then.

Now? He let the tears trail down his face. He did not sob; his mother was in him, and she had, in her way, been the more reserved, the more private, of his parents. But he met the stranger's gaze without shame or demur, and in answer—another act of generosity, so unexpected it could rob one of breath—like tears trailed down the dirty face of a sailor. A warrior.

"None but the men of the *Ice Wolf* know," he told Angel. "None. But, boy, we know. Your father was Weyrdon. And Weyrdon is waiting." He turned, then, and he let Angel go.

But even the parting words were a gift, of sorts, for he spoke the name Weyrdon with a respect and a certainty that not even his father had done, and it robbed

Angel of some of the fear that he'd been holding onto
so tightly. He'd hidden it, of course—if the Northerners
knew how to cry, they knew better than to show fear. To
them, fear was weakness, a lack of commitment.

Alaric was waiting; he had turned, and he had listened, but he had not spoken or interfered. When Angel
met his eyes, the older man nodded. "Your father was
much loved here," he said gravely.

"Then why was he asked to—" He bit back the
words; there was too much anger in them, too much
confusion. These, too, had to be hoarded. Alaric led and
Angel followed, and this time the sailors moved to one
side or the other, forming a tunnel as they did.

Their hands rested on their weapons, but they did
not lean against the rails or the great pole that seemed
to impale as much of the ship as Angel could see; they
stood, and they bore witness. Even in the heat, their
faces dribbling sweat, they looked . . . proud. Certain.

Angel straightened his shoulders, aware of what they
offered in silence, and aware, as well, that he had to
offer them something similar in return. For just a moment, he had to be Garroc's son—because he was all
that was left of Garroc, a man they appeared to have
known and respected.

Kalliaris, he thought. *Smile, Lady.*

She smiled. He didn't trip or stumble. He walked
the deck of the ship until he came to a short flight of
stairs, and he mounted these as well without incident,
although the deck was slippery and wet in places.

But he stopped when Alaric stopped. He could see
the man's arm lift staff and turn it sideways, and he
could see the staff—perfectly steady—as it lay in the
air a moment.

Then Alaric walked again, but this time, he walked
to the side of a man whose back was toward them both.

The back of his hair was long, and braided; it was—or
it would be, when cleaned—pale, a light shade of gold.
But the peaks of his hair rose, bound around wire in an
odd and familiar spiral. He wore a chain shirt, even in
this weather, and no obvious tabard, but the shirt was

large; the man's shoulders were broad and straight. He wore a greatsword across his back, and a belt meant for some sort of weapon girded his waist; it hung loose at the moment.

When the man at last turned, his hands fell from the rails to his sides. His face was scarred, but the scars were clean lines across his forehead and the left side of his face, disappearing into a thick and unkempt beard; he had both eyes. His nose had the angularity that suggested it had been broken a time or two, and it wasn't small, but it suited the rest of his face.

But it was his eyes that demanded attention, for his eyes were golden. Golden like the sun, like wheat at harvest, like fire in winter; golden, Angel thought, like Alaric's. God-born. Two such men, here.

He was not handsome, but had he been in a crowd of thousands, he would have commanded attention instantly simply by existing. It wasn't his height, although he was taller than Angel's father; it wasn't the weapon that he wore at his back. It wasn't his armor either; he could have worn sackcloth with equal ease. He just . . . demanded attention.

He was Weyrdon. Angel understood the truth—the implacable and undeniable truth—of that as if he'd been born to it, and nothing else.

"Alaric, clear the deck, and give the men leave to go ashore."

The older man nodded.

"But do not leave with them," Weyrdon added.

The older man hesitated for a fraction of a minute and then nodded again. He turned briskly; Angel saw his robes and his staff out of the corner of his eye. He could not take his eyes from Weyrdon.

Weyrdon smiled down at him when Alaric had left them. "Angel, Garroc's son," he said quietly.

Angel nodded, unsurprised by sound of his name. The syllables were Rendish in pronunciation, although the word itself was Weston.

Weyrdon's gaze lifted, shot past Angel's shoulder. "Garroc is dead." No question in the words. But . . . an invitation lurked between the syllables. "And he sent you to me."

Angel nodded. He had never been chatty, but words had completely deserted him, and he struggled to find them while the ship's decks slowly—and completely—cleared.

But Weyrdon did not wait for long.

"You've come to ask me why I sent your father from my side."

Angel said nothing.

"It is not why your father sent you," Weyrdon added.

"No."

"Do you know why he sent you?"

Angel had thought about little else on the road to Averalaan. He was—he couldn't say the word out loud—orphaned. He had no kin, either in the Free Towns or in the City, that he knew of. His mother's family must be in the Empire, if they existed—but if they existed, she had never, ever chosen to speak about them.

And he thought his father might have sent him because in some fashion Weyrdon was his family, but even thinking it felt wrong. ". . . No."

Weyrdon nodded. Turned back to the sea. What he said next was not what Angel was expecting—if he had, indeed, expected anything from this man.

"We will see war in our lifetimes."

Given that the sailors bore so many scars and so much obvious weaponry, the statement almost made no sense. Angel hesitated, and then said, "You've already seen war."

Weyrdon turned and lifted a brow, one bisected neatly by a slender scar. His smile was deep and sudden. "Aye, we have at that." His eyes were bright and clear. "And no doubt we'll see more." The smile dimmed. "But those battles were merely a foundation.

"And the war I speak of will touch the entirety of the Empire—no matter how tenuous its hold—before it runs its course; it will stretch to the West, as far as the Western Kingdoms, and to the North, where not even my kin go. It will reach to the South, beyond the

Empire, and," he added, gazing a moment at the water in the bay, "to the East, upon the Islands.

"We will fight in the North," he added softly, "as we can, and where we have the power to do so. Here, in the Empire's heart, such a power exists, and here, too, war will come. I think . . . it may end here, one way or the other. But of that, I cannot be certain."

Angel frowned. "My father—"

"Your father knew what I knew," Weyrdon replied.

"But who—who could start a war that's fought everywhere? Who could lead an army that could destroy the Empire?"

"That," was the soft reply, "is the question. We do not—I do not—have the answer, not yet. And in some small measure, I'm grateful; when we have the answer, the war will be upon us all."

"And this has something to do with my father."

"Yes. And no." Weyrdon's eyes, as he turned, were the color of the sea. It was a trick of the light, but for a moment, on the decks of this ship, he seemed to encompass the breadth of an ocean that not even the horizon could break. He lifted a hand and gestured, and Alaric, standing down-deck, joined them, his staff a counterpoint to the rhythm of his steps.

"Alaric is Wittan," Weyrdon said. "And counted wise beyond even the lands that Weyrdon knows. All that I know, he knows, although the inverse is not true; he keeps much to himself."

"Indeed," Alaric said, with the faint hint of a wry smile. "And in part because Weyrdon dislikes secrecy and politics, however much these may be necessary."

Weyrdon frowned; the frown did not seem to upset Alaric so much as amuse him. The amusement caused his weathered skin to fall, for a moment, into different lines. They were etched there as well, and even the passing of the smile could be seen for a moment. "But he can lead, and where he leads, men follow. He is what he is," Alaric added, "As am I. But you, Angel, Garroc's son, are not bound as we two are bound, to this war in the North."

Angel was silent for a moment, gathering what might have been called courage were it not so feeble. "Weyrdon," he said gravely, "why did you send my father into exile?"

Weyrdon glanced at Alaric.

"He leads men," Alaric said, "but as always, in difficulties that do not involve Cartanis, he is content to let others speak."

Weyrdon grimaced. "Alaric is not entirely just in his portrayal of my leadership. Very well. This will make, perhaps, little sense to you. It makes little sense to me; there is too much of hope and fancy in it, and not enough blood and bone.

"We face war, as I have said. But it is not a war of men, or not of men alone, and there are some fell things of which I cannot speak, even in your fair city."

It wasn't Angel's city. But he nodded anyway.

"Understand that we are, Alaric and I, the sons of our fathers. We are bound in some measure, by blood and birth, to our fathers' world—and it is not your world, not Garroc's world." He hesitated. "Understand as well that what the gods know, men cannot fully understand—and we are men. Gods speak in riddles, and often the unraveling of their meaning is not done until after the events of which they speak have transpired."

Angel frowned and Alaric snorted.

"Alaric," Weyrdon said, looking pained. "It is for this reason that I had the men go ashore. My dignity is, unfortunately, necessary, and Alaric's care of it lessens the farther away from a field of battle we travel.

"We have traveled far, indeed, to be here, Angel, Garroc's son. We had word that you would come to this port, to meet the *Ice Wolf*."

"You knew my father was dead."

"Only by that; not while he was alive would he have sent you to me." His expression lost all of the exasperated amusement he had shown his adviser; for a moment, it was as pale as it might be in the land of Winter. "I would have had him by my side to face the endless night, had I the choice." His hand rested briefly on the rails.

Angel said nothing, waiting now. He didn't try to mark the passage of time; there was no contest in the pause, no quiet battle of wills.

"But I did not have that choice. We are given little advantage in the battle that is—if all fails—to come, and what very, very little we have is not to be found on the field of battle, or not on a field that Cartanis understands. Not even on a field that Teos does," he added.

Cartanis was a name that was familiar to Angel, if for no other reason than that his father had often invoked the god when he was particularly annoyed during his long weeks teaching the Free Town boys to hold, and wield, swords. Teos, however, he did not know.

"The god of knowledge," Alaric said, correctly divining Angel's ignorance.

"Does he know everything?"

Weyrdon laughed out loud and Alaric frowned. It was Weyrdon who answered. "He knows what his sons know. He knows what his Priests know. He knows what his Priests since the dawn of time have known. But he does not, and cannot, know everything that occurs in the world of man—no god can, and in that lies our hope. But it is, I admit, a scant hope, and not one to my liking; there is too much that will be decided in lands that I will never personally see, and too much of the war itself fought in the same fashion. It is not to my liking to leave so much to chance or the leadership of strangers, but what we cannot change, we accept.

"Some years ago, when we were young and my armies were a fraction of the size they now are, word was sent to Alaric, and from Alaric, to me. Signs were given, and they were signs that Weyrdon would know and recognize; I understood that the word itself could not be challenged; it could be questioned.

"We questioned it," he added. "Alaric risked the displeasure of his parent not once, but thrice, and in the land between the thunder and the snow, the air was thick with the god's annoyance when we took our leave the third time.

"But in the end, we could not ignore what was asked of us, and we summoned Garroc."

"Why?"

"Because Garroc's duty lay in the Empire, or in the city at its heart."

"But—"

Weyrdon lifted a hand. "It was not to fight that he was sent; he was my best, but one man is not an army. It was not to gather information; we have those who could serve in that capacity. It was," and he frowned, now, lines framing slightly tightened lips, "to find a worthy lord."

"He had one."

"Oddly enough," Alaric interjected, "those are not dissimilar from Weyrdon's first words when he learned of the task that he must set Garroc; nor are they dissimilar from his final words. It is not easy for Weyrdon to consign men whose oaths he has taken to serve another. Nor," he added, "is it easy for Weyrdon to imagine, in the end, that there could be any other who might deserve Garroc's service, if Weyrdon himself was to forgo it. He is a great leader of men, but he is not known for his humility.

"Garroc, however, accepted with grace what Weyrdon could accept only with difficulty, and when the *Ice Wolf* sailed, he was upon its decks. He assumed that his task was to find a worthy lord within the heart of the Empire; we all assumed it. We also assumed it would take time, if it proved possible at all—the North and the South are different."

"But he was sent into exile."

"He was sent into exile. Only those who sailed the *Ice Wolf* understood that he served Weyrdon, still. His name is spoken only here."

"But—"

"Tell me, Garroc's son, did you not encounter Northerners upon the farm that was your home?"

Angel fell silent.

"So. You understand."

No, Angel thought. *No, I don't understand.* But ... those men had died. They had come and they now lay buried in the soil of Evanston. But so, too, Angel's father, and his mother, and half of his friends.

Weyrdon said nothing.

"And ... if he found this lord," Angel said, thinking of Terrick's anger. "What then?"

Weyrdon's silence was different. At last he said, "He did not find his lord."

"How do you know?"

"The same way," he replied, "that we knew you would come, seeking the *Ice Wolf*. The same way," he added, "that I knew that when you came to me, I would offer you in the end none of the respect that your father's sacrifice deserves." He turned, then, to Alaric.

"Angel, Garroc's son," Alaric said, the words like a chant, their pronunciation wrong. "You are of the Empire, and of Garroc. The only thing of Weyrdon you will have—should you choose it—is the mark; we will not hunt you and we will not kill you for your presumption in assuming it.

"Perhaps what Garroc sought, in the end, was a Lord of the North; perhaps what he sought, and what he measured, he measured against the truth of Weyrdon, and against such truth, all men might be found wanting. We burden you with no such comparison; we burden you with no such struggle.

"We thought it was Garroc's duty, but we see clearly now.

"If you will take up Garroc's duties, seek what he sought, and seek it as a citizen of the Empire; perhaps you will see clearly what Garroc, in the end, could not, and thus prevent your father's duty from ending in failure."

Failure. Angel closed his eyes. He could hear the lap of water against the ship; could hear the raucous cry of gulls, could smell fish, sweat, and the sea breeze. Everything but the sweat so different from Evanston; he had stepped into a different world.

But that world, and this one, were anchored by one

man: Garroc of Weyrdon. The man he had known as
father. The man who had sworn his life to the service of
the god-born.

"If I refuse?"

Alaric said nothing.

"Can you?" Weyrdon asked softly.

"I . . . don't know."

"No," the Rendish warlord said. He nodded. "You do
not know, not yet, what we face."

"And you won't tell me."

"What it is safe to say, I have said."

"You told my father more."

"Your father was mine," Weyrdon replied. "I took—
and knew—his full measure. You are merely his son.
The nights are growing longer," he added in Rendish.
"And if my words or judgment seem harsh, take comfort in this: you have not taken my measure. I am not
served by fools; while it might at times be convenient,
I expect no blind obedience. You will find truth in my
words, or you will not, but you will not forget what I
have said."

"No." The single word was soft. "If I—if I do as my
father did not live to do, what then?"

"What then?"

"If I find what you seek, what do I do then?"

Weyrdon glanced at Alaric, and the older man's
robes rose and fell as he shrugged. "We do not know,"
Alaric said at last. "It has never been clear to us what
the purpose of such a lord might be; whether it be to
lead armies, or no. We know only that in some measure
it will be significant, if you both survive."

"If?"

"Many will not," Alaric replied. "Even here, in the
heart of the Empire, where the god-born rule the Isle
and the cathedrals, many will die. There is a shadow that
is growing here; my lord Teos cannot pierce it. It spreads
across the City, like mist, but night follows in its wake.
Here, in Averalaan, sons of my father also labor; we are
not kin, but the language we speak is not dissimilar for
all their foreignness."

"Where? Where do I start?"

Alaric's smile was gentle. "Angel, Garroc's son, if we could answer, we would not have surrendered Garroc to exile—and death—in a land that barely knows Winter. But if what we were told can be understood at all, it is in Averalaan that you will begin to unravel the answer, and in the end? You will know more than the sons of Teos." He bowed. "It is almost time for you to depart." Reaching into his robes, he pulled out a small leather bag. "Imperial coin," he said. "We have nothing else to give. No advice, no warning, no words of wisdom."

"We understand that you have not yet made your choice," Weyrdon continued, when Alaric had placed the small satchel into Angel's shaking palm. "And we will not therefore ask you what decision you have reached; if you offer your sword, I will not take it. Not yet. You will return to me," he added, his eyes glinting for a moment, as if they had caught sunlight, although the sun was at his back. "And what you offer then, I will consider." He turned his back upon Angel, and did not turn again. But he had not finished, and what he said surprised Angel.

"Have you spoken with Terrick?"

Angel nodded, and then, realizing that Weyrdon did not, in fact, have eyes in the back of his head, said, "Yes."

"Ah. And he warned you not to chance these decks?"

Terrick had offered him hospitality and shelter. Angel did not choose to answer Weyrdon's question.

After a pause in which Weyrdon accepted silence as the only answer he would be offered, the son of Cartanis spoke again. "You will speak with Terrick. Understand him, Angel, and perhaps you will have more of an answer than either I or Alaric can give you."

There was respect in those distant words. Respect, and something else, but not anger, not disapproval. Something softer, or sadder. Angel couldn't identify it.

"Would you—would you take Terrick's service now if he offered it?"

"He will never offer it," Weyrdon replied.

"But if he did?"

"That," Alaric said, taking Angel gently by the shoulder and turning him toward the stairs, "was as much of an answer as Weyrdon will give. You are not of the North, boy, although the North has touched you."

Angel followed; Alaric's hand did not leave the boy's shoulder, so he had little choice. But as they reached the bottom of the short flight of stairs, Weyrdon spoke again.

"I cannot command you, not yet," he said, as both Alaric and Angel slowed. "But I ask that you do as your father did. Leave what I have spoken of on these decks."

Angel straightened his shoulders. Nodded. He did not look back as Alaric began to walk again. He did not look back until he had reached the bottom of the gangplank, and Averalaan once again reigned.

But when he stood, alone, upon the empty dock, he gazed up to see Weyrdon's eyes, robbed of color by distance, and he lifted a hand, not in salute, but not—quite—in farewell.

The Port Authority was not yet a press of angry people; it was crowded, by the standards of Evanston; by the standards of Averalaan, however, it was sparse enough that the air, farther away from the doors and the scant breeze that wafted in, still felt like air when one took a deep breath.

Angel stood in the line that led to Terrick's wicket. He could see the Northerner, his height lessened by his position on a stool and the framing window of the wicket itself; could see the way his hair darkened in the internal light of the building. He could see his eyes, from this distance, although he couldn't clearly see their color; he could see lips move, although no sound carried this far back. Paper came and went, as if it were coin.

The line shortened as Angel waited, thinking now of gathering eggs from the hen house. Thinking, as well, that he might never have that chore again; he had seen no farms in the City itself, and where there was land for the gardens one tended for one's own family, there was no food; just grass, and flowers, and trees.

He had come from Evanston, walking in the heat of summer and resting when the heat was at its worst; he had asked for directions from passing merchants, found the road most traveled, and following it, had arrived in Averalaan. He had dreamed of the *Ice Wolf*, and he had dreamed of death.

But he had walked and waited, waited and walked. He wasn't ready to walk into the nowhere that his life now led, not yet, and he could not turn back to the ship. So he stood in line until the last back before him broke away. He watched it recede, seeing folds of a deep blue that looked almost purple as it caught light; seeing, as well, the salt stain white across its textured surface. He watched it as the minutes passed, and when the colors shifted as movement changed the caught light, he stepped forward.

Terrick looked up. At this distance, his eyes were all of gray, the color of clouds just before thunder breaks.

Angel started to speak, and stopped. He did this three times before he spread his hands, palms up.

Terrick smiled. It was an odd smile, and reminded Angel more of pain than joy or amusement. "So," he said, "You're back."

Angel nodded.

"And you still have—"

"Hair, yes."

At that, Terrick chuckled. "Meet me when the horns sound lunch," he told the boy. "Second lunch, as it happens; if you try to come into the back during first lunch, you'll probably trip over Barriston. The man you first spoke to," he added. "Barriston is very finicky, and very precise. He will no doubt eject you, possibly with the help of the guards."

They sat on either side of Terrick's massive and cluttered desk. Most of the clutter, on the other hand, was lunch. "It's not our custom to entertain guests in the back rooms," he offered, by way of explanation. He was careful to keep his tone light and neutral as he once again broke bread, divided cheese and meat, and poured water.

They ate in silence. Angel ate the way calm men

breathe; slowly, naturally—and continuously. But when he spoke, he surprised Terrick. Even now.

"What will you do?"

Terrick could have pretended to misunderstand the question, and had he been asked it a day earlier, would have. But he met the boy's steady gaze with his own. "Work."

"Garroc is gone." He spoke as if Garroc and his father had been two different men. Fair enough; to Terrick, they were. But they were both dead. The loss was new to Angel; to Terrick it was not so much new as finally acknowledged. He drank his wine the way the boy ate, and stared, for a moment, into the distance of writing and paper and furled sails.

"He is."

"I'm not Garroc." He set his food aside, and looked up at Terrick. "I'm never going to be Garroc."

"No."

"Were you waiting for him?"

Terrick said nothing. But he gave up the pretense of food, and set aside the wine. "Do you serve Weyrdon?" The question was direct and clear, for all that it was spoken softly.

There was a pause, but Angel didn't look away, and in the muted light of the office, his eyes were almost gray. At last he said, "I don't know."

There was so much about the boy that was foreign and frustrating. Terrick had time for neither, but it was a struggle. "Did you offer him your service?"

"No."

"Then you do not serve him."

"No, I guess I don't."

"Your hair—"

"He said I had the right, in my father's name, and for my father's service," Angel replied quietly.

"For his service."

"I told you, he was asked to leave. He did what Weyrdon asked of him. I'm not of Weyrdon. I imagine that if I were living in Arrend, I would have a very short life unless I never left that ship."

"And what did he ask of you?"

Angel's eyes widened in surprise; his skin flushed slightly. "He asked me not to speak of what he said," he answered quietly, and for the first time, his eyes slid away from Terrick's. And then they slid back, and the boy's jaw tightened. "But I will," he said, in the same low tones, his eyes blue now, his gaze steady. "Because I know you never will."

Terrick listened while the boy talked. Listened, seeing Garroc in him, and seeing, as well, the wife and mother that Terrick had never—and would never—meet. But the boy's slow, quiet words were not Garroc's words, and the intensity with which Garroc burned in his youth was also absent.

How it must have angered Garroc, to know that he had failed, and that he would remain, to the end of his days, an exile in these lands. And how it must have weighed on him to place that task on the slender shoulders of a boy who had never seen battle.

And who had, even now, only seen one.

"What will you do?" Angel asked, when the last of his words had trailed into silence.

"Work," Terrick replied.

"I mean, what will you do now?"

"Work."

"But why?"

Terrick shrugged. "Because I can. Because Garroc is not coming back. Because I don't choose to serve another. Not yet. Maybe never." He shrugged, and then added, "Work is something to do while you wait. If you can't find answers, if you can't find direction, it puts food on the table, a roof over the head."

"And that's all?"

"It's not what I wanted when I was young, but we seldom get what we want." He watched Angel's face for any sign of comprehension. When he found none, which was oddly comforting, he said, "What will you do?"

Angel's smile was wan. "Work," he replied. "If I can find it."

"And you will not search?"

"How can I?" Bitterness, faint but unmistakable, seeped into the boy's words. "My father at least had the Kings' Challenge on which to stand when he looked for someone—anyone—worthy. I have nothing; no money, no family, no land; I can hardly use a sword, and I don't have many useful skills.

"Even if I knew what to look for, I have nothing to offer. If this worthy lord has guards, I wouldn't get close to him."

"You will not always be this young," Terrick began.

But Angel frowned, and the words fell away. The silence was pointed and cool.

"But you won't leave the City."

Angel shook his head.

"Neither will I." Terrick rose. "Lunch will end soon. If you need a place to stay while you settle in, I'm not moving."

Angel nodded, his shoulders turning down toward the ground, the years falling away from his pale face. His hair was awkward; far too stiff, too defined, for his age. "I have to try," he said in a low voice. "For my father's sake. I have to try."

"I know," Terrick replied, equally quiet. The lunch horn blew, low and loud like a flatland cow. "Stay here if you want. Or meet me after my shift ends." He turned, not expecting a reply, and made his way back to his wicket.

He didn't know how long Angel would stay.

But he knew that he would wait for the boy. For Garroc's son. He had waited, day after day, the Port Authority consuming his life in the slow march of hours, for Angel, although he hadn't known it; he knew it now. What Angel had told him he understood in some small measure, and he resolved to practice with swords again; to build the type of endurance that battle required.

To be ready to face the endless night when Garroc's son, the last of his line, finally returned to the Authority and bid him leave it.

Chapter One

Angel

A MOMENT IN TIME, fixed and unchanging. He can return to it, and often does, trying to make sense of his life.

More often, it returns to him, sometimes as a whisper, sometimes as a shout, sometimes as a slap in the face. He's never sure when it will come, and when it will leave, and sometimes it's damn inconvenient—but not now.

5th of Morel, 410 AA
Twenty-fifth holding, Averalaan

Angel opened the windows. Which meant, in this case, grabbing faded strips of cloth—from an old shirt, maybe; it was kind of hard to tell—and tying them 'round both the shutter and the hook in the wall. It had to be done four times. There were actually two windows in this room, but the apartment had been old before Angel's father had been born, so the shutters were warped; they liked to close. *It'd be a lot easier if people would move,* he thought. But if he were trying to be fair—and given this was the third shutter, he didn't much feel like it— he'd have to acknowledge that there wasn't much room

to move *in*. Jay wanted the entire den in one room. They
did fit, but not easily, and as usual she wanted everyone
as close to the kitchen as possible. So they'd all congre-
gated in one room, finding floor space to sit on or wall
space to lean against—the wall was safer, unless you
liked to be stepped on. Sadly, the windows were part of
the wall, which made the chore harder.

He would have given up, but no one else cared, and
Angel liked being able to breathe.

Now, people were talking in that half-shout they used
when there were too many other people talking; the
room, which wouldn't have been large back home, was
crowded with people sounds and people smells. Obviously, some idiot had told Carver to cook, because one
of those smells was something burning.

Angel moved toward the bucket in the corner, just
in case, and stood idle, leaning against the wall. This
should've taken more thought than it did, but, well.
It was Carver, and Carver was trying to cook. Which
meant he was trying to own part of the conversation,
an effort which demanded more of his time than the
stove and the pot on it. Anyone who let Carver cook
when it was this crowded *expected* to put out the occasional fire.

"Want me to watch?" Finch asked, standing on her
toes and shouting in the direction of his ear; her breath
tickled his collarbone. She'd probably asked the question at least four times, but the noise of colliding conversations was so damn loud it was easy to miss her. She
didn't have much of a voice, not compared to the rest of
the den. Only Teller was quieter, but he had other ways
of making himself heard.

Angel shrugged and watched her hover. Her eyes
were so dark a brown, the dim light made them all
black, but it was a warm black, infused by an immediate and urgent desire to be *helpful* that was so strong it
was almost its own color. He liked Finch. It would have
been damn hard not to like Finch, and in this, at least,
Angel was lazy.

Jester muttered something, and his words made a

wave in the eddies of other conversations, other gambits
for attention; laughter followed, enveloping everyone
except the sullen silence that was Duster. Duster habitually sat beside Jay, or stood by her shoulder, her hands
in fists at her sides. She seldom smiled, and the only
time she laughed? Not worth the cost. Today, everyone
was crowded around Jay, and while Duster had her own
special way of staking out space, when people started
laughing, they pressed into it.

Angel didn't understand Duster, and mostly, he was
certain he never would. But sometimes—sometimes
he thought he might, and that was worse. It made him
uncomfortable.

When he was uncomfortable, he remembered. A
month, two months—no, maybe six now. Or seven.
Whatever. The time didn't matter; it just marked a
boundary. Before it, this room and these people didn't
exist as part of his life, and after? Well, he was the one
standing beside the damn bucket.

So he leaned against the wall, not that there was a
lot of wall to lean against; he folded his arms across his
chest, let his chin tilt forward toward his heart, as if it
was the center of gravity. Who knows. He wasn't a doctor and he wasn't a healer—maybe it was.

Angel

A moment in time.

Where does it start?

Not in the Port Authority. Not in Terrick's apartment, although the heat of the smithy permeates every
memory of that place. Not in the Common, and not in
the shade of its giant, unnatural trees (trees which, he
has been assured, are entirely natural). For some reason
people like to talk to him about the trees: the magisterial guards, the merchants coming to their stalls, the old
women who seem to gird the Common with their daily
presence (and if there's a better way to tell time than
Mrs. Gallaby's tapping cane, he hasn't seen it yet).

Maybe it starts with money. Or with having no money.

Maybe it starts with the job he also doesn't have.

Maybe it starts with the streets of the City, because they stretch out forever, longer than fields, with no fields in sight. Yeah, maybe it starts there.

Angel knows what hunger feels like. But he's never lived in a place where you can't even *grow your own food* because there's no land at all that isn't part of your windowsill—if you even have that much you can call your own. He knows that most of your land is used to grow things that other people want—but having *nothing* that other people want? It's something the City teaches him, daily. He doesn't like the lesson.

There are other things he learns.

He learns that having no family is hard—he knew it, but he learns it again, over and over. He forgets, for minutes at a time, that his mother and father are dead. He forgets, for the same minutes, that he'll never hear their voices, or see their expressions, or feel their arms, and when those moments pass, and he is alone again, he regrets bitterly the embarrassment he felt at his father's open affection. *I'm not a child* echoes in the empty room when Terrick is at the Port Authority.

Sometimes he hates the echoes enough that he leaves. He goes exploring, as if he were a child again, without the strength to help his father in the fields.

The City is larger than anything he dreamed of as that child. There's a river that cuts through the City, but it's surrounded by buildings and bisected by bridges. People live on its banks when it's warm. They fight there and die there as well. Far enough downstream, people don't even blink when a body works free of the mud and rises, dragged along by the current. He's seen it, once. He doesn't want to see it again.

He discovers that there are a hundred holdings. He asks the old woman who tells him this how she knows which ones are which—and how he's supposed to—and she shrugs. People just know, she tells him, nodding sagely. He doesn't. There are streets all over the place, and the boundaries of the holdings crisscross them, claiming one part for the twenty-fifth, and one part for the thirty-fifth in a way that makes no sense.

But the boundaries mean something to the people who live inside them. As if these patches of city, invisible to Angel's eye, are their fields, they roam the boundaries in packs, like feral dogs. They're called dens, here. Angel doesn't know why—it's a stupid word for what they actually are. What they are? Dangerous. He watches for them, but the buildings and the alleys get in the way; he's spent some time running from them as a result.

There are some days his life seems to be all about running.

Sometimes that makes him angry. It's better than crying. It's better than staring at walls and trying to figure out what there is to do in this smelly, hot, crowded, noisy corner of the Hells.

He spends a month being angry. He spends two months being angry. In the City there are so many things to be angry *about,* walking down the street is an exercise in fury; it's like he's wounded and every single thing he sees rubs at the wound, catching its edges and making it bleed more.

He can remember the first fight he gets into; he can't remember why it started. Because after the first fight, there are *so many* of them. He does remember Terrick's silence, and that's harder; Terrick is silent the way his father would have been silent, at least to start. But Terrick isn't his father, and the second time, the third, he starts to try to teach Angel the things his father didn't.

He teaches Angel how to fight. There's no honor in it, and no attempt to teach morals. It's just about the fight itself, and that much, Angel can focus on. The morals? Not so much. Not when he can walk the streets and see people thin with starvation, begging, hands or bowls in their laps, all dignity lost in the face of hunger and their inability to make themselves useful to people who have money. Not when he can leave the Common and walk half a mile and be surrounded by buildings that his family might have used for firewood if the wood itself weren't so rotten. Not when he can turn the wrong corner or cross the wrong street and come face-to-face with boys little older than he is, waving daggers, strutting across the landscape like roosters.

Not when right and wrong have become so damn blurred.

Sometimes he remembers that it wasn't always blurred. Sometimes remembering helps, but it gets harder and harder to remember the *when*, and the why, he thinks, is buried with his parents. He doesn't think about Weyrdon often. He doesn't go to the port, doesn't stand on the docks, doesn't look for a glimpse of the *Ice Wolf*'s long shadow. He doesn't replay the conversation about war and endless night—because in some ways, he's already living it. Here, on the ground, as the heat fades and the sea air turns damp and chill. The beggars are desperate now, and he watches and listens until he *cannot stand* to listen to another word.

He should be grateful. He thinks it, in the dim light of Terrick's kitchen. He *should be grateful*. He's not in the streets; he's not begging; he's not starving. But he feels he has more in common, in the end, with the people who *are*. And the day that he can't meet Terrick's gaze, that he forgets *how,* is the day Terrick looks at him across empty plates and air thick with silence, and says, *Have you forgotten Garroc*?

And he's out in the street, the Common empty, the stalls looking thin and forlorn as new beggars; he's out through the gates that are still patrolled, out past them, circling the Common streets. He knows this close to the Common, those streets are safe—but even if they weren't? He wouldn't care. He sees the facades of merchant buildings, runs past the Merchant Authority; sees his reflection in the windows of the permanent shops that Terrick would never frequent. He hates his reflection, hates the running, slows to a walk. But even walking, he's a coward; he's running. He knows it.

There are tears on his face, but that could be the rain. He doesn't believe it, but he doesn't know what to believe anymore; he just knows that someone else might, if they saw him. He knows, takes comfort in knowing. Someone *else* might believe it. Someone who isn't Terrick and isn't Angel, might not understand just how weak he really is. Garroc's son? Garroc, the man who put swords in their hands in the heat of summer, and taught them how to handle them so they didn't cut off their own damn feet?

He doesn't know where he's going. He doesn't even care.

But he isn't surprised when he stops before the gated courtyard of one of the larger cathedrals in the City. It's not one of the three, and it's not as fine as the cathedrals on the Isle—cathedrals that he's never seen because he's not rich enough or stupid enough to cross the bridge and stand in the shadow of *Avantari*, the home of Kings. But it's close enough, and the gates aren't locked; this close to the Common, this close to the heart of Averalaan's wealth, they won't be.

He walks into the courtyard that leads to the arched peaks of its doors. The wood is dark, but it's dark anyway; lamps burn to either side. He follows the steps as if they're a footpath, cleaving to their center, and as he approaches the doors, he sees that their stone sides are carved. To the left and the right, at equal distances, swords are raised; they will never be lowered to bar entrance. But that's not the point, is it? At the peak of the architrave, in the same stone relief as the swords, he sees a shield; it is carried in the pinions of stone hawks. None of these carvings are particularly ornate, and the hawks are smooth, their wings unbroken by the actual texture of feathers. No paint colors them, and they are small, but it doesn't matter; Angel recognizes them.

He knows where he is.

Looking up a moment at the shield, he raises his palms to his face and wipes the rain away. The water, curse it, has gathered in his hair. It'll take its damn time trickling down the sides of his face, but there's nothing he can do about it now; he can either stand in the rain or get out of it.

He walks up the last three stairs, taking them one at a time, and he touches the closed door.

It swings inward, silent. Even so, he stands a moment in the darkness before he accepts the invitation. He steps across the stone threshold.

Before him, the building stretches out forever. There is light here, and it is the even and diffuse light that only magic can grant. He can't see where it starts, although he does try. The only church he visited in the Free Towns was the Mother's. It was smaller than this, although not much tidier. The first thing he could see, when he entered her hall, were the walls of the vestibule. To either side of the open arch, that wall was lined with candles. Some of them were made by the Priests and the Priestesses, but not all—some were made by the congregation. Different sizes, different shapes, different colors. One of them was made by his mother, and whenever she came to the church, she would light it.

But there's nothing on these walls besides names.

People don't light candles, not in this church. They don't pray for their sons or daughters that way. It's not for *safety* that you come to Cartanis, after all.

You come to serve.

You come to be found *worthy* to serve.

God of Just War.

Angel passes the vestibule itself, which is easy: it's small. There are doors recessed into the wall to the left and right. They don't matter. He looks at them anyway, and then takes a breath. Without the drum of rain, it's bloody quiet here. The Mother's church was never quiet.

But it was small, that church. Full of small people. They brought grain, wheat, corn—he remembers that. What do they bring Cartanis here?

Not the harvest.

He passes the walls, shadowed for a moment by the width of a great stone opening that is grander and taller than the arch of the outer door. Gray and smooth, unadorned by carvings, it rises toward a ceiling that seems to stretch on forever. The light follows that stretch, and

he can see—as if the sun were housed here—the paintings that adorn the ceilings, following its curve. He can't
see support beams or joists, and he wonders how it is
that the ceiling doesn't fall down.

But clearly it doesn't, because there's no dust or
plaster, no stone or wooden beam, across the rows of
benches. The benches themselves are broken by aisles,
and at the end of each bench, a wolf sits, like a silent
sentinel. The dogs of Cartanis. Unlike the birds, these
bristle with fangs, and fur seems to rise slightly from the
tufts of their ears and the width of their neck.

He walks between them, toward the nave.

Toward Cartanis.

They don't leave much to the imagination, when
it comes right down to it. Cartanis is carved in stone,
larger—far larger—than life. His hands grip the pommel of a greatsword, point to the base of the statue; it
gleams, as if it were real. He wears a shield across his
back, and his face is helmed; he wears plate chest, and
epaulets, as well as shin splints. No wolves sit sentinel
beside him, and no hawks soar above; nor do they sit on
his shoulders. Armored, he is unadorned. And he looks
down. It's a long way to look.

Angel feels every inch. He stops walking for a moment; looks away from Cartanis to see the braziers to
his right and left. They gleam yellow in the light, and
smoke rises from them in a lazy, skyward plume. There
are windows along either wall, beyond the benches:
beveled, colored, held in place by bars. No light shines
through them and they are curiously flat and lifeless.

He shouldn't be here. He thinks it, knows it, and
takes a breath. But he keeps walking, and only when he
reaches the base of the statue does he stop.

People don't come to Cartanis to pray.

They don't come to Cartanis to scream or shout
either—but he has to stop himself from doing both. He
is *so* angry at the god.

My father served you all his life, and what did he get?

The god doesn't answer, of course. Gods generally
don't.

But absent the god's answer, the answer is there: death.

Of course. Death.

Angel would leave, but another thought comes to him as he glares at the helmed visage of Cartanis. Death is all you get, in the end. There's no point in serving one god or another if you just want to avoid death.

It's life he wants to avoid. And people who want to avoid life? They don't come to Cartanis. He raises a hand to the god, palm exposed; it's like a salute, but there's no strength in it; if it weren't for the angle of the palm itself, it would be a beggar's gesture. A plea. But he can't make it here. He can't even ask the question. If it's life he wants to avoid, he *knows* where to go.

Yes, Garroc served Cartanis. Yes, Garroc died in Evanston, defending his town, and his home. Angel has no town. No home; it's Terrick's, after all, and Terrick doesn't *need* Angel. Nobody does.

He turns, sees, for a moment, lightning illuminate the church, sharp and harsh through windows that night can't penetrate. Hears thunder, as if it's the tongue of gods. But it has no words for Angel, no wisdom, no command.

He turns toward the arch, and beyond it, the door.

No Priest comes to stop him. No novitiate. There are only Cartanis and Angel, and the rows of empty benches, their stone wolves staring straight ahead. The rain slants, slapping glass; he hears the howl of sea wind. He doesn't want to go out again; the anger's spent, and without its heat he's cold and damp.

So he slumps across the nearest bench.

5th of Morel, 410 AA
Twenty-fifth holding, Averalaan

"Angel?" Finch said, and he blinked.

"Sorry. I was thinking."

She hesitated a minute, as if she were picking through

her words and tossing out the bad ones before she used any of them. "Help me in the kitchen?"

Kitchen was the wrong word for the cramped, crowded room. It was Jay's space; she did her writing and her reading there. If she wanted to have a talk, it was always *kitchen*. Still, he was standing closest to it, given that Carver was cooking. Carver had vacated the room; he'd done his damage and he'd moved on.

"What do you want me to do?"

"Help me cut stuff. Teller can carry it. Jay wants us to eat fast. She's got a surprise," she added, lowering her voice. Given that no one else had stopped talking, it meant Angel almost missed the words. But he shrugged and nodded.

Finch handed him a knife, taking care to point it at the floor. His mother had always done that.

Sometimes it was hard to be the outsider. Sometimes he forgot why he wanted to be here.

Angel

But when it's hard, he remembers, and he dives back into the moment more carefully than he holds on to the knife that Finch has finally let go. She doesn't like the sight of blood.

The windows look different at dawn. They overshadow the gray stone of wall, and their colors spill across the farthest benches, reflected by gleaming wood. There are deaths writ large and flat in glass. *Good* deaths. *Noble* deaths. He's heard the stories; everyone has.

But he never wondered, hearing them, about the husbands—or the wives—those deaths left behind. He never wondered what happened to the children, because there were children, must have been children. Did they starve? Did they grow up wondering why serving Cartanis was more important, in the end, than staying at home?

He's spared that. It's a small mercy. His father was going to die anyway. He was one of a dozen men in Evanston who knew his way around a weapon; he was one of far fewer who had experience with raiding.

Angel pulls himself off the bench; his neck is stiff, and his arms ache. The church is still empty, still silent. He walks away without looking at the statue of Cartanis, but as he reaches the door, he feels the hint of a breeze, and the light from the windows, the glass-blue skies, makes him feel—for just a moment—that he's walking *into* the world; that the world is more contained, somehow, than the cathedral.

And then he's in it, and the rain is gone; the sun is low, the sky a wash of colors that haven't yet faded to blue. The air is clear and cold; the ever-present taste of salt across his dry lips is the only thing that reminds him of the sea.

He is *so tired* of the City. Of what it means to be here. Of what it says about Angel, Garroc's son. Terrick is at the Port Authority; Angel could go back to a blessedly empty room and sleep until sundown. He starts to do that. He means to do that—he could swear he means to do that—but the streets twist unexpectedly beneath his feet, like a sudden turn in a conversation that you didn't want to have in the first place.

He's not where he should be; the Common's trees are way the Hells across the City. The sun is higher, and he's dead tired because pew benches are not the same as the floor above the foundry. He turns toward the trees, sees the stretch of road, narrower and lined with brown weeds. They're the only growing thing that survive the wagons, horses, and shoes that tread back and forth across the cracked causeway. He recognizes them, even transplanted; here, no one bothers to get rid of them, because nothing useful grows where they grow.

That was one of his jobs.

To weed.

He stops; the weeds are obscured for a moment by feet, by passing people. He hated weeding. He hated it, complained about it, got cuffed on the side of the head for forgetting to do it as he got older. He can feel the rough hand, meant to sting, not hurt.

And gods, he misses it. He misses the weeding. The planting. The feeding. He misses the anger and the resentment and the love and certainty of *home*—there's no word for what home meant, no word for the loss. He stares at brown weeds in a street that's growing more crowded.

Then he does something stupid. He walks against traffic, toward those weeds, and he kneels in the wet street, placing his fingers at the base of the flattened shoot. He pulls it free of the dirt that exists between cracks—more mud than anything right now, and cold—and he tosses it over his shoulder. Then he stands, and he looks at his fingers, looks again at the street. It's stupid. It's worse than stupid.

But the longing is like a hunger, like the hunger the beggars expose, day in and day out, in the shadow of the Common, except it's worse—there's nothing at all that will satisfy the ache. Nothing. Not even the next weed, or the next, or the next—and he knows, because damn it all, he *tries*. He has to try. He doesn't know why. If someone asked, he'd probably hit them.

But no one asks. They never do. Maybe they think he's stupid enough to try to eat them; some weeds, you can eat, if you're hungry enough. Not these, but it doesn't matter; it's not about the damn weeds. His hands are shaking and his arms hurt and he's cold and bone-tired and it's like he's falling, and the only thing he can grasp to slow his fall are the weeds themselves, and he *tries*.

Because he knew who he was, when he last did this. He knew who he was, and what he was supposed to do, and what he believed in, even if he never thought about it much. Because he has fallen into *this* life and he doesn't want it, and he wouldn't be here if—

If—

His mother hadn't died. He should have stayed. She wasn't the one with the sword, and he *should have stayed*. But he didn't.

And when he hears the voices—the voices—when he hears the shout, broken mid-word into something like a whimper, his hands freeze at the base of another useless plant; his fingers are dark with dirt, and shaking as he rises. He sees the people moving away, hears the taunting, the brief curses, the orders. Boys' voices, so like his, so unlike his.

He's in the City again; the streets coalesce around him, emptying just to one side of two buildings that form an alley. He knows what he sees, but he sees it askew: Boys with clubs and daggers. They aren't using the daggers, but they don't need them; their victim is already on the ground, and she's not putting up much of a fight.

He recognizes them, knows where he is: This is the twenty-fifth holding. They're Carmenta's den. He's run from them before, skipping fences and almost eating dirt in his rush to be gone. But the dirt beneath his nails—it's like an anchor. For just one moment, everything is clear: the cathedral, the weeds, the mud, the den—and the woman on the ground. An old woman, because it's always the old women who stop to talk to Angel. Maybe because they sense that he's lost; maybe because they're old and they've lost everyone else and they need to talk, too.

It doesn't matter. It really doesn't matter.

He doesn't have a sword with him; it's at Terrick's, under the bed. But he doesn't need a sword here, and if he didn't have a dagger, it still wouldn't matter. He sees the old woman, and he finally understands. She's not that far away. They're not that far; the road in the twenty-fifth isn't wide. His legs lose their cramped ache as he stretches them, breaks stride; he doesn't have to push other people out of the way, and for that, he's grateful.

He doesn't even shout as he hits the first boy, and the second; they don't shout until they're tumbling because they don't see him. Clumped together like this, the only thing they listen for is the metallic sound of a passing patrol, and right now? There isn't one.

Just Angel.

Angel is enough. The sheer surprise of him, the unexpected strength of one. They cluster together, shoulder to shoulder, and three go down; the other three swear as they stagger, shout, one snarls—and then he stops, and he looks, and he finally sees Angel.

This is when Angel should run away, because he still can, and if he doesn't, he won't be able. But he's done with running. He's finally done with running. This is a place to stand, and if he stands here long enough, maybe their victim will crawl away. Maybe she'll call the magisterial guards. Maybe she won't—but it doesn't matter. He's not doing this for her, not really.

He hefts his dagger, he uses it as they close, he even draws blood and a snarl of surprised rage. He feels good. He feels beyond good. The cold is gone. He has no rage and no fury; he thinks clearly, now, sees clearly. It's clarity he wants, has wanted. He knows the pain will come.

The bleeding boy pulls back, still snarling; his words are syllables devoid of meaning. The den circles him, and he counts them again: six. To one. Not bad odds—impossible odds. He knows it.

But the moment stretches, time seems to slow; everything is so clear.

"Arann, Finch, go!"

Everything is *so* clear.

The first words, a girl's voice, more bark and urgency than language. He can pick them out of air, and he does it now. They make no sense; he has no context in which to understand them. He's shifting on his feet, back and forth, side to side. Carmenta's den is circling, and Carmenta, hair pulled back off a lean face, sun-dark except where the scars stand out white, stops, his head turning in the wrong direction. Turning away. What the den leader sees robs him of motion, but not of expression; there's anger there, and just the faintest hint of fear.

He shouts and his den turns, and there's just enough of an opening between their shoulders that Angel can see what they see.

*   *   *

Experience only heightens the moment: gives him names and personalities to pin to what he sees. What, he admits, he always wants to see, even if he hasn't known it till now.

He sees Jewel Markess, her flyaway hair half in her eyes, even though it's pulled off her face; her skin is flushed and her eyes seem both dark and luminescent. She's short. Later, he'll remember she's short; he's even peripherally aware of it now—but it doesn't matter. She says two more words: *Carver. Duster.*

He knows them as names because two people step out from behind her, as if they were standing in her shadow. One is a little taller than Angel, and about as thin, but his hair is a dark flap over one half of his face. Stupid, fighting like that. The other? A girl, almost Carver's height, hair just as dark but longer, and eyes— her eyes make Carmenta seem friendly and sane.

They both have knives; Duster has two. They step toward Carmenta's den, and as they do, Fisher and Jester—red hair gleaming in sun that's already added too many freckles—join them, to the left and right. They're armed as well. It's all daggers. But that's all Angel's got.

Jewel has a dagger as well. She steps forward; it's five to six.

No, Angel realizes, looking at his hand, still as Carmenta is still.

It's six to six. It's an even fight.

Carmenta can count, give him that.

And when Arann has helped the old woman to her feet, when Arann has handed her over to Teller and Finch, when he turns, face set, and towers over Carver and Duster?

Well, Carmenta can count him, too.

He lifts one hand, sharp and curt, and his den pulls away from Angel; a blond boy spits as he withdraws, the shape of their group changing from a circle to a line. Angel thinks about knifing him. Doesn't. Instead, he watches as Carmenta begins to signal retreat, to back away. There are no dead, and the only blood that was spilled? A knife scratch to the forearm. Not much, not really.

Not like Evanston.

Jewel watches Carmenta. Duster starts to follow, and Jewel says a curt *No*. "We've got what we came for."

"Take Carmenta out. Let *me* take some of them out," Duster says. "He's going to be trouble."

"No. I'm not willing to risk you on garbage."

Carmenta stiffens at that, and Angel waits; he can see how close it is. Carmenta's like any other den leader—he can't afford to lose face. His power? It's carrion power. It's tentative.

But Jewel Markess *isn't* like any other den leader that he's seen in the City—and he's seen a lot, wandering through the hundred holdings, listening to old women talk. Jewel's people? They stand, and Angel realizes that they're going to stand if she tells them to stand, and fight if she tells them to fight.

He wants to see it. It's visceral and painful, the desire to see it for fact.

But he knows, as Carmenta says, "I'll be waiting," that he won't. Not now.

Carmenta's den back away, bristling. They don't run. But walking? They're running. Angel knows.

And Jewel hasn't said a word; her eyes don't leave them.

Not until the old woman mumbles something. Then, she turns.

"Can you walk?"

The woman nods, but she wobbles, and Arann breaks away. He's taller than she is, and he offers her an arm. She takes it, no hesitation there, and Teller? He's got her cane, and her basket, or what's left of it; the side's staved in.

Finch comes to stand beside her, and it's Finch that she turns to, although she doesn't let go of Arann's arm.

"That boy," she says, and she nods to Angel.

Jewel nods as well. "We'll walk you home," she tells the woman, and just like that, they form up, and they walk. It starts to rain, and the rain is cold—but it's clean, this rain. It hits Angel's face, travels down the spirals of his hair; he feels the hint of ice trail down his neck, and he doesn't care.

He watches them walk away, his knife in a hand that's slowly relaxing. But . . . they walk slowly, and they look back, in ones and twos, and Teller, mousy-brown hair, pale face, touches Jewel's shoulder; says something that doesn't travel. Carver says something as well. That, Angel can catch, but he can't hear the words.

He knows, in the now, that Lander and Lefty are home—and he knows, in the now, that the apartment had better be *clean* when Jay gets back, or there'll be noise. But what he sees, even now:

Jewel turns. "You," she says. "What's your name?"

"Angel."

She raises an auburn brow, and shoves her hair out of her eyes. "Are you an idiot?" Half smile on her lips, and in her appraising glance.

He shrugs. He knows what she's talking about. The old woman, on the ground. Six of Carmenta's den. One boy. "Seemed like a good idea at the time."

"I'm sure that's what all the suicides say in Mandaros' Hall." She shakes her head, adds, "My kind of idiot. You have some place to stay?"

He has Terrick's.

But he shakes his head. No.

"You have one now, if you want it." She pauses, and then adds, "It's not much, but it beats the rain, and we even have food. Some. You eat much?"

He lies.

She snorts; she doesn't believe him. But she motions toward the retreating group.

Maybe, he thinks, as he starts to walk, gods don't answer prayers, and anyway, he didn't pray. But maybe they hear it all—all the things you don't have, and can't find, words for.

"Hey," he says, and she stops; he catches up.

"Yeah?"

"Why did you—" *save me*. He can't bring himself to ask the question.

She doesn't need to hear it. "Don't know. Seemed like a good idea at the time. Were you born here?"

"Free Towns."

"You're a long way from home. You've got family?"

He shrugs, falls in beside her. She takes quick, short, staccato steps.

She glances at the side of his face, and then away. Her breath is a short mist. "Yeah," she says. "Mine are gone, too." For a minute, she looks older, but the creases in her forehead ripple into smooth skin and the expression's lost as she glances at the rest of her den. "They're my family, now. They're my home."

"And me?"

"If you want," she says. "But if we don't move, there won't be any food left."

And . . . he wants. So he follows.

5th of Morel, 410 AA
Twenty-fifth holding, Averalaan

"Angel?"

He blinked. Finch turned her wrist and touched his forehead, beneath the locks of white that trailed just above his brows.

"I'm not sick."

"Just checking. You're really quiet today."

He shrugged. "I don't like shouting." And smiled when she grimaced. His point. He put the knife down, took a look at what he'd been cutting: cheese, some sausage—which was more or less not meat—and the very crusty bread that was so common in Averalaan. You could cut your mouth eating it, but at least it didn't much matter if it was stale, because you couldn't really tell the difference when you were trying to chew it. Too early yet for decent fruit, and what there was was damn expensive. Later. Summer food. There were also potatoes and carrots here, the latter bitter; they were cooked. Some of them were *very* cooked, but none of them were black; Angel wondered, briefly, what Carver had burned.

There was never going to be enough room at the table for everyone to sit and eat, which was good because there weren't enough utensils; on a bad day, there weren't enough plates.

But only on a very bad day was there not enough food, and this? Not a bad day. Not yet.

Picking up plates, he stepped his way across a few legs. It wasn't easy, and Carver cursed him, but that was fair; he'd stepped on Carver deliberately. He handed both of his plates to Arann, because Arann had the longest reach, and left them there, making his way back to the kitchen. He avoided colliding with Teller, and picked up more plates, stopping a moment at the edge of the kitchen to look out into the room.

And there they were. His den: Arann by the window beside Lefty, who was sitting directly beneath the eastern one, his extended legs butting Jester's elbow; Lander on the floor between the windows, on the other side of Lefty. Neither Lander nor Lefty were talkers, but they signed almost all the time, and days like this, it even seemed smarter; Teller, walking toward the kitchen, and Finch, in whose hands the plates looked much larger; Carver and Jester sprawled out in the middle of the floor, arguing about something; Duster, sullen—or bored, it was hard to tell the difference—arms folded across her chest as she leaned at a slant against the wall. Fisher, to one side of Carver, was most of the way through his food before Angel managed to find some floor to sit on; Fisher didn't eat so much as inhale.

In the center of them, Jay.

Jay turned a chair toward the wall and sat on it, draping her arms over its back, and crossing her legs on the seat. She took a plate and had to shift position again to eat, pausing to drop food on the floor for the cat. It purred. And drooled.

Angel didn't much care for cats, but they didn't have a mouse problem when the cat was around. Which, mostly, he was; he could disappear for a week at a time, but he *was* a cat.

Duster shoved the cat out of the way and sat, hard, on the floor to Jay's left.

The cat batted her knee with its paws, claws sheathed. Then it crawled into her lap. It was the only living thing in the place that could do that and still *be* living. Duster glared at everyone, as if daring them to say anything. The cat didn't notice and didn't care—but even the cat was careful when it came to Duster's food. Duster reminded Angel of a feral farm dog—too accustomed to people to be afraid, and too hungry and wild to be anything but dangerous. Months, he'd lived here, and he didn't understand her any better than he had.

But he was the newcomer here.

He held his peace; he was good at that with anyone but Carver. Jester finished second and started in on an impression of Carmenta which made it hard to eat. He pulled Arann into his farce, and although Arann did nothing but stand there and look at Jester as if he was insane, it worked anyway.

Even Duster laughed.

And Jay, Angel thought, watching the den leader, noticed. Jay noticed everything, and as if she could hear the thought, she looked up and met Angel's gaze. He shrugged. Neither of them were laughing at Jester, but then again, Jay rarely found any mention of Carmenta amusing. Carmenta's den had become a big problem in the last six months; Jay wouldn't let anyone head out to the Common alone. She wouldn't let them head out to the *well* alone.

Still, she let Jester go on, let everyone else laugh, let Arann pick Jester up by the back of his neck and dangle him a few inches off the ground. She promised she'd break arms if he dropped Jester on any of the plates that were still on the same ground, which sent Teller and Finch scuttling to pick them all up, and made clear to Angel why they were sometimes short plates.

But when the plates disappeared, Jay stood and cleared her throat. Her glance strayed to the kitchen, and Angel's, following it, went there as well; Finch and Teller were working side by side, but he couldn't see what they were doing.

He couldn't hear them either, because Jester, in his infinite boredom, launched into an impression of Old Rath—and that one did make Jay laugh. Angel had only met Rath once, but he could see his cold, almost autocratic presence, his weary annoyance and his very obvious condescension, in Jester's performance. In particular, the exact and perfect pronunciation, the bored, half-lidded expression, as he listed the flaws in Carver's dagger work. Carver grimaced. If Angel had to bet, it was word-for-word what Rath had said to Carver on the day that Angel had been introduced. Jester had a memory for the spoken word that was astonishing. What he *did* with the memory? Not so much.

Of Angel, Rath had merely said, "Another one?"

It still stung, but Angel had said nothing, as if it were a test.

Rath's lips had quirked in what might have been a smile on another face.

Jay cleared her throat again, and this time, her hands settled on her hips. Arann leaned over and dropped his fist on Jester's head. Jester fell over.

Finch and Teller came back into the room carrying plates. They were the same plates, but there was different food on them. Cake.

"What the Hells?" Duster said, eyes narrowing.

Jay turned to Arann, who crouched down and pulled something flat from behind Lefty's back. Lefty waved at Duster, as Arann handed the flat package to Jay.

"What *is* this?" Duster said again, looking from face to face in a room that was—for one miraculous moment—silent.

It stayed silent.

Jay took an audible breath and said, "Happy birthday, Duster." She handed Duster the parcel; it was long, narrow, and flat.

Duster looked at it as if it were a snake, and its fangs were bared.

"Take it," Jay told her. "It's a present."

As if that much weren't obvious. On the other hand, Duster was still looking at the package with a mixture of fury, fascination, and horror. Her mouth opened, like a trap with no hinges.

More silence, and it was unbroken until Duster swore.

It was, as far as cursing went, impressive, even for a sixteen year old who'd spent all her life on the streets. She reached out and slapped the parcel out of Jay's hand. It landed on the floor, but the noise it might have made couldn't be heard over Duster. "I'm not some *fucking* birthday girl!"

Jay took a less audible breath. "It *is* your birthday."

"It's my birthday if some godsdamned Priest didn't lie! What bloody difference does it make?" She swore some more, but as everyone had already cleared the ground at her feet, there wasn't anyone she could easily kick.

Without another word, she turned on her heel and stormed out of the apartment. If Angel had ever wondered where that phrase had come from, he now knew: she looked like the type of lightning-heavy cloud that blocked out all light. But less friendly.

The slam of the door was almost a relief.

Jay waited for the sounds of stomping to recede, and then she winced. "Well," she said, as she bent down and picked up the present, "that could have gone worse."

"Yeah, no one's bleeding," Lefty added helpfully. "Can we eat that if she's not here?"

"Might as well. But save her a piece."

They all looked at Jay as if she were crazy.

Angel, on the other hand, pulled a plate off the floor and walked it to the kitchen. "This one," he said, placing it on the counter, "is Duster's."

"The cat's going to knock it off and eat it," Lefty pointed out.

"The cat's not stupid enough to eat Duster's food."

Lefty shrugged; it was true.

"Everyone else," Jay said, easing herself back onto her chair, "eat. She won't be back for at least two hours."

"A copper on morning," Carver offered. "... It was just an idea."

Jay let the silence tell him just how good she thought the idea was.

"You knew she wasn't going to like it," Finch finally said.

Jay crumbled a piece of cake between her fingers as if forgetting it was supposed to be edible.

"Jay—"

She shook her head. "Yes, I knew she wasn't going to like it. But it's been three years. Maybe more. Everyone else has birthdays. She's—" She shook her head again, and this time, she pushed her hair out of her eyes.

"She's better than she used to be," Teller said. "She's always that little bit better than she was. We know it's not easy. For her. For you."

Angel had cleared his throat, and said, quietly, "She never relaxes unless we're fighting, about to be fighting, or running from a fight." He leaned against the wall. "But ... she's there, when we're fighting. She's there when we need her. She hates taking orders, but Jay—she takes them. From you."

"I should order her to eat her damn cake and take her damn present."

"If you did," Angel said with a shrug, "she'd do both." That much, he'd seen. If he could find nothing else to say about Duster, he could say that.

"I am *not* going to order someone to eat cake!"

"She doesn't understand why it's important to you." Angel didn't personally understand why it was important to Jay either. But it was; he could see that. "If you can make her understand it, she'll eat."

Jay could still surprise him. Maybe she always would. "I don't want her to feel left out." It was something that

Finch might have said. Or at least that he wouldn't have been surprised to hear Finch say.

"I don't think she cares."

"*I* care. Look, she's never going to be entirely comfortable with family things, but this *is* her family. I want her to understand that. What family means to her—meant to her—it has to change. We're her family, now. And yes, I know she'll take orders, especially in a pinch. But it can't just be about that."

"Why?"

Jay looked up, met Angel's gaze. "You tell me," she said evenly.

He grimaced, acknowledging her point. His chin dropped toward his chest as he slid, slowly, down the wall. "She's afraid." He looked up and added, "And don't repeat that unless you want me dead."

Jay laughed.

Angel didn't. "She's afraid of being happy. This—all of this—it's like a reminder of everything she doesn't think she is. She's not comfortable when people are relaxed and happy."

Jay nodded. Angel looked up to see Teller and Finch; they were watching him carefully. Sometimes he felt like everything was a test. But at the same time? He felt like passing—or failing—didn't really matter.

"It's hard, to trust." He shook his head, clearing the wrong words, trying to grope his way toward the right ones. "I don't mean it's hard to trust you. I trust you. It's . . . easy to trust you, Jay. You have a foul temper," he added, still musing; he almost missed her grimace. "But it's not an ugly temper. Mostly.

"It's hard to trust . . . this." He lifted a hand, waved it, encompassing in that gesture all of the den who weren't actively part of this conversation: Fisher, Lander, Lefty, Arann, Jester, Carver. Encompassing, as well, the small, cramped room, the warped shutters and open windows, the plates on lap or floor, the bedrolls which had been tossed in a large pile in the corner—even the kitchen. Perhaps especially that.

He gazed at his knees. "I lost my family in Evanston. My family, the farm, some of my friends."

Finch touched his knee. "You don't need to talk about it if you don't want to," she told him.

He knew. He knew Jay's rules about the past. But he smiled at Finch as he spoke. "Not even my nightmares were as bad as the truth. And it took me months to realize that it *was* true: they were dead. I had no home, no life, no chores. The chores? I hated them, but they were *what I did*.

"You found me," he continued, his gaze tracing wood grain until it ran into Carver's leg. "I followed you home." He kept the bitterness out of the words without effort; the shame still tinted them. "How long have I been here?"

"Four months, give or take a few days," Jay replied.

Four months. "It feels longer," he told her, not looking at her. "But it feels real. I wanted—I needed—to find a place to belong. A home. A family. But there are some days I wake up, and I see the signal fires burning, and I see the smoke of bigger fires, and I hear the bells ringing—and I hear them stop—and I know, I mean, *I know* it can't last. This," he added, again waving his hand around the room in a circle. "And sometimes, when I know it, I'm afraid to want it too badly because if I want it, something will take it away." It was hard to say the words out loud.

Hard to hear them. But Jay had asked.

"Duster's more afraid of that than I will ever be. And when Duster's afraid something bad will happen, she tries to make something bad happen, because then it'll be over. The worst will have happened. She'll have something to face down or fight." He looked up at Jay then.

Jay nodded, her lips curved in something that was almost a smile. Not a smile, though; it was heavy with some sadness, some worry, that a smile couldn't quite hold. "And you said you didn't understand Duster."

"I don't. But I recognize my own fear when I see it in someone else."

"Fair enough. But it is really any better to have nothing?"

"No. But if that's all you're certain you'll have, sometimes you think it'll hurt less if you bring it on yourself."

Jay looked at him for a moment, and then nodded. "Thanks."

"For what?"

She stood, picked up the plate that still had mostly cake on it, and gave him a rueful smile. "It's not the way *I* think. Sometimes I need the reminder."

Angel rose as well. "How would you see it?"

She shrugged, made her way to the kitchen. "I lost everything," she told him. "I should have been able to do something. I didn't. Or couldn't.

"But I wouldn't have made it this far without help. I had help." She nodded in the general direction of the den. "This is my family. The only thing that scares me, these days? I'll lose 'em *because* I don't do something, or because I see something but I don't understand it in time. It won't be because I'm afraid they're important, or even too important—they're everything I've got. I'm not ashamed of that."

Chapter Two

6th of Morel, 410 AA
Twenty-fifth holding, Averalaan

SINCE NO ONE HAD BEEN STUPID enough to take up Carver's bet, Carver was no richer when the apartment door opened in the morning.

It was impossible to open that damn door quietly, even on a bet; it was, however, possible to sleep through the creaking. If you were in the room, where Jay, Finch, Teller, Lefty, and Lander usually threw down bedrolls, there was a good chance you'd miss it if the person who opened the door was trying to sneak in.

Arann, Carver, Jester, Fisher and Angel usually took up the floor in the big room. Arann could sleep through a fire. Jester could sleep through a flood. Fisher and Carver paid attention, though. Angel could probably sleep through either a fire or a flood, but this was never put to the test; Angel was not asleep.

City time and Town time were measured slightly differently, in part because the Common required the farmers and merchants *on* Town time to actually travel to the City itself. The Port Authority had been on Town time; Terrick's early mornings had been some part of Angel's days for the months that he'd lived in Averalaan.

Four months with the den, in much more crowded

quarters, hadn't changed this. Admittedly, sleeping at all had been difficult for the first few days; Angel wasn't used to this many people crammed into this little space for any reason other than deep and bitter cold. But after four days of almost no sleep, exhaustion did what comfort couldn't, and after that? He slept. He told himself it was better than being alone and, mostly, he believed it.

Carver and Fisher were awake. They weren't *obviously* awake, but their breathing shifted as the door slid open. They didn't move, though, and Angel, propped up by arm and wall, slid quietly back to the floor.

The shutters were closed, but they leaked light in precise beams. Those beams didn't reach the door, but they didn't have to; Duster moved slowly and cautiously into the room. He could see her face for a brief moment as it was caught, and cut, by light; could see the slight darkening of a bruise across her cheek. Her lips were swollen, and her left eye, swollen as well. She had to step carefully if she didn't want to wake Arann. Arann was about as easygoing as anyone in this den ever got— but he didn't always wake well. And when he woke badly? You remembered that he was also the biggest person in the den.

Lefty could usually calm him down, but they took their cue from Lefty's attempts, all of which involved keeping as much space as possible between himself and the not-quite-awake Arann. Arann frequently slept closest to the door because it was farthest away from anyone else.

Duster sidestepped him neatly, and with the practiced ease of long habit. She didn't like to be confined. She couldn't be. If she woke at night—and she often did—she would sneak out the same way she was now sneaking in.

She stopped for a moment, until the floorboards had settled, and then she retraced her steps slightly, and turned toward the kitchen. Angel could see that much, but not more unless he wanted to get up and follow her. He didn't; he listened instead.

Heard the very quiet movement of dishes. A pause,

another movement. In the darkness, the sounds gathered, told a broken story. Plate against plate. Plate against plate. Plate against counter. No fist against counter; no swearing. Angel took a breath, a slow quiet breath; held it a moment. He heard something that wasn't a plate hit the counter; wrong sound for a hand. It took him a moment before he realized what it probably was: Jay had left Duster's present there, with the cake.

She had picked it up, put it down. Not with force this time; no one was watching.

He listened hard, and after a moment, heard movement, heard Duster walking quietly toward the room. She slept there—when she slept at all—between Finch and Jay. In another hour, it would be moot; they'd all be awake and tripping over each other's feet. In two hours? Out in the Common, or anywhere else they needed to be.

He waited, listening, until Duster found some room; heard Finch's sleepy mumble, Duster's genial curse. It passed for an apology around these parts. He heard cloth rustling, wondered—briefly—if Duster was getting changed. Waited.

When it had been silent for at least ten minutes, he slowly pushed himself off the ground, and traveled the length of the wall, taking the same care that Duster had taken to avoid touching Arann.

He made his way to the kitchen.

The cake was still sitting on its plate on the counter; she hadn't touched that.

But the present? Gone. She'd taken it with her.

He wondered if she'd open it.

Jewel hated mornings. In particular, she hated mornings that started—as this one did—with Duster's cursing. If Jewel hated morning, Duster *loathed* it with unbridled passion. The fact that this morning occurred an hour after Duster had finally come home probably didn't help; the fact that the night had occurred like an accident—and judging from Duster's blackening eye and puffy lips, not a harmless accident either—helped even less. Finch was doing her best not to notice Duster's face. Jewel, annoyed enough to be awake—again—didn't care.

She shrugged herself out of her bedclothes, and out of the newest bedroll in the room, and scrounged around for clothing that wasn't too dirty. She didn't particularly relish the thought of laundry, but it was warm enough; they could head to the riverbank, and they could beat things into shape after they'd hit the Common.

Duster, on the other hand, was wearing pretty much the same clothing she'd worn yesterday, and the day before. It was distinctly dirtier at the moment.

"Jay?" Teller's voice.

She answered, finished pulling her tunic over her head, and answered again. "What?"

Teller was standing to her left, crouched over the iron box.

"Never mind," she told him. She knew what he was looking at. Or, more specifically, what he wasn't looking at. Duster's birthday had not been cheap. Or affordable, really. "Just dig out some of what's there. It'll get us through the week."

He nodded, and picked through the coins.

Farmer Hanson was waiting for the den, as he so often did. The market guards were less obviously waiting, and made some show of checking for things like shirts and shoes; it was just on the edge of too crowded for it to be a good show, but they had to make their point.

Jewel shrugged her way past the guards, smacked Jester across the back of the head because he had that *I'm going to do something funny* expression and the guards had that *We've already been here too long to find cheeky amusing* expression, and walked directly to Farmer Hanson's wagon. Duster followed close on, the way she always did; the only thing that got between Duster and Jewel in a crowd? Jewel's shadow.

She knew it shouldn't have been a comfort, but it was. She couldn't count on Duster to be normal, or happy, or civil—but she could count on Duster. Sometimes, on the other hand, she could count on Duster to break the hand of a passing thief, and she'd gotten used to saying *Don't break anything* the minute Duster swiveled her head in a certain way.

Arann pulled up the rear, as he always did, and Carver walked shoulder to shoulder with Duster. Of all of her den, it was Carver that Duster was most comfortable with. Carver and the newest member, Angel. Angel walked on Jewel's other side, when there was room, and Jay watched him, briefly. He never tried to steal much.

Which was good, because they didn't need to steal much just now; let some other hungry kid do the stealing and get away with it. If things didn't pick up, they'd be stealing just ahead of winter. And stealing for ten? Way, way more trouble than stealing for one had ever been.

But she didn't regret having the ten. She just hated not knowing how to *keep* them. And that was something she didn't want to think about today. Because she could see, jutting slightly against the blouse of an oversize tunic, the pommel of a dagger, and she knew that Duster had not only opened, but kept, the present given to her.

She didn't ask; no one would. It would be just like Duster to pull it off and throw it away, and in this crowd, it would be gone. But . . . still. She was wearing it. She'd kept it. That was a start.

That and, as Lefty had cheerfully pointed out, no one was bleeding.

She put a hand on Duster's elbow, and when Duster looked at her, she signed, *No trouble.* Duster grimaced and nodded, but added, *Won't start any.* Jewel knew she wasn't going to get better from Duster today.

Jewel approached Farmer Hanson and waved. He shouted hello in between the sentences he was shouting at an older woman who had perfected convenient deafness, and she waited until he was finished.

He counted. He always counted, these days. "Where's Finch?"

"Back home. With Teller, Lefty, Lander, and Fisher. With any luck, they'll be down riverside, washing clothing so we don't frighten the guards."

"Mrs. Keppel said you had a bit of a run-in with Carmenta's den?"

Mrs. Keppel, Mother be kind to her, had a very big mouth. "No, *she* had a bit of a run-in with Carmenta's den. We had a bit of a nothing." She turned half her attention to food. The carrots were small, but the potatoes were solid. There were some early berries as well, and Jay wanted them so badly she could almost taste them—but they were expensive, and she couldn't buy enough for ten.

"Bit of a nothing?"

"No one was hurt. Besides Mrs. Keppel."

"That's three times in the last four months, Jay," the farmer said.

She handed the basket, which was growing heavy, to Carver, and continued to pick idly through the stock. Lemons. Ugh. But, mindful of Rath's advice, she bought them, thinking that even limes weren't as bad.

"They didn't used to bother the older folk," the farmer said.

"That's because the older folk generally have no money."

"So what's changed?"

Jewel frowned. "I've been wondering that, myself. Normally, they wouldn't bother—the older people are more likely to call in the magisterians, if nothing else." She shrugged. "But—there aren't as many guards in the streets these days, and it looks like they pulled the best of them off the holdings and put them outside the Common gates." She didn't want to add the rest of the truth: Most of the dens, when things were lean, picked pockets and the odd bit of merchandise from people in the Common, which of course meant people like Farmer Hanson.

The farmer notwithstanding, she preferred thieving in the Common; the chance of a fight was minimal. But with the newer guards at the gates, it was hard to even get *in* on a good day. And on a bad day? No luck.

"So you've been running interference?"

"No. We just happened to be in the right place at the right time. Or the wrong place at the wrong time."

"Jay—"

She lifted both hands in surrender. "We can take care of ourselves," she told him quietly. "And it doesn't hurt us to keep an eye out for those that can't."

He was proud of her; she could see that. But he was worried as well. He barely counted the money she put in his hand, barely paid attention to the produce she'd slipped into the baskets.

"Jay," he said, after a pause that was just a little too long, "have you talked to Rath lately?"

She was instantly on her guard. "Not recently, why?"

Farmer Hanson didn't answer for a moment. It was a long moment. "It's nothing," he finally said.

She lifted a brow, and then shoved hair out of her eyes. "Nothing?"

"It's none of my business."

Jewel almost snorted. But he deserved better than that, this farmer with his inexplicable sympathy for the starving. "No," she said quietly. "But it's still mine. I'll go see him."

"Don't mention my name."

"Wouldn't dream of it," she replied, with the hint of a rueful smile. She wouldn't have to mention Farmer Hanson; Rath was no idiot. He'd guess.

Jewel split off from the rest of the den when they were near the edge of the Common. "Go home by street," she told Carver. "I'll follow later."

Carver hesitated, which meant he stopped walking, which meant Angel ran into him, which caused the usual scuffle. Jewel reminded herself, while she waited, that she *really liked* both Angel and Carver. *"Guys,"* she said, when the reminder failed to be appropriately calming, "go home."

"Carmenta—" Carver began.

"Carmenta doesn't know about the undercity; he doesn't know about the tunnels. I'll take 'em most of the way back. And most of the way to where I'm going. I'll be good." She would be. The den, over the past eighteen months, had done both exploration and contingency planning; most of the exits and entrances into the maze beneath the City now had rope, a pack, and bandages. If Jewel had had the money, these little emergency supplies would also have included magelights. She didn't. But she carried hers with her; it was small and of no apparent value unless it was dark. In the dark, however, its glow was unmistakable.

Duster split off from the den, and came to stand beside Jewel. Jewel sighed inwardly and shook her head. "Not you, Duster. I'll take Angel."

One of Duster's brows drew closer to her hairline; both were so dark a brown in some light they looked black. But while she opened her mouth, no words came out, and when she shut it, it stayed shut. Thank *Kalliaris* for small mercies. Duster didn't particularly like Rath, and although Duster had proved herself countless times over the last three years, Rath did not like Duster.

Jewel had some suspicion about what she'd see when she finally spoke to Rath, and she didn't care to expose that to Duster, or she would have taken Duster with her.

"Angel," Duster said. It had taken the better part of three weeks before Duster was willing to use his actual name, but the months since then had made it natural.

Angel glanced at Duster. Nodded.

"You have a dagger?"

"Always."

"Good." She stepped back, joining Carver.

"Carver," Jewel said, "straight home. If you run into Carmenta, lose him."

Carver nodded. "Any message?"

"Yeah. Save some of the food for us."

*　　*　　*

They dropped down an unused chute tucked between two of the standing merchant storefronts in the Common. The chute, once meant for the type of mundane delivery that came by dirty, common laborers, was recessed far enough back from the street that the more genteel and monied of the custom could safely ignore it. It was old; the type of deliveries that had been made here had long since ceased.

Angel lifted the chute's warped hatch and Jewel dropped to the ground ten feet below; he followed, and made less noise landing than Jewel had, although he was larger in all ways. She tried not to resent it as she dusted herself off and pulled the magestone out of the pouch she had strapped to her waist on the inside of her tunic. The pouch was leather; the tunic appeared to be mostly dirt. She grimaced, thought of the riverbank and the heavy stones they used to beat clothes clean. Oh, well.

She picked up the backpack with the rope; they'd come back this way tomorrow or the day after and replace it.

Angel almost never complained. She wondered, as she walked, if he felt that he couldn't, in safety; although he'd been with the den for four months now, he had to know that everyone else had been together for years. On the other hand, he seemed comfortable enough with Carver; they argued, on and off, like brothers.

Not that she had personally had any.

She handed Angel the magestone for the next leg down, and caught it when he threw it after she'd landed. They didn't come by this entrance often, but Angel didn't seem to need to see anything more than once.

Only when they had settled into the downward slope of actual stone did Angel speak. "What's up with Rath?"

Jewel shrugged.

"You worried?"

And nodded. "Some. He can take care of himself."

"But?"

She shrugged again. "I worry. I'm good at that. Take the left," she added.

"Left?"

She thought back a bit. "You haven't come to Rath's this way before."

"No."

"Left, sorry. I forget what you've seen and what you haven't. We don't have much in the way of secrets and anything I know, I assume everyone else knows."

"Any gaps here?"

"Not this way. Well, maybe, but it's only a couple of feet; we can step across it."

Except that it wasn't, and they couldn't.

Angel stared at the fissure in the ground. He thought it was eight feet across, and it traveled to the left and right as far as the eye could see. Admittedly, given that the only light was the magelight, that wasn't far. He glanced at Jay's face before he spoke. "Did we take a wrong turn?"

He could see furrows in her forehead, and counted the seconds until she shoved one hand up into her hair and pushed it out of her eyes. Usually she used both hands, but currently one of them was gripping the magelight just a little too tightly.

Teller and Carver had both warned Angel that geography was not one of Jay's strengths. He didn't relish the idea of being lost in the undercity with only Jay as a guide, but as he studied her profile, he knew she wasn't lost. And that she knew it.

He looked at the fissure, sinking to his knees and laying his hands flat against the ground about six inches before it ended. "Good thing you brought the rope," he told her quietly.

"Can you clear the jump?"

He nodded. "Unless the edges are fragile, yeah. Even if. It's not that big a jump if you take a run at it."

"Good." Her shoulders eased slowly down her back and she lifted her chin; she spoke a single word and the magestone brightened, casting both light and shadow across anything in its radius. "You run," she added. "I'll throw you the rope when you're on the other side."

He shrugged, backed up. He hadn't lied; it really wasn't that big a jump, and he cleared it easily before he turned to look back.

"I'm going to toss you the stone and the rope."

He nodded, waited. Watched her, and it came to him as he did that she didn't want to make the jump. "Jay, are you afraid of heights?"

Her reply: she fumbled a moment with the magestone before setting it on the ground beneath her feet, and wrapped the rope around her waist, crossing the ends and pulling them tight. Then she tossed him the rope. He caught the end, looped it around his waist, knotted. It wasn't a *good* knot; a good knot would require that he hold all of the rope. On the other hand, hers was probably better, and he didn't expect to have to *use* the rope.

"Back up farther," he told her quietly. The good thing about the undercity was that you never had to shout to be heard. There was no sound here, no sea wind, no other voices.

"I can't," she replied, in a flat, tight voice. "Rope only goes so far."

He nodded. Waited for her to toss the stone across the chasm. It bounced five feet behind and to his right, skidding against the oddly smooth stone. He retrieved the light. Then he held it up, examining the fissure. "It's narrowest here," he offered.

Her turn to nod. She took a breath sharp enough to cut, tensed, and then ran. He saw her eyes close just before she bent into her knees and pushed herself up and forward. It was a good jump; she cleared the crevice by at least a foot. Angel reached down and offered her a hand, which she took as soon as she could open her eyes.

"Yes," she told him, as she stood and began to unknot the rope, "I *hate* heights." She was trembling. Angel tried not to notice. Instead, he dropped her magestone into her palm, all business. Thinking that this crack had been six feet narrower the last time Jay had come this way, and wondering what had widened it. He couldn't

come up with an answer, which was just as well; he had
a suspicion that any answer he did come up with would
be worse than not knowing.

"Next time Carver complains about rope," she muttered, as she began, once again, to lead the way, "remind
me to tell him about this."

The rest of the way to Rath's was clear, or as clear as
the undercity ever was. Jay frequently let the den forage
in buildings or around the edges of them, but not today;
today she was in a hurry. Angel knew they were short
on cash, which meant they'd have to come back to the
undercity soon, but something was eating at Jay, so he
separated *soon* from *now* and followed.

Jay entered the subbasement that led to Rath's, and
pulled up short. Angel bumped into her, but not hard;
they could never move quickly in these basements because they had to walk hunched over, even Jay, who was
never going to be tall.

She crouched, folding into her knees, and brought
the magelight to ground level.

"Angel," she said quietly, "tell me that I'm not seeing
a line of white salt on the ground here."

Angel obligingly looked. "I don't think it's salt," he
said, at last. "Or sugar. It looks like ... dense ash." He
crouched closer to the light and reached out; Jay caught
his wrist.

"Don't touch it."

"Why?"

"Just ... don't touch it." He could see her grimace
in profile, and whistled slightly under his breath. She
elbowed him backward.

"You seeing something I can't?" he asked.

She nodded. "Not—it's not feeling or *knowing*. It's—
there's light there, and it's golden."

To Angel it looked like white powder. Whatever light
she could see, he couldn't. But that was Jay; she could
see things that none of the rest of the den could. She
unfolded. "Step over it carefully; don't scuff it."

"Poison?"

"Not to us."

"Then who, rats?"

"Probably something like that."

Jay, Angel thought, taking a very large step over the fine, slender line, and leaving it as unbroken as Jay had, was the world's worst liar.

They made their way, much more slowly, toward the trapdoor and the crawl space. When they opened it, Rath was waiting. Funny, how neither of them was actually surprised to see him.

Jewel pulled herself onto solid floor with little help from Rath. Angel pulled himself up the same way, and when he was clear, Rath let the trapdoor drop. Then he stumbled, and leaned heavily against the wall.

Even in the darkness of the basement, Rath didn't look good. Jewel opened her fingers, and the magelight brightened in her palm as she whispered a word above it.

Rath's hair had always changed color with the help of hennas and dyes. At the moment, however, it looked a natural shade of brown. And gray. His skin was pale, and his face, in the light, look discolored, although it was hard to say how. But his left arm was in a sling, and his hand—or what could be seen of it—was purple, black, and yellow. He was standing.

But then again, he was leaning against the wall while he did.

"Rath," she whispered. "What happened to you?"

Rath didn't answer. From the forbidding quality of his silence, she knew he never would. And also knew that she was breaking one of the few rules that, unacknowledged, had governed her life with him.

"Angel," Jewel said. "Help him to his room."

When Angel hesitated, she cursed. "Just do it now and try not to step on the crap he's left lying all over the floor." She walked down the hall and into the kitchen. It was a larger kitchen than the den now claimed, but it wasn't cleaner, and it wasn't as well organized.

It was, however, familiar, and it was—as it often had been—lacking certain amenities.

"Jewel," Rath said, his voice traveling down the hall like a little blast of winter wind. "Why are you here?"

She ignored him. "Angel, I'm going to the well. I'll be back as soon as I can; try to get him to rest."

"I *was* resting," Rath replied, with a certain amount of annoyance, "when someone chose to attempt to sneak into my home."

"So go back to resting. I'm just getting water." She hesitated, mentally counting change. "And food."

He started to forbid it; she could almost hear the tone of his silence. But . . . Rath had always tried to teach her to be practical, and he was, in Jewel's opinion, standing only by dint of sheer, stubborn will. "Don't take the tunnels," was his compromise.

"With buckets?" she snapped back.

"Jewel, I have very little patience at the moment. Try, please, not to tax it."

"Yes, Rath." She opened the three bolts that *any* Rath door always had. "I'm leaving Angel with you. Don't argue."

"I wouldn't dream of doing so, given the remote chance it would have of changing your mind."

Jewel snorted, opened the door, stepped into the hall, and tried very, very hard not to slam it shut behind her.

To Angel's surprise, Rath did not immediately return to the bed.

It was hard to tell what Rath's version of *resting* meant, because his bed wasn't exactly clear of debris; clothing lay across it in piles of texture and color, and paper seemed to nest at the upper corner, closest to the wall. Books occupied the floor near the bed, and also stood in precarious stacks on the desk; there was a table in the room, and across it, curling in on itself, leather parchment.

It was to the table Rath repaired, while Angel hovered.

"Sit down, boy, if you're going to wait here."

"Jay told you to rest—"

"And when I have at last taken leave of my senses and I'm sleeping in the same room with five other members of your den, I will, with alacrity, obey her commands." He tried to unroll the parchment, and after a tense minute said, in perfect, clipped tones, "take the other end of this."

Jay is going to kill me, Angel thought, but he did as Rath ordered, because it was very hard not to obey Rath. Carver, Angel, Duster, and Fisher came by Rath's place when Rath had time. Since Angel had joined Jay's den, that had been twice. But Carver had pointed out that in the early days it had been twice a week.

He had taught them to fight, then. *You missed the important stuff,* was how Carver put it. What Rath had done, when Angel had gone with them, was something less martial. He had taught them to vanish. Or rather, he had criticized them for their inability to vanish. His criticism was muted when he spoke to Duster, but to Angel's eye, Duster was better at losing people. Probably because losing her was safer.

"Hold the map steady for just a few moments, and then help me move the paraphernalia from my bed. I'll be lying down by the time Jewel returns." He ran a hand across his brow, and it came away red.

Angel was silent, but the silence was different. He did exactly as Rath asked, noting what Rath marked on the parchment, and noting the fact that the parchment seemed to glow in response. Magic.

Then Angel did clear away the clothing, handling it all with care under Rath's pinched direction. Rath settled into the bed, adjusting his weight and shifting his arm into a less uncomfortable position; from the look of the arm, the choice was between less uncomfortable and painful.

"When she returns," Rath said, closing his eyes, "tell her to take the unguent from the top shelf over the mantel. She can dress a few wounds; it will make her feel useful."

"It won't stop her from worrying."

"Nothing short of death will stop Jewel Markess from worrying," was the quiet, bitter reply. "And I will thank you not to repeat that."

Jewel came back two hours later, carrying two buckets that dangled from a slat across her shoulders. Only one of these was filled with water, and it had been a good deal fuller when she had started the trek back to Rath's place. She opened the door, which no one had locked behind her. That fact told her more than she wanted to know about Rath's current condition.

She wasn't Rath; she couldn't easily find a doctor. Even if she knew where one worked or lived—and she did, at least in the twenty-fifth holding—finding one that would let her across the threshold when she wasn't actively threatening to die in the door by, say, something as obvious as bleeding, was next to impossible. That, coupled with Rath's almost legendary dislike of strangers—of anyone—knowing precisely where he lived meant food and water were *all* she could safely do.

She was Jewel Markess; she did what she could.

But it was hard, to open his door, to close it, to pick up the bucket and march it into the kitchen; it was hard to empty the food she'd managed to negotiate from Farmer Hanson out of the second bucket. It had been years—*years*—since she'd lived with Rath, but sometimes this place, this empty quiet space, still felt like home.

She was not, now, the girl she had been then. She was not as frightened, not as uncertain. She could read, and even Rath grudgingly admitted she read *reasonably well;* she could handle enough of numbers to budget, and living on her own, with an iron box of constantly diminishing coin, had made clear to her that budgeting was not optional. Rath had taught her that, picking up the strands of her father's earlier lessons; he had taught her how to read, how to write. He was—when he saw her at all—teaching her how to speak, and given that she knew damn well how to speak, this said something. Teller and Finch often accompanied her for these lessons, although neither of them appeared to enjoy the constant outburst and argument that some of his instructions provoked in Jewel.

Rath, on the other hand, liked Teller and Finch. He was quiet with them in a way that he was not quiet with the other members of her den; it was a silence of appraisal, but with no edge, no cutting judgment. Where, with Jewel, he was curt and sometimes heated, and with the others, dismissive, with Teller or Finch he was more measured in his reply, and he often took a few minutes to consider the questions they asked as if the questions themselves were inherently worthy of thought.

Jewel, on bad days, envied this horribly.

But, she thought, as she began to put wood from a noticeably tiny pile into the stove, that was a different type of bad day. Because on one of *these* bad days, she would have been sitting in her room, in silence, listening and waiting and wondering. Would he stay in bed? Would he recover? Would he go back to wherever it is he'd come from so injured? Would he never come home at all?

And as she thought it, she looked down the hall. Stupid, to waste the time. She found a pot, started water boiling, found some rags that did not look conspicuously dirty, and headed toward his room, trailing water from the bucket she had cursed so roundly at the wellside.

Angel jumped slightly when she opened the door. Whatever he saw in her face didn't instantly make him relax, and she grimaced, trying to school her expression. "I'm only here for a couple of minutes while the water boils." She saw his pale, raised brow and added, "Soup. He didn't open his mouth enough that I could see that he had all his teeth." She kept the words light, on purpose.

But he nodded gravely, and instead of returning to the chair over which he'd draped himself with a characteristic floppy grace, he walked over to the wall above the mantel, and stretching to his full height, he pulled a jar down.

She grimaced as she saw it; she couldn't quite help herself.

"Bad?" he asked, as he handed it to her.

"It's the smell," she replied, as she struggled to remove the lid. "And the texture."

He didn't even wrinkle his nose.

"You can't get this stuff off for weeks, I swear." She paused and turned to Rath, who lay still across the bed. "Look, Angel, do you want to cook?"

He shrugged, his lips quirking in an odd smile. "Thankful you brought me instead of Carver?"

"Not really. If I'd brought Carver, *he'd* be using this . . . stuff, and *I'd* be cooking." But she smiled as she said it, and he lifted the surprisingly heavy chair and put it down, quietly, by the side of the bed, taking care not to catch anything on the floor under its stout, round legs.

"Get me a cup," she told him, and Angel disappeared. She sat, heavily, and then touched Rath's forehead with the inside of her wrist.

He opened his eyes. Just his eyes, but they were ringed and dark. Not bruises. Care, she thought. Or age. Rath looked old. And tired.

"Rath," she said, very quietly.

He smiled, but it was slight, and it left creases at the corners of his mouth that spoke of pain, not amusement.

"Your arm?"

"Fractured. It looks worse than it is."

"Your hand . . . "

"That looks about as bad as it is," was the wry reply. Rath's voice was low, and his eyelids drifted down.

Jewel, inspecting his face, drew a sharp breath which Rath didn't choose to acknowledge. But she pulled a rag from the bucket, and very gently began to sponge his forehead clean. The cut an inch above his hairline wasn't deep, but it hadn't yet closed completely. This, she began to dress with the unguent. It was familiar and almost soothing, even given the smell.

He knew. He must have known; he lifted his hand—his uninjured hand—and placed it almost gently over hers. Hers stilled. "You've seen worse, Jewel."

It was true. She'd even seen Rath worse. But the only time that had happened? It was the night she knew he would send her—send them all—away. She'd lived in fear of it for months and months.

It was gone, that fear; he could only do it once. But he had. And truthfully? The hurt had been buried so deep beneath the fear and panic of having to feed, clothe, and house her entire den, she hadn't had much time to dwell on it.

But . . . she hadn't done it on her own. Rath had been there, while she looked for a place—any place—that would take their money and not toss them out the minute Rath's back was turned. Rath had answered her questions, prodding her to ask more, and to ask them herself, first. He had helped her forage in the undercity for the first of the things he could try to sell, and he had given her the money he had made when he had completed the transaction; he would not take her with him to negotiate, nor tell her where he was going.

And he'd made her promise, again, that she would bring things to him to sell—and only to him. He'd been there for her. He just hadn't been willing to have her in his space, and his life, in the same way he had when he'd first found her.

She hadn't understood *why*.

Seeing him, hand broken, arm fractured, forehead bleeding beneath the welt of sticky, smelly unguent, she suddenly did. Like the previous injuries, these weren't the result of an accident. But the last time? She'd believed that those injuries had finally reminded him of what he was called: Old Rath. He'd lived by wits and cunning and caution for his entire life in the holdings—and probably outside of them as well—and he *knew* when to cut his losses and back away.

She saw, clearly now, that he *hadn't* backed away. Whatever it was he'd been doing before he'd thrown her out of his apartments, he was *still doing*. He'd never meant to stop.

And if he wasn't going to stop, he put them all at risk *if they lived with him*. Hand still sticky with unguent, she looked away from his bruised face, his closed eyes. She could feel the slow unknotting of pain.

It stopped before she could let it go. Because she felt a sudden certainty as she gazed at his face, at his skin, at the lines around his mouth and eyes. He would go wherever he went, and he would not come back. That's the way she thought it: *not come back*. The other word, she shied away from, although it was there in its stark and empty simplicity.

But he must have felt it, or seen it; his hand was still on hers, and his eyes were still watching her face.

She worked for the words, for the breath to *say* the damn words. These words, she had *never* been good at.

His hand tightened. "Jewel," he told her softly, "I know."

He did.

The knowledge didn't comfort her; it absolved her of *nothing*.

"You *don't* know," she began. She broke off, met his gaze, and held it. Then she pulled her hand away, rocking the chair backward as she stood. She caught it as it teetered; slammed it down hard. He was injured. He was hurt. She shouldn't be angry—shouldn't be shouting—but she couldn't, damn it, stop.

He closed his eyes. "No," he replied, letting his uninjured arm fall to his side. "But what you tell me will not give me *knowledge,* either. You see what you see, Jewel. But I see what I see."

"What do you see?" Her voice was low, almost wild. She had to curb it, had to hold it in.

He shook his head.

"Rath!"

"Jewel, leave it be." He paused, and then added, "I am not your father. What your father would not hear, he would not hear because he did not believe. The failure you fear is not, in the end, your failure. What you say to me now—if you even know *what* to say—will be true. I'll understand it, little urchin, because I have *always* understood it. I did not come to this life by accident, nor do I pursue my curent goals by accident. I am not driven

by the need for money; I've always had enough to eat,
I've always had a place to live."

"Liar."

He frowned, and this time, it was not a frown of pain.
"Your manners are somewhat lacking of late."

It was not what she'd expected to hear, and her laugh
was, like her voice, wild, unexpected.

"I told you, Jewel: You cannot save everyone. Learn
to accept this."

"I'm not trying to save everyone. I'm trying to—"

"Very well," he told her, lifting a hand. "You cannot
save *me*. If that is why you came, I apologize for wast-
ing your time. I do what I do because I can. I even tell
myself it's because I *must*. I believe it," he added softly.
"And because I believe it, I do not require you to do
the same."

"It's not why I came."

"Ah. If you came for lessons, I fear that I must
disappoint."

She shook her head.

His eyes, as he gazed at her face, were clear, and the
pain left them. "Angel," he said, although he didn't look
at Angel. "Help me stand."

Bad, Jewel thought numbly. She hadn't even heard
Angel reenter the damn room.

Angel came up behind Jewel, and then hesitated for
a moment before sidestepping her. He handed her the
cup that was dangling from two fingers, and she took
it automatically while he waited. And he waited, Jewel
thought, for her order, or rather, her countermand.
She had no words to spare. All of her words were on
the inside of her mouth, her throat; they were a messy
jumble of anger and fear. She wanted to believe that if
she untangled them, if she chose the *right* words, Rath
would understand. Rath would *listen*.

Wanted to, and couldn't.

Angel took Rath's good arm, put a hand behind his
shoulder, and pulled him to his feet; he let Rath lean
against him as Rath moved to the head of his bed. He

gripped the rounded wooden end, but didn't let go of Angel, and Jewel watched him as he twisted the head of the post off. "Come here, Jewel."

She did. He handed her the knob, and pointed at the post. It was hollow. She had seen it before, of course. She'd even taken pleasure in it; it was a secret, a way of communicating with Rath if she needed to do so.

"If anything happens to me—"

"When?"

"If you prefer. When I die, and you are certain I am dead, come here. What I can leave, I will leave."

She said nothing.

"Jewel—"

"It's not a game, Rath."

"No. I merely display a sense of humor. I do not, however, require that you develop one. If I need information to reach you, and only you, I will leave it here." He held out his hand, and she handed him the top of post. He replaced it, and then shuffled, with Angel's help, back to bed.

"Angel," she said gruffly. "You finished in the kitchen?"

Angel said nothing, but he did retreat.

She listened for the sound of the door. When she heard it, she came back to the bed, and the chair she had vacated. She picked up the rag, picked up the unguent jar—the latter from the folds of a cape which lay over jackets and shirts—and began to tend him again. She worked in a silence that was part mutinous. The other part? Didn't matter.

"You do what you can," he told her. "You've always done what you can. You're blameless here."

"Does it matter? I'm not trying to lay blame."

He grimaced. "Your point," he told her, as if they were keeping score. And maybe, she thought, one of them was.

Fifteen minutes went by. Maybe more. Rath had a clock that a mage had given him, and Jewel had learned to read it. And to watch it.

Rath.

"I don't want you to die." When the words left her mouth, they surprised her. And embarrassed her, a little.

He reached out again, placed his hand on one of hers. "I don't particularly want to die. If I thought what you would tell me would preserve my life, I would listen— but you'll tell me to stop, to quit, to retreat."

"Only for now," she began.

His hand tightened. "Only for now, Jewel?"

"For now." But her gaze slid off his face, slid away.

"What are my rules for visitors?"

"Never lie to you."

"Very good. Jewel?"

"Why is it so important? What's worth dying for?"

He chuckled. It was not a happy sound. "You sound," he told her, "like a younger version of me." His hand tightened again. "Never become that. There are things in your life that you would die for."

She heard the door, this time. But she had to ask. "What do you think I'd die for?"

"Your den," he replied. "You would die, without thought, for your den."

"If I died without bloody thought, I wouldn't *deserve* them."

"No. And perhaps we come to the crux of the matter. I, Jewel Markess, don't deserve you."

"Because you haven't done anything bad enough?"

"Oh, be a good girl and shut up." But his hand relaxed, and the tone of his voice invited words, instead of rejecting them. "You'll tell me to stop or to flee, Jewel."

She swallowed. Nodded.

"I can do neither. And perhaps, one day, you will be proud of the fact; perhaps, one day, my ancestors will know, when they meet me in the Halls of Mandaros, and they, too, will forgive my desertion.

"Why did you come, today?"

"I meant to come earlier," she told him. "We're broke, and we want to head into the tunnels; we need to sell things."

He hesitated. "You'll go?"

She nodded.

"You, personally."

"Yes."

"Then go. But don't linger, Jewel, and trust your instincts while you're there. I . . . may not be in a position to fence much in the next few days. If you require money, borrow some. From me," he added.

"If it comes to that, we will." She swallowed. "Rath—"

"Stay," he said abruptly. "Stay, feed me. Read to me, if you like. Do not talk to me of death. Do not offer me your fear. I have fear of my own to drive me, and if my own fear is not strong enough to keep me from my duty, yours will only grieve me, girl. It will give me guilt and no rest, but it won't preserve my life."

And she swallowed. "Angel," she said softly, "go home." She paused. "Can you get home, from here?"

"I can walk."

She hesitated. "Carmenta—"

"I'll circle around the holding. Jay—I spent months outrunning random dens. I can make it home."

So she read.

She read from one of the books that graced the shelf above Rath's mantel, taking comfort from its aged leather, the faded brilliance of its letters, the occasional pictures. Rath had taught her well; she saw the parchment maps of the undercity, half-furled on the table that also held the magestone by which he worked. Saw, as well, the clothing that lay scattered around the room, and could pick out the pieces that had probably seen recent use. His boots were dusty, and the leather was badly gashed, as if someone, or something, had slashed at his retreating feet.

She thought of the widening chasm that she and Angel had had to cross, and shuddered, but the words on the page still left her lips.

She got up once, and went to check the soup in the kitchen before returning to Rath's room. There, she gave him water, watched to make sure he actually drank it, and read some more.

It was hard, to sit and read. He did not correct her mispronunciations, and he did not catch the words she missed; she missed them deliberately, a kind of test. His eyelids drifted down, and then sprang open, several times, but he said very little.

When she had finished reading, and checked the soup again, she spoke to him, her voice as soft and low as it had been when the text had provided boundaries for it. She spoke of Helen, in the Common, and of Farmer Hanson; she mentioned Taverson. She talked about the summer squalls which had been unseasonal and had caused gossip about the port for a few days.

She didn't ask him about the undercity. Most days, she would have. But today?

She wanted to tell him to stay out, to keep away, to abandon the tunnels on which his wealth was based. She wanted to tell him to *go home,* and since he *was* home, the words would make no sense, but they were there, waiting. Vision was strong.

And she almost hated the undercity, because she could see his death in it. He had already suffered because of what he'd taken from those silent streets; something was hunting him.

But maybe life was like that: it held your death, waiting, and you had no choice but to walk toward it if you *wanted* a life. She touched his forehead when his eyes were closed.

Then she rose again, and this time, the soup was as ready as it would be; if she let it simmer forever it would be a sort of mushy stew, with bits of disintegrating potato for ballast. She scooped some out of the pot, put it in a cup, threw a spoon in, and headed back to the room.

His eyes were open; his gaze was on the door, and although he wasn't fevered, she thought he was delirious. Because he smiled—a real smile—as she entered the room, and he whispered a name that she couldn't quite catch. She wanted to: to catch it and hold it as if it were hers.

But it passed. She came back to the chair, sat in it, the cup in her hands, and waited. When he tried to push himself up, she set the cup on the table, and helped him, rearranging the pillow at his back. All of this, wordless. It was hard, to be wordless.

She remembered the first few weeks she had lived with Rath. The silence had been so hard, because no home, no *real* home, was silent; it was full of frustration, and joy, anger and gossip. It was full of interruption, intrusion, and care. It was full of people you wanted to strangle and hug.

But she had been at home here, regardless.

He took the cup from her hands and then grimaced and held it out; she retrieved the spoon, which he could barely use. He could drink, and he did.

"You will not always be here," he told her.

"I can stay a couple of days if you need me."

He raised a brow. She knew what he meant, and she had chosen to ignore it. But politely, as he had also taught her. After a moment, he smiled. "I am feeling somewhat refreshed," he told her. "And you are obviously bored. Tell me the names of the Kings."

She stared at him.

"And," he added, "of The Ten."

"With or without their current rulers?"

"Without, for the moment. The last time we attempted this, you knew perhaps six."

She shrugged. "It's not going to make much difference to me," she told him softly. "And the things that do take up most of my time."

"Not enough of your time that you didn't pick up Angel."

"Angel was different."

"They always are. The Kings?"

She thought about telling him to stop. She thought hard about it. "Cormalyn and Reymalyn," she replied. "They're *always* Cormalyn and Reymalyn."

"Good. The Queens?"

"Siodonay the Fair and Marieyan the Wise."

"Good. The Ten?"

Really, really thought hard about it. "Look, Rath—"

But she saw his expression. She couldn't even describe it because she didn't understand what it meant: it wasn't pleading, and it wasn't desperation, and it wasn't fear, or love, or pride. It was maybe all those things. He didn't want her to stay to feed him or dress his wounds; he *allowed* that, for her sake.

But this? He wanted this for his own, somehow. For his sake.

And she hated it, because she hated exposing her ignorance. But in the end?

She would do it, for Rath. Because if she did, he would let her do the other things: feed him, dress his wounds, watch him sleep, and clean his damn kitchen. She could come here during the day, after the market. He had money, and she was willing to borrow it against future earnings, at least until he was on his feet. Maybe a week. Maybe two. Then she'd take Duster and Carver and head into the undercity.

"The Ten, Jewel."

"I'm thinking, I'm thinking." She exhaled. Yes, she could do that; the den would understand. "Terafin. Darias. Kalakar. Berrilya. Korama . . . " She grimaced.

"Five?"

"I told you—" she was probably going to have to stop herself from strangling Rath before the end of the first week, however.

Chapter Three

IT HAD BEEN YEARS since they'd lived with Rath. Duster had no idea why he'd given them the boot, and Jay didn't—or wouldn't—say. None of the den had stolen anything, and none of the den was loud; none of them wandered into Rath's personal rooms—well, maybe Jay sometimes—and they didn't eat much or leave a big mess. Besides Arann, who did the odd job for Farmer Hanson in the Common, no one worked out of the basement rooms.

But he'd taken them in and he'd spit them out. For Duster, it was no big deal; she'd been kicked out of a lot of places. Jay had taken it hard, though.

Still, if he'd spit them out, he continued to insist on teaching them what he could; Carver, Arann, and Duster, along with a taciturn Fisher, would show up in front of his door for lessons, as he called them, in fighting. Most of it was smart, a lot of it was dirty. Which suited Duster fine. Arann didn't like it, but he went.

Rath still taught Jay as well, and Finch and Teller sometimes went with her. Jay could read really well now, and she could handle the numbers he gave her. Lander didn't like to leave the apartment, and Jay let him stay, but she often dragged Jester out with them. By the ear.

The streets at this time of night were pretty damn quiet, which was both good and bad. The type of noise you usually got was loud and drunken, and that type of loud could get damn ugly, depending on who'd been doing the drinking. They weren't that far from the river, and they weren't that far from the thirty-fifth holding; the den knew the thirty-fifth well enough they could walk the holding in their sleep.

Which they were practically doing. It was chilly and damp, but it wasn't cold—that would be months away. And if the streets were less than comfortable, the tunnels that led to the maze were warmer and—mostly—drier.

The maze was their secret. The den's secret, and Rath's. Beneath the older holdings, underneath basements and catacombs, tunnels existed that led, in the end, into a city. It was a city that saw no sky, no sunlight, no star or moonlight; its streets saw no patrols, and the fighting that existed between dens who were staking claims to whole holdings was nonexistent there—the dead didn't need much. They certainly didn't have voices.

But buildings—some whole, and some worn and tumbling, girded streets in the silence. It went on for miles and miles, and almost any basement that existed where a building was old enough had some entry into the tunnels.

On the rare occasions when they ventured into the undercity to scout around—or, be honest, take anything small enough to be moved and solid enough to survive it—Rath would examine what they'd found and take it away. He gave them some of the money he got for selling the pieces. It was always a lot, but they didn't find much, and in truth, Jewel wouldn't start looking until they were almost out of silver.

It was to the maze that Carver and Duster now went, finding an old building that had been broken up into dozens of ratty apartments, much like the one the den now called home.

Duster kept the magestone pocketed, her hand

around it, until they approached the old wooden chute that led to the basement. It had been boarded up against rain, but time had rusted through the nails that had first kept it in place, and no one cared enough to replace them. Duster pulled the slats up, and Carver gave her a hand down; she dropped five feet and landed in a roll. She palmed the magelight and spoke a single Weston word above it until it brightened in the gloom. Carver leaped down after it. Come tomorrow, they'd replace the flat slats. Because, among other things, it did keep the rain out.

This particular building had a decent basement that only rats used; it was tall enough for Carver to straighten out in. It also had another trapdoor, and this one, they didn't replace often, because it was the way they usually entered the maze. Duster liked the maze; she liked the tunnels that started out half-dirt and ended in worn stone, liked as well the broken arches that suggested that this buried place had once had a courtyard that saw light.

And she like the dead old buildings—stone, all—that implied wealth, because obviously, wealth hadn't done the previous occupants a whole lot of good. Their fancy homes were buried and forgotten by all but a handful of ragged orphans and a skilled thief.

Old Rath even said their language was dead.

Duster had never had much, and she hoarded her resentment. She railed against the lucky, and she scorned the unlucky; after all, luck was something you made. And you didn't whine about it after.

But in the maze—she never really liked the name "undercity" much—no one was left to whine. Teller often wondered what had happened to create this city-beneath-a-city. Duster didn't care.

"Duster."

She turned, and stopped. She had the only light in the maze, and she'd started to walk quickly, leaving Carver behind. She shrugged. Realized, after a moment, that she wasn't even going in the right direction, and grimaced.

"Where were you headed?" Carver asked, as she turned and walked back down the street.

"Probably nowhere."

His turn to shrug, and he did. "Let's go to Rath's," he told her. The unspoken *Jay is waiting* hovered a moment in the air. Duster nodded and set off at a brisk pace down the right road.

Jay was waiting for them; they didn't even have to crawl out of the basement to reach her.

"How's Rath?"

"Enraging," she replied. It was a terse word, and didn't invite questions. But as she climbed down to join them, Jay made a face and added, "I apparently don't 'retain enough.' He's frustrated."

"He been out at all?" Carver made room by flattening himself against the nearest wall. Which was mostly very wet, very dense dirt.

"Not during the day," Jay replied with a shrug. "I have. I apparently take either too long or not enough time, depending on his mood. Which is near to foul."

It didn't much surprise Carver that Rath was not a good patient. "What've you been doing?"

"Reciting lists of names."

"Which names?"

"All of them. I mean *all* of them. Swear to the gods he's going to expect me to list the name of every damn ratcatcher in the City some day soon."

Duster snorted, which was her version of laughter.

"The Ten," Jay said, as she made her way down the tunnel. "The guilds, and the guildmasters. The churches. The gods."

"What, he thinks you don't know the names of the gods?"

Jay shot Carver a look. Duster snorted again.

"Okay. So . . . maybe you don't know the names of all the gods."

"The Merchant Authority. The names of the officers of the Authority. I didn't even know the Merchant Authority *had* officers. Let's see . . . military ranks. I drew the line at House crests."

"Did he ask you for the names of all the ruling lords of the other noble houses?"

"Please don't give him any ideas. He's capable of making me totally miserable with the ones he already has."

Duster snorted for a third time, which was about as much mirth as Duster ever showed.

"You sure you want to do this tonight?" Carver asked. Even in the scant light, Jay didn't look great. She was tired.

"There is no day or night in the undercity. And we're broke."

Which more or less settled that.

Duster liked the maze.

Given that there were no fights to be found here, and nobody that had to be taken down a peg, this surprised a lot of the den. Duster knew it, and mostly didn't care. Lander had asked her why she liked it, because he was probably the only person who could.

She couldn't answer. Maybe she didn't want to. Liking things? It made you vulnerable, if people knew about it. But she liked the secrecy of it, the hidden things, the fact that everyone who had ever lived here was dead. And she liked the fact that Jay almost never came here without her. Even though there was no need for muscle, no need for Duster's known skill.

She didn't particularly mind if Carver came along as well; he could carry the rope. But she led. These days, when they reached the maze proper, it was always Duster who led. Duster had a better memory than Jay, and sometimes she thought she could *feel* familiar streets beneath her feet. She didn't share this. Not with words. Not any way but this one: she walked, and they followed.

"Where do you want to start?" she asked Jay. She always asked Jay.

Jay shrugged. Duster could hear the movement in the rustle of cloth; she didn't bother to turn around to see it. She felt restless, but she knew it was late and Jay was tired. Two weeks of Rath would make anyone tired, except maybe Teller. Still, she wanted to go somewhere different. See something different.

So she began to walk down the streets of the maze. She could see the facades of buildings disappearing into the constant darkness, but they had two stones tonight; she had Jay's and Jay had Rath's. She could afford to walk ahead a little.

She heard Carver's voice, heard Jay's, didn't pay much attention to the words. They were quiet; no panic, no anger. Nothing she had to worry about. They liked to talk. Duster didn't. But she no longer hated it when everyone else chattered like insane animals. That was something, wasn't it? And unless she was actively angry, they didn't shy away from her; they didn't look at her as if she were insane and dangerous—and that was something, too.

But sometimes it was peaceful, to be here. With Jay, who didn't care. With Carver, the only other person she was sure she could rely on in a fight. She paused, touched a wall. It was part of a row of buildings, with narrow fronts—for the maze. The buildings in the maze all seemed to be wider than the ones on the streets above.

"That one?" Carver said.

Duster frowned. She headed toward the short flight of steps that led to the door. The steps were stone, and they took her weight. But not much else in the place looked like it would. She backed out and shook her head, and they continued walking. Walking, stopping, checking the buildings.

They also looked at what lay in the streets, lights bobbing as they navigated their way around chunks of fallen stone. They saw, as they often did, the writing that Jay called Old Weston, but it was all attached to stone that the whole den working together wouldn't have had a hope of moving.

They kept walking. The streets widened, and Duster

took the second left, veering off from the central maze. They sometimes had better luck on the narrower streets, although the buildings were often barely standing.

"Have we been down this street before?" Carver asked her.

She shrugged, and then thought about it. Took a few steps, testing the ground. There were places in the maze where it wasn't entirely safe to walk, but this felt firm enough. It didn't feel familiar, though. And she wasn't about to put that into words. Instead, she said, "Don't think so." Which was safe.

Carver stopped walking and set the pack down. He pulled the rope out, and tossed one end to Duster. Duster hated ropes. But she knew why they were necessary, and it was either wear the knots, or give the lead to Carver, who didn't hate them.

She chose to wear the rope, today; Carver held the other end. Jay was like a shadow, but she accepted Duster's lead. Here, in the dark places of the world, who else but Duster? The street narrowed as Duster walked it, testing it for cracks, for breaks. Here, the facades of buildings had fallen, and the parts of those buildings that were not stone had rotted away, leaving only the detritus of their fall.

Duster stopped.

"Dead end?"

"No."

"What?"

"I think I can see past the blockage."

Carver said, "How much blockage and how much can you see?"

"A lot, and a little. Jay?"

Jay slid past Carver, stepping almost exactly where Duster had stepped, and stopping about five feet from Duster's exposed back. Duster didn't expose her back all that often.

"See it?" Duster asked softly.

Jay, squinting in the light of two magestones, hesitated. "Yeah," she finally said.

"See what?" Carver asked.

"Something shiny."

He whistled. "Worth it?"

She drew a breath so sharp it was almost a whistle. "Maybe," she said. To Duster it sounded almost like no. They must be *really* broke. "I think there's a chance Duster and I can get through the gap—if nothing falls on us when we move things. You won't fit."

"Teller or Finch?"

She hesitated. Lifted a hand in den-sign. *No.*

"Jay—"

"Go home, Carver. We'll check it out."

He clearly didn't like it, and he waited a few minutes.

"Carver." She turned, sliding her hands up to her hips, where she perched them.

"I don't like it," he told her. Which was obvious, but sometimes Carver was like that.

She shrugged. "I don't like it much either, but—we're good. Go get Lander; the two of you can scout elsewhere." She covered her mouth as she yawned, destroying her posture. "Or, better yet, get sleep. We're good."

He handed her the rope, and she handed him the magestone.

Jewel tied the rope in a knot around her waist. She sometimes tied it around her arms, but it took longer and it was less convenient. Duster, used to this, was busy shining light into the cracks that always existed when large chunks of rock fell on top of one another. When Jewel was ready, she gave the rope a tug. Duster stepped back immediately.

"Just hold the light up, let's look at what's on top."

Duster nodded, and opened her hand; Jewel spoke a simple word and the light the stone shed increased. In the dark, it seemed blinding, but it wasn't; magelight was weird that way. Jewel could increase the brightness by quite a bit, but she never chose to do so; light could attract unwanted attention.

Rath had taught her that, and even when Lander had sensibly pointed out that the brightest of lights, here, was unlikely to disturb anyone, Jewel had thanked him, and continued to keep the light down.

"It's straight to the top from this angle," Duster finally said. "But I think if we head to the left a bit, we might have a chance at climbing. You want to try climbing?"

She didn't; she hated climbing. Duster, on the other hand, was good at it. "I'm not sure we can get through the cracks here. What's to the left?"

"Narrower, at least to start."

"Anything look like it's likely to fall on us if we jiggle it?"

"Not here."

Jewel cursed softly. "Let me try going in."

Duster nodded and handed Jewel the magestone. One day, when they were very rich, they needed about eight of them. Preferably attached to chains you could hang around your neck. She adjusted the rope, turned sideways, and began to inch her way, with care, around the ragged edges of stone. She hit one snag, and scraped the skin off her shoulder, when the very minuscule opening veered sharply to the right and she had to both stretch and flatten herself against the rock in order to navigate herself free.

But after that, it opened up enough that she could walk, rather than sidle, and she turned back, positioning the magestone. She gave the rope two tugs.

"It's tight," she said, pitching her voice back the way she'd come. "But you can stand in it; there's no crawling." Which wasn't always the case. "It looks clear, here; we couldn't see much because of the bend."

Duster came through. It took her about ten minutes to scrape herself round the one sharp corner, and she made certain that any listening god got an earful while she was doing it.

"Never heard that one," Jewel told her den-kin when she at last pulled free.

Duster snorted. And swore. "I left half my skin on that damn rock."

"I left half mine on the inside of the shirt I'm going to have to pound clean."

"Why? No one can see the inside of your damn shirt." Duster snorted again. "Let's hope we can get out; I'm not going back that way."

"I can probably push from this side."

"Not and live."

Jewel laughed. Her shoulder stung, and she noticed the skin around her wrist was also raw. "Let's go find gold. Or something we can sell." She started to head out, testing the rope to make sure it was secure.

The space between fallen chunks of rock never narrowed as badly again, and in places the path was wide enough that Jewel could see the street, or what had once been street, beneath her feet. She bent once or twice to examine the ground, and Duster bent with her; it was odd. It wasn't flat stone—Rath had told Teller, on one of their many runs into the undercity, that the larger chunks of rock were probably from fallen causeways— and it wasn't the oddly cobbled stone that the engineers of the narrower streets had employed. Here, without sun, and without much in the way of water, nothing grew between the stones. Bats sometimes flew in the air above their light, but if Jewel were honest, the only other living things she'd glimpsed tended to scuttle. Quickly.

She shook her head, reached out, and tracked grooves, deep grooves, in the rock just in front of her boots. She'd mistaken the rock for very large cobblestone, but it was all of a piece, and she traced the curve with her fingers until her fingers hit the edge of sheared stone. "I think these are letters," she told Duster.

"Old Weston?" Duster had never been willing to sit and study Old Weston. Truth to tell, only Teller and Jewel had put in the time; Finch was interested in it, but she preferred to get the concise version, and Rath was never concise while teaching.

"I think it must be—there's not enough visible here, but maybe once we get out." She looked left and right, and saw the irregular edge of sharp rock in both directions. She wanted a glimpse of the buildings that had once stood in their place, because that would tell her how wide this particular street had been. If it even was a street. Rath had once pointed out the cloisters of a building that must have once been a towering cathedral; since not very much of the building remained, what was left suggested alley. And wasn't.

Jewel stood and began to walk forward again; it helped that there wasn't any other direction to walk in, because back was all Duster. "You know the part where I said it all looked clear from here on?"

Duster swore. She was useful, that way.

It took about half an hour to clear the rocks. In the last stretch, they did, in fact, have to crawl, but the crawling was easier because nearer the ground, the space was at its widest. Small slivers of stone that had probably never been disturbed lodged themselves in Jewel's palms and knees, but Duster, flattened almost entirely against the ground, left off cursing for a bit to save breath. "I am *not* going back that way," she said, in that tight voice that meant she was talking through her teeth. "So there'd better be another bloody way up."

Jewel, for once, had nothing to say.

After Duster was no longer practically biting Jewel's boots, neither did she.

They emerged into a room. Into, in fact, what looked like a giant hall. The ceilings here had not been sheared off by the fall of stone and other buildings, and they rose and rose until their heights could only be glimpsed by almost falling over. Which Jewel did.

Duster, who still had some dignity, put a hand out and caught her den leader's shoulders before she toppled.

The walls here were the color of dry earth. Cold, dry earth. They rose into arches that seemed to support the world. Jewel frowned, and then spoke a single word. The magelight in her hand guttered.

But the halls could still be seen, and seen clearly.

Jewel turned to look back the way they'd come. The

rocks that had blocked the last of their passage were, like the walls of the hall itself, the same pale brown; she could not see past them or above them.

"Jay?"

"You can see, right?"

Duster nodded. "Why are the rest of the walls standing?"

"Funny, that's what I was wondering." She hesitated and then added, "we might end up crawling back out."

Duster grimaced, but understood: whatever it was that had preserved this hall didn't extend to the rest of the undercity, and it was in the rest of the undercity that ways up were found. She shrugged, and took a step toward the nearest standing wall. "Where are the lights?"

"I don't know. Possibly in the ceiling." It had to be magelight; it was too even, too regular, for anything else. That, and it was still shining.

"Too bad. We could use a few."

It had been Jewel's second or third thought as well. And even if they'd no personal need for them, they could easily sell a magestone. But the ceiling was never—ever—going to be accessible to anyone but a mage. Or a whole horde of men with scaffolds and ladders. She didn't have access to the former, and Rath would slowly murder her if she tried to bring the latter here.

But glancing at the floor, she saw grooves in stone, and although they were long and deep, they did, in fact, form letters. They were not, however, Weston letters of any vintage that Jewel recognized.

"Jay?"

Jay looked up.

"Rope?"

Jewel nodded, and they both untied their respective ends. Whatever had stopped the walls from being crushed had clearly preserved the floor; it was unlikely that they'd hit a crevice or thin stone here. Carver, on the other hand, had taken the empty pack. Jewel grimaced and coiled the rope, tying it into an awkward circle. She stuck her right arm through it, and tried to perch its mass over her shoulder. "Next time, remind me to bring parchment." Rath had a bunch, and given the past week, she'd feel no guilt *at all* for borrowing some of it.

Duster nodded.

They were standing at what might have been the entrance, and the hall stretched out before them, not into darkness, but into the distance.

"Do you think their Kings lived here?"

"Or their gods," Jewel replied, without thinking. Thought caught up with her, and it was a cold thought; she felt it settle uneasily around her body, and drew her shoulders in.

"You think this was a temple?"

Jewel didn't answer.

After a moment Duster shrugged; temple or palace, it didn't matter to her. What did—what always did—was what, if anything, could be carried. In this case, the answer was: not much. Whatever they took would have to go back through the accidental passage created by the fall of large slabs of solid stone. Jewel watched her walk toward the wall on their right, and, shaking herself, she moved toward the wall on their left. Walking this way, they began to traverse the hall.

The first thing they discovered as they walked were the faintly luminescent symbols engraved on the walls. They were identical on the left and the right, and they appeared in pairs. Jewel's lack of parchment and coal frustrated her greatly, here. She knew damn well she wouldn't remember them; they were too damn complicated. And she knew, when she told Rath, that he would want the information.

Duster, on the other hand, was Duster. She had taken out her knife, and she was picking at the wall.

"Duster!"

"I think this is gold," Duster said, without looking up. "In the grooves."

Jewel hesitated. What had Rath said? The dead wanted for nothing, needed nothing. She believed it, most times. They didn't need bowls or scraps of rotten armor. They certainly didn't need gold, if Duster were right. But . . . the rest of the undercity felt like an empty place. This hall, with its diffuse light, its intact ceilings, its standing walls, didn't.

Jewel walked over to where Duster was chiseling stone, and grimaced. It was, among other things, hellish on a knife edge if you weren't careful.

Duster glanced at her. "You going to stand there and watch me until we starve, or did you want to help?"

Since starvation was not entirely theoretical at this point, Jewel brought the magestone out of her pocket and whispered the activation word. It glowed as she held its more focused light above the groove at which Duster was chipping.

"I don't think it's gold," she said.

"If it is, it's not coming off." Duster sheathed her knife almost reluctantly, and unfolded. "This isn't so bad," she said, stretching her arms. "We could live here. It'd save us rent money."

"If we could find a way in that didn't involve crawling."

"There's got to be another way in. And out. And there's got to be other stuff in this place that we can sell. C'mon."

Duster was pleased with the idea of moving the entire den here—but Duster had always liked the undercity; like Lander, she found its utter silence and endless night peaceful. Jewel, walking down the long hall and wondering if it would ever truly end, was less enthused. Mostly, she grunted, made a show of looking at the walls. It wasn't entirely show; she would have liked to see a door or two open up, just to break the monotony.

But she found the symbols disturbing. Duster didn't seem to notice the difference between the symbols, but Jewel did, and some, inexplicably, made the hair on the back of her neck stand on end. Those, she didn't touch. She didn't let Duster touch them either, although that was harder; Duster was good if Jewel could say she had a *feeling,* but bad if she thought it was just superstition or fear.

It was still very important to Duster to show no fear; always would be. She was sensitive, in her way—it just didn't cause her to be any kinder. Jewel tried to sit on her growing unease. But Duster was Duster; she could tell.

They reached the end of the hall, and stopped in front of a tall, narrow arch. It, like the hall, was stone, but the stone was gray to the previous pale brown; there was no door, but beyond the arch, the hall seemed to taper, losing, in that glimpse, some of its stark grandeur.

"Jay?" Duster pointed.

Jewel nodded. Studding the stone frame of simple arch were magestones. Five in all, three of which they couldn't reach if they'd been standing on each other's shoulders, and two of which were embedded at shoulder height. Well, at Duster's shoulder. At first, they appeared to be gems, but the light they gave off was the same, in quality, if not brightness, as the light cast by the stone in Jewel's hand.

"I think they're glass," Jewel said.

"For *magestones*? What a waste of glass."

Jewel nodded; it was. "They probably didn't need to worry about the money," she said dryly. "Just the looks. It's not gold," she added, "but if we can get them out, they'll do." She kept her voice even, on purpose, but it was hard. She was excited—and relieved—because it had occurred to both of them that anything large or bulky might be hard to actually get home.

They set to work. Duster once again drew her knife, but she approached the magestone with care. It was larger than Jewel's, and the glass was cut, like a gem, with a flat and eight distinct sides. Jewel drew her own knife, but she let Duster take the lead, let Duster try to use her blade as a lever.

They worked in silence for a long time. Jewel was hungry and tired, but she was often hungry and tired, and if some of her attention wandered to home and bed, she could forgive that. Especially when the magestone finally popped out of its socket and into her hand. Duster gave a wordless shout of glee.

And then the lights went out.

"Shit."

Jewel carried her own magestone. The heavier glass one still glowed, but the hall was now as dark as the rest of the undercity. "Here," she said, and handed Duster her stone. She whispered it into brightness, and the light increased—but only in the one stone.

Which, damn it, made sense. *This* glass wasn't crafted by a mage in Averalaan; who even knew how it worked? The thought had occurred to Duster as well, and probably at the same time.

"There's no damn way these stones were lighting the whole damn hall," she said.

"No. But there was probably some spell linking all the lights."

"That's stupid."

Jewel nodded. It seemed stupid to her. Then again, whoever had designed these halls probably wasn't thinking about the convenience—or lack thereof—to a couple of would-be thieves. "We've got this, and it's still working. I think it's good enough, for now." She examined it as carefully as she could in the light of her magestone. It was clear glass, the edges still sharp, but at the base of the stone a single rune had been engraved.

"You want to try to grab the other one?"

Jewel hesitated, and then shook her head. "I want to try to crawl home for a couple of hours before Rath wakes up."

Duster shrugged, looked at the arch, and then stepped through it. When Jewel called her name, she stopped, but didn't turn. "We might as well see where this goes; maybe there's an exit closer to an actual street."

The hall through the arch did, as their glimpse of it implied it might, narrow signficantly; the ceilings were lower, although the walls that the light could easily reach curved upward at the heights. The heights themselves could be seen through a veil of darkness; Jewel whispered the light to its brightest output, which caused Duster, who was holding the stone, to curse in surprise. She dimmed it again, but didn't apologize; Duster had very little patience with apologies, and when she was in a mood, they could be actively harmful.

With the light dimmed, they started walking; Duster paused when the hall turned, slowly, to the right.

"Floor?"

"Solid." She took a few steps forward, as if uncertain, and then repeated the word. Jewel saw her crest the bend, and followed. Because they always moved more slowly in the dark, she avoided running into Duster's back, and only because of that.

And she could see why: the hall, which inclined slightly up, ended at the mouth of what appeared to be a room, and the room was so brightly lit, the sun might have been directly above it in an absolutely cloudless sky.

What darkness didn't do, with Duster, light did. She hesitated. Jewel understood why; if they were anywhere near the surface, she was Queen Marieyan the Wise. Which meant magic. Which made her teeth ache, but only because she was grinding them. If she had been with anyone else, she would have said, *Let me go first;* with Duster, she couldn't. But she could, in fact, take the lead without putting it into words; Duster would allow that.

Duster was always going to be prickly. But if she was content to let Jewel quietly take the lead, and the possible risk, she was no more than three steps behind, and in the glow of magelight, the glint of her dagger was unmistakable when Jewel glanced back. Jewel smiled, because she recognized the knife. She kept that to herself.

She couldn't change the brightness of the stone in her hand, but as she approached the room, Jewel realized it didn't matter. At its brightest, her stone would have been completely useless; the room was almost white with light, and painful to look at. But it was the pain of eyes acclimatized to shadow, and as her eyes teared, and they did, they grew accustomed enough to the light that she could ease them out of their defensive squint.

Duster pulled up to her right, and stayed one step behind. Didn't matter.

This room was not empty.

It had coffins in it. Or cenotaphs. Or whatever it was stone coffins with statues on top were called; Rath had told her, but the word fled, as words often did when she needed them.

Duster whistled. "Fancy crypt," she said softly.

Jewel nodded, silent, as she stepped into the room.

The room itself was large; certainly larger than the entire apartment the den now called home; it was also almost circular in shape. Reaching out carefully, Jewel touched one wall. It was almost white in color, but hints of smoky gray veined it. Marble, white marble. No bloody wonder the room's light was so harsh. It couldn't *all* be marble, could it?

"Jay . . ."

"Sorry."

There seemed to be three ways to enter, and she and Duster were standing at the mouth of one of them; the largest exit was girded by a plain, tall door, which rose to a peak. There was another exit, this one framed by cracked and broken stone; it led into the familiar darkness of the rest of the undercity. But the walls were otherwise unbroken, and they rose and curved into stellar vaulting above the center of the cenotaphs.

The cenotaphs themselves were arranged like rectangular clover petals. There were three, each bearing the likeness of a body. The feet of those elegant, perfect bodies pointed in, their heads toward the walls. But they weren't exactly men; they were taller than any man she had ever met. Even though the figures were lying on their backs, she could see height and majesty. *Makers,* she thought.

"You think the maker-born made these?"

Sometimes, the division between thinking and speaking wasn't sharp enough. "I think they must have," she told her den-kin. "Look at their hair. Look at their armor. I've never seen anything like the armor." It was true. The armor was faintly blue, and gilded. They bore shields which obscured their breastplates, and they carried helms in their folded hands. Hair trailed the length of their bodies, like capes, and curled around their narrow, fine-boned faces.

"Are they male or female?" Duster asked.

Good question. Jewel couldn't tell.

She took a step forward and stopped. Around each of the standing stone coffins, circles had been engraved in the ground. Three concentric circles, and between each ring, writing caught light. But the circles were dark, and seemed to grow darker as she approached. She stopped walking and lifted a hand.

But Duster, relaxed, had seen what she had seen, and Duster interpreted it differently. "That *is* gold," she said. She passed Jewel, headed to the nearest circle, and knelt before it. The dagger hovered above gold runes, gold symbols, as Duster looked for a good place to start.

"Duster, *no!*"

The dagger touched, seemed to touch, floor, and Duster cried out, briefly, as the light flared to a searing, painful white. She was thrown across the room. Her dagger went flying and clattered, skipping like a stone, across the surface of marble floor.

As it did, Jewel heard words. They were not words she understood, not clearly, but they hit her the way a gong strikes a bell: she resonated with them. She would have raised her hands to her ears, for all the good it would have done, but Duster was half a room away, and might be injured. So she ran instead, while the syllables underscored her frantic steps.

But she remembered the words. They were not the only words she would take from this place, but she would not repeat them to anyone save Rath, and even to Rath, only a few at a time, until she could make sense of them without alarming him.

Jewel ran over to where Duster had fallen; Duster was already slowly gaining her feet. She was too surprised to swear. Much. And stunned enough to wordlessly take Jewel's offered hand.

"Okay," she said. "No gold."

"I think," Jewel replied, "no room. I don't like the feel of this place."

"You couldn't have said that before?"

Jewel grimaced. "Let's just stay by the walls and see if we can get out."

Duster nodded, and then looked down at her empty hand. She cursed. Jewel, looking down at it as well, saw a white mark across her palm and the skin between thumb and forefinger.

"Duster, wait—"

Duster didn't answer. Instead, she headed back into the room's center.

"Duster, what are you *doing*?"

"I'm getting my knife," Duster snapped, without a backward glance.

"No, forget the damn knife; you can have mine. Duster!"

Duster froze for a second; her feet were at the edge of the circle that enclosed one coffin. Jewel managed to catch up, and she could see, resting against the farthest corner of the bier, the flat surface of naked blade.

She wanted to leave this place.

But Duster said, quietly, "I am not leaving without that knife." It was a stubborn quiet. An implacable quiet.

Gods damn it all, Jewel thought, furious with herself. She knew *exactly* why Duster wasn't willing to leave the knife, and she knew that Duster would never admit it. She tried to say, *Leave it, we'll buy you another one,* but she couldn't force the words from between her clenched jaws.

Because she knew that it would make no difference

to Duster. Duster couldn't be talked out of something she was unwilling to admit existed.

This is what you wanted, her Oma said curtly, rearing up in memory as she always did when things were bad. *You wanted to give her a present. You wanted to give her something tangible that she'd use. You wanted her to value this kind of thing.*

So live with it.

Living with it, Jewel thought grimly, might not be the problem. "We can try pulling it with the rope. We can toss the rope over, see if we can get it that way."

Duster said, without meeting Jewel's gaze, "I won't step on the circles. It should be safe."

What was the worst thing that could happen? Duster could go flying and hit a wall? Jewel said, "Do it quickly." And held her breath. It wasn't hard to hold her breath; she often forgot to breathe when she was afraid. And she *was,* now. She couldn't say why. She understood that it was, as they called it in the den, the *feeling.* And also understood and accepted that in spite of it, she was going to take the risk.

But things often worked out so badly when she ignored her feelings.

Duster jumped over the three circles. Her landing was awkward, because she was also afraid. She sprinted, head down, for the dagger, and reached for it without quite stopping. She missed. She slowed herself down by grabbing the edge of the damn coffin.

Jewel bit her lip, to stop from crying out. Because the statue on the bier, the one that Duster was touching, had *moved.* Not a lot. But his fingers had moved around the curve of his helm. "Duster, damn it, *hurry.*"

Duster grabbed for the knife a second time, and this time, she got it. She pivoted and made a running leap out of the circles.

Jewel watched the statue for any other sign of movement, but it was still again. "Come to the wall," she told Duster.

Duster sheathed her knife, and followed.

*   *   *

"What are they?" Duster asked, her voice low.

"I don't know."

"Magic?"

"I think so. I know we're not coming back here." She waited for the *I'm not afraid*, but it didn't come. Whatever these were—fancy golems, living statues, enchanted creatures—she didn't want to meet them, speak with them, be seen by them. That was all she was certain of, and that was all she needed.

"Jay?"

"What?"

"Are they sleeping?"

Silence. Just like Duster, Jewel thought bitterly, to give voice to something that she herself had been trying damn hard not to think. She didn't answer. Normally, that would have been enough.

"Jay, are they—do you think they're the—the Sleepers?"

The Sleepers. *Yes, damn it.* She forced herself to shrug. "What are the Sleepers, anyway?"

Duster didn't know. "End of the world," she finally said, with a shrug.

"End of the world?"

"Yeah. When the Sleepers wake."

"It's just a saying." And it was. *When the Sleepers wake* meant, pretty much, never.

"Yeah. Just." Duster cast a glance at the cenotaphs, and then shivered and turned away.

"Tunnel or door?" Duster asked, her voice subdued.

Jewel hesitated. Out of habit, she had begun to walk to the familiar dark patch that suggested broken stone and possible tunnel, but she stopped against the curve of a wall. "Let's try the door," she said at last.

"Problem?" Duster asked, after a minute.

"It doesn't have a handle." She shoved the cut glass magelight into the inside of her shirt and looked at the door. "Duster, is this glowing at all to you?"

Duster shook her head. She nodded toward the third exit, and the darkness, and Jewel almost said yes. Opened her mouth to say it.

What emerged instead was *"No."*

They both looked a little surprised. Duster said, "All right, then."

But Jewel felt that particular shock that comes with strong intuition; the cold of it, and the certainty, made her ball her hands in fists. "We have to get out of here," she said, dropping her voice. Looking, as she did, at the cenotaphs, and the vaulted ceiling above them. At shields that were, in her vision, strangely blurred; at faces that made a hollow mockery of beauty, because they *were* beautiful, but somehow terrifying as well.

She turned her attention, and her body, toward the closed door. Unlike the figures, and the room itself, it wasn't beautiful. It wasn't grand. It was just a door. But as she touched it, both of her hands spread, palm out, against its sturdy, unremarkable surface, she felt warmth, saw light.

She could never have said what color the light was, not then, and not after. But she felt it almost as gold; the gold of harvest and plenty, not the gold of the banker.

She gave the door an experimental push. "Duster?"

"What?"

"You said you lived in the Mother's temple for a little while."

"When did I say that?"

Jewel rolled her eyes; it was safe, as Duster couldn't see them. "I don't remember when—next time I'll take notes. Look, it isn't an accusation. I don't care where you lived."

Duster hesitated; it was almost physical. But after a moment she gave a very noncommittal grunt.

"I went there with my mother and father a few times. Not often," Jewel added softly, "but a few times."

"Why are you telling me this?"

"Because—don't laugh—it reminds me of that."

"What reminds you of what?"

"The *door*. It reminds me of the Mother's temple."

Duster's hands joined hers, and Duster came to stand beside her, her narrowed eyes examining the wood grain as if it were writing and she had actually bothered to learn it. "You're crazy," she finally said.

"Tell me something I don't know," Jewel replied.

"It looks like a door, to me."

Jewel bit her tongue, hard. A thousand sarcastic words jammed themselves into the backs of her teeth, and stayed behind closed lips by the sheer dint of will. "It *is* a door. It's a wooden door. How many of those do we see in the undercity on a normal run?"

None, of course. Duster knew the answer, and didn't offer it.

"But this one is standing. This one is still here. It feels solid, but old." The pauses could kill a person. "It's either been replaced, been oiled and repaired, or it's magical. Which of the three do you think is most likely in a room like this?"

Duster grunted. After a few minutes, she realized that Jewel expected her to carry at least a small portion of the conversation. Looking harassed, she said, "Not the first two."

"Right. So. Do you remember anything you were taught in the temple?"

"Why the Mother's temple? It's a *door*."

"I *don't know,*" Jewel said, and then, forcing her voice back down from its brief climb, added, "it's what it *feels* like, to me."

Silence. It was always like this when you asked a question Duster didn't expect; she had to examine it to see if she could figure out what your game was. Only if she couldn't—because in Duster's world, that meant there wasn't one—would she risk answering. "Yeah, some."

"Do you remember any of the prayers?"

"Prayers? Are you serious?"

"Yes. I only know street prayers, and those are all short and to the wrong gods."

Duster shrugged. She was uncomfortable. If Jewel

had missed Carver, she was glad she'd sent him home now.

Jewel waited. She waited while the hair on the back of her neck rose. The only warmth in the room emanated in some measure from the door, and she didn't lift her hands. But neither, she noticed, did Duster.

"Some," Duster finally said. "There was a lot of stuff about food." She hesitated, but the hesitation was different, and when Jewel looked at the side of Duster's face, framed by black hair, she saw that it was the effort to remember, and not the fear of mockery, that held her tongue.

"There was some other stuff. About health. I think there were things about babies."

"Were they all Weston?"

"The ones I could understand, yeah."

"Were there other ones?"

"Yeah."

"Did you ever have to—to recite them?"

"Only one." Duster's lips had thinned in annoyance.

"Often?"

"Every day." Very thin.

"Could you repeat it?"

"Jay—"

"I'm not asking because I'm bored and it'll kill time," Jewel said softly, each word distinct and low.

"It'll kill me," Duster snarled. Her eyes were that particular shade of dark they got when they narrowed, but she didn't snap. Instead, she took a long, slow breath. In the first year, she'd have tried to stab the door. "Why do you need me to do this?" She spoke each syllable carefully and precisely.

Jewel exhaled. "I know this is going to sound stupid—"

"Good."

"—But I don't think the door will open if you don't."

Duster turned to look at her den leader. Jewel waited.

"Mother's blood, Jay!" She lifted a hand and pounded the door once. As if she were knocking. "What if I remember, and I say it, and it's the wrong damn thing?"

"Then we go out the way we came in."

"Why don't we just go out the way we came in *anyway*?" But she knew the answer. Jewel didn't want to go back. For some reason. And asking her why wouldn't get answers; that wasn't the way the strong *feeling* worked.

"Duster, *please*."

Duster exhaled. Jewel, watching her, realized for the hundredth time that she could ask Duster to risk her life a thousand different ways much more easily than she could ask her to dent her pride. This, for whatever reason, was pride-denting in a big way.

"I don't know why I'm still here," Duster told the door.

Because the door's closed. Jewel, however, kept that to herself.

Duster began to speak. Well, to mumble. She had both hands on the door, and Jewel put her hands there as well. But Jewel also bowed her forehead, leaning it against the wooden surface. She waited, in silence.

Nothing happened, and she winced.

"There," Duster said bitterly. "Satisfied?"

"No."

Duster swore. "I'm *not*—"

"Say it slowly again."

"Why?"

"Because you need to teach it to me. I need to say it, too."

"What the Hells?"

"We're both in here. Whatever it is needs saying, it needs saying by both of us."

"Godsdamnit, Jay. You'd better be sure about this."

"Sure as I ever am."

Duster spat, which Jewel found shocking in the perfect white of the room. The shock cheered Duster immensely.

She started to speak the unfamiliar syllables slowly. Jewel repeated them back. "How many lines are there?"

"It's three sentences," Duster said. "If you could see 'em, you'd know that."

"You couldn't read them."

"No, but they were carved on the damn wall."

"Look, I'm sorry. Give them to me slowly again. First line first."

Duster stared at her for a minute, and then she seemed to relax. It was a slow unwinding, but teaching Jewel the prayer, syllable by syllable, was leading her into unexpected terrain. Not back to whatever she had suffered—and if there was suffering to be had in the Mother's temple, Jewel wasn't sure she even wanted to know—but somewhere else, somewhere she had never expected to be.

"Here," Duster said, "sit down. Just close your eyes and listen." As if she'd been told that, and had listened, once.

Jewel nodded. She was afraid, now, and couldn't say why. Didn't want to know.

But want or not, she felt the beginning of an answer beneath her: a tremor in the ground. She opened her eyes and looked at Duster, who had fallen momentarily silent. They waited. Silence.

"Jay—"

And sound. The distant fall of rock.

Jewel swallowed. "Duster."

Duster nodded. Any peace the act of teaching had offered, and with Duster all peace was tenuous, was gone. She began again, her voice low, her lips very near Jewel's ear. Jewel repeated the syllables, trying to feel them as rhythm and sound, trying to pick a pattern in cadence that would make it easier.

The ground trembled again, and this time, it was stronger.

Duster cursed, and Jewel caught her hand—the unburned one—and pressed her fingers into it. Touch sometimes upset her and sometimes steadied her. This time, it steadied; it was a familiar and unthreatening hand. She kept speaking, slowly, and Jewel, frustrated at herself, repeated what she heard.

This time, when rock broke, it was undeniably closer,

as if whatever was breaking it was moving, slowly, toward them. Jewel stood, and put her hands firmly against the door; it stilled their shaking. Duster did the same.

"Try it," Jewel told her. "I'll try to follow."

Duster did. And Jewel tried.

The door, however, remained shut. Frustrated, tense with fear, Jewel said, "Duster, what does it mean?"

Duster looked at her. "Is that important?"

"I think so. What does it mean?"

"It's just a prayer. We called it the orphan's prayer."

"Which we both are. Tell me, if you remember."

The hesitation was very small; it was there, but necessity made it easier to step around. *"Mother, guide and guard your children as they walk the longest road. In darkness, hunger, isolation, in the lee of war and death. Mother hear us, lost and wandering, lead us, lead your children home."*

Jewel took a breath and closed her eyes. Those words, she could remember. They were way too long for street prayers, but she promised the Mother that she would say them every bloody night if the Mother would only *hear them* now.

She sucked in air, and then said, "Okay, Duster, again."

And rock fell, closer now. The ground shook with it, accompanying the sound.

"Kalliaris," Duster whispered. "I think the hall is coming down."

Jewel nodded. "Duster," she said.

Duster began again, and this time, while Jewel followed her, pronouncing each syllable, she mapped them: the meaning and sounds. The door against her palm grew warmer, and the sense of harvest and hearth, nearer. She held them as she could, because the ground was now shaking beneath her feet and in the distance, she thought she could hear more than just the roar of falling stone.

A different roar; an ancient voice.

She didn't raise her voice, but Duster did. And it helped. She needed Duster's lead here, needed to con-

centrate, needed to give the lead to someone who knew
what she didn't know.

And it was hard. It was always hard. Didn't matter.

Duster spoke clearly. Jewel, less so, but Jewel's words
were distinct. She felt heat now, as if the door's warmth
had spread throughout her entire body. For a moment,
the warmth was stronger than the fear; for a moment,
she felt cocooned and safe, and the tremors at her feet
and back, the sound of crashing rock, receded; they
were outside.

She saw her hands beside Duster's hands, and knew
she would remember them for a long time.

And then the door dissolved, and both she and
Duster fell through the arch where it had stood.

They got to their feet in silence. The breaking of stone
had either stopped, or they had stepped somehow beyond it into a familiar, silent darkness. Duster reached
into a pocket and pulled out Jewel's magestone, holding
it in one palm. Jewel whispered the word to brighten
it, and then remembered the heavy glass she carried
against her stomach, in the folds of her shirt. She pulled
this out as well, although she could not change the
brightness of the light it shed.

"We're not coming back here," Duster said, echoing
Jewel's earlier words.

Jewel nodded. "Not that I could find it again, without you or Carver," she felt compelled to add. Duster
snorted. She reached for the sheath at her hip, touched
the familiar hilt of a new dagger, and then relaxed a
little. But when she turned to look back, she stopped.

Jewel, caught by the quality of her silence, turned as
well.

In the frame through which they'd both just fallen,
stood a door. No, not a door; two doors. Nothing
about these doors was familiar. They were tall, and
they stretched from ground to a ceiling that magelight
did not quite illuminate. Across the seam where the
two doors met was a symbol, a complicated symbol
encircled by a spiral that started at its center. It was

glowing with gold light, and as they watched, the light slowly faded.

They watched it until it could no longer be seen, even as an afterimage. Then they turned and began to make their way down the hall.

It was a long damn hall, and there were no doors to break it; there were also no junctions. They walked slowly in the magelight, and Jewel only tripped once on the bulky rope that wouldn't quite stay in a convenient wreath. They didn't speak, partly because they were listening, and partly because they were examining the ground.

"Rope?" Duster asked her, when they'd been walking for a few minutes.

"I think we're good. There are no cracks at all in the stone."

"There might be soon."

"I don't think so. I'm not even sure we're anywhere near the room we left."

Duster shrugged. The door was so clearly not the same door to her eye that she couldn't argue. Besides which, neither of them particularly liked the confinement of knots. They walked for several minutes and came, at last, to stairs.

The stairs were not wide, but they weren't that narrow. They were stone, and they headed up into darkness in a slow, curving spiral. Up was a good sign. Duster took the lead.

She put her weight slowly on the second step up, testing it.

And jumped back down almost instantly.

A clear note had sounded in the darkness. It was not something you normally heard when walking up the stairs. Bending, Duster brought the magelight closer. The step, to her eyes, and to Jewel's, was solid rock.

She tried again, and again, a single note sounded. It wasn't harsh, and it wasn't horribly loud; the shock came from the fact it happened at all. "Magic?" Duster asked.

Jewel muttered, "Oh, probably. But I don't see any magical auras very clearly."

Duster muttered something about music and fear, and then began to walk; Jewel didn't need to hear it to know what it was. Every step she took sounded a note, and each note was deep and long. Jewel began to follow, and found that her steps produced the same notes.

"Think this is some sort of early warning?" Duster asked.

"Yeah. Hopefully they've got nothing against would-be grave robbers."

Duster snorted. It was slightly more nervous than the usual snort, but not by much; the closed doors and the lack of obviously disintegrating walls had put her in a better frame of mind. That, and the notes themselves; there was something soothing about them. The music created by the act of walking was neither too loud nor too harsh, and as they climbed their way through even—and changing—notes, they discovered that the notes created song, one that was soft and melodic. Sad, Jewel thought, but in a melancholy way.

They reached the top of the stairs, and the last of the notes faded into stillness.

Chapter Four

THEY HAD CLIMBED FOR A *LONG* TIME.
Jewel couldn't be certain how high the stairs were,
but she was almost certain that they must be close to
an exit—if an exit from the undercity existed here. She
had always wondered how far the undercity went. Did
it stretch past the demiwalls that in theory girded the
farthest reaches of the City, burrowed and hidden by
dirt and stone roads? It certainly couldn't extend into
the sea.

The landing that led from the stairs was composed of
a different stone than the stairs themselves had been; it
was dark, and its surface, veined with hints of colors that
might only be found in stone, reflected the magelight in
Duster's hand. Jewel bore the heavier, cumbersome cut-
glass light in her hand, and held it aloft as she knelt to run
her fingers across the floor.

"Marble," she said quietly.

Duster had never been hugely concerned with what
things were made of if they couldn't be carried, but she
waited while Jewel looked.

When Jewel rose, they approached the frame—or
what was left of the frame—of an arch. It was not a
doorway; no doors, except possibly those in *Avantari*,
the Palace of Kings, were this damn wide.

And no rooms, Jewel thought, as magelight moved in
both of their hands, were this damn big. Not even, she

felt certain, in *Avantari*. She couldn't see ceiling. "More light?" Duster whispered.

But Jewel shook her head. "Not here."

Duster nodded. And whistled. "Look," she said, "that's gold."

Jewel, glancing at Duster's hand, shook her head. Had it been anyone else, she would have laughed and dared them to try to remove it; with Duster, that was only a guarantee that she *would*.

Duster nonetheless felt the need to say, "I'm not afraid."

Jewel said, "No, *I* am. On the other hand," she added, pushing a little, "I'll try, if you want."

Duster shook her head. Lifted one hand off dagger hilt. *Not you.*

Jewel signed back, *Not anyone.* Duster nodded. Gold was good, but hands were better.

The walls couldn't even be seen, although they must have existed. Great runes were carved into the surface of marble, their edges undamaged by time and debris. Like the symbols in the first hall, they were unfamiliar to Jewel, and the scope of their size was so vast, she could not immediately identify them as single runes. But there were also circles, similar to those that had enclosed the cenotaphs; these circles, however, were broken in places, and the central figures they encircled seem to be parts of statues. She couldn't read the writing at their bases, but they seemed to be Old Weston.

"Do you think this was all a temple to the Mother?" Duster asked.

"Probably," Jewel replied.

"Which means you don't know."

"Which means I don't know."

Duster snorted, and wandered ahead; Jewel followed. She followed for a while, lost in marble, and in thought, until Duster said, "Dead end." They'd reached a wall, the beginning and end of which couldn't be seen.

"Go right," Jewel told Duster. Duster obliged, and they followed the wall, stepping over the occasional broken ridge of stone, until they reached a corner.

"Back?" Duster asked, and Jewel nodded. She was, by this point, so tired she could have curled up on the marble and slept. She was also hungry, and wondered if there was any food left in the apartment. She wanted to go home and stay there. Forever.

But she often wanted that, and with a sigh, she began to follow Duster, and the wall, until they reached another corner.

This corner, however, was different.

For one, the marble stone that covered the entire hall stopped here, and the stone that did cover the rest of the floor? It glowed.

Given the way that Duster approached it so carefully, it was a glow that Duster could also see. "Jay?" she said.

"What do you see?" Jewel asked in reply.

"It looks like . . . white rock."

"That's it?"

"No. It looks like liquid, white rock. But not boiling, not hot. It's what rock would look like if it were water."

"That's what I see as well, but I see more color in the white."

"Which color?"

"Almost all of them; it's like a rainbow, but moving."

"Throw something in?"

Jewel nodded. She walked back along the wall until her toe hit fallen rock, and she picked through the sharp, smaller bits until she found something heavy enough to make a splash and light enough that she could carry it. She brought it back to the oddly luminescent corner of floor. "Stand back," she told Duster, who shrugged and moved.

She threw the rock.

It hit the floor and sat that there for a second; it made no noise, and it didn't skip. And then, as they watched, it sank. They both edged closer.

"Please don't tell me you think this is the way out," Duster said quietly, still watching the ripples left in the wake of the piece of stone.

"Let's keep looking," Jewel told her, instead.

*   *   *

An hour later—if it had been only an hour, and Jewel privately had her doubts—they had crossed every inch of wall and had passed over every inch of exposed floor. There was no way back through the doors; they had even gone back down the stairs to check. There were no other halls, no other doors, no other exposed tunnels.

They sat not far from the unusual patch of floor in the corner, watching it.

"Does it feel safe?" Duster asked quietly.

"It doesn't feel dangerous," Jewel replied, aware, at this late hour, of how pathetic the answer was. "But I do think this is the way out. It's not water," she added. She reached out and touched the surface with the flat of her palm. Duster grabbed her waist and held tight, but nothing happened.

"It feels like stone," Jewel told her. "Cold, hard." She reached out again and this time, she pushed.

The whole of the white surface undulated.

And for that moment, distant and just barely audible, they both heard the cry of . . . gulls. They looked at each other, and then Jewel stood and began to unwind the rope. She tied one end around her waist, being careful with the knot.

Duster, wordless, did the same.

"I'll go first," Jewel said.

"Two tugs, follow?"

"Same as usual. Pull me back if I tug it once." She didn't add *if you can,* because there wasn't much point, and Duster wasn't stupid. Jewel took a deep breath, as if she were about to dive into water, and Duster said, "Check the knot."

Frowning—and exhaling—Jewel looked down at her waist.

And as she did, Duster jumped.

"Duster!"

Duster turned as her feet began to sink, and she smiled. It was that quirky, pained, and angry smile that suggested smugness rather than pleasure, and as such was wholly her own. "If it's safe," she said, with a shrug, "I'd just as soon get out first."

"And if it's not?"

"I'd just as soon get out first." She met Jewel's gaze and held it, daring her to speak, to argue, to order.

Jewel, stunned, was silent.

"You can't always take all the risks, Jay."

"I don't—"

"You do, whenever it's possible. You think we don't notice? You rely on your feelings too much," Duster added. "And *we* rely on them too much." She was now waist-deep.

"Can you—can you move?" Jewel asked, struggling for calm.

"Some. It's not like water," Duster said. "It's not as cold. It doesn't move as easily."

"And your feet—you're not touching anything?" It was *so damn hard* to speak calmly. She almost said, *Let me pull you out,* but she knew what Duster would say, and without some help on Duster's end, Jewel didn't stand a chance.

"No. But Jay?"

Jewel nodded.

"I can hear things. People's voices. Gulls. Can you hear them?"

Jewel hadn't tried. Too many of her own words were getting in the way. She took a deep breath, forced her shoulders to relax. Tried not to panic as Duster continued to sink.

"Don't," Duster said, as Jewel took a step forward. "Let me do this. Wait."

"Does it matter?" Jewel shot back. "There doesn't seem to be any other way out."

"Let me do this, Jay."

Jewel folded her arms across her chest and waited. Her hands bunched into fists when the white stone hit Duster's chin, and she watched as Duster swallowed air. She said nothing. Duster was not a person you could thank. She wasn't a person you could fuss over, and she loathed and despised tears, for any reason. Jewel only despised her own.

The pale white stone closed over Duster's head before Jewel exhaled again. She picked up the rope in both hands, and waited as it grew taut. *Come on, Duster.*

She waited. Counted seconds, and then minutes: five. Which wasn't that long to get bearings, if bearings were needed. But it was an eternity to Jewel, in the silence and darkness.

Waiting was hard.

Jewel wondered if it were as hard for the rest of the den as she found it now. The reason she went ahead? Because if it were her *own* life in danger, she knew. She always knew.

But theirs? No.

It was practical. She was practical.

And Duster? Hells.

She crouched, settled her elbows on her knees, her hands still holding the rope that bridged the distance vision couldn't. *Come* on, Duster. *If this is your sick idea of a joke, I will kill you slowly myself.* She would have paced, but there wasn't enough slack in the rope for it. She stood anyway, because her knees were becoming cramped.

Kalliaris, smile. Smile, Lady.

Kalliaris, capricious god of luck, did smile. The rope in Jewel's hands grew taut, loosened, and grew taut again. Tucking the cut-glass magestone back inside her shirt, where it nested awkwardly above the rope and her stomach, she took two steps forward.

18th of Morel, 410 AA
Sanctum of Moorelas, Averalaan

She had expected to fall slowly, because the stone gave way slowly, like thick, cool mud. She had expected that as she finally sank through it, as Duster had done, her feet would magically touch the ground, and she would be standing someplace else.

Unfortunately, when she at last felt the liquid stone close over the top of her head—which had taken just a little bit longer than was comfortable, given the lack of air—she passed through whatever it was that had been holding her up, and she dropped into sudden, painful light—sunlight, as unlike the darkness of the undercity as any light could be.

She landed as well as she could, given the sudden lack of anything beneath her feet, and rolled, cursing, to those feet. Her eyes were tearing; she rubbed them, covering them until they had acclimatized to daylight.

The first thing she saw wasn't Duster. It was the pedestal of a vaguely familiar statue. The statue's feet started just above her head, and she looked up, shading her watering eyes, to see the sword arm of Moorelas, against the perfect azure of cloudless sky. He wore armor, although it was all of stone, but no helm and no shield; the sword was a greatsword.

At his feet, carved in stone in eight directions, were reliefs of Moorelas writ small; the one Jewel had landed on was a scene that depicted a young Moorelas wielding sword against a demon. The demon was taller and grander than Moorelas; it had wings. Jewel moved her feet slightly because she was standing on its tail.

A shadow crossed the demon, and, like a child, she leaped out of its path, but it wasn't Moorelas' shadow, and she returned to the relief. Demons, she thought. And ancient heroes. Things she never wanted to see. But she felt uneasy, because she was here, and because they had both—she and Duster—been disgorged from the undercity into a wholly unexpected place.

I should tell Rath, she thought.

The sun wasn't high; it was, Jewel thought, not far off dawn.

She turned to look for Duster, following the rope from one end to the other. Duster was leaning against the base of the statue. She had untied the knotted rope from her waist, and now held the end in both hands.

Jewel, shaking, did the same. She started to wind

the rope, and Duster let it go, one hand sliding into her pocket and one dropping to the hilt of her dagger. She winced, and pulled the hand back.

The gulls were out in force, loud and raucous. They eyed Jewel and Duster like thieves eyed careless people in the Common. Duster said something rude, and made a throwing gesture; she had nothing in her hand, but the birds startled slightly, before settling in to make even more noise.

"Come away from the statue," Jewel said quietly.

Duster snorted. "Are you afraid of its shadow?"

"On bad days," Jewel replied, "I'm afraid of mine."

Duster snorted again, but she followed Jewel to the seawall, and leaned back against it on her elbows. Jewel climbed up on its flat top, and dangled her feet off the seaside. Salt wind blew her hair off her face; the air was cool and bracing.

From here, you could see *Averalaan Aramarelas*. The three Church spires. The Palace of the Twin Kings. From here, you could see the ships in harbor, and the Port Authority; you could see the bridges that led to and from the Isle.

You couldn't see the twenty-fifth holding, and the Common was only visible because of its trees. She would have gone straight to the Common, but had very little money with her; certainly not enough to do the daily shopping. Besides which, she was dead tired.

She looked across at Duster. "Let's not do that again."

Duster shrugged.

18th of Morel, 410 AA
Twenty-fifth holding, Averalaan

They walked back to the apartment in the open air. The streets were crowded, and they skirted the Common to avoid the worst of those crowds. Home, however, was also crowded, and most of that crowd surged to the door when it opened. They surged back when they saw that

it was Duster who entered first; Duster looked about as
tired as Jewel felt, and it was always a good idea to give
her some space when she did.

But there were hugs all around, and explanations
demanded, before Jewel asked who'd gone to market
in the morning. If she'd hoped to have something to
complain about, she was out of luck; Finch and Teller
had organized a small outing, taking Lefty, Arann, and
Angel with them. They had also sent Carver, Fisher,
Jester, and Lander to the riverside, to wash clothing,
which privately made Jewel cringe. Still, there was food,
and Finch was in the kitchen before Duster cleared the
small hall, so they didn't go hungry for long.

There was something that was comforting about
Finch in the kitchen. Jewel wasn't sure what it was, or
why, and it didn't seem fair that there was something
totally wrong with, say, Carver in the kitchen, because
Carver wasn't actually an idiot. But fair or no, she liked
watching Finch. Duster, true to the earliest of her words,
seldom helped in the kitchen.

Jewel showed the den the one prize they'd taken
from their outing in the maze, and then went to sleep
for a couple of hours. She needed to go see Rath, but
she wanted to be awake when she did.

When she got to Rath's, taking the maze with Carver
rather than the open streets, Rath was awake. The
weeks had improved his color, soured his temper, and
made him extremely impatient. His hand was now
mostly a sallow yellow, with a bit of purple around the
knuckles, but the cut on his head had healed, and hadn't
infected; they found him in the practice room, throwing
knives and cursing.

As Rath didn't often curse, they waited a bit for silence before they knocked on the door. He knew they
were there, of course. He answered the door at the
second knock, and Jewel, who had already been to the
kitchen with the food she'd purchased for him, handed
him a plate. "Eat," she told him.

He lifted one silvering brow, but he nodded toward

his room, and Carver and Jewel followed him. He sat on the chair at the map table. It hadn't always been the map table; it had once been almost a second desk. But these days, it carried maps of the undercity.

Rath sat in front of them, and Jewel said, "Rath, can I see the maps?"

He glanced at her, and then nodded.

She walked around his chair, and began to examine the maps; there were three. Rath had added his own marks to the thin leather parchment over the years, but for the most part, he left them alone; they were, he had once told Jewel, almost complete. The ruins of old buildings and fallen causeways were an echo of these maps; these had been made by people who had known the undercity before it *was* under the City. Or at least so it seemed.

Jewel was never going to be as good at reading maps as Rath was. The buildings and facades that she had seen didn't collapse into lines and rectangles in her mind with any ease at all, and it was difficult for her to translate them into something she could read on a map. But she'd brought Carver with her for a reason. She waved him over, signaling *Come here* without really thinking about it.

"Yesterday?" he asked.

She nodded.

He grimaced. While it was true he was better at this than Jewel, he hated to make mistakes in front of Rath; they all did. But he touched four spots on the maps, all of them at the edges. "One of these, I think."

Carver hadn't been inside the great hall. Jewel had, and of the four possibles she narrowed it down to one. She touched the map, and pressed down. A blue line grew slowly from beneath her finger.

Rath frowned. "You were there?" he asked softly.

Jewel nodded, and almost as an afterthought, she pulled the cut-glass magelight out of her clothing. It wasn't the most comfortable thing to carry because the edges were sharp and they cut into her stomach. She handed it to Rath.

He whistled.

"Where did you get this?" he asked her.

"Here, I think. If this is the right place." She hesitated. "The street here wasn't clear; there was a lot of heavy rubble, but we managed to crawl through it. When we made our way through the fallen stone, we were in a huge hall; it was lit. That stone came from the hall," she added. "We kind of had to pry it out of a wall, and when we did, everything went dark."

He whispered his own magelight, perched as it always was in a holder on the desk, to brightness, and he examined the glass in its glow. His fingers traced the rune at the back of the gem.

"I thought it would be useful," Jewel admitted, "but we don't know the activation words for it."

"No, you wouldn't," he said softly. "I don't recognize this rune."

"It's not Old Weston."

Rath shook his head.

She hesitated for a moment, and then said, "Rath, I think we found something . . . else there."

His expression didn't shift at all, but he was paying more attention.

"I think—there was a crypt, at the end of this hall. And . . . " She hesitated.

"And?"

"Three cenotaphs. Three figures on stone biers. They looked like painted stone, maybe painted marble. The room they were in was lit so brightly I thought it might come up above ground."

"Go on."

"But they . . . they moved. When we came near them, they moved."

He fell silent for a moment, and then he looked at Jewel. The glance was brief, but there was worry in it; Rath had a way of being almost motionless when something was serious. "Do not go back there," he told her softly.

She nodded. "I'm not even sure we can," she added.

"Why not? Did the hall outside collapse?"

"Yes." She frowned, and then added, "But I don't think it collapsed on its own."

He became utterly still. "What do you mean, Jewel?"

"I mean—I don't know why, but I think something was pulling the walls down."

He rose. "If they knew you were there, of all places," he mused, "they might." He reached for the map that her fingers still touched, and after a moment, she lifted her hand. He brought the map into the light, running his hands across his eyes before he examined it. "Jay," he said. Just that.

"It's bad news?"

He didn't appear to have heard her; the map had his whole attention.

"Eat," she told him. "Rath, eat. You need food."

"I need information," he said bitterly.

Jewel glanced at Carver, and Carver signed, *Leave?*

She nodded. When the door closed, she turned to Rath, who had not eaten, and had not looked away from the map.

"Rath. Eat."

He glanced at her, then. "Don't go into the maze," he told her softly. She had known he would.

"Rath—what's happening? What's happening with the maze? Who are the 'they' you're talking about?"

"I am not entirely certain," he replied. This much, at least, was true. But it was also not the whole truth. Since so much of her life depended on the maze, she said, "What do you think is happening?"

"If I knew, I wouldn't tell you." This was also true. "I have a feeling the knowledge would not be conducive to survival." He paused, and then he set the map aside, as if aware that its presence would only invoke more questions, none of which he wanted—or intended to— answer. Then he sat, and he began to eat. Jewel watched him in silence.

"What information do you need, and can we help gather it?"

"No."

"Rath—"

"No, Jewel." He lifted a hand, finished chewing, swallowed, and then said, "I regret that I showed you the maze, as you call it. I regret, on certain days, that I discovered it. But, yes," he added, "the magestone that you brought is worth money, and I will make it a priority to sell it."

She exhaled, and he offered her a small, grim smile. "The need to eat and sleep under a roof often causes us to do things that we later regret." He hesitated, and then said, "I trust you to know when things are too dangerous, Jewel. If you cannot trust yourself in this regard, stay out of the maze."

"Because of those walls?"

"Because of the hall, yes. Think about what it takes to tear down walls of that size. Age may make them somehow more brittle—although with stone, I fail to see how—but not so brittle that they are easily leveled." He looked at her and added, "how certain are you?"

She shrugged. "Not certain," she offered, at last, testing the words. They were true. "I thought—I thought I heard roaring, but I couldn't tell. Because the stone makes a lot of noise when its falling and hitting other stones."

Rath nodded. "Where were you when you heard this?"

"In the crypt. Rath, we had to *pray* to get out of that room."

"Pray?"

"A prayer taught in the Mother's temple. Duster remembered it. You can imagine how happy she was to have to *repeat* it."

That invoked a smile with a bit of an edge; he could, indeed, imagine it. "This rune," he said at last, lifting the magelight Jewel had pried from the undercity as he spoke. "I have a suspicion of what it might mean, and your prayer confirms that. I will take the magestone to the Isle, and see what can be learned from it."

"Will you tell me what you learn?"

"If it's relevant."

Which pretty much meant no. But as Jewel had no

connections on the Isle, it didn't matter. She took a breath and then said, "When we left that part of the undercity? We came out at the Sanctum of Moorelas."

"Came out? What do you mean?"

"I mean we stepped into something that looked like it was liquid rock. Not molten," she added quickly. "Just liquid. We sank into it, and we kind of fell out the other side. At the foot of the statue near the seawall."

Rath frowned.

"You never went there?"

"No. There are whole sections of the undercity that I haven't explored, and that one would require someone of smaller stature than I."

"What do you think brought the hall down?"

He didn't answer.

It frightened her, and he knew it. He put a hand over hers, just one, and he offered no words. After a moment, he ate. "If I had never met you," he told her, "I would still be here. I would still be in the undercity, and its mystery—and its danger—would still be mine."

"If I had never met you," Jewel told him, after a few minutes of silence, "I would never have found Finch. I would never have had a place to bring Lefty and Arann. I would never have built my den. Yes, I would never have discovered the maze on my own.

"But I wouldn't have the life I have now. I don't regret it," she added, in case that wasn't obvious. With Rath, it was hard to tell, sometimes.

"I hope you never have cause." His smile was slight, and wan; he was tired. "I promise I will finish eating," he added, "And I am almost at the point at which your visits here are purely social."

"Meaning?"

"You don't need to come to nurse me back to health."

"Could I do it anyway?"

He laughed and shook his head. "Not if you want to sell this," he told her, setting the odd glass to one side. "I'll come to you, when I have word of a buyer. Or, if you prefer, I can buy the stone now."

"No. Find a buyer. We already owe you too much."

"Jay—"

"You won't be here forever. We have to be able to stand on our own sometime."

He nodded.

She let herself out when it became clear that he had no intention of leaving his desk or the work he had set for himself. Carver was lounging quietly against the wall. "How bad is it?"

"I think it's bad," she replied. "But I don't understand how."

Carver nodded. Rath's moods and his temper were unpredictable at the best of times, but he was particularly fussy about the maze. "Should we walk home?"

Jewel hesitated. She hated to walk into the twenty-fifth when there were only two of her den. "I think," she said, stalling for time, "that someone else has finally discovered the maze."

Carver whistled, but after a moment said, "It had to happen sooner or later."

She nodded, thinking. "I don't know where Rath was injured. I don't know how; he won't say."

"You asked him?"

"About a dozen times over the last two weeks."

"He must have been really bad."

"He was. Of course, the last time I asked, he told me he'd eject me physically if I bothered him about it again."

"He had to get better sometime."

Jewel laughed. "We'll walk, for now," she told Carver. She headed toward the familiar door, with its three bolts. She no longer needed a stool to reach the highest one, although it helped. Carver, who was standing behind her, tactfully did not reach above her head to pull the highest one free.

She wondered if she would ever grow taller. She was already taller than Finch, but that was it; even Teller was her height, now. She remembered her father as a large man, but the last time she'd seen him she'd been so much younger. His actual height? She didn't know. Sometimes it bothered her. Today, it didn't.

Rath, she thought, *who are they? Who are they, that you thought they could pull down the damn walls just because we were poking around in a crypt?*

But she didn't say it out loud; there was no point. She didn't want to worry Carver, and Rath would never, ever answer that question.

She slid out the door that led to the hall, waited until Carver had followed her, and then closed the door behind them both. She didn't bother to lock it; Rath didn't trust single locks, and he'd come out of his room sometime to push the bolts home.

But she paused a moment outside the door, looking at its worn surface. As doors went, it wasn't great, but it was better than the door she opened daily. It wasn't a window, though. She could look at it for hours and see nothing.

"Jay?"

She shook her head.

"The worst thing about the feelings," she said softly, as Carver bent to catch the words, "is that you can't *make* people listen. They hear as much as they want to hear, and they do what they're going to do anyway."

Carver, quiet in a way that Duster was not, said, "Rath?"

She hadn't meant to say so much. She didn't intend to say more.

But she looked up at her den-kin, and she felt her throat tighten, her lips compress. She nodded.

Carver wasn't much for comfort; he didn't ask for it often, and he didn't offer it. But that was good, in its way, because he knew there was *no* comfort he could give, and he didn't try to tell her that she might be wrong. He didn't try to argue her out of instinct or her belief in it; he couldn't. The den relied on it, and trusted it.

He said, instead, "Do you want us to try to talk to him?"

It should have made her laugh. Give Carver his due, it *almost* did. But she couldn't work a laugh out of her throat just now, and walking away from this basement apartment in the thirty-fifth holding didn't put any distance between her and the memory that it now evoked: Her father, and her father's death in the shipyards.

It had been so damn long since she'd felt this helpless, because building her den had been both an act of faith and an attempt to use what she could see, in nightmare and sometimes in rare waking vision, to *save* lives.

And she had saved their lives. "Let's go home," she told Carver.

He nodded, and he led, although they both knew this part of the City so well they could walk it blindfolded. Not that that would have been either practical or safe, but it was possible.

25th of Morel, 410 AA
The Common, Averalaan

Farmer Hanson smiled when he saw Jewel, but he always did. What was different about this smile was the way it dropped from his face after only a few words had been exchanged. He asked her how she was, of course, and he asked after Lefty; he didn't ask after Arann because Arann was with her. Finch was chatting with his scary daughter. The farmer often worried about his daughter, and Jewel privately thought he was crazy; his daughter could freeze a would-be thief in his or her tracks simply by looking at them.

But the daughter liked Finch, and they often chatted while Jewel was talking with Farmer Hanson. Today, however, the chatter was sparse. He was worried about something.

She finally asked, "Is something wrong?"

The smile that came up in response to the question looked like something dredged out of one of the Common's less savory puddles. Like, say, the ones near the butchers' stalls. "Wrong? Why do you ask that, Jay?"

She looked at him, and raised a brow.

He lifted both of his hands in mock defense, but he dropped them slowly. "You aren't the only kids I keep an eye on," he said, as if it needed saying.

Jewel nodded, because clearly it did.

"There's a young girl and her brother," he said.

"How young?"

"About your age. Maybe a year younger."

"The brother?"

"Two years younger. They're not doing as well as you are," he added quietly. "But they manage."

She didn't ask how. He probably didn't ask them either. Just fed them when he could, or more likely ignored their thefts when he could.

"Her name's Marion, and his is Mouse."

"Mouse?"

"Mouse."

"Seriously?"

Farmer Hanson shrugged. "You've got Lefty, Teller, Carver, and Duster," he pointed out.

Fair enough. "What about these two?"

"I haven't seen them in the Common for the last three weeks."

"Do you know which holding they live in?"

The farmer shrugged. Which meant no. "They don't talk much," he added, "and I get the impression they're like Lefty and Arann were—they find a place they can hunker down for a while, and they move when they have to move."

Arann was listening with half an ear. Which really meant the farmer had the whole of his attention. The mention of Lefty's name often had that effect.

"You think they've been co-opted by a den?"

"I don't know. It's just not like them to be gone quite so long."

"They can't freeze to death at this time of year."

"No," the farmer replied, scanning the crowd as he often did when he talked. "Marion's about your height, but thinner. Her hair's a brown-black, and it's straight, but straggly. Mouse is shorter than you are, hair's the same color. It's too long," he added, which was just like Farmer Hanson, "but he mostly keeps it off his face."

"I'll keep an ear out," Jewel told him. "If they're running in the twenty-fifth at all, we might be able to find them."

The farmer nodded. It was clear that he didn't think Jay would find them, and if she were being honest, he was right.

"Just keep an eye on your den," he told her quietly.

"None of my den is likely to get lost any time soon."

8th of Lattan, 410 AA
Twenty-fifth holding, Averlaan

Later, Jewel would remember the longest day in the year of 410. The longest day, the eighth day of the fourth month, when sunset took its time, and the sky was a clear azure that only slowly tinged purple, and even pink, before the stars could be seen. She would remember, as well, the longest night, because the former marked the beginning of the end, and the latter marked the end. The end was easier to mark and easier to remember, because endings were.

But not so, the former. The beginning of the end, the point at which things started to unravel—after so much effort, so much hope and planning—was harder to pinpoint.

The eighth day of Lattan was always a busy day in the Common, because it started at the regular painful predawn hour, and continued well into the night. There were candles, and charity was such on the longest day that even the beggars had them; there were the special pastries that, adorned with melted butter and dusted with sugar, also found their way through the milling summer crowd. There was sweet water, sweet wine, and apple beer, although it was true that even the charitable had their limits, and apple beer, while it could be scented upon any moving breeze, remained in the hands of the few with enough coin to spare.

The bards, taught and housed in the famous Senniel College upon *Averalaan Aramarelas*, crossed the bridge, carrying small harps, lutes, and pipes, and they traveled toward the Common, where they came to rest, for minutes at a time, in the crowd. They offered their songs, when asked; they played for copper and silver, although they were accustomed to commanding purses of gold. They started at dawn, and they continued until the moons were high, as if their voices alone could cajole another hour or two of daylight.

Here, in the Common and at its edges, the Priests and Priestesses of the Mother also came, often at the head of small groups of the orphans they fed, housed, and clothed.

The great trees of the Common were decorated, from the lowest to the highest branches; the mages, of course, oversaw much of this part of the festivities, and it was always interesting to watch them work.

Jewel loved the longest day. She always had.

On the longest day, even her dour grandmother would gird herself with something that passed for a smile and enter the Common to stay a few hours. Her father, her mother, and their friends, children in hand, would also leave the safety and certainty of their small apartments. They would sometimes—Jewel remembered this clearly—walk toward the sea, and they would stand on the seawall, gazing for a few moments out at the Isle, where the poor did not go.

Jewel remembered the first time they had done this, because the Isle, with its towering cathedrals and the palace that was home to the Twin Kings, looked like something very much out of story. *There,* her father would say, *live the sons and daughters of gods.* And he would point.

There was no work to be had on the longest day, unless you were a merchant or a magisterial guard, in which case the day must have been long indeed. Jewel wondered, as she grew older, if the children of those merchants and guards hated the longest day as much as she loved it.

But after a glimpse of the Isle, the home to the scions of gods, they would go to the Common, walking slowly, chatting and playing as they moved.

It was a good day for thieves and beggars, as well. This year, the den didn't have to be thieves, but it was close, and the temptation to turn someone else's holiday into a lesson about caution and attention was stronger than it had been in years. But it wasn't an overwhelming temptation, for Jewel, and she made it clear that they were to leave be. Only Duster complained.

She didn't lead her den to the seawall. She didn't lead them anywhere; she was content to let them wander.

For herself, she chose to watch the mages work at the base of the great trees, because they could—with effort—gain the heights. When they did, she could see, if she watched carefully, the sudden burst of color that surrounded them. She could see the orange or the gray, and gray was a color she seldom saw. They would not so much fly as float, and they would place, upon the higher branches, light. Not candles, of course; no fire. They would also argue. A lot. It made them seem human.

Finch and Teller chose to accompany her, and to watch, although they didn't see as much as she did. They could, however, hear the raised voices and the bickering, and they found it as amusing as Jewel. Lefty and Arann had gone to talk to Farmer Hanson, and Duster and Carver had taken Lander in search of gods only knew what. Fisher and Jester, Angel in tow, had gone in search of food.

It was peaceful in the Common. Loud, of course, but it was the type of noise that put one at ease. There were children here, and grandparents, parents, uncles; there were small dogs and large dogs, the latter tightly leashed. There were horses, but these horses, taller by far than anyone else in the crowd, were accustomed to people, and the men and women who rode them, in their very fine uniforms, served the Kings.

The flags of the Common flew all night, hoisted on poles at the top of buildings, or in the Common itself. he flagpoles were further decorated by streamers and ribbons, and sometimes garlanded, although the mules and goats often took care of that. There were games and dances around those poles, erupting and ending in shrieks and laughter, and sometimes, where the younger children were involved, in tears; there were prizes given and received, and sometimes, as the sun began to wend its way toward the horizon, kisses.

Somewhere close by, a bard began to sing. Bardic voices stilled chatter, but even wordless there was a hum in the crowd that listened. Poor or rich, the longest day was a day of contentment in the Common. Oh, there were more guards, and the guards could be testy by the time the Common finally emptied, but on the longest day, they turned a blind eye to the shoeless, and the often shirtless.

Finch passed Jewel a pastry, and Jewel took it as the mages began their descent. They wouldn't leave, though. It was the mages who would, when the evening finally fell, turn their hands and their talent to the serious business of light. Their light, their foreign, brilliant light, would speak to the passing day, and brighten the sky in a flurry of color.

And then, when the last of that light faded, the longest day would be over, leaving a pleasant ghost in its wake. *Make memories,* her mother had said. *In the end, they're all we have. Make good memories. The bad ones will come on their own. Choose, as you can, what you remember.*

She couldn't clearly remember her mother's face on most days, although she could remember the feel of her arms, the warmth of her smile, the slight thunder of her anger and her worry. She could remember facial expression, but couldn't hold it long enough to examine chin, or cheek, or shape of forehead.

Mostly, she could remember her mother's voice, the texture of her words. But her mother and her father returned seldom; her Oma, often.

Enjoy what you have now, her Oma said. *Because now is all you have.*

This longest day, this now, was Jewel's answer, to

both of the women who had raised her. Her father's voice was silent. She bit into pastry, left white sugar on her cheeks—it had been an overly ambitious bite—and raised her hand to sky; Finch and Teller followed her wordless direction. Light, blue and green and red, exploded above even the highest of the great trees.

Voices came in a rush, a roar of sound that seldom surrendered distinct syllables. Small children rode shoulders, grabbing hat and hair at the unexpected vantage of height. For a moment, magic was spectacle, miracle, and benison. For Jewel, it was also memory. If she couldn't see the ghosts of her dead, she could feel them, here. This was how she introduced her den to her family, how she built a bridge of the present that would reach backward and extend forward for as long as they lived.

When they at last gathered and returned to the apartment, they spilled in, their voices still street-loud. Because of this, it was clearer than usual when all talk suddenly trailed into silence. Jewel was at the back of the pack, but she pushed her way through to the front— and in the very small space near the door, that took both time and effort.

Seated on the sill of a window they hadn't bothered to shut because in the humidity of summer, the shutters were too warped to stay closed, was Rath. His arms were folded loosely across his chest, and his eyes were shut; his chin was tilted down as well. He might have been sleeping; Rath had once said he could sleep standing up.

But as they spread out, hesitant to disturb him, he opened one lid.

Jewel crossed the room. There was no uncertainty here; this was her place. "Rath?"

He nodded. He looked old and tired, but he hadn't sustained any new injuries. Or at least not any obvious ones. "Jay," he said, deferring to her preferred name while the den was present. He eased himself off the sill, and stretched.

"We were out in the Common," she told him, signing to her den while she talked. They were curious, of course, but they drifted as far away as the small space allowed. "It's the longest day," she added, by way of explanation.

"It is, indeed," Rath replied gravely. "And there are rites and observances that were ancient before the Empire which are also apparently kept." He grimaced. "I would have been earlier, otherwise."

She thought for a moment, and then brightened. "The stone?"

He nodded. "Come," he told her. "Walk with me."

She'd been on her feet since just before dawn, but the look on his face forbade mention of the fact. She exhaled, and signed to Finch, who, lingering by the bedroom door, nodded.

They left her home and headed down the hall to the stairs, and from the stairs, into the hall that led to the street. Rath walked slowly, because it was hard to walk quickly in these streets. Although the Common had begun to empty, the taverns had opened their doors, and the streets would not be clear until morning, if that.

Because he walked slowly, Jewel kept pace. She didn't speak, waiting for Rath; Rath didn't speak until they had crossed a large stretch of the City, wandering from the poor holdings into holdings in which the respectable might choose to live. It was a far cry from the expensive buildings near the Merchant Authority, but the buildings here were not in poor repair, and the streets were both cleaner and emptier.

Rath didn't seem to worry about being followed, so Jewel relaxed enough to ask him where they were going.

"To the sea," he said quietly.

"Why?"

He shrugged. "I spent most of today in a cloister, waiting. I need to stretch my legs."

Jewel didn't. She wisely said nothing, holding her peace. But she faltered when she saw what he approached: the Sanctum of Moorelas. "Yes," he said, although he did not look down to see her reaction. "I haven't seen Moorelas since I was . . . younger." He stopped walking when he reached the foot of the statue, and looked up. Even in the moonlight, Moorelas was intimidating. "The hope of the world," Rath said.

"I wonder if he wanted that."

"What?"

"To bear the weight of the world's hope."

Rath chuckled. "You have no desire to be a hero, do you?"

She shrugged. "I did when I was four," she told him.

"And you are not four now."

"No. But—it's hard, I think. To be the only hope the world has. And," she added softly, "to fail." She looked up at his stone face for some sign that he understood that burden. His expression, of course, didn't change.

"He did not fail," Rath said, looking at the same thing, although what he made of it, Jewel couldn't tell.

"He didn't succeed," Jewel replied.

"No?"

"No. He wounded the god, but even gifted with the sword, he didn't kill him. And so the god lives."

"The Hells would be a difficult place without its ruler."

"I don't know. It's the Hells," she added. "How much worse could it get?"

He laughed.

Jewel, caught in the moment, said, "Maybe you're right. Morel was human," she added, using the simpler name. "Maybe humans just aren't meant to kill gods. And if he didn't kill the god, he weakened the god enough that he could be defeated."

"By the other gods."

"By the other gods combined." She shrugged again. "Maybe it's just about trying."

"And not succeeding?"

"He wasn't a god," she told Rath again, slightly annoyed. "He did what he could. He did *everything* he could. And we're still here," she added. "So maybe it was enough. I hope he knew that, before he died. That he'd done his best. That he'd done enough."

Rath was silent for long enough that Jewel's gaze dropped from the statue's face to seek his. She found him watching her in silence, his expression as remote as graven stone. "Would it have been a comfort?" he asked her softly, nothing in his face changing.

"I hope so," she replied.

He reached into his tunic and pulled out a small bag. This, he handed to her.

"You couldn't have given me this in the apartment?" she asked, hearing the familiar jingle of coin.

"I could," he replied. "But I wanted to walk." He did now, leaving the statue and its many untold stories to walk to the wall. She shoved the bag inside her own shirt, where it nestled against her stomach. Then she trailed after him, sparing Moorelas one backward glance.

"So, you came here with Duster," he said, leaning on his elbows, facing the sea.

"Yeah. But it was morning, then." She hesitated and then said, "The stone?"

He nodded. "The rune," he told her softly, "was not, as you suspected, Old Weston. It was not," he added, "in any language that was spoken by man."

"How do you know?"

"I went," he said quietly, "to the Exalted of Cormaris upon the Isle."

She was speechless for a long moment. He was not the only son of the god to walk in the City, but he was the spiritual leader of almost all the others, and almost-brother to the King Cormalyn. The Lord of Wisdom. The first words that came, when words returned, were, "And he had time to talk to you?"

"For this, yes."

"You didn't go to the Order of Knowledge?"

"No. There are men and women there who might have been able to answer the question, but not with any secrecy."

"But—but why—"

"A friend suggested that the god-born might know. I did not have the time or leisure to ask the Teos-born;

they are not perhaps as civic minded, and they are not easily found when they are absorbed in their studies."

Teos was the god of knowledge.

"What language, Rath?"

"They call it the Oldest Tongue," he replied. "It was the tongue the gods spoke, when they walked the world."

"But—but—"

He turned to look at her. "You understand," he said softly.

"No. No, I don't." She climbed up on the wall, and crossed her legs there, facing his profile. "If this—this stone—was engraved in this tongue ... "

"Yes?"

"What was it doing in the undercity?"

He chuckled. It was a thin, dry sound. "See? You *do* understand."

"Rath, don't make fun of me. I don't."

"You don't want to," he replied. But the amusement left his voice when he spoke again. "I think it not an accident," he said, "that you discovered this, and that the hall from which it was taken was destroyed."

"But, Rath—"

"The gods no longer walk the world."

Jewel didn't privately believe they ever had. If they had, how in the Hells had man survived? She started to say as much, but there was something about him that stopped the words from leaving her mouth. This man was not the man who had found her in the streets, and not the man who had insisted on nursing her back to health.

He was the man, she realized, who wouldn't heed any warning or plea she might make.

He was the man who had insisted she learn about The Ten, and the Kings, and the gods themselves; about the guilds, and the ranks of the army; about the Merchant Authority, and the way it handled the currencies of different nations.

Recognizing him, she surrendered. "They don't want

people to know. About the gods. About the gods walking the world."

Rath nodded.

"I don't really understand why it's important."

"No more do I," he replied. "But the fact that it *is* important may change things." She heard the lie in his voice more clearly than she had ever heard it. And she could not call him on it, not here.

"Jay," he said softly, "I think the time has come that you avoid the maze. Tell your den to do the same."

"But we can't—"

"If you're careful, the money there will keep you for some time."

She wanted to tell him that it wasn't enough; they needed to eat, and they outgrew all their clothing; they needed a place to sleep, and things to sleep in. She wanted to tell him that he was wrong. She even tried.

But she understood why he'd brought her, by seeming accident, to the Sanctum of Moorelas. Because ever since she'd seen the crypts, she had been uneasy, and this was his subtle way of forcing her to confront that.

"Rath," she said, staring out to sea, and seeing, in the bay, the height of the towers, the lights of the day. "What can we *do* that can support us? We live off the maze, and what we can find there."

"I took the liberty of leaving a few books in your apartment. Read them. I will be less available for the next little while; do not use that as an excuse not to read. No doubt Teller has already discovered them. Or Finch. I left them in the kitchen," he added, "where, I suspect, neither Carver nor Duster go, if not forced at knifepoint."

"Oh, Carver'll go—but we can't afford to have him burn the building down around our ears."

Rath chuckled, and then stood. "I'm serious, Jewel. The maze, unless there is no other alternative, is done."

She was silent, but he was not yet finished. He caught her by the shoulders, and held her firmly, but gently, as she sat on the seawall. "Tell me that I'm wrong," he said. "Tell me that you think I'm wrong. Say it, and I'll let you be."

She tried. She honestly tried.

And he watched her, and he knew. But she had grown, and she was not always kind, this Jewel, this den leader. "What are you afraid of, Rath?"

He let her go, withdrawing more than just his hands and the intensity of his demand. He had almost hoped she could do what he had demanded, which was a fool's hope, a wayward dream.

"Afraid of? The usual things," he replied.

"The usual?"

He glanced at Moorelas' face. "Come, Jewel. Home. It's late."

She said, "Rath, the gods—" and stopped.

He turned, and he felt, in that moment, the certainty of his own death. Here, across the carvings that detailed the myth and legend of mankind's greatest warrior, he stepped across the winged backs of the demon-kin, above the blazing swords of the *Kialli*, and he wanted to turn and walk away; to leave Averalaan, to leave Jewel Markess.

She said, her voice shallow, her eyes in that peculiar wide gaze that he had come, with time, to recognize, "The gods will walk."

"I've been told," he said softly, "that that's impossible."

She didn't hear him. She didn't answer.

Answer enough. He did not leave her, and he did not leave the City, but he waited until she could breathe again before he walked her home. She asked him no more questions about the gods, then or ever; he asked her no more questions about the gods, then or ever.

But she had spoken his fear, not her own.

Chapter Five

6th of Emperal, 410 AA
The Common, Averalaan

DUSTER LEANED AGAINST THE GIRTH of a great tree, and folded her arms across her chest. She hated the damn heat, and she hated the damn humidity, because the shade wasn't much good against humidity. She didn't particularly love the Common; it was too damn crowded all the time. But she liked eating, as long as she wasn't doing the cooking.

She watched Jay at the farmer's stall. Angel, with his ridiculous hair, shadowed her, keeping an eye on the crowd. He was the only member of this misfit den that Duster hadn't known for years, and she could never quite figure him out. He'd only gone to Rath's a couple of times, but he knew how to handle a blade; he even knew how to handle a sword, which Rath noticed, although he hadn't said much.

Jay had her basket, and beside Jay, almost lost in the crowd, Finch had hers. They filled them methodically but slowly; there was always so much damn *chatter* at the farmer's wagon. Fisher was with Finch, but it was hard to tell if he was paying attention. He hadn't been one to talk much when they'd first come to Jay, and unlike the rest, time hadn't loosened his tongue.

It's not that he didn't talk; he was just lazy.

She let her hand drop to her dagger when a couple of kids a few years younger wandered close. They had that clothing-found-in-a-gutter look; everything too large and mismatched. They had shoes that wouldn't see the end of the season, although they were still mostly in one piece.

The kids left, looking for easier pickings. Duster watched them, just to make sure. She was restless.

Aside from three run-ins with Carmenta's gang, only one of which included Carmenta, things had been quiet in the twenty-fifth. Quiet, that is, everywhere but home. Home was always loud.

But it was the wrong kind of loud, these days. Jay was worried. Well, Jay was *always* worried. But this worry? Money. They had money, at least for a few months, courtesy of Rath. Well, courtesy of Duster and Jay's expedition to the undercity. Usually, when they had a few months' worth of money, Jay relaxed.

Jay was not relaxed now. The first thing she'd done with the damn money was march them all, in shifts, to Helen's. Helen had been surprised to see them, but not unhappy; she liked practical people, and she nodded while Jay gave instructions about, of all things, clothing. From there, she went off to the cobblers, with a similar set of instructions. They *had* decent clothing. They didn't need to fuss about it now.

But Jay had insisted they fuss while, as she put it, they had the money. This was new, and it was unwelcome. When Finch asked her why, Jay had avoided answering the question. Which meant that Finch stopped asking.

Duster started, instead.

We've got money. We've got a lot of money. Loosen up.

"We've got money *now*. But we won't have a lot of it if we spend it all."

"Then we go and get *more*."

Jay had said nothing.

"Look, what is your problem? If we run out of money, we go on a run. We don't have to leave it as late as we did last time. We can borrow money from Rath. He knows we're good for it."

"No."

"No, what?"

"No, we don't borrow money from Rath."

"So, we don't borrow money. We go to the undercity—"

"Leave it, Duster."

Duster glanced at the rest of the den. The rest of the den glanced at each other. It was awkward. Even Jester, prone to sticking his neck out for the sake of a badly timed joke, had been silent.

It was Teller who said quietly, "You don't want us to go into the undercity."

Jay hadn't answered. Enough of an answer, from Jay; she liked to talk. But she didn't say no. She just didn't say anything.

At the end of three days, it became clear that she wouldn't, either. The subject was closed, as far as Jay was concerned.

But Duster was pissed off. Her hand had stopped hurting, and the scarring wasn't bad; she hadn't lost any fingers, and she hadn't lost sensation. She hadn't been afraid of anything they'd found, and if she didn't particularly like being dumped on her butt in front of Moorelas' damn statue, it hadn't broken anything.

They'd gotten *out*. They'd gotten out with something good enough to sell on their first go.

The worst thing about it had been the damn prayer, and Duster was willing to say anything to anyone for that kind of money; it was all just words, anyway.

But something had spooked Jay.

Things were quiet at home. Or what passed for quiet, with this many people in a small space. The windows were open, because it was hot and humid enough that the slats had swollen and wouldn't stay closed. In the colder weather, they stayed closed because someone made the effort to tie the flapping shutters together; it wasn't worth it at any other time of the year, unless the rain was wicked.

Finch shuffled off to the kitchen; Jay followed her, and they spent a bit of time in the small space, trying to find room on the counter for the contents of each basket. Always seemed like a waste of time, to Duster, since most of what was in the basket was just going to disappear in a meal or two anyway.

Teller carefully closed the open books on the den's single table and set them in a pile on the floor, up against the wall. He also gathered the candles, which Jay only used when someone was out after dark; if someone was going to be late, they took the magestone. In the last few days, that had been Duster, Carver, and Fisher. And in the last few days, they'd come in to find Jay, candlelight flickering, bent over the pages of one of Rath's books. She hadn't looked happy to see them, but when she was working that hard, she rarely looked happy to see anyone.

She had blown the candle out as soon as Carver had produced the magestone, but she'd also closed the book. It was dark, which meant it was late, and even if the days *were* getting shorter, dawn still came early.

Jay didn't go to sleep until everyone was home and she could put the magestone in its holder—a gift from Rath—in her room. When Duster went out on her night runs in the holding, she left after Jay was snoring, because if she left before, Jay didn't sleep.

She'd sit up and wait.

And when Jay hadn't had enough sleep, she was the Hells on earth. Not that Duster cared all that much what anyone else suffered; she was hellish on *everyone,* which included Duster. It was just a bit of self-preservation at work, and she would have told that to anyone who asked. Anyone who was stupid enough to ask.

Today, bedtime was a long way off. Duster was restless, and knew it; she found a corner of the room to occupy and defended it by glaring. She ate there, in a sullen silence. Lander didn't break it, but he did drift by and sign a bit. He talked now, it was true, but he *liked* the den-sign, and he used it about as often as he used words.

She shrugged, and took a plate from his hands; she also didn't bite him when he settled against the wall to one side of her corner. They ate in silence. But everyone did. People were watching Jay.

Duster hated chatter. Always had. It was what people who were afraid of silence did, and Duster wasn't afraid of anything. But there were silences that were, for all intents and purposes, a lot like chatter, and she hated those, too. She ate, brooding, until she caught sight of Lander's fingers moving, deliberately and slowly, in his lap. He wasn't talking to her, but she could follow, if she wanted.

She was bored enough that she looked across the crowded damn room, to see whose hands were dancing in response. Mostly, she saw legs, and she shifted against the wall to better line her gaze up with Lander's. She snorted when she saw who was signaling. Lefty.

Lefty was still the runt of this particular litter. He was no taller than Duster, and most days, he looked shorter than everyone but Finch and Teller. This would be because he slouched, and he walked with his shoulders hunched up, as if to ward off blows. No one hit him, not here, but even years here hadn't killed that reflex.

If she were being fair, it hadn't killed many of hers, either. It was hard, most days, not to snap at Lefty. He didn't keep his maimed hand tucked under his armpit anymore, but he still fell silent when Duster walked in, or even walked by him. He practically screamed, *Hit me,* just because he was a walking cringe.

You couldn't count on him in a fight, ever. You couldn't count on him not to eat your food (if he didn't know it was yours; no one ate Duster's food otherwise, not even the cat) or actually *get* clothing clean, because apparently, even beating cloth with a rock was too hard for him. He actually had a bit of a mouth, but he only really used it when he was standing right under Arann's armpit.

And he lived here, in her space, and she hadn't beaten or killed him yet. She shook her head. Maybe miracles happened.

She stood, with her plate, paused to scoop Lander's, which was empty, out of his lap. She had never learned to cook, and she hated cut-up in the kitchen, but she was willing to help clean up, because everyone else did it.

She stopped short of the kitchen. Something Lander had just signed caught her attention. *So,* she thought. *Maze?*

She glanced around the room to see if anyone else was watching. Fisher and Carver, but neither of them added much. In Fisher's case, that was no surprise, but Carver?

As if he could hear the thought, he glanced at Jay, who was seated at the table. She was the only one who was, and she was lost in what passed for thought in these parts. As if to underscore this, she pulled out a slate and found some chalk. Duster shrugged, and carried the plates to the counter. She set them down, and took a closer look at the slate: it had columns of numbers. Duster hated them.

But she understood that those numbers were at the heart of this den. Without them, they ran out of money, food, or clothing. Anything they'd picked up in the undercity became, by Rath's grace, more numbers. Anything they needed was transformed into numbers as well, and making those numbers all add up to something that left room for food and rent—that was hard work and magic.

Both of which made Jay cranky.

Finch could do some numbers; Teller as well. Duster suspected that Angel was more than passingly familiar with them, but he kept the hell away from those slates because, like the rest of the den, he was both lazy and aware of what put Jay in a foul mood. She glanced at him; the bastard had strolled across the room and taken up squatting in her corner. She would have gone and pulled him out, but she saw why: He was signing with Lander.

Angel, new to the den, had not quite mastered this silent tongue. He asked questions, using words because they were faster, and Lander answered with gestures, slowing them down so Angel could see the whole of them.

Duster hated Angel's hair, but she was all right with him otherwise. Angel, on the other hand, seemed to have no problems with anyone else in the den except Duster. She made him nervous, and they both knew it.

Fair enough. She made everyone else nervous at times, and they'd known her for years. Everyone, she thought, but Jay. Jay worried about almost everything else, but not Duster, at least not that way. Duster's hand crept over the pommel of her dagger and rested there. It was sharp and clean; she had no reason to draw it; she wanted to, but didn't.

Because it was still important. Not to want things. Not to let people know how much you *did* want them. Not even these people.

But she'd lived with them for three years, now. Maybe more. Day by day, she'd eaten and slept with them; she'd hunted for a place, and she'd worked with them, in the undercity. She'd fought back to back with Carver a couple of times, once when things were dicey. He hadn't run, hadn't left her open.

She'd considered running, then. Hadn't. Couldn't really say why, except maybe she wasn't willing to be the *first* to run, and he wouldn't while she wouldn't. But Jay had come, with Arann and Fisher and Jester, and then the odds weren't so bad.

Ah, hells. She drew her dagger and held it up to whatever light she could find, just to see its edge.

After dinner, when Lander and Lefty rose, Angel and Carver rose as well. Carver palmed the magestone, and Jay caught his wrist; they fenced with stares, but Jay didn't say whatever it was she wanted to say. Duster, lounging against the wall, got to her feet and headed toward the door.

This brought the other four up short, but Duster said,

clearly, "You're not sticking me with the cleanup," before walking out. They milled about for a few minutes, but eventually they followed.

Only after the door was closed and they were most of the way to the stairs did Duster sign.

It was Angel who hesitated, not Lefty. But Angel's signing wasn't great. "You want to come with us?" he finally asked.

She shrugged.

He shrugged as well, but it was a different shrug. He didn't really care. They bounced a slow nod among themselves, and then they headed out, streetside.

"Jay's not going to like it," Angel said.

"She hasn't said we *can't* go. Precisely."

There was a lot more silence. Duster broke it, with a snort. "She's afraid of the undercity," she told them.

Jay's fears were never taken lightly by anyone but Duster.

"But she's afraid of being broke, as well."

"Yeah, but she's always afraid of that," Lefty said, cautiously.

"She's trying to get better at reading again. I think she thinks she can get some kind of job that pays her to read. Or do numbers," Duster added. "I can't do either. The rest of you can't read half as well as Teller or Finch. Some of us can fight, but we're sure as the Hells not going to get jobs with the magisterial guards, even if we can.

"But this? We can *do* this. We've all gone on runs in the undercity before now. We can head there. Just for a few days. We can scrounge around for stuff, give it to Rath later." Since it's pretty much what Lander and Lefty had been discussing in the silent apartment, no one should have been surprised.

"Come on," Duster said, when no one spoke, not even with their hands. "We can do that much, for her. It's only a few days. We'll want money for the rainy season. Look, we've been doing this for three years now. She's been doing it for longer. Nothing bad's ever happened before. She hasn't told us *not* to go, but she'll work her way up to it sometime this month, so if we're going to do this, we've got to do it soon. And," she added, as she headed down the street, "it's not like we've got anything else she'd ever let us sell."

Echoes, in those words, and she knew it.

Lander held the magestone. In the undercity, he often did. Not always, because he liked to wander, and when there was only one source of light, wandering wasn't an option.

Lander liked the undercity. He liked the quiet, and the empty spaces; he liked the stones, both fractured and whole, with their broken words, their engraved runes. Duster liked the undercity for different reasons, but there was something about Lander's open wonder that was comfortable, for her.

In the streets above, he often talked with his hands, which was sometimes a problem, because he wasn't much for repeating himself. But in the dark, he often used words, and no one forgot that it was in the undercity that most of the den had first heard him speak.

Not Duster; Duster had heard him someplace else first, before he had realized that words, especially his, served no purpose and offered no help. He had abandoned them, just as he had been abandoned. But his return to speech had come here, first, as if the boundaries between below and above controlled his mouth.

They made their way to the Stone Garden, because Lander held the magestone and they were forced to follow him. The Stone Garden never changed. The den had, and most of the changes, even in Duster's cynical view, had been good ones—but there was something calming about the garden's immutability. They could return to it, in any weather, and at any age, and it would be like this: Stone flowers, vines, and small trees, arrayed around a courtyard that was larger than any building they had ever lived in.

You could feel wind in the bend of stem and the slow turn of petal; you could feel sunlight, even in this endless night. You could smell the earth beneath stone roots. Even the downward drift of petals was captured; it was as if a mage had found the perfect gardens, and transformed them, in an instant, to stone.

There had been some discussion about that, among the den. There had been questions about how the maker-born worked. But even the answers they'd managed to dig out of Rath hadn't really done much to quench curiosity, because Rath was very definite: this was not made by the mere maker-born. The Stone Garden, Rath had said, was the work of an Artisan— and Artisans were both famously mad and inexplicably magical.

The Twin Kings held a rod and a sword that had been Made by Fabril, the first and the best known of the Empire's Artisans, so it wasn't as if the den had never heard of Artisans. Everyone had, no matter where they lived, or how. But those, the rod and the sword of Kings, were the stuff of legend, and therefore properly the work of Artisans.

The Stone Garden, though? It made no sense.

They never tried to take anything from the Stone Garden; the Stone Garden, likewise, never took anything but their mute admiration from them. Even Duster, who liked to hold herself aloof, was not immune.

But Duster, unlike the rest of her den, could only bear to wander here for so long before she grew restless, and it was therefore Duster who eventually called a halt to Lander's progress.

The building beyond this garden, they did not enter. Duster had tried once or twice, but the farthest she had ever gotten was with Jay, and Jay had stopped at a closed door and shaken her head.

"Dangerous?"

"Might be."

"Too bad."

It was. Anything they could find *here* was guaranteed to be worth money. But it wasn't, as Jay pointed out, worth injury. Healers in the Empire weren't easily found, and they were never cheap. Doctors were more easily found, but they still weren't cheap, and Duster privately thought they weren't worth what they wanted to charge. Duster had old scars from injuries that no doctor had ever seen, and she'd survived.

"Duster?"

She looked up, away from a glimpse of the interior of the building. Lander, stone cupped in his left hand, was waiting. She shook her head and wandered toward him, taking care not to step on anything. Duster was careful here. Sometimes it irritated her, but she reasoned that she could be careful at all because the flowers here *were* beautiful and they would never hurt her.

And the only *people* you could say that about, for sure, were dead.

But as she followed Lander into their secret city, she wondered if that was still true. Because *these* people had been in her life for longer than anyone else, and they didn't hurt her either. They pissed her off a lot, but on the right day, the weather could piss her off.

They spent time wandering from building to building in a loose group. Carver had picked up the rope by the entrance, and they ended up having to use it a few times, which always made the going slow.

"These are wider," Carver said, when they'd crossed the third large gap and he was untying the knot around Lefty.

Duster nodded. "Think there's some kind of earthquake that's causing them?"

"Something that we can't feel streetside?" He shrugged. "Maybe Jay's worried this whole place is going to collapse."

Duster snorted. "If she were worried about *that,* she'd make us move. We're living above the damn undercity, and if it all comes down, so do we."

Carver started to say something, shut his mouth, and glanced at Angel. Angel shrugged. "She's making sense to me." He nodded toward Lander's back, because Lander had already started to move. "I think we should head right a bit—this is all familiar."

Carver glanced at Duster, who nodded. Familiar

meant it had probably been gone over at least a few times.

When they finally crawled out of the undercity, dirty and not a little tired, they had one candlestick to show for the effort. It was heavy, and caused arguments about whether or not the previous inhabitants had actually used candles, but since no one could think of what *else* it might be used for, they dumped it into the backpack that was used to carry rope.

Lefty reasoned that if they couldn't sell it, they could use it as a club. Which was about as much reasoning as Lefty was up to, but Duster had to admit that the damn thing *was* heavy. She wanted it to be heavier, because then it might be gold; it was some sort of metal. Not silver, because old silver was always black. It also had space for three candles, so maybe Jay could make use of it while she studied those damn books, if it didn't end up being worth money. There were letters on it, but no one recognized what they were, which was a good sign, in the undercity. Streetside, it made Jay cranky.

"We can come back tomorrow," Carver told everyone as they reached the small door that separated home from the rest of the twenty-fifth holding. "After market, before dinner."

Angel said, "I'm out."

"Why?"

"My turn to cook."

Carver shrugged. Then he smiled. "I'll drag Fisher." He opened the door and walked in.

One run to the well, and one dinner later, Jester and Lander chased flies around the apartment, accidentally swatting half the den. Or not so accidentally; with Jester, it was hard to tell. Crawling around the undercity had quieted everyone but Lander. Most of Lander's chatter was sign, so it wasn't exactly noisy—but he wanted people to pay attention. Hadn't always wanted it either. But . . . he did, these days.

Jay sat on the ground for dinner and joined in general conversation, trying to look relaxed, which meant she knew how strained she was. Carver had handed her the candlestick holder, or, as Lefty called it, the club, when he'd entered the apartment; she'd taken it with a slight widening of eyes, and then set it down on one side of her table. She looked as if she wanted to say more, and clearly she did—but for tonight, she bit the words back.

But when Teller and Finch were cleaning up in the kitchen, she said, "I'm making everyone worry, aren't I?" Duster, lounging rather closer to the cleanup than she usually did, heard it clearly.

Teller nodded. "You haven't told us what's wrong," he added. "So no one knows what to do."

"What do you mean, do?"

He glanced at her slates. "You don't want us to farm the undercity. But you don't know why. We don't know how to do much else."

She looked at the candlestick holder and her shoulders sank. "I'm afraid," she said softly, aware that Duster was listening. "Because I don't know that I'm good for anything else either. No," she added, lifting a hand, "I'm not fishing for compliments. I *can* do other stuff. I just don't know how to convince someone with enough money to pay me to do it. And without money, Teller . . . "

"And the undercity?"

She shook her head. "I . . . just don't know."

Lame. Duster snorted.

"It's Emperal," Finch piped in.

Jewel frowned, and then she smiled. "I almost forgot."

"We've got ten days to mooch stuff from The Ten at the Festival." Finch loved The Gathering. "We can keep our costs down that way while we try to think of something else to do." She added, "It's not raining, it's not cold, we're not starving, and we all have shoes. Smile."

Pretty pathetic smile, Duster thought, as Jay tried.

But when it got dark again, Jay put aside slates and books, and rose. She stretched, because she sat like a pretzel in the chair when she worked, and then she padded off to the bedroom to toss her clothing in a pile and slide into her bedroll.

Jay dropped the magestone into its stand on the small block of wood that served as a night table. Finch, Teller, Duster, and sometimes Lander would sleep in the room on the blankets and bedrolls that existed for only that purpose. There was often a bit of argument about who got what, but not tonight; tonight it was warm, and Jay had tried, however pathetically, to be a part of the den.

Duster didn't care for the room; she didn't like sleeping with the lights on. Night was supposed to be dark. She generally shed less clothing than Jay or Finch, and if had been up to her, she'd have slept on her own, her back as close to the wall as she she could get. But . . . this is where Jay slept. And if Duster didn't care for the room, she had one job she took seriously: she watched over Jay.

She listened for Jay's nightmares—the ones that weren't the *feeling,* the ones that didn't come in bloody threes. She knew where the normal nightmares came from; she'd been there at the start. It had been partly her fault, but Jay had never thrown it back at her, never thrown it in her face. There was nothing—nothing *at all*—that Duster could do for Jay in return, but this: wake her, when it was bad.

She didn't even hate the part of herself that *wanted* to somehow do something for Jay that would make all the old pain worthwhile. Something big. Something *only* Duster could manage. Like, say, killing Carmenta.

Jay wouldn't let her kill him. Duster accepted that.

But . . . something *big*. Something like that.

When she had first started sleeping with the den, she had refused to fall asleep until she could hear the even breathing of every other person in the room. Now? She took the sleep she could get, because there was no guarantee that there would be much of it. Jay had nightmares.

She wasn't the only one who had nightmares; they all did. Some, like Duster, were quiet about it; some, like Lander, were as loud as Jay, but more bewildered. No one said much; they woke you if it was safe, and they let you be if it wasn't. She thought of Arann, and grimaced. Not even Duster was stupid enough to wake him.

Duster slept with her dagger. Sometimes she slid it under the pillow, if she had one; tonight, she didn't, and she tucked it, sheathed, under her shoulder instead.

She could have slept in the other room. Carver, well aware of her dislike for the night-light, had offered. She always said no. Didn't stop her complaining about the things she didn't like.

No, Duster couldn't fight Jay's nightmares. She couldn't calm her down—that's what Teller and Finch were for.

But she could roll out of bed with her knife in her hand, and she could stand watch, where Jay could see her and know that she was ready to fight for her, in all ways, at any hour, in any circumstance. That she could be, still and always, what Jay had wanted from her in the early days.

It was important, to Duster. Important because it said all these things without words, without exposure.

She curled up on her side and closed her eyes.

And woke with a start. Her body rolled her to her feet while her eyes focused. Jay was screaming, and Duster, dagger already gleaming in the light, took a deep breath, and listened.

Teller was already awake, and Finch had thrown off her bedclothes; they were both slow to climb to their feet. The screaming banked sharply as Jay shot up, sitting stiff and white, bedroll twisted beneath her arms in chunks. In the hall, Carver had gained his feet, and Angel as well, and both had come to the mouth of the doorframe, waiting. For Duster's word.

Duster, watching Jay come back from nightmare, saw that she had swallowed the screaming in just such a way that it now sat within her widened eyes.

"Teller," Duster said.

Teller nodded. "Kitchen."

*　　　*　　　*

The last to wake was Arann because, as usual, no one wanted to wake him until they'd cleared enough floor space that they could throw things at him from a distance. Teller led Jay to the kitchen table, stubbing his toes on the chair in the process. Duster had scooped up the magestone and its holder, following closely behind.

Finch brought Jay a cup of water and set it in front of her, and Teller reached for the closest slate, taking care to pick up the one on the top of the pile. He would write what she said, if she started to talk about the dream. He would do this for three nights, because significant dreams often came in threes. No one knew why; they didn't need to know why.

Jay looked at the magestone, her eyes half-closed. She drank the water Finch had placed before her without ever looking at the cup. She said, "It's dark."

Teller started to write.

"It's dark enough I can't see. I can hear, though. Voices. Talking. Movement."

"A lot of movement?"

"Heavy stone, I think." She frowned. "Yes. Stone."

"Where are you standing?" Angel's voice, quiet and direct.

She drank again. "It's . . . " Frowned. "Dirt, I think. I'm standing on dirt. It's dark," she added. "But after a while, I can see light. Just a little light, glowing faintly."

"Magical?"

"I think . . . it must be."

"Why?"

She shrugged. "It's a dream," she told him, as if that explained anything.

No one pointed out that *their* dreams did not intersect with reality the way Jay's did.

"It's a stone. Above the ground. I think—I think it's a keystone," she added.

"A what?" Duster asked, trying to imagine a magical stone that could be used to lock doors. It had a certain appeal.

"A keystone. It's the top stone in an arch, the one at the height of the curve, if it's curved."

Duster liked her version better, but said nothing.

"It's glowing," she added softly, "and I can move toward it. I can almost see it. The stone isn't great—it's rough stone, and I can't see the color; just the rune. The rune is the source of the light."

Duster hesitated. No one was watching her, so no one else noticed.

"Can you see stars or moonlight?" Angel again.

Jay frowned. Closed her eyes. Shook her head. She ran her hands through her hair, shoving it out of her eyes as she opened them again. It sprang back almost immediately, because in this weather, the humidity made the curls thick and tight.

"So, you're inside."

She nodded, but it was a slow, doubtful nod.

They waited, because so far, nothing was worth screaming yourself awake for.

"And then," she said, almost unaware of the quality of waiting, "there *is* light."

Teller's scratching was the only sound in the room. It was a constant sound, a quiet one—the equivalent, in writing, of heartbeat or breath.

"And she's standing in it."

"Who?"

Jay shook her head. "I don't know. She's not human," she added. "Maybe some minor god—I don't know. I *don't want* to know. But she's tall, and she's surrounded by red light and shadow. She has a red, red sword."

"Blood?"

"Not yet. Light, I think. Red light. Her hair is all black, and it flies around her face and shoulders without ever getting in her way. She's beautiful," Jay added, as if beauty were a curse. "And she points at the arch—and it is an arch, and the keystone is glowing brightly now."

"She doesn't kill anything?"

"She doesn't have to. I can see what the arch contains." She shuddered. "It's like darkness, but it's not—there's light in it, but it sheds nothing, it just roils. And it's moving," she added softly.

Silence. Jay'd had a lot of dreams in the years they'd

been together, but this one was new and disturbing. "Toward me. It's moving toward me, and I can't move—I
want to run, but I'm afraid because if it sees me—" She
closed her eyes, tight, and wrapped her arms around her
shoulders.

"And then it speaks."

"What does it say?"

"I don't know. I can't understand it. But it's not one
voice—it's like every ugly thing any voice has ever said."

Okay, Duster thought. *That was worth a wake-up
scream.*

Teller finished writing in the silence. Then he took
the slate and set it apart. "One night," he told Jay softly.

"Good. Will it make sense in the morning?"

"I don't know. It doesn't make much sense now."

She nodded. Emptied her cup. She didn't tell them
not to speak about it; they never did. Rath had made
clear, years ago, that Jay's visions, Jay's feelings, were
unique as far as he knew—and Rath knew *mages*. He
had also made it clear that if other people knew about
her visions, Jay might not be in the streets much longer,
her own wishes notwithstanding.

"Maybe she could work for someone," Teller had
said. "Someone powerful."

Rath nodded his approval, as if Teller had said anything that everyone else wasn't thinking. "She could. If
she could find the right person, and prove herself."

"And if she finds the wrong person?"

Rath hadn't answered. But that was answer enough.
Everyone in the den had found—or been found—by the
wrong people before. They knew what it meant.

"Come on, Jay," Finch said gently. Jay nodded. Nightmares like this only happened once a night, although
the regular nightmares could still happen afterward.
They slowly returned to their patches of floor, trying
not to think about Jay's vision, and what it might mean.

Especially Duster, who thought she could guess.

7th of Emperal, 410 AA
The Common, Averalaan

Jewel rarely went to the Common alone. It wasn't entirely safe if you took the streets. She hadn't. She'd slid down into the undercity, taking a route that was seldom used by her den. She wasn't sure why; maybe she wanted to prove something. To them, or to herself, she wasn't certain. But they'd gone, they'd found something that Jewel was certain was worth money, although Lefty still called it a club. What they dared, she had to be able to dare.

Why? her Oma asked from across the veil.

There was no *good* answer to the question, so Jewel didn't bother; her Oma had never been particularly kind when she'd offered a bad one.

The morning outing to the Common had come and gone, and there was food for a day in the kitchen in baskets on the floor. The well had been visited, and Finch had undertaken the laundry with whomever she could collar.

The walk through the solemn—and silent—streets of the undercity had passed without incident; it was peaceful and private. Jewel had even meandered a little, and stopped to visit the Stone Garden, in which peace could sometimes be coaxed out of hiding. Even on a day like today.

She missed the undercity.

It wasn't the foraging, because on those days she had half of her den in tow, and they had to be careful of things like the floors and the ceilings. It was the quiet. The sense of secrecy, of hidden things. It wasn't their home; she doubted anyone but Duster could live in continual dark. But it was, in some ways, an extension of home, and losing it was hard.

She knew they all felt that way. She knew they had gone there yesterday. She knew, *knew,* they would go back today. And she knew, as well, that she should forbid it. But she wasn't their owner or their captain.

Forbidding them, ordering them—it made her uneasy. It felt wrong.

Not that she didn't order them around half the time—but that was little stuff, and they could snap back at her at any time (and often did). This was bigger.

She carried the candleholder in her backpack as she traversed the much more crowded streets of the Common. She was to meet Rath in two hours. She knew he wouldn't be pleased. She wondered if he'd be angry. Knowing Rath, probably. But would he be angry enough not to fence what they'd found?

Without him, the den had no way of selling the things they could pry out of the undercity and carry home. He had connections to merchants in the Common and mages in the Order of Knowledge, and none of the den suffered under the illusion that they could build their own if he withdrew his aid. Hells, they couldn't even afford to cross the bridge to the Isle that housed the damn Order unless they were willing to give up a day's worth of food.

Two hours. Jewel stood for a moment, like a rock in a stream comprised of people, before she turned on her heel and made her way to the outer edge of the Common, where the merchants with actual storefronts worked.

The streets were marginally less crowded here, but the guards were more numerous, and they eyed her with tired suspicion as she walked. She wasn't dressed as a customer. But she had shoes, and her clothing, if somewhat mismatched, was in decent enough repair; they had no call to stop her, and they didn't.

She found the store she was looking for, paused just a moment in front of the closed door to look at her reflection, shoved her hair as far out of her eyes as it would go, and then pushed the door inward. Bells rang as she did.

It was true that she hadn't had cause to enter many shops in the Common. The guards that often stood outside the doors would have put her off, even if she'd wanted to. But the owner of this particular store—

which sold bolts of fine cloth and custom dresses—wouldn't call the guards.

He barely looked up at the sound of the bells, and she walked over to the counter at which he did much of his work in the front of the store. The back room, in which the rest of the work was done was a study in clutter and mess; it wasn't dirty, but there wasn't a square inch of visible tabletop or chairback in sight.

He was not, however, in the back room at the moment. Instead, he was perched on a stool, his lap covered in a fine purple cloth that seemed blue and green as it caught the light at different angles. His lips were pursed around pins, which jutted out of his mouth in a fan, and the counter was occupied by glass beads and small pearls. In his hands, needle and thread moved slowly and completely steadily.

Jewel had always liked to watch Haval work, and she watched him for at least five minutes before he looked up, moving only his eyes. He looked down to his work again, and finished the stitching before removing the pins from his mouth; these, he wove into the seams of what looked a very fine skirt.

"Jewel," he said, and nodded.

She had given up telling him to call her Jay.

He was a fastidious little man, although he wasn't actually that small. She knew it was partly an act, a presentation meant to either ease or comfort, but she liked it enough to accept it.

"Excellent timing. It's almost lunch," he told her, as he eased himself off of his stool. "Will you join me in the back room?" Before she could answer, he raised his voice. He didn't actually shout, but he had the ability to project that voice across the distance of a few rooms. "Hannerle, young Jewel Markess will be joining me for lunch."

She slid her backpack off her shoulders, and dropped it behind the counter in the front of the store. This was practical; anything she dropped in the back of the store was likely to get buried by bolts of cloth, lace or beading, and it would take some time to find it again.

She was the one who was going to be moving most of those bolts. Haval directed her, often by the simple expedient of lifting something and dumping it, without warning or ceremony, into her arms. This happened any time Jewel visited Haval's back room, because space for visitors had to be cleared. In Jewel's opinion, space for Haval also had to be cleared, but since Haval owned everything here, he was unlikely to be furious at himself for any damage he caused while he moved things.

"You're alone today," Haval said, while he carefully gathered stray beads and dropped them into a round, leather container.

"Yes. I'm meeting Rath," she added. She didn't look up from her chosen task, because she was picking up pins.

"Why?"

She hesitated.

"Come sit, Jewel. Here. There's room—no, wait, just move that carding to the desk. The desk by the wall."

Since the desk by the wall had been buried in bolts and colorful debris, Jewel didn't feel particularly stupid for not having recognized it.

But there was now room on a real chair, and there was space—on a small round table that looked so spindly anything would knock it over—for whatever lunch Haval's wife had prepared. Jewel took the chair. It was at a slight angle to Haval's, and the table formed the third point of a lopsided triangle.

Haval sat. "Why are you meeting Rath?" he asked again.

Jewel grimaced. "I've something to deliver to him." She knew he'd marked the first hesitation, because he missed *nothing*. She half-suspected he knew about the undercity, but if he miraculously didn't, she wasn't about to betray the confidence.

"So this visit is simply killing time? I'm hurt."

"You know Rath doesn't like it when I visit."

He chuckled, at that. "I should say that Hannerle doesn't like it when *Rath* visits."

"Why are you talking about Rath?" Hannerle had entered the room, carrying a heavy tray. A wide, well-worn apron covered her not insubstantial girth.

"To tease you," Jewel replied. "Haval is teasing you," she added hastily. "I wouldn't have mentioned Rath."

Hannerle snorted. It was one of the few manner-isms that she and Duster had in common. "We've seen enough of Rath in the last little while to last a lifetime," Haval's wife added as she set the tray down. "But, to be fair, he hasn't asked for much."

"No?"

"No," Haval said smoothly. "He is aware that it's Emperal. It's a busy month for us. And no, Jewel, that was not a hint. Even when it's busy, I still have to eat."

"You think you'd remember that first thing in the morning, when breakfast is congealing," Hannerle re-plied sharply. She wiped her hands in her apron, and offered Jewel a tired smile. "He likes company," she said. "I'd have more over if there was any place to put it." She looked around Haval's workspace as if it were a particularly dirty kitchen she'd been both ordered to work in and forbidden to clean.

Haval, accustomed to this, lifted the teapot with great care, and poured two cups. He offered one to Jewel. He offered one to his wife, who declined to join them because it would, in her words, take until dinner to find another chair. To be fair, Jewel thought she was underestimating.

But she touched Jewel briefly on the shoulder, telling her to make sure Haval ate well, before she retreated.

Haval said, "She's a good wife, for me."

Jewel nodded, because she agreed. Her Oma would have liked Haval's wife, and Jewel had no doubt that Hannerle would have thoroughly approved of her Oma—although neither of the two would have been comfortable living under the same roof.

"You've grown again," Haval said, when Jewel had put the small sandwiches Hannerle liked to make on his plate.

"Have I?"

"At least three inches, although it's difficult to tell when you slouch." The last was said with slight reproach.

"There's no reason not to slouch, and the backpack is heavy."

"And you're not to tell me what's in it?"

"No."

"Ah, well. I did have to ask."

"You could ask Rath."

"There is no chance whatsoever that he would answer."

"There's no chance *I* will either, if he won't."

"True. But the way you refuse to answer tells me much," Haval replied, this time with a smile. It was an old smile, but it was friendly enough—just—that Jewel didn't bridle. "And if you did not come to regale me with information, you must have come seeking it."

Jewel started to say, quite truthfully, that she had come for no such thing, but she stopped herself. "What information would I be seeking?"

He chuckled. "Very good, Jewel. Very good. We will make a politician of you yet."

"You'd have to make me rich first. And powerful, if they aren't the same thing."

"They are not, as you know, the same thing. A man, or woman, can be rich and never leverage wealth to gain power. A man, or woman, can be titled, and never leverage title to gain wealth. Power comes in many forms. Some power extends itself as far as a sword can swing. Some power is more subtle, but it extends further."

"One of these days, you'll tell me how you met Rath."

"I hope not," Haval said, in mock horror. "Hannerle would kill me."

Jewel was silent then. "Haval—"

He lifted a slender hand. The humor left his face, and his eyes were dark and clear as he studied her in the workshop's light. It was good light, bright enough to do fine work in, but it cast sharper shadows.

"Do not tell me anything that Rath would not tell me," he said softly. A warning.

"Why not? You're the best liar I've ever met. If you

know it, and you don't want him to know you do, it won't even occur to him to ask."

Haval simply watched her.

She said, "Can I talk about myself, instead?"

"It is not for yourself that you're concerned," he replied. He took a loud sip of tea, but his eyes didn't leave her face.

"I'm always worried about myself."

He raised a brow. "Because I'm the best liar you've ever met," he told her, "I take a professional interest in the lies of others. Yours are so far beneath rank amateur that I suggest you not bother. Lies are not, and will never be, a part of your armory." He took another sip of tea, and watched her through the rising steam. "Why did you come?"

"To visit. To kill time."

"Ah. And you are just now bothered by something?"

She picked up her tea and put it down again. She disliked his cups, because they had so little handle and the surfaces were always hot. "Rath listens to you," she said. She looked at the little sandwiches on her plate, and began to eat one. Because she was with Haval, she ate slowly. He disliked it when she shoved the whole thing into her mouth, even though each one was only two bites' worth of food.

"He listens when it serves his purpose. If you mean he obeys me, you have failed entirely to understand the nature of our relationship. If you want me to tell him not to do something," he added, his eyes narrowing slightly as Jewel's widened, "I will have to refuse."

"Haval—"

"I understand some small part of his purpose," Haval told her gently. He, too, ate, and he ate with exquisite care; no hint of a crumb escaped either his plate or his mouth. "And while I am merely a designer and purveyor of fine clothing, it is not, in the end, a purpose of which I disapprove."

"He's told you what he's doing?" She leaned forward in her chair, food almost forgotten.

"Ah. No, of course not. But I am a man—one of

many—from whom he obtains information. He uses—
and you must pay attention to this—several different
sources. It is not, as it might at first appear, because
there is no overlap in the information these sources
might provide. Tell me why you think he does this,"
Haval added.

With Haval, everything was a lesson. Jewel was not
of a mind to be lectured, but he was feeding her, and he
never did anything without reason. She chewed, swallowed, and thought. "Rath is serious about his privacy."

"Very good. How is that pertinent?"

"He can't ask for information without giving information first. Even if it's insignificant. He'll have to give
you a name—or names—unless it's a general request,
but even if it's general, he has to tell you what he needs."
She hesitated, and then added, "He could ask you for
information he doesn't need, as well, to muddy the
waters."

Haval's grin was as good as applause. "He could, indeed. And that would serve what purpose?"

"Well, if he asked you for information about three
things, and he already had decent information about
two of them, he could figure out how good your own information is. He could also figure out if you were lying."

Haval did clap, then, which bought Jewel time to eat
two more sandwiches, and check her tea. It was still hot.

"And?"

"And in any case, you wouldn't know which of
the three things he already knew, and you would
take note of all three things, in an attempt to discern some sort of pattern. If he wanted the pattern
to be less obvious, he would choose things that were
both interesting—because he says you're a notorious
gossip—and unrelated."

"All these years, I thought you weren't paying attention," Haval replied. "Tell me why I might know some
part of his purpose, given that he would be this careful."

"Because you also talk to most of the City, and you
know both rumors and the truth behind those rumors.
You probably know—or at least suspect—the identity

of anyone else he talks to, so you can filter out anything he doesn't really need or want to know. Not all of it," she added, "but enough. You can pick out a bit of a pattern, and you can enlarge it by making your own inquiries."

"Indeed. You have earned a better lunch than I am giving you. Let us agree that I owe you a much better lunch, in a future month that does not include The Gathering." He paused, and then said softly, "He knows what he does, and I believe he understands the risks. He is called Old Rath for a reason."

"He won't survive," she replied. Just that, but starkly.

"And you wish me to convince him that his survival should be his only imperative."

"Yes."

"You cannot know that he won't survive, Jewel. And even if you did, and I was certain of it, he wouldn't listen." He lifted both hands, after setting the cup down; it was a type of surrender. "I will be frank with you, although you will have to judge for yourself whether or not my earnest words are truthful. I have given him just such advice, and with varying degrees of seriousness. You credit me with too much influence," he added, picking up his cup again. "Or perhaps it is just hope speaking."

"If I've earned lunch, have I earned information?"

"Perhaps. What information? I will not tell you of Rath's doings," he added, as if it needed to be said.

"In the last couple of months," she told him, "people have gone missing in the lower holdings. Not many, and a lot of them are people who wouldn't be noticed by anyone who would care—I don't think they have family, and they live wherever they can find a roof that hasn't collapsed."

"Where?"

"I don't know where. I don't know which holdings, but—it's rumor. At the wells, and in the Common. I've heard it in the twenty-fifth," she continued, "and some of the people speak of the thirty-second, the thirty-fifth, as well."

He listened. "That's not a question," he told her.

"No. Let me try that again. Have you heard anything about people disappearing or bodies being found? There aren't *more* bodies," she added, because there were often one or two in the hot, dry months, dredged out of the river as it receded from its banks.

"I haven't heard about bodies being found," he said. He picked up a sandwich, paused, and said, "And your den are not among that number?"

"My den has me. And each other. If one of us disappeared, we'd make a lot of noise."

He nodded again. "Understand, Jewel, that most of my information involves parts of the City that your den does not normally see. But this is not always the case, and I will keep an ear out. Have you moved?"

"No."

"I will send word, if any word of interest reaches me."

Chapter Six

7th of Emperal, 410 AA
The Common, Averalaan

RATH MET JEWEL BY THE FOUNTAIN in the southwest of the Common. It had a couple of advantages as a meeting place, the most important one being that it was used by everyone *as* a meeting place. Standing around the fountain, or sitting on its edge, or even removing your shoes and dipping your feet in the water, were all commonplace, because inevitably some of the people gathered here were going to have to wait a while.

Because it was hot, Jewel was one of the people who did remove her shoes and dip her toes in the water, and because she was Jewel, Rath showed up the minute her feet were actually wet.

He didn't look amused.

She apologized, retrieved her feet, and dried them with her socks.

"You came alone?" he asked, when she shrugged her shoulders out of the backpack's cumbersome straps and handed it to Rath.

She nodded.

He looked, if it were possible, less pleased. He wasn't stupid. He didn't ask her what route she'd taken to get here, and she didn't tell him. But they knew each other well enough to fill in the words. Instead, he offered her lunch. Since she'd already eaten with Haval, she was tempted to say no, but Rath had never liked discussions in public spaces, so she nodded instead, and followed him.

The Common boasted a number of restaurants without inns attached to them, and Rath chose the Bough, which was pricey enough that Jewel fretted in the entrance. Rath, however, was dressed decently, and if the owner cared about the condition of his dining companion, he didn't so much as frown. Instead, he led them to a booth in the back corner of the room, where Jewel's attire was less likely to be spotted.

When they were seated and the owner had gone away, Rath untied the strings that kept the backpack closed. He glanced at what it contained, frowned, and then tied the strings again. He hadn't taken the candleholder out, but Jewel hadn't expected that.

She had, however, expected the look that now settled into his familiar features.

"Where," he said quietly, "did you find this?"

She hesitated. Thought about lying. Thought about how well it was likely to work. "I didn't. Duster and Carver did."

"You let them go to the maze without you."

"It's hard to stop them, Rath. Without being able to tell them *why,* it's hard. We've been doing it for years. We're careful, and we almost never go down alone. I know that you've said it's dangerous. Duster was with me when—when part of the labyrinth started to collapse, and damn it, she's not afraid to go back.

"They don't listen if I don't *feel* it. And they know the difference."

He said nothing for a long moment. And then he relaxed. Or seemed to; his expression was still remote. "I will sell this," he told her. "But after this piece, Jewel, it will become more difficult for me. You know better than to ask why."

She did. It almost didn't stop her. Of all the things she had dreaded hearing, this was the worst.

"Have you finished the books I left with you?"

"Almost. Teller and Finch have been helping me."

"With?"

"The lists. The memorization. Teller's better at it," Jewel added.

"Because he's interested in the content, no doubt. I'll bring a few others by in the next couple of weeks, but I will be absent for much of those. If you need to reach me, leave me a message. Do not take the tunnels to my apartment. Come in whatever numbers you feel wise, but take the street."

She nodded.

Everything tasted like dust, but she ate because he was watching.

Haval looked up when the chimes rang and the door was pushed open. He immediately set aside the beading he'd been working on, and set aside as well the glass that he wore to do the work; it was technically a jeweler's glass, but it served him well.

"Ararath," he said, nodding.

"Haval." Rath was tired, and he looked older. He wore summer linens, and these were cleaned and, apparently, pressed; he wore a light jacket. And he carried a backpack that Haval had seen scant hours before.

"I've had some word," Haval said, dispensing with idle chat entirely. He retrieved an envelope from under the volume of powder-blue silk that had occupied most of this week's afternoons; he had graduated from purple silk, a color he disdained, as the day had progressed. He handed the envelope to Rath.

Rath took it, and placed it casually inside his jacket.

"Jewel was by," Haval said quietly.

Rath frowned. "A social call?"

"A social call. She is not in a situation in which any of my other skills might prove useful to her."

Rath nodded.

"She's concerned about you, on the other hand. She thought that I might have some influence with you, where she does not."

"And you offered her what comfort?"

"None. She is not a child."

"You could lie."

"I could," Haval replied affably. "But any lie I tell her will comfort her for as long as she is in my presence, no longer. The truth will crush the delicate illusion that I build, and she's not capable of maintaining that illusion, however greatly she desires it. I am, as you are well aware, famously lazy. I won't go through the work of lying to her when it will serve so little purpose."

Rath exhaled.

"You," Haval said, "are also, I see, indulging in laziness today."

"Oh?"

"You look haggard, Ararath. I'm aware that you could look hale and dangerously energetic if you so chose, and I am also aware that you intended this visit to last no more than a handful of necessary minutes. A few minutes of acting is not more than I have come to expect."

Rath shrugged. "Perhaps on another day. Today, it's beyond me. I came for information," he added, "not a lecture."

"No. No man ever comes for a lecture. I will tell you, however, that I think your Jewel is wasted here."

"You've said that a hundred times. If we're tossing accusations of laziness back and forth, you might come up with something more original."

"Oh, very well. But remember, Ararath, that you insisted."

Rath raised a pale brow, and his lips turned up at the corners in something that might, by a different man, be mistaken for a grin.

"She thought to ask me if I had word of any unusual disappearances, or the discovery of a larger number of bodies than would be usual, in the holdings."

Rath cursed. "And you answered?"

"I explained as gently as I could that the holdings in which she currently resides are not my area of expertise. And no, before you turn grim, I did not explain that her inquiries and your own are not, in this case, that disparate."

"Good."

"Rath."

Rath closed his eyes. "I know," he told Haval.

"She is worried for you, and it is a peculiar type of worry. I understand the shallow insecurity of the young, and I understand the insecurity that a hard life imposes. Her worry is neither of these things. I know the nuances of her expressions, because one can hardly *not* know them; she is not good at hiding. I find it painful to watch her try.

"And I understand that she does not *fear* your death. She knows it is coming, the way she knows Winter will come. It is a certainty for her, and it grieves her. I am not Jewel. I take no responsibility for either your life or your death. I will feel no guilt when word at last reaches me. She will, however."

"I should never have brought her here."

"No," Haval replied. "You did her no kindness, there."

They had never spoken of Lord Waverly's death. They never would. Nor would they speak of the events that surrounded it. But Haval, in his way, had now been as blunt as he had ever been. What Haval guessed, he guessed—but Haval missed little.

"What will you do, for her?"

"Have a care, Haval."

Haval was silent for a moment, but the moment didn't last. "As I can, Ararath." He slowly unfolded from his habitual slouch, shedding years and the slightly dotty demeanor that he so often adopted in the store. It was easy to think of Haval as a quirky, curmudgeonly older man.

But it was easy because Haval desired it. At the moment, he shed the pretense, and when he met Rath's gaze—and held it—he was no longer the comfort-craving dressmaker. He was no longer old, and he was no longer harmless; he was no longer the nonjudgmental wise man.

His face was a mask.

The smile Rath offered him was genuine. It was informed by, of all strange things, delight. The delight of discovery, or of rediscovering something you had thought lost. "So," he said softly. "You wear your age less poorly."

"Less deliberately, certainly," Haval replied, the subtle inflections transforming the agreement into a distant neutrality. "It is not entirely an act, which is why I am successful. Truth has its own feel, and where it is possible, it should be used. A careful blend of truth and the expectations—even the unconscious preferences—of one's audience have always been powerful, in a quiet way."

"And now?"

"Even now, old friend," Haval replied, "what I have just said is true. You are not, however, that audience."

"Which audience, then?"

"You are Ararath Handernesse," he replied, and he bowed, just slightly, at the name. "What you were three years ago, you are not now. I offered Jewel no comfort because she would take none; she is afraid, both for her own future, and of the end of yours. But she cannot understand what she sees in you, and I see it clearly."

Rath's smile was slight, a thin edge composed in part of lips and bitter humor. "Clumsy of me," he said. "How did I fail, this time?"

Haval smiled in return, and there was some kinship in the expression. "The nature of your inquiries, and the breadth. Three holdings, Ararath."

"I believe I inquired after ten."

"Indeed. And a disparate ten, at that. But of the ten, three are held by a Patris Cordufar. The thirty-second, the thirty-fifth, and the seventeenth. It is unusual," he added, "that a lord who owns three holdings should have no residence upon the Isle; he does not."

"Haval—"

Haval lifted a hand. "You have come to ask me a favor. You will indulge me before you ask."

"Very well. Should we adjourn to the back?"

"No. I prefer the front of the store. I can see the street, and anyone who watches or approaches."

Rath nodded.

"The current Lord Cordufar is a man one approaches with caution, if at all. He is like his father, in that regard. For well on thirty years now, Cordufar has amassed wealth in the Empire, and yet, were it not for the acquisition of two of the least significant of the hundred holdings, the family has done little with that wealth; they have not advanced the family or its political rank. Given Lord Cordufar's obvious interest in the powerful, this is strange. Still, strange things often happen.

"But, and this is interesting to me because it is in territory about which I know so little, the two poor holdings that he owns have had some difficulty with their native precincts of magisterial guards. You may correct me if I am wrong," he added, in the tone of voice that clearly said such correction would never be forthcoming. "It is a tricky difficulty, and in this regard, a *political* one. The magisterial guards in theory report to the Magisterium. In practice, in the Cordufar-held holdings, they seem to report to no one. Oh, some reports are filed, but the reports filed do not represent the complaints received by the offices in the holdings. They no longer keep a morgue, and when questioned, explained that cost cutting has led them to transfer bodies for identification to other precincts. This, at least, appears to be verifiable.

"The duty roster is skeletal; it is impossible for the magisterial guards in these holdings to run a full street patrol, and many of the older and more experienced guards have been transferred to different holdings."

Rath nodded again.

"And last, Ararath, your own interests in antiquities. You are not the only man to have such interests, but you are at the moment, the only man whose interest runs counter to the current trend: You find, and you offer."

"Why are you telling me this, Haval?"

"Because I wish to admire my own cleverness for a moment, and I seldom have the opportunity."

"Liar."

"Yes, habitually. It is a modest skill. There are other rumors. These are much harder to find," he added softly, "and for that reason, harder to trust on the surface."

"And those?"

"Lord Cordufar, or someone in his direct employ, is a mage."

"Given his wealth, that would not be a stretch. All Houses of note employ mages."

"Do not insult me."

"Very well. Yes, old friend. I admire your cleverness."

"I do not understand the game you play, Ararath. I understand, at this juncture, that it ends in death. It is not coin that you seek; it is not gain of any type that I can perceive. It vexes me. And it worries me. If I guess correctly, you have enough information now to unravel the most heinous of plots; you do not, and have not, done this."

Rath said nothing.

"I must ask you why."

"Ask, if it pleases you."

"Very well. Why do you hold your hand so close to your chest, now?"

"Because, old friend, I can prove nothing. And if I attempt to bring what I now know to light, I will die, and my death will serve *no purpose*. I have, as you have not suggested, allies in this fight. I have, as you suggest, information that, *were it to be believed,* would force the highest hands in the land to action.

"But my enemies are cunning, and they have operated unseen and undetected for decades, at best guess. Patris Cordufar serves The Darias," he added bleakly.

"The Ten," Haval's voice was soft. "You suspect Darias, in this game?"

"I suspect everyone."

Haval watched Rath for a long moment.

"But The Darias, in this as in much else, is canny and wary, if shortsighted; the rumors of Cordufar's mage, while not widely circulated, are believed. Inasmuch as a lord trusts his liege, there is trust—but it extends only to a point." Rath waited a beat, and then said, "Old friend, what if, in the Empire, there existed magics that could transform a man completely, so that he might replace another man, and take by that transformation, all power and title?"

"Such sorcery does not exist."

"Ah. And if it did, and you believed in it?"

"I would, as you guess, remain silent."

"For what reason?"

"I am not overly fond of charges of insanity, and I am attached to my existence, meager though it might be. I would also be loath to spread the type of panic that is sure to follow such announcement."

"If I had proof," Rath said, "I would make my move. But proof is a complicated thing, and even with the help of the Magi, it has eluded me."

"Ararath—"

Rath lifted a hand. It shook, but only slightly; a man less practiced in observation might have missed it entirely. Haval was not that man.

"I accept what I cannot change," Rath said. "This war—and it *is* a war—will touch us all before it is, at last, in the open. It is my hope that it will not kill everything it touches. Had I not abandoned my family and my birthright, I would not now be in possession of the knowledge that drives me. I consider it a bitter act of fate.

"And Jewel, as well. A bitter act of fate, but for all that, important to me. I have already failed her once, and if I abandon my fight here and now, I will fail her again."

"She would not count it a failure."

"No. Not while she lived. Not while I lived. But I have always been an arrogant man, and it is *my* opinion, in this, that holds sway. You have said she is wasted here. She would disagree, and vehemently. If she had not been *here,* she would never have gathered her den. It defines her, in ways that you might not entirely comprehend.

"But it is not my intent that she remain here."

"Ah." Haval bowed his head for a moment.

Rath thought the conversation at an end, but he should have known better; Haval decided when a conversation was at an end.

"You do not question her," Haval said.

"I frequently do."

"And you misunderstand me with such grace I will assume it was genuine. Ararath, she has spoken to you of your death, and you accept, now, that it *is* your death."

The quality of the silence in the enclosed shop sharpened and changed in that instant.

"So," Haval said, lifting a hand. Placing it, palm out, between them, a gesture that implied surrender without the embarrassment of actually offering it. "I will not speak of this further. Trust me or not, as you deem wise."

"If you think that it is because of her knowledge that I value her—"

"No. I understand well what you see in her. I knew it the first day you brought her to me. If you die, as you now expect you will do, will you send her to the Isle?"

"If it comes to that." Rath added, "I am weary, Haval. I had not known how weary I could become, and still continue to fight. I did not come here today to ask more than I have already asked of you.

"But we live in a world that confounds our expectation, time and again. Where she goes, I cannot follow. It is my one regret. I might offer her advice, if she were of a mind to hear it, but she sees only her own small world. Do," he said softly, "what I cannot do. Go where I cannot go. If she is lost, help her find her way."

"Where she goes, if she does indeed go where I suspect you will attempt to send her, I cannot follow."

"No. But she is Jay. She will come to you, because you're familiar. She'll clean out your back room looking for a place to sit, and she'll answer your interminable questions and engage in your verbal tests because she will long for the comfort of people who knew her, and helped her, when she was just another orphan in the streets of the twenty-fifth."

"I will be that, for her. And perhaps more, as I am allowed. For your sake, Ararath Handernesse."

"And not for hers?"

"For hers, in years to come, but for yours, now." With that, he surrendered conversation.

The Placid Sea was quiet in the midafternoon hours of High Market commerce. Rath was underdressed, but not of a mind to be concerned; he was seated in the much more casual room in which one met with friends and associates for drinks, rather than meals. He had, under his arm, the pack that he had taken from Jewel. In his hand he toyed with the slender stem of a wineglass, which contained chilled plum wine, suitable for the warmer climate.

He had taken care to shave and to plait his hair, which had grown wild over the past few months; it had also grayed considerably. Rath had his vanity, and the obvious silvering pained him, but not enough that he was willing to resort to permanent dyes.

He looked up when movement caught his attention. The longer, oiled robes that warded off the worst of the rain afforded a certain protection and invisibility when one traveled in the High City; it was not, unfortunately, a day for rain. A day for sun, yes, and as was the fashion in the courts at the moment, parasols were all the rage, but a parasol, like a hat, was a statement. It was not a statement that Rath wished to make, and likewise, the long-haired, almost feline Meralonne APhaniel; he wore his hair in a straight fall from head to waist. It was all white; if it had once had another color, even the hint of it was gone.

But his white hair suggested austerity and gravitas, not age. Age, he left to his companion, Sigurne Mellifas. She, however, carried a folded parasol in one hand. She wore simple, summer robes, and no obvious adornment that spoke of her affiliation with the Order of Knowledge; indeed, she had forsaken even the pendant that all members wore.

Rath rose.

It was not habit, although the grace and the depth of the bow he offered Sigurne was informed in all ways by the harsh and rigorous etiquette lessons he had so despised in his youth; nor was it flattery, for without her emblem, she came to him shorn of title or rank. It was a gesture of genuine respect and admiration, one he seldom offered.

Sigurne had, in any case, refused the styling of House title to which her position all but entitled her; she had not been born to the patriciate, and she had no pretensions in that regard. Rath suspected that there was more to it than a mere lack of pretension. She was a woman who had made difficult choices, and accepted onerous responsibility, in service of her life's goals; she did not wish to be burdened with more of either.

He took her hand and walked her around to the front of a heavily cushioned armchair before surrendering it.

Meralonne had already taken a chair, and was now padding the bowl of his pipe with new leaf. He paused a moment as Rath resumed his seat, and taking from his pocket a mid-sized stone, he placed it upon the table. It was not their custom to shield conversation by magical means, but then again, it was not their custom to meet at the Placid Sea, although this was not the first time they had chosen to do so.

Rath glanced at the stone and grimaced.

Meralonne, catching both the direction of the glance and the implied criticism, shrugged and returned to his tobacco.

"Were you followed?" Rath asked. He asked the question of Meralonne.

Meralonne nodded. "I will add that it took some *time* to be certain that we were followed, and we are therefore somewhat late."

"I find that hard to believe."

"As you will. I do not question your skills in this regard; I will trouble you not to question mine. However, since you have, I will point out that the resources of those who might consider the departure of Sigurne from the Order for the afternoon of significant import are probably stretched greatly; they hunt you."

"I will also remind you that I consider this enterprise unwise."

Rath nodded. "The stone," he said at last. "Is rather obvious."

"That was the intent, I assumed."

"What will they hear?"

"Silence, if they use no magic. As this is obviously magical, and assuming that they will trouble themselves to use magic, they will hear a conversation that is not entirely unlike the conversation we are now having."

"And if they are careful?"

"Silence," Meralonne replied. "There are only so many games that one can play. What we actually say, they will not hear."

Rath was uneasy. Stones that blanketed a conversation in silence were used, frequently, by the canny and the political who could afford them; they were not considered a forbidden magic. More subtle stones could be found or made, and these would broadcast conversation to those who listened for it. Both stones radiated a similar magic. This stone radiated magical silence, and beneath that silence, magical conversation. It was unusual, and it had been made at Rath's request.

If, however, a mage listened, he might penetrate the layers of the magical conversation—or the silence—and listen, at last, to what was said. It was a dangerous game, because that intrusive a magic was detectable *if* the conversation was being conducted by mages.

And this one was.

"The conversation they *will* hear is interesting enough," Meralonne said at length, "that I do not think they will delve further. They will hear what you want them to hear."

Rath nodded.

Sigurne, silent until that moment, reached out and touched his arm. "It is not wise, Ararath."

"No."

She nodded and withdrew her hand, placing it in her lap. She looked as tired, and as frail, as he felt.

"You have had no further success with Cordufar or his associates." It wasn't a question.

Meralonne, however, nodded. "We have had, as you say, no success. The fact that magic is used, and in quantity, on his estates, we have determined—but the nature of the magic is largely protective. There is some element of illusion involved, but in private estates, and in private homes, illusion is in and of itself not forbidden.

"We have, however, at your request sifted through the Order's records. We have," Meralonne added darkly, "undertaken this task on our own time, and without assistance, at Sigurne's insistence." He cast a glance at her, which she failed to notice. He lit his pipe. Which she also failed to notice.

"Sometime in the year 368, Lord Cordufar—the present Lord Cordufar's father—hired a member of the Order of Knowledge. He entered into a contract with the Order for the services of Davash AMarkham, a mage of the Second Circle."

Rath frowned. "What need had he of a mage of that level of power?"

Meralonne shrugged. "Davash AMarkham was not a First Circle mage, and not Magi." He spoke as if the Second Circle was of no consequence. Rath was often impressed with the depth and certainty of Member APhaniel's arrogance.

"Meralonne." Sigurne's voice was gentle. She turned to Rath. "Many of the Houses, The Ten among them, will undertake the hire of a mage of import within the Order as a symbol of status. The duties the mage owes the House are not onerous." She paused, and then added, "In the time of the Blood Barons, when mages were also rulers, mages could be called upon in emergency to defend their House. This custom is seldom invoked now, but it is still in effect in older families. Cordufar," she added, "has some pretensions."

"And this Davash?"

"He worked for three years out of the Order upon the Isle, and after those three years, he accepted a more exclusive term with the Cordufar family, and removed himself to the Cordufar estates." She hesitated, and then added, "The last time he was seen was in the year 375; there was a row about it, in the Council chambers, and a very furious Lord Cordufar demanded compensation for the abrupt—and under-negotiated—departure of his mage."

"What did Davash AMarkham study, Sigurne?"

"Our records indicate that he had some interest in fire, and in the manipulation of earth. He was also interested, in some fashion, in the ancient branches of magical lore, which are not studied now."

"Demonology?"

"If we had records of his study in that school, we would know when, and where, he died," she replied firmly.

"You think he died."

"Yes."

"He did not leave the City?"

"If he left, he left in secrecy. We are well aware that this would not be the first time this has happened," she added, "but our informants in the South do not indicate that he traveled to the Dominion; our informants in the Western Kingdoms have likewise failed to unearth information about a new mage in their demesnes. Some searching was done," she added softly, "to placate Lord Cordufar."

Meralonne lifted his pipe, and studied its stem for a moment. "I do not mean to alarm, Ararath," he said softly, "but I believe we now have an eavesdropper."

Rath nodded. He glanced at Meralonne but did not otherwise look around the room; if their interloper was a mage, the room would surrender nothing to Rath's vision.

"Can you see him?"

"No. But he is not demonic."

Rath nodded again. "Continue, then. Davash AMarkham died in the year 375. His disappearance was in-

vestigated at the instigation of Lord Cordufar, on whose
estates he had been living and working."

"That is correct," Sigurne said.

"And you now believe that he met his death on Cordufar lands?"

Sigurne's lips thinned. "It would seem likely. We have
less information about Lord Cordufar and the Cordufar
family than you can access through your other sources."

"Meaning?"

"You tell us."

"Lord Cordufar the elder, the man who appeared
in the Order demanding the return of either his con-
tractual fees or his mage, was not an overly ambitious
man in his middle years. He became more subtle, more
canny, and more dangerous in the years that followed."

"Starting in the year of Davash's disappearance?"
Sigurne raised her head, and glanced around the near-
empty room. From the far wall, a neatly and demurely
dressed man appeared, and he walked directly—and
quietly—toward the table they now shared. Sigurne
ordered, to Rath's surprise, a glass of a red wine that
Andrei would not have consumed for money. She also
ordered something more refined for Member APhaniel,
who couldn't be bothered to remove the pipe from the
corner of his lips to ask for something as insignificant
as drink.

The man both left and returned, placing glasses in
front of both Sigurne and Meralonne APhaniel; the
utter silence at the table during this procedure caused
him to withdraw instantly once he had finished.

Rath, accustomed to these small breaks in conversation, began again only when he had returned to his
position by the wall. "Starting perhaps a year later. The
exact time cannot easily be traced. Could he have studied forbidden arts?"

"Davash?"

Rath nodded.

"Anyone with talent and the ability to find information is capable of it, yes. Understand that it is something
we watch for, and we watch closely."

"It is understood. This would, however, be before your tenure."

"Not before my involvement in the Order," she pointed out. "But he would not be the first mage to make that choice. Nor would he be the first to flee the Order."

"But he went only as far as Cordufar, no farther."

"Ararath, will you not tell us why this does not surprise you?"

"Not yet, Sigurne," he said softly. "Not yet, but the time is coming when you will know everything I know." He paused, and then added, "The hands of those in control of the demons must be forced."

"And how are we to force their hands when we cannot discern either their identities or their motives?"

"Does it matter? The Kings and the Exalted have, in your estimation, some ability to defend the Empire against the kin. We are decided that the kin are involved; there is *no question* in any of our minds, and no room at all for doubt, however comfortable doubt might be."

She nodded.

"Both you and Member APhaniel feel that the kin that are involved are not trivial in nature, and that they are not, lamentably, *few*. And no sane man can assume that the kin do not mean danger, grave danger, to the Empire, even if we cannot discern the use to which they are being put. Cordufar, we are agreed, is at present the most *likely* source of danger."

She nodded again, this time more stiffly.

"Yet we have not brought the Kings into play because of the subtle discouragement of The Darias in what he considers *internal affairs*."

Sigurne glanced at Meralonne, who smoked his pipe in a moody and uncharacteristic silence. "I understand the degree to which this pains you," she said softly. "But The Ten have jurisprudence over their own affairs, and until one of The Ten seeks intervention, the Kings' hands are tied."

Rath cursed The Ten in bitter silence. "They play

foolish, political games, and it will be costly. Do the Twin Kings know?"

"They know some of what we know, but the avenues we have taken to feed them information are not, in any way, direct." She hesitated and then added, "You must also understand that magery as it exists in the Empire exists at the whim of the Kings; were it up to the Astari, no power of any note would be left standing that could theoretically pose a threat to the Kings they protect.

"We are loath to be more heavily scrutinized than we already are."

"Then we are left, again, with the problem of intervention, and again, with the problem of motivation, if we must prove beyond a doubt that the demons who plague only the darkest reaches of the City are a threat, not to Darias, but to the Empire itself." Rath attempted to cool the heat in his words; it was difficult. He understood, better than most, the necessary political dances by which the Houses gained, and shed, power. But to play those games *now* . . . He closed his eyes.

"Let me return to more recent history," he finally said. His wine had grown warm in the still air. "You are both aware of my difficulties with Patris AMatie."

They were. Meralonne watched him thoughtfully while he smoked. "He did not cause you so much difficulty that you are not now with us."

"No. But not for lack of trying. He was capable, he used what you have both agreed is magic, and in the end he revealed himself to be demonic, rather than human."

"Continue."

"Patris AMatie, as far as the rest of the City is concerned, was a merchant who owed allegiance to Lord Cordufar. His sudden disappearance failed to be either noted or investigated, to the best of our knowledge, which, at the very least, implies some knowledge on the part of Cordufar."

She nodded again. "Agreed."

"But AMatie's concerns were not obvious, demonic concerns; I encountered him the first time because he sought historical artifacts that existed long before the founding of Averalaan. We do not know why. But he was known throughout the Order and the Common for both his interest and the depths of his pockets in procuring such items.

"So. We have mages, served by kin," he continued. "They are interested in the ancient, they have access to very large sums of money, and they have access, as well, to a seemingly endless supply of demonic names. Given these things, Sigurne, can you not discern some part of what they intend?"

"Mages are *men*, Ararath. Their motivations are complex, and often self-delusional. But the *kialli* value power, and the knowledge that will grant them power. If the mages themselves are careless in their arrogance, the *kialli* can act, with subtlety, for their own purposes, not their master's."

"To what end?"

"The reaving," she said, softly. "But beyond that? I do not know. There is much about this mystery that makes no sense to me. You have personally killed almost two dozen of the lesser kin, and two that I consider—from your description—to be powerful. They know that you know, of course, but they sit secure in the knowledge that they will be unhindered by your discoveries. Such certainty speaks of Darias, to me; they are certain that Darias will cover anything that comes to light before it can cause their destruction.

"Our own security has tightened, if that's possible, but we have not found, within the Order, men or women who could summon what you have faced. Among those who might have taken to the study of the forbidden arts, very few have exhibited the power necessary to summon."

"Not all who have the power to do so might display it openly."

"No. There are perhaps two or three who have the will and the focus to both summon and suborn another being in this fashion. To summon and control not one, but many?" She shook her head. "It takes power to exert that level of control over even one such creature."

"It has been done, in the past. My understanding was that the only immutable requirement was the demon's name."

"That is a flawed understanding. The name *is* required, but simply *speaking* the name does not call a demon to the plane. A path between the Hells and the caster must be built; such a path is entirely magical in nature. You would not see it at all. The building of such a gate requires no little power."

"Then let us look at power, and only at power. Let us look not at magery, for they clearly *have* that. If Cordufar has *extended* its influence over the past several decades, the mages need political power. How have they gathered it? If, as we now suspect, the Lord Cordufar who first hired Davash AMarkham was a mage—or a demon—it is clear that our enemies have the ability to mimic those they kill and replace them, for he was not always what he is now. Nor was his son. If one could do this, one could rule empires without the messy impediment of an obvious war. One could not replace the Kings or the Exalted; the gods would know, and their followers and children throughout the Empire would bear warning.

"But one could replace other men and women of power, and subvert those Houses from within."

They were silent.

"Ararath," Sigurne began, but he lifted a hand.

"House Terafin retains the services of the Magi?"

She nodded, little liking where this was going. He knew, of course, and knew why.

"Whose service, Sigurne?"

Meralonne lifted both pipe and head. He also blew rings of smoke in the half-dark room, each smaller than the last. "My service," he replied. "The Terafin requested the service of Sigurne Mellifas, and she made the referral."

"Were your presence to be required *immediately,* how long would it take you to arrive at the estates?"

At that, the Magi smiled. It was an odd smile. Sharp and cunning as it was, it nonetheless conveyed a very real pleasure, even anticipation. "Terafin is older than the Empire. I could arrive—without exhausting myself—the instant the message was sent. I could not, however, arrive without a summons, and such a summons would not be undertaken trivially."

"If an incident of a highly magical nature occurred within the Terafin manse upon the Isle, you would be the mage summoned?"

"Indeed."

"And you could deal with a demon, if so summoned?"

Meralonne APhaniel raised a silver brow. "If what they send is what you have hunted? In my sleep."

Rath stared at him for a long moment. "If I didn't know better," he finally said, "I would say that you almost—almost—look forward to such a contest."

"Ah."

Rath rose. "Be prepared," he said softly. "Be prepared to move quickly. Be prepared, as well, to launch a full-scale investigation that will cover most of the City—not upon the Isle, but in the holdings."

"Magical?"

Rath nodded.

Meralonne glanced at Sigurne. "We have done what we can to be, as you say, prepared," she told Rath quietly, "but it is difficult; preparations are noticed, and the members of the Order are fractious when asked to devote time to something that comes with no attendant explanation."

"I will send word, if I am able. You will receive word, if I am not."

Meralonne nodded, and then, tapping ash from the bowl of his pipe, said, "We have just lost our eavesdropper."

"A pity. I hoped I might notice him when I leave this place. Did he listen for long enough?"

"Long enough that he is now aware that it is you who are hunting demons, and that you are the natural brother of The Terafin. As you requested."

"Good." He bowed stiffly to Meralonne, and then, less stiffly, as if it were an entirely different gesture, to Sigurne Mellifas.

Sigurne met his gaze, held it a moment. "Ararath," she said quietly.

"I will send a messenger to House Terafin. The messenger will not be well-versed in the political, but it is my hope that Amarais will see fit to retain her services."

Sigurne did not look away from his face, and with Meralonne present, this was awkward, although the gray-eyed mage did not speak. More significant, he did not light his pipe again.

"As you can be, you have been the best of allies, Sigurne."

"And you," she replied. "Will you not reconsider?"

He glanced at the stone on the table; answer enough for both of them.

"Keep an eye on her, if you can. Both of you. Keep her safe."

"The Terafin?"

"The Terafin as well."

She stood, and taking from her robe a nondescript sack, handed it to Rath. He knew what it contained: consecrated daggers.

"I am not entirely certain," he said gravely, "that I will be able to uphold my side of our agreement in the foreseeable future."

"I will take that risk," she replied, "and I would not see you face our enemies unarmed." She nodded as Rath slid her small bundle into the backpack he had taken from Jewel.

Rath bowed, briefly, to both of the members of the Order of Knowledge. He then left them.

"I am uneasy," Meralonne said quietly, as he picked up the stone he had set upon the table and slid it into his robes.

Sigurne said nothing for a long moment. "What will Ararath do?"

"I cannot say. I wonder instead, if he will do what he intends in time."

"In time?"

"Can you not feel it? There is a shadow growing

across the City, Sigurne. Something in it reminds me, much, of my distant youth. I cannot say, for certain what, or why, and it frustrates me."

She glanced at him, and then away. "If it will ease you, follow him. But I suspect you will meet with the same success the kin and their masters have had, where he is concerned."

Meralonne nodded. "I will visit House Terafin," he added.

8th of Emperal, 410 AA
Undercity, Averalaan

Angel cursed as rope slipped across his palm. He tightened both hands, and the rope slowed, but not enough that it didn't abrade his skin. Beneath him, over the edge of cracked and broken stone, Lefty almost shrieked.

"I've got you," Angel said, raising his voice. Duster and Fisher were across the gap; Carver was beside him. Carver caught the rope in both hands as well; he was better braced than Angel. Angel had slid two feet, and he could feel the edge of the gap against the thinning undersoles of his boots. He hadn't been prepared for Lefty's fall, and rocks dislodged by Angel's momentary stumble dropped toward Lefty's upturned face. They were neither heavy nor large, but they were sharp-edged, and Lefty raised one hand to cover his eyes as they fell.

"Sorry," Angel said, the word more grunt than speech. "I've got you."

Lefty said nothing. He dangled for a moment, eight feet below Angel. Then he put both hands on the rope, and began to search the side of the crevice for footholds.

The weight lessened as he found them, and increased as one—Angel couldn't clearly see which—failed.

"I swear these gaps are getting wider," Carver murmured. "I've got him, Angel," he added. "Pull back. Duster!"

She nodded. She was utterly silent. She held the

magestone in one shaking hand, and its light was not kind; it exposed everything. What Angel saw in her expression, he couldn't say. Not fear; Duster didn't show fear even in nightmare. But close enough, for Duster.

"See if the gap narrows anywhere. I don't think he can make this jump."

Duster nodded, and then hesitated.

"We've got Lefty," Carver told her, grunting as Lefty began to try to climb. "We don't need to see much, because we're not going to move. Go."

She nodded. She didn't argue, and she didn't tell him not to give her orders. Fisher followed in her wake.

As the light ebbed, Lefty continued to climb, to lessen the weight on the rope that was probably making it difficult to breathe. Carver and Angel put their backs and shoulders into the narrow line that connected them all, and pulled.

Lefty came up slowly; rocks went down as he scrabbled along the edge. It was now dark enough that they could barely see his hands, but it didn't matter; they held him. They didn't try to reach for him, but in the dark, he made it back up.

He paused for breath, and then crawled away from the edge, his chest and limbs flat against the ground. "Let's not do that again," he said, as the rope went slack in the hands of his den-kin.

Angel nodded in the dark night of the undercity. His stomach growled.

Carver snorted and smacked the back of Angel's head; lack of light didn't seem to affect his aim.

"What? We've been here for hours."

"You eat more than the rest of us combined," Carver answered. "You'd be making that noise if we'd been here for less than ten minutes."

Angel sat, folding his legs. "Lefty?"

"I'm good," Lefty replied. "Well, I'm not dead, at any rate. Sorry."

"Why? You've made that jump a hundred times. We'll find a narrower gap, and we'll try it from there."

8th of Emperal, 410 AA
Twenty-fifth holding, Averalaan

Candlelight.

It wasn't magelight; it wasn't steady. It flickered, and it illuminated only the small space around its wick. It didn't, and couldn't, banish the darkness of night sky at a single word. But Jewel liked candlelight; it reminded her of her family, long dead. Magelights, of course, had existed then, but only in lampposts that towered above the streets, or in buildings that existed for the convenience of the wealthy.

Her family had had candles. Lamps, and lamp oil, were too expensive; candles were cheaper—but even they weren't free. They were seldom lit, for that reason. Her mother and her Oma made as much of daylight as they could, and when the sun sank, and the moons took to the skies, they retreated to bed, and sleep.

When Jewel was ill, they would light candles, briefly, and stand over her, expressing worry by silence, or the softness of their voices. She could remember their faces, lit from beneath by orange light, noses throwing shadows across the familiar.

Lamps were better light than candles for reasons that weren't entirely clear to Jewel, but she put off buying one, even when the den was flush. She worked, instead, by candle, if any one of her den, except Duster, was out. The work was long and tiring, and in truth she would have put it off, but it was important to Rath. She could do nothing else for him, so she read, and wrote, and worked through numbers that seemed more arcane, and more unapproachable, than Old Weston ever had.

The numbers she did on paper that Rath had provided. She could leave them on the table, and when they returned from the Common or the well, he would have them annotated. Sometimes the words in the margins of her messy columns were more real than Rath; they reminded her of the early months. Terse, yes, but sometimes encouraging. She both dreaded and looked forward to them.

The candle was almost a stub when she at last stoppered the inkwell and took the pen to the bucket; she very carefully cleaned the quill and returned it to the table. She closed the books, and made a neat pile of them, pushing it to one side. Then she rose, and went to the windows, stepping over Lander and Jester, who were snoring. Arann was, as usual, a bit closer to the door, and Finch and Teller slept a room away.

The rest of her den?

Pushing her hair out of her eyes, she levered herself up onto the windowsill and looked out at the still face of the moon in the night sky. The bright moon's light silvered the City, even in shadow. She could see, by its position, that it was late. Very late and edging into early.

She lowered herself gently, creaked along the floorboards, and made her way back to the candle that was burning itself into a small puddle. Then she sat, carefully, in the chair that she had vacated, yawned, and rubbed her eyes.

Kalliaris, she thought, giving in, at last, to the hour. *Lady, smile.*

The candle guttered.

Duster came back after a full ten minutes, and her light trailed past them on the opposite side of the crevice as she followed its edge in the other direction. Not one for words, not Duster. If she'd found something, she would have let them know. She didn't turn, and didn't speak; she might have been an apparition.

But as they watched her go, Lefty suddenly sat up, his supine back stiffening. He didn't shout, not to Duster. But he spoke loudly enough for either Angel or Carver, who bracketed him, Carver cross-legged, and Angel standing.

"Where's Fisher?"

They looked, as the last of her light grayed and faded. "Carver?"

Carver shook his head, black hair obscuring his eye just before darkness did. In the undercity, darkness had meaning, and it was absolute.

"I didn't see him."

"No," Angel said. "I didn't either. But he followed Duster when she left."

"Maybe he saw something, and she kept walking." Carver's voice held no conviction. It held hope. "If he did, he'll stand and wait."

Duster came back, the faint light of slowly moving magestone gray again. They felt the distance keenly, and her approach was so slow it was almost agonizing. You couldn't begrudge it; the crevices weren't simple, straight lines, and the stone along their edges wasn't solid. But even so, they held breath until she could be seen, magelight trailing the underside of her chin.

"Duster!" Carver shouted. His voice, the two syllables distinct, echoed in the silence.

She looked up. "I think I've found—"

"Duster!" Carver shouted again, but this time not quite as loudly. "Where's Fisher?"

She frowned then, and her eyes left the crevice along which she'd been searching. She turned to look back the way she'd come and Carver shouted her name again.

"He didn't come back the first time. He followed you when you went to the right, but he didn't come back."

She cursed. More loudly than Carver had called her name. "Why didn't you say something?" She started to head to their right, lingering only to hear the reply.

"Lefty noticed as you passed us." He turned to Angel. "You want to stay here, or should I?"

"Either way."

"Stay." He walked back, away from the crevice, and approached it at a run. He cleared it by at least two feet on the opposite side, landing in Duster's shadow.

Duster passed him the stone without comment, and he hesitated before holding out his palm to catch it. They left, and Angel watched them until there wasn't anything to watch.

Jewel didn't light another candle. No point. She wasn't working, so she didn't need that type of light. The light

from the street and the light from the moon were good
enough.

She sat in her chair, and she waited.

She had always hated waiting.

It wasn't the first time something like this had happened. Carver knew it, and knew as well that Duster
needed reminding. Because he held the light, it was his
face that was exposed, but even in the shadows it cast,
he could see enough of her to know. She was tense as
a bowstring. Her hand had found its perch on her dagger's hilt, and nothing would separate them. Carver
didn't try. He followed her, held the light, saw the buildings and the crevice and the fallen shards of stone that
lay across the street, taller than a man.

Neither of them raised their voices; they called Fisher's name every few feet, and they checked the rubble
and fallen rock, although it was pointless. If more rock
had fallen, this close, they would have heard it. And felt
it.

They walked to the end of the crevice, or rather, to
the last passable point; here, slabs of rock had fallen
across it. Had they been flat, or even, they would have
formed a bridge; as it was, they formed a small moun-
tain.

Duster started to climb, and Carver called her back.

She said nothing, but her lips were compressed in a
line so thin they were almost white.

"He's the laziest member of our den," Carver told
her. "No way he'd try to climb anything."

Duster snorted. But she nodded, and she turned
back, following the light and the edge of the crack in
the world.

Three times they went back and forth. Angel traded
places with Carver, and he followed Duster as she
searched. The search grew longer, and wider, but they
found no sign of Fisher. No sign that he had fallen—and
even the taciturn Fisher would have made some noise if
he had. No sign that he had stopped to wait. They broke,

walked with Lefty to the far left, where the chasm, as Duster noted, was narrower. It was a long trek, and they would have left Duster standing there to mark the spot, but Lefty wouldn't agree to that.

"No one stays alone," he said, almost inaudibly.

Duster opened her mouth to snarl something, and shut it again hard. The snap of her teeth was audible.

"Mark it with stones," Angel told her. He picked up a few loose rocks and began to make a standing pile on an open patch of ground. Duster watched him for half a minute, and then she joined him. They didn't take their time, but the pile was big enough and irregular enough that they could easily find it on the way back.

They got Lefty across, put the rope into the pack that hung, slack, across Carver's back, and then began to search in earnest.

The sky changed color, and the moons paled, and Jewel sat in her chair. It was an anchor, it was what she knew and what she did when her den was not gathered under the safety of this roof, when they weren't all sleeping in bedrolls and blankets across the length of the floor, like a human carpet.

Had they ever been gone this long? In silence, she could expose the heart of her worry. She could poke at it, prod it, test it against other worries, other fears. She could lob facts at it, as if trying to pierce it somehow. As if, in so doing, she could suddenly shake loose the knowledge and the *certainty* that was both curse and gift.

But nothing came, in the slow graying of darkness.

Not the *feeling,* and not her den.

They did not separate again.

Carver held the magestone, and Lefty stayed at his side, as if he were Arann. Angel and Duster moved ahead, fanning out as far as the light would reach, and circling back in silence. And it was silent. They spoke, when they spoke at all, with den-sign and movement: the curt shake of a head. Whether it was followed by the trail of moving dark hair or the sharp spires of white didn't matter; it meant the same thing. No luck.

And, goddess, they wanted luck. If they didn't speak, they thought the words: Her name, and a plea that the face she showed was her smile.

The only word that broke their self-imposed silence was a name, and it echoed against fallen and standing buildings, whose occupants had long since vanished. They widened their search, narrowed it, crossed the same ground again and again; they listened for any sign of movement, huddled together around the light.

They didn't so much lose track of time as ignore it, as if by ignoring it they could buy more, or could—even better—turn it back to the moment when Fisher casually turned to follow in Duster's wake.

But after hours, they regrouped. This time, they whispered, argued, held on to both their tempers and their fear. No one wanted to leave, not because they felt their presence would suddenly change things, but because they would go home, without Fisher, and find Jay waiting.

No one knew what they could say to her, or even what they would say, but in the end, home is where they retreated, gathering and guarding each other as they took their light and its foreign illumination from the undercity that had, in the space of one night, become as unknown, as mysterious, and as uncontrollable as the City that rested above it.

Teller woke when the sun's light lay across his brow and eyes. He rolled over so it was on his neck, but that didn't help, and eventually he sat up, blankets falling away from his chest. He pushed his hair out of his eyes—a gesture they'd all picked up in their years of watching Jay. No nightmare last night, he thought with relief, and he turned to look at Jay's bedroll.

It was empty.

Finch was still asleep a couple of feet to his right, but Duster was already up; her space was conspicuously empty. Which was unusual; Duster didn't like morning much, and she had to be dragged into it, which was only a little less risky than waking Arann. Arann, on the other hand, was awake; Teller could hear the boards creak in the other room, and they only creaked that loudly for Arann.

Teller rose, found his clothing, and slid into it. He opened the door carefully, and stepped into the main room. Jester and Lander were still sleeping against the wall. Arann was ... pacing. He paused when he saw Teller, and something about his expression caused Teller to look at Jay's table.

Jay was still on her chair, her arms wrapped around her upper body. He couldn't see her face, but he looked at the rest of the room, then. Carver, Angel, Fisher, and Lefty were missing.

He opened his mouth, closed it, and tapped Arann's arm; when Arann turned, he signed.

Arann shook his head.

How long?

Arann's gaze flickered to the window and back.

No nightmare, Teller thought, but this time with no relief, and with a curious hollow sensation that had nothing to do with hunger. No nightmare, no second dream, because Jay hadn't slept yet.

Duster was often out at night, and she was good enough to wait until Jay was in bed before she left. But only Duster. Not half the den. And even Duster didn't stay out all night unless she'd managed to get into a fight that involved injury, running, and hiding.

This was the time they usually began to assemble a crew for the Common. Teller didn't bother; he knew they wouldn't be going anywhere until everyone returned.

He turned back to the bedroom to wake Finch.

Finch was never a heavy sleeper. She might have been at one time, but years spent sleeping in the same room as Jay had destroyed that. Like Teller, she hadn't been expecting a full night's sleep; like Teller, she'd expected Jay to wake them all in that state of panic that followed those dreams that weren't quite dreams. She hadn't expected sleep; she'd expected the odd dread that came from spending too much time in the darkened kitchen, while Jay spoke and Teller captured her words.

But unlike Teller, she felt no relief at the sight of morning sun, because the first thing she saw was his face. "What?" She whispered. "What happened?"

He lifted a finger to his lips, and she lowered her voice, although she hadn't spoken loudly to begin with. "They didn't come back last night."

He slid out of the room while she changed, and she joined him and Arann in the main room. Then she woke Jester and Lander, finger to lips, and waited until they were dressed. They looked at each other, and fingers flew as they glanced at Jay's bent back.

Lander nodded, and he and Arann went to the well, taking Jester with them. Even with the streets busy, Jay hated anyone to travel alone unless there was pressing need. Only Jay and Duster did.

Water returned in buckets and silence. Arann entered first, glanced around the room, and then set the buckets to one side in the kitchen. He approached Jay, but he didn't speak.

There wasn't much point. They couldn't go into the undercity without a magestone; that was death. They had candles, but candles were almost useless unless you didn't plan to actually move; they had no lamp, and lamplight cost money. Finch came to draw Arann away, and he went, but he looked at her once and she had to turn away from his expression.

It said, naked, all the things that everyone was afraid to even think.

They were sitting in the center of the room when the door opened. They looked up—all of them, even Jay—as Carver entered. He walked over to the kitchen table and set the magestone flat upon its surface. But he didn't meet Jay's eyes.

One by one, they filed in: Angel. Duster. Lefty.

Lefty went straight to Arann's side and stood one

step behind him, as if they were alone again in the City, and he didn't know, and didn't want to know, what to do.

Gods, Finch thought. *Kalliaris.*

Jay stood. Her eyes were dark with lack of sleep, and dark with something else as well. But she asked the question they were all silently asking. "Where's Fisher?"

And she got the answer they were all silently dreading.

"We lost him. In the undercity." It was Angel who spoke, not Carver, not Duster. The words were flat, and he bowed the odd spiral of his hair slowly, lifting a hand to his eyes.

Jay hit the table with both hands; it was the only sound in the apartment. Then she rose and she headed to the other room, slamming the door behind her.

Fisher did not come home.

Not then. Not later. Not ever.

Chapter Seven

DUSTER DID NOT DARE THE UNDERCITY. She left the magelight in the stand on the kitchen table, surrounded by the flapping tongues of books; the sea breeze was heavy, and the windows were open. She thought about tying them shut. It wasn't raining. It wasn't her job.

Her job.

Glancing around the room, she saw the den. Saw the awkward space and silence that surrounded each person. Even Lander's hands were quiet in his lap, as if he'd forgotten all forms of speech in this daylight room. She looked away before he could meet her eyes. Hells, she looked away before anyone could, as if their gaze was painful. As if it would burn. And in this tight little constricted cage of a space, it was just pain and suffocation. She *had* to get out.

To get out of here.

No one tried to stop her. Not Jay. Not Lander. No one else would've dared. She said nothing as she made her way to the door. Maybe it took her a little longer to open the damn thing than it should have. Maybe she stayed in the frame, listening for something—some sound, some word, some question. Whatever it was, it either wasn't coming, or it would take too damn long, and hells if she'd wait.

But the door sounded loud as she shut it. Had she slammed it? Hadn't meant to, if she had. Didn't matter. She strode down the hall, down the stairs, and down a different hall. Sunlight opened up as she stepped into the street. Sunlight swallowed her.

It didn't swallow enough of her, though. Here, the streets crowded with too many people, too many smells, and too much damn noise, she was haunted by the silence. Silence of the undercity. Fisher had followed *her*. She wasn't his keeper, she told herself that. Fisher never listened to anyone, and he didn't cling like a baby to anyone either. He wasn't great in a fight, but he wasn't bad; he was just damn quiet.

Too damn quiet.

She headed toward the Common because it was the Common, and because that's where most of the people were going. She could fight the crowd, or slide through it, or dodge it—but she had nowhere else to be, and if they weren't her den, there was still some safety in numbers. If she wanted safety.

Fisher had followed *her*.

She'd lost him. She hadn't even been aware that he was gone. She'd wanted to run back, run to where she might have lost him—

No. No one goes alone. We need to stay together. And Lefty, runt of the litter, had been the first to notice. Lefty. He should have shut up, let her wander off alone. Maybe get her ass lost, same as Fisher's. He should have. Didn't.

Her hands were fists. She couldn't uncurl them. Didn't try. She'd lost Fisher. Fisher was gone.

Maybe, she thought. Maybe he'd come back. Maybe he'd find some way out of the dark and the silence, maybe he'd be home when she got home, and the den would be loud again, and Jay would finally sleep. She wanted to believe it. Hated herself for wanting it. There were way better things to want.

Or there had been. There had been way better things to want. She knew; she'd wanted a lot of them. But she'd seen Jay's face. She'd seen the look in her eyes, and she knew, just as sure as if it were Duster cursed with the feelings, not Jay, that Fisher was never coming back.

Duster found it hard to breathe. Is this how it started?

She didn't even *like* Fisher all that much, not really. He was just another body on the floor, come rain or shine, just another mouth to feed, another voice to ignore. That's what he was, right? That's all he'd been?

But he was gone. He was gone. She hadn't had enough time to learn to hate him. She'd learned how to hate almost everyone else she'd met before the den. Not Fisher. She hadn't hated him enough to make his absence a thing of joy or triumph. All she had was this—this horrible sense of nothing, this break, this uncomfortable tightening of throat and chest.

And they'd all be there, silent, trying to figure out how to comfort each other.

She didn't *need* their comfort. She didn't *want* their comfort. She wasn't crying, because she didn't. Nothing made her cry. But . . . she couldn't breathe. She was—she thought it, *loathed* thinking it—afraid. She was never going to share that with anyone. She was afraid. He was gone. She didn't know what his loss would do to the den. She couldn't even tell herself she didn't care. She tried. She knew she could tell any of the rest of them—any of them, even Jay—that she seriously didn't give a shit. But she couldn't say it to herself.

Home, hey? *This* is what home was? *This* is what Jay wanted her to learn?

Here, in the open sun, as far from the darkness and the quiet of the undercity as she could possibly get, she found a small gap beneath the trees of the Common and knelt, forehead against bark, eyes closed.

She could wait here for as long as it took.

9th of Emperal, 410 AA
Twenty-fifth holding, Averalaan

Jay woke, shouting, in the middle of the night. She sat up in bed, threw off her bedcovers and turned, almost wild, toward the magelight.

Teller, Finch, and Duster were awake before she reached out to *grab* the magestone and pull it, in her fist, to her chest. She sat breathing heavily, her hair in tight curls dangling in front of her eyes. She didn't even bother to reach up and push them out of the way.

Duster was off the floor first, but she always was; she kicked off blankets and rolled to her feet. Even with the magestone's light dampened by Jewel's fingers, the edge of Duster's dagger gleamed.

Teller touched Duster's shoulder gently, and she pivoted on her feet. But he stood very still and waited until she relaxed. Duster didn't wake up quickly; she could move, and talk, and fight, when she was still half-dazed by sleep. Since movement or fighting weren't usually required, the den waited until she was actually awake; when she was awake, she could tuck in the fury that characterized almost anything she did.

The day had been hard.

Jay hadn't spoken two words side by side. She did eat, but she didn't eat much, and she didn't study at all.

Guilt had taken Fisher's place in the den. It was an unwelcome addition, but no one had any idea of how to get rid of it. Teller, glancing at Finch who was now standing at the foot of the bed, nodded. *Kitchen,* he mouthed.

Finch signed agreement without lifting her hand, and gently put an arm around Jay's shoulders. Jay blinked, then, and slowly released her death grip on the magestone. She also shoved her hair out of her eyes, as if it were sleep.

"Duster," Jay said, still seated.

Duster looked up.

"It wasn't your fault."

And shrugged. But it was an awkward shrug. Teller's

mother had never been violent, but in a rare moment of clarity, Teller thought it would be easiest for Duster if Jay slapped her or shouted at her, bringing her fury into the open.

Jay swung her legs to the side and slid out of bed. "Kitchen," she said, although they were all heading that way anyway.

They picked up the rest of the den on the way to the table, which added ten minutes. Jay took her usual chair, and Teller brought one of the chairs that rested against the far wall. He also picked up a slate and chalk as Jay deposited the magestone on the table, whispering the light to an almost uncomfortable brightness. She stared at it, wide-eyed, as if she were seeing something else. Which was fair, because she was.

"It's dark," Jay said.

Teller began to write.

"It's not like the undercity. It's night dark, but *dark*. Everything smells funny," she added, wrinkling her nose.

"Where are you?" Finch asked.

"I think I'm in a forest. But it's like the *idea* of a forest. The trees are so thick-trunked, they look like buildings. I think that's why it's dark," she added. "So many trees. But there's room between those trees. And stuff growing between them as well. I'm running," she added softly.

"From what?"

"I don't know." She frowned, closing her eyes. "A hunter, I think."

"You can't see anyone?"

"Not yet."

"Hear anyone?"

She nodded slowly. "Voices. Distant voices. And ... horns. I run faster. I break branches and things close to the ground; I can't see them," she added. "But I clear the big forest, and I'm out in the open. The moon is full," she added. "So there's light.

"But there's also someone standing in the clearing, and I've seen her before."

There was a pause in the transcription as Teller
looked up.

"She looks at me. Same woman as—as last night.
Long, dark hair, perfect, pale skin. Perfect teeth," she
added. "No sword, this time. But her hands are red with
fire, and shadows drip from her hair. She smiles when
she sees me."

"Does she have a name?"

"Yes. Two names. I *know* this, but she doesn't give
me either. Instead she holds out her burning palms and
says, "The gods are coming, and it is *too late* to stop
them. She throws the fire—but not at me; she throws
it at the forest. And it starts to burn. I can hear the
screams and shouts of men and animals." She paused,
and then took a deep breath.

"One of those animals clears the fires, and enters the
clearing to the left of me. He passes *so close,* I want to
run and hide, but I can't move because if I move I might
catch his attention. It's focused on her."

"What kind of animal?"

"Huge."

Teller's hand stilled. "Ummm, anything more con-
crete?"

"I can't really see him clearly. It's like he's a bunch
of different animals, and they all overlap, so he's blurred
at the edges. Giant, different animals. But he has horns.
Not like cow horns," she added.

"Antlers?" Angel offered.

Jay nodded. They thought she was finished, but she
spoke again. "But he tells me to *run,* and I can't help it;
I run. Except I'm not running through forest anymore.
I'm running through the holdings, and the streets are
disappearing at my back."

"Disappearing?"

"Into shadow," she whispered. "Except it's *not*
shadow; there's no light to cast it, and no light to penetrate it. It's like the undercity would be if magestones
did nothing. It is eating the whole damn City almost as
fast as I can run."

Silence, then, broken only by the sound of Teller's

writing. He looked at Jay, and then looked at all of the den. "Day two?" he asked.

"It's not exactly the same," Carver began.

Jay lifted a hand before anyone could agree or disagree. "Day two," she said heavily as she pushed herself out of the chair and stood. "Are we betting on day three?"

"Can't," Jester said cheerfully. They all turned to look at him. "You've got all the money," he added.

Someone smacked him, but it wasn't Jay; Jay had already turned to stumble back to bed.

10th of Emperal, 410 AA
Twenty-fifth holding, Averalaan

It almost wasn't worth the effort of going to sleep.

Jay did, because her sleep was going to be interrupted, and she reasoned she might as well start "early." Everyone else sat in the main room, lounging against found wall space, or sprawled across patches of floor. Lefty lay beneath the kitchen table, his elbows against the wood grain, his hands propping his head up.

There wasn't much talk. Even Lander's hands were still. They listened, hard, for the sound of steps outside in the hall; they glanced far too often at the very uninteresting door.

Finch watched them all, her arms wrapped, as they often were when things were awkward, around her chest. She had done all the cleaning and tidying there was to do, but even that had been difficult; one less plate.

She walked past Arann, who was sitting to one side of the kitchen table under which Lefty lay; she stepped over Carver's extended legs and walked around Angel's crossed ones; she touched Teller's shoulder and glanced at Duster.

Duster's version of talking was a little bit more animated than Fisher's, because it *had* to be; Fisher just didn't like to talk. But in the past two days, Duster had hardly spoken a word. Not to the den. Not to Jay. When she did bother, it was sharp and harsh, a shadow of her early days in the den.

Finch, who had never been Duster's victim, grimaced. When Duster was this withdrawn—the last time it happened had been after a run-in with Carmenta's den that had not gone particularly well—the only person who could reach her was Jay. And that was partly because Jay didn't find the sharp edge of Duster's tongue all that threatening. She didn't apparently find the sharp edge of Duster's *dagger* all that threatening either, which was good, because Duster pulled it every time she had an argument.

Jay, however, had been almost as silent as Duster.

"Any point in going to sleep?" Jester asked.

Angel shrugged. "I'm not going to bother," he replied. "And if you fall asleep and start snoring, you aren't either."

Jester laughed. Angel, using the sign language of the street, rather than den-sign, made plain what he thought of that.

Finch wanted to hold on to this: It was normal. It was the way things always were. And it gave her hope that in the end, they could find normal again.

But the boys fell silent, and it was a heavy, gray silence that darkened as the sky did. Finch waited for a while, and then headed toward the window, where the moon lay above the tall buildings across the narrow street. Silver moon, shadowed face, it seemed so impersonal.

It was.

Fisher was gone and the only people who knew, or cared, were in this apartment. But his absence robbed them of words, which was a bitter irony; he would have *liked* the silence. If she disappeared, if she vanished into the utter night of the undercity, the last thing she wanted to leave her den was this silence; it was so like a wound, but there was no blood, and nothing to tend or bandage.

She might have said it, might have told them how

she felt, but Jay shouted instead, and they rose almost to a man—the exception being Jester—pausing as they neared the door to let Duster and Teller through. Finch, lingering at their backs, simply moved to the table to wait.

Jewel sat on her chair, with the soft glow of light in her face. She missed fire, sometimes, because with fire came heat; she would have raised her hands to cup even the smallest of candle flames, because it would have eased the ice from her fingers.

Instead she clasped them loosely in her lap. Her shoulders were bent and curled, as if to ward off blows; she knew this, but couldn't bring herself to straighten them. Maybe no one would notice, in the dark.

Teller whispered the magestone to a brighter light. Not its brightest, but he needed light to work with, and she knew Teller well enough to know that he gave her as much space as this small, crowded room allowed. Tonight, she wasn't sure she wanted it, but couldn't bring herself to say as much; that's not what he was here for.

Not what any of them were here for.

"It's her," she said bluntly. "She's back."

She could hear Teller's breath break; it wasn't a sharp inhalation, but it was a pause. After which, he started writing. She couldn't remember whose idea it had been to write things down. She couldn't even remember when they'd started. But now? It was part of the vision, part of the nightmare—the last, and best, part. She could listen to the even scritching of chalk against blackboard, and even when she spoke, she was aware of what it meant: people were *here,* they were *with her,* and they believed enough in what she said that they were willing to transcribe it.

"Still no name?"

She shook her head.

"I don't know what she is," Jewel whispered, "but she's not a god."

Teller's hand paused. "How do you know?"

"Because I saw gods."

"Gods. As in plural."

"I think so."

"Sorry," he added. "I didn't mean to interrupt."

"Tonight," she said softly, "Interruptions are good." She turned in her chair, draping one arm across its back. "Interruptions are good because it's *too damn big*. What can we do about gods?"

"Die?" Jester suggested.

She heard someone hit him. "Don't."

"He was joking," Angel said.

"I know. But it's not really a joke. If these dreams can be trusted—if we can even *figure out* what they mean— what can we possibly do about them? I can't even protect my own," she added bitterly. "And gods aren't likely to give a damn about something as insignificant as one den in Averalaan."

"We won't have to say anything," Teller told her. "If the gods do *anything*, the god-born will know. They're not a den in the twenty-fifth; when they speak, the Kings will have to listen."

Everyone nodded. Everyone.

She wanted to leave the table. Instead, she put her hands across it and splayed the fingers wide. "She's there," she said, waiting for Teller to start writing. He did, and she continued, feeding him the stream of her words. "She's red and black; she's taller than Arann. She has a sword, in this one," she added softly. "And a red dress that's all of one piece."

"Sleeves?"

"I don't think so. Does it matter?"

"You could ask Haval."

She could, at that. She probably wouldn't. He'd just ask her why she wanted to know, and that led places she wasn't willing to go with him.

Instead, she concentrated, because the dream might slip away. "Long sleeves, or at least they look like sleeves; they're so close to her skin they might as well *be* skin. Did I tell you she's tall?"

"Yes."

"But she's not."

"Where is she?"

"In the darkness," Jewel replied. "It's—it looks like the undercity darkness, not the streetside night." A shudder took her, momentarily robbing her of words. "But it's not the undercity; that's not what the darkness is. I think I can see the moons, but they're warped and twisted, and they look Summer red.

"They're not moons."

The silence contained only the movement of Teller's hand, and this, too, came to a close.

"They're eyes," Jewel said softly. "And suddenly the woman is way too short, and the thing towering behind her is—the size of nightmare. And it speaks, and I hear it, and I can't understand what I hear—but I try to plug my ears. Doesn't help. Nothing does."

"Where are you?" Teller asked, gently.

"Alley, I think. Some place with walls on either side. I turn to run. There's nothing I can *do* but run, and I *know* this." She drew a deeper breath, raising her hands to push her hair out of her eyes. "But . . . I run into trees, of all things, into forest, and . . . someone is waiting for me."

"He steps into my path. There's moonlight here, but he's hard to look at, and I realize it's hard to look at him because he's constantly changing. He's always tall," she added, forehead briefly creasing in frustration, "but his body shifts in place. I can't describe it," she added. "But it's strange, not terrifying.

"I try to move past him, but he lifts a hand, palm out, and I stop. I look over my shoulder," she added. "I can't help that.

"But he knows. He tells me that: *I know what you're running from.*"

Duster was restless. Out of the corner of her eye, Jewel could see the glint of steel in her hand.

"He's a god, Duster," she said, more sharply than she intended. "I can't exactly tell him to drop dead."

Duster shrugged.

"He says, 'I know what you're running from. And you know that you can't run from him, in the end; there is nowhere safe to go if he is free.'"

"And I tell him that I *can't do anything else,* and he says, 'I know. Understand, now, that you *cannot* do anything to fight him. You are not, yet, armed, if you will ever be. This fight *is not your fight,* and you must have the humility to accept this as truth.

"'But it *is* mine. Lead me out of this forest, lead me into your grove of standing stone and dead wood and stunted tree, and I will stand where you cannot.'

"I turn back, then, but it's all damn trees as far as I can see.

"'Find a way,' he says. 'Only you can.'

"But I *can't.* I can't even see the City anymore. I can just hear the screaming.

"And I know that everything—*everything*—that I care about is dying, or will die, and I can't do *anything*—" She lifted her hands to her face.

Teller finished his writing, then. He added this third slate to the others, making a careful pile of them. "Rath?" he asked her softly.

She lowered her hands, and nodded.

11th of Emperal, 410 AA
Thirty-fifth holding, Averalaan

Jewel went to Rath's by street after the daily trip to the Common. She didn't go alone, although she did, briefly, try. She took Carver, Duster, and Angel with her, but only after they agreed to wait outside. The slates hung on her back in a pack, but she had bundled them with as much care as possible; chalk smudged.

No one talked much. Duster was silent, but she often was; Carver was silent, which was unusual. The silence of Duster and Carver silenced Angel as well, and Jewel was not up to shouldering the entire weight of conversation. She walked in silence, surrounded by the noise of the streets as they crossed invisible holding boundaries on their trek.

When she arrived at Rath's apartment building, Duster, Carver, and Angel, as promised, took up lounging positions to one side of the door. They looked clean enough—just—not to seem too threatening. She hoped.

She still had keys to Rath's place, and she used them all. It wasn't the first time she cursed his locks, because in her opinion, one would have been more than enough, and the third one was still a little high. But she opened them, took a breath, and opened the door.

She was very proud of herself; Rath was standing inches from the arc the opening door made, and she did not start or scream. Instead, she slid the pack from her shoulders and handed it to him.

Rath's hair was pulled back, which wasn't unusual; it was shining in the magelight, which was. It was also darker than it had been the last time she'd seen him. His skin was the type of smooth and pale that only makeup could achieve, and she could only see his scars because she knew where to look. He wore a jacket that was mostly burgundy velvet to her eyes, and a shirt.

"New jacket?" she asked, as he took the pack from her hands and stepped to one side to let her in.

"Relatively."

"You're going out?"

"Not immediately." He glanced at her face, and his tone softened. "Why are you here, Jewel?"

She gestured at the backpack. "In there," she told him. "Three slates."

"Ah." His expression softened as well, and he turned and walked the length of the hall to his room. Jewel trailed in his wake like a slightly detached shadow.

When he reached his room, he set the backpack on the bed, untied it, and carefully retrieved its contents. He unbundled the slates from the blanket with more care than Jewel could have managed, and then took them to the table. There, magelight shone.

"Sit," he told her.

Nodding, she walked to the bed and sat on its edge. After a few moments, she eased backward, until she was lying down, staring at the ceiling. She could hear the slight clack of slates as they were separated; could hear a slightly different clack as he discarded them. When she heard it for the third time, she pushed herself up on her elbows.

Rath turned in his chair. "When did you have these dreams?"

"The past three nights."

"Three," he said. He rose then and went to one of the boxes on the mantel; from this, he pulled his pipe. Jewel watched him line the bowl with leaves taken from the same box. She closed her eyes until the faint and oddly comforting aroma of smoke drifted toward her.

"I don't know what it means," she said softly.

He nodded. "This woman," he said quietly. "Does she remind you of anyone you've ever seen?"

"You couldn't forget seeing someone like her," was the quiet reply.

"No. I don't imagine you could."

Jewel's eyes narrowed. "You've seen her?"

Rath, silent for long enough that Jewel thought he wouldn't answer the question, finally nodded. "I have."

"Where?"

He shook his head. That question, he would not answer. But after a moment, he added, "Someplace you will never be. I admit, however, that she does not obviously carry a sword or cloak herself in shadow." His lips turned up at the corners in what might have been a smile.

Jewel closed her eyes again.

"It's too much, Rath," she whispered. "It's too much for us. Do you know what it means? There were *gods*," she added, raising her arm and settling it over her closed eyes.

"I think," he said, words drifting and mingling with that familiar scent, "I have some idea of what it signifies." His voice was quiet and soothing, and she heard no lie in the words. "But you are right; it is not information that you, or your den, can use to any purpose."

"Can you?"

"I can. And if not I, the Magi of my acquaintance. It is important information; I do not mean to lessen its significance. But it is something that they will be both familiar with and competent to analyze, if you will allow me to retain the slates."

"You might as well. We haven't been using them much."

"You mistake me. Which you do not often do. Take mine in their place; I will keep these." Smoke eddied as Jewel removed her arm and slowly opened her eyes. "If you will allow it, I will take responsibility for what they contain. You may, of course, feel free to attempt to further interpret them."

She shrugged. "I'll see what the others have to say."

"If anything they say strikes you as interesting, write it down."

She nodded again.

"You're upset, but not about the dreams," Rath said. He had always been too damn perceptive.

"I am," she whispered. Then, aware that she was not to lie to him in his own home—the first rule he had established—she added, "There's something else, as well."

He waited in silence while she tried to find words. The ones that finally came out were, "We lost Fisher."

What the dreams hadn't done, these words did; he was utterly still for a moment, his face that mask that meant his expression would show exactly—and only—what he wanted it to show. "What do you mean?"

These words were harder to force out. She didn't manage before he asked one question.

"Where?"

"In the undercity."

"While you were there?"

No lying to Rath in his own home. Jewel stood. *They're not my pets and they're not my children. I can't just keep them locked up in the apartment, waiting on my permission to even breathe.* She was angry, and it was like a Summer storm; she shook with it. But she did not say the words.

Because she only *wanted* them to be true.

If he had shouted at her, it might have been easier. Because then, she could have shouted back. Instead, after the silence, heavy with unspoken words, had gone on too long, he said, "Who was with Fisher?"

She exhaled. "Duster, Carver, Angel, and Lefty."

"They heard nothing?"

"Nothing."

"And saw nothing?"

She nodded.

He rose. "When?"

"On the eighth of Emperal. Or maybe really late on the seventh."

"I will not lecture you," he told her quietly, walking over to the mantel and opening the box again. "I can't say anything to you that you haven't already thought."

She opened her mouth and closed it again. "Is he dead, Rath?"

"You don't know?"

"No. I felt *nothing*. I saw *nothing*."

Rath's back was turned toward her; she couldn't see his face. But after a silence, he offered what he could. "He is almost certainly dead."

"But *why*?"

"I don't know," he replied, and this time he did turn. "I have to leave soon, Jewel. You can remain here, if you want."

"I can't. Carver, Duster, and Angel are outside, waiting."

He raised a brow. It was the same dark that his hair now was.

"We don't go out in the streets alone, if we can help it. And I wasn't sure I could make it here on my own if I—" No. That wasn't true. What was true was this: she was afraid to go into the maze. "The streets of the undercity have changed."

"Yes," he said. Just that.

He let himself out of his apartment quietly. He did not linger by the door, and did not listen for her familiar, if slightly heavier, footfall. Her gift and her talent made it very difficult to lie to her, but Rath had the advantage of knowledge and experience. He had not spoken a lie.

But he had acted one. He had been quiet, reasonable, suggesting a calm acceptance of the three dreams that he in no way felt.

Fisher had helped, in this. A better man would have hesitated to take advantage of her pain, her guilt, and her fear. But she needed to be quit of this, and he needed to be certain that she was. That he left her with guilt and desolation was insignificant in comparison; he wanted her to remain *alive*.

Rath had intended to visit the Order of Knowledge with the candelabra that Jewel had given into his keeping. Because of the destination, he had made the effort to shave his face, dye his hair, and mute the white of his scars. He had also dressed in a way that suggested moderate wealth, but not in a way that suggested power.

Jewel's visit did not change his destination, but he went quickly, and his mind was no longer on the candelabra that would, at one time, have been a marvel. A lucky find, even in the undercity. It had been many, many months since he had felt the thrill of discovery, and he knew that the time for that had passed.

The time for much had passed, was passing, even as he walked. Old Rath, he was called, and although he had done much to lessen the visual impact of age, he felt it keenly in the Summer air. The streets that he walked were crowded, but that was not unexpected at this time of day; he nodded and smiled at those he passed, occasionally taking care to lift his hat. The crowds dispersed as he approached the footbridge that led to the Isle and vanished by the time he'd paid its onerous tolls.

He crossed the bridge, and made his way to the Order of Knowledge.

Sigurne looked particularly frail when she met him. He retrieved a chair for her and held it while she sat, before taking one of his own. The room, with its large and perfectly waxed great table, was otherwise empty; light flooded in through the bank of windows that took up most of the surrounding walls.

"I almost dread these meetings," she told him softly. Her hands lay across her chair's armrests, and he could see the way her fingers curled slightly into the wood.

"I know. I have other business here," he added, "but this would not wait."

"What, then, have you come to tell me? Have you come to return more daggers?"

"No. I've been careful of late, and have spent more time socializing than fighting."

She raised a brow, but did not ask.

"It is almost time, I think," Rath told her quietly, "to play the only card I hold. I wished, however, to ask you if, in your researches, you have come across any descriptions or depictions of Lord Cordufar's mistress."

She raised a brow. "The current Lord Cordufar?"

"His father," Rath replied. "I have briefly seen the current Lord's mistress."

She stiffened. "You believe they are the same woman." It was not a question. "Why?"

He seldom rehearsed speech. Today, he had, in the silence of his walk. But those words, whatever they had been, deserted him; he grimaced as they fled. "I have an acquaintance," he said at last.

"You have many. What makes this particular acquaintance significant?"

He straightened, words teetering on the edge of his lips as he tried to find a way to steer them between truth and lie. "Three dreams," he finally said.

"Three."

He nodded.

She did not tell him that this was impossible. He appreciated the tact. "I will assume that these three were consecutive."

"Yes." He hesitated. With Sigurne's conversational guidance, it was difficult to say too little, and entirely too easy to say too much. She understood that he habitually lied, that he hid, almost unconsciously, most of what he knew. He therefore read her expression with care, and found information wanting. Still, old habits were difficult to break. "It is not the first time in our history that men and women of unknown significance have been visited with the dreaming Wyrd."

Her expression shifted slightly, but it did not sharpen, and he was not entirely certain—yet—that he had said too much, or spoken too clumsily. "As you say. Let us assume that these three dreams are indeed such a Wyrd. Fate," she added, a hint of bitterness in the word, "has seldom taken care to be kind. Tell me of the dreams."

"The element the three dreams had in common was, if I interpret them correctly, Lord Cordufar's mistress; the dreams offered no name, of course, but the description is exact. I no longer believe she is human."

Sigurne nodded.

"Sigurne, what happens if what we are facing is not, in fact, a rogue mage? All of our plans, and all of our investigations, have assumed that we are dealing, at base, with another Ice Mage. But if Cordufar's mistress has been here for two consecutive generations, the man—or woman—who summoned her must have been barely out of childhood when he did so."

Sigurne closed her eyes. "Or she is not leashed."

"Or, as you say, she is no longer enslaved." Rath set his hands upon his legs, palms down.

"I will be careful, in the future, to wish wisely. I dreaded word of another demon, and the return of another quenched blade."

He waited for a moment; because she looked so weary, he felt a sharp hesitance to add to the burden he'd placed on her shoulders.

But she was the head of the Magi. Fragile, even delicate, yes, but there was steel in her that time could not touch. "There is more."

Sigurne lifted a hand. She rose, as she often did when she was troubled, and she walked the length of the room, passing the table to come to the windows which overlooked the quiet City. There she stood, framed in light, and exposed by it.

He waited; he did not speak until she turned to face him. "The news you have already brought me," she whispered, "is dark enough, Ararath. It is far, far worse than the daggers."

"My pardon, Sigurne," he replied.

"No. I will not grant what you have no need to ask of me. It is I who should ask yours. If I desired a life free of trouble, I would not now occupy the position I hold. Tell me," she added.

"Gods," he replied.

She closed her eyes.

In the silence, Ararath of Handernesse accepted death. He had accepted it in theory, when Jewel had first begged him to leave his pursuit of the demons, although she did not know what she asked. He had accepted it in the troubling conversation with Haval. But accepting the unknown, accepting the risk—and calling it certainty—was not the same as choosing. As knowing.

Is this what Jewel always felt? he wondered, as he watched Sigurne's veined lids, her closed eyes, the way her hands trembled.

He would have left her, but knew that she would not allow it. Frail or no, she would hear what he had to say. And in truth? He required it. He required the knowledge, the certainty that she could offer.

"There are two," he continued, "and I do not understand the second."

"The first?"

"The first I understand well," he replied. "The god we do not name. To see his hand in the work of demons is not a stretch," he added, "If the demons are free."

She nodded.

"But the nature of his influence is not clear to me. In all three of the dreams, darkness figures prominently, but—and the dreams, even of prophecy, cannot be said to be literal—the darkness is devouring the City."

Sigurne said softly "That is not possible."

"As you say," was the quiet reply. A minute passed in a silence so still words would have shattered it. Rath waited until that stillness had eased before he chose to continue. "In the second and third dream, however, another god—my informant believed it to be a god, and my informant's instincts are seldom wrong, although they are frequently fractured—appears, and it is a god, in aspect and description, that I cannot name. I admit that I have done little research," he added. "I came directly to you upon receipt of this information."

"Tell me of this second god."

"He had no name. He did not name himself, and my informant likewise could not name him. However, he told my informant that this fight, in the end, was his fight." He hesitated. He was weary of subterfuge.

But he was not yet willing to expose Jewel's talent-born gifts to this woman. Not even to this woman, whom he trusted. He had all but said he would send Jewel—as a messenger—to Amarais. To House Terafin. But he could not bring himself to speak of her abilities; not directly.

"What aspect did he choose?"

"Ah. He had no fixed form. The first time she saw him, he was a giant beast; a giant antlered beast. But in both cases? Forest figured prominently."

Her frown was a frown that could be found on the countenance of any member of the Order of Knowledge, and it lessened the pain and fatigue. He had presented her with a riddle.

"Hunters?" she finally asked, and the way she asked caused Rath to raise a brow.

"In the first dream, yes, if I am not mistaken. They were not seen in the vision, but horns were heard, and dogs. You have some suspicion of who he must be?"

"I have, but, Ararath, what I know makes *no sense*." She turned back to the window that framed the street.

"How so?"

"The Hunter God is worshiped in one of the Western Kingdoms, the Kingdom of Breodanir. He is worshiped nowhere else," she added, "But he is considered the god of the hunt, and it is not in the interests of the members of the Order to question his existence while they work there. One of his aspects, the most feared, is that of a giant beast; it is said he causes the deaths of his Hunters annually."

"You have members in the Western Kingdoms?"

"We have members anywhere that it is relatively safe for them to study. Not all of those members, by any means, are mage-born."

"And they do not believe that the Hunter God is a god?"

"He has no mortal children," she replied. "Not even in Breodanir, the kingdom in which the whole of his worship resides. The term hunter-born, which is used with frequency, refers merely to the sons of the ruling nobles. None of the hunter-born are golden-eyed; they are not, in any way that we have been able to determine, born *of* the god they worship."

"They do not put the golden-eyed to death there, as they do in the Dominion?"

"No. They accept the existence of our gods, and in general, the worship of our gods in Breodanir is similar to their worship in the Empire. The mother-born work in the Mother's temples in the King's City, and possibly elsewhere in the Kingdom, and they are treated with both respect and understanding of their divine nature. It is because the true gods are accepted, and even worshiped, that Breodanir has long been a puzzle to us. It is seldom that a country accepts the existence of true gods while venerating, by their side, a god that cannot exist."

He frowned. "So. A god that doesn't exist offers the key to the defeat of the plans of the god we do not name."

"I will confer with my colleagues," she replied. "It may be that some part of the mystery will be unraveled by those who have made Breodanir their study."

Rath stood, then. "Sigurne," he said softly, grasping, at last, at straws. Seeking a way out, a way to survive. "Will you not take this to the Kings?"

"I would take it," she replied, "had I access to your informant, and some way of ascertaining the truth of Wyrd you have claimed on their behalf." She raised a hand to her eyes for a moment, and then lowered it. "I could go to Duvari. The political caution that must be exercised with The Ten would not trouble him."

Rath flinched at the use of the name. He did not, however, argue.

"But if I go to Duvari, he will demand the name of your informant. If you are not ready to surrender it, you will no longer be free. And if you are ready, and you pass this information to the head of the Astari, your informant will almost certainly not be unencumbered again." She hesitated. "Ararath."

"I think it likely you could sway the Kings by belief alone, given your position and your reputation."

"About the demons, yes. But in order to reach Cordufar, we would have to cross The Darias in the Council, and without proof—as you have long known—that is not an option to us.

"And not even I would be able to claim, by belief alone, that the gods are literally involved." She rose. "It is not, however, by belief alone that I would operate in that realm. Remember, I am on the Isle."

"You will speak with the Exalted?"

"I will," she said softly, tiredly. "If it concerns the gods, who better than the children of the three to consult? But there is much that involves the gods that the gods will not divulge. I will speak," she said quietly, "with the Son of Cormaris." She walked toward the door, and then turned back.

Voice gentle, she added, "But if, indeed, the god we do not name is involved, it is my belief that the gods would know, and they would bespeak their mortal sons and daughters. If this were the case, word would have already reached the Kings."

"And you do not think it has."

"The Kings have not approached the Order of Knowledge with this information." She lifted a hand before he could speak. "Nor would they hesitate, Ararath. The Magi are part of the first line of defense against those that serve the unnamed god; they are part of the first line of defense, hampered as they are, against the demons.

"But I will speak, now, with the Exalted of Cormaris,

should he choose to grant me audience. If it will ease you, accompany me."

"I am hardly dressed in an appropriate manner to speak with the Exalted."

"No," she replied, "You are not. But I will cede, for the moment, a robe for your use. It will be of lesser quality than the jacket you now wear, but it will mark your presence as one who aids me in my journeys. Come."

When a robe had been found—and the search had raised brows and caused some dire, and thankfully largely inaudible muttering—Rath slid it over his clothing. The outer halls of the first floor of the Order of Knowledge were decorated in a way that suggested wealth and its obvious extension, power. There were, therefore, mirrors into which he might look, adjusting the fall of shoulders and the drape of hood, both of which were large, even considering the jacket he wore beneath its folds.

While he was thus occupied, Sigurne approached him at the side of another member of the Order.

"This is Matteos Corvel," she said. "Matteos, this is Ararath. His style of dress is entirely a courtesy to the Exalted."

Rath bowed. "Member Mellifas felt that speed was advisable and I was not otherwise able to come up with suitable attire on short notice."

Matteos Corvel raised a dark brow. His hood did not obscure his face; it was dark, and the lines across his brow, white in comparison, spoke of battles that had not managed to kill him.

"Matteos," Sigurne told Rath, "is often charged with my safety. Member APhaniel is not currently in residence," she added. "But in any event, Member APhaniel is not always the ideal choice for the formality of the Church of Cormaris."

At this, Matteos Corvel grimaced and looked as if he would speak; he held his peace, but with some effort. Instead of words, he offered Sigurne his arm, and she nodded gracefully, placing her hand upon it.

*   *   *

The cathedrals of *Averalaan Aramarelas* could be seen by travelers long before they had reached the demiwalls which girded the outer City itself. At that distance, they were evocative; they hinted at wealth and the serenity of distant, benign power. It was not, however, as such a traveler that Rath now approached them.

Nor was it as such a traveler that he was granted entrance. Unlike the palace, with its obvious guards, its obvious foreign dignitaries and the wing of *Avantari* occupied by its multiple bureaucracies and their attendant employees and visitors, the cathedral was dramatically silent. What bustle there was existed behind the walls of the open nave. Visitors, of course, did not use those halls. They walked, instead, beneath the spread wings of an eagle in flight, and passed beneath the rod he clasped in curved talons. That all of this was done in stone was expected; that the stone did not rob the eagle of intelligence, focus, and the sense that it was living, was not.

But here, of course, the maker-born had toiled. If any could afford their services, it was the cathedrals upon the Isle.

Gold leaf had been laid upon the carved runes of welcome, and startling blue stones had been laid at their points. Rath gazed at them a moment, but did not linger. It had been years since he had come to sit on the magnificent and gleaming benches that spread out within the space formed by three walls. The cathedral was never dark. Even in Henden, at midnight, magelights shone, reflected in gold and warmed by aged ivory and polished silver. The Mother's cathedral observed the strict tenets of the Six Dark Days, as did the cathedral of Reymaris, but Cormaris was the Lord of Wisdom, and in the darkness, wisdom was light.

Or so Rath had been told. Funny, to think of that here.

Sigurne had passed beneath the towering arch that led to the pews, Matteos by her side. The younger mage—Rath had no doubt he was mage-born—had relaxed perceptibly upon entering the cathedral. Rath envied him; he hadn't.

Nor was it required. Sigurne had not been in the building long before two Priests came from the recessed doors to either side of the great nave. They wore robes that were not dissimilar to the Order's robes, but where the Order's robes were functional and plain, the robes of the Priesthood were subtly embroidered with gold. The men were silent as they approached, but they tendered Sigurne a deep bow; it was also genuine.

"Member Mellifas," one man said. "The Exalted is waiting."

She nodded in turn, and Matteos offered her an arm.

"Your companion?"

"Ah. He is, as you have divined, new to the Order, and he is here at my request."

"Very well." He glanced once again at Rath, as if words were about to spill into the silence and he hoped to catch them. The silence, however, remained unbroken. Long past the point it would have been awkward under merely social circumstances, the Priest nodded and turned.

The halls that were traveled by Priests and novitiates were not as finely accoutered as the areas meant to instill awe in visitors, but they were by no means plain, and they did not suggest humility. They were wider than the servants' halls that wound like warrens through any of the great manors, and the sconces that held torches—or, in this case, magestones—were gleaming in the light. The floors were stone, as were the walls, but they were broken by any number of architectural flourishes: small alcoves in which statues resided, arches that were not structurally necessary, molded cornices. There were also hanging tapestries and framed paintings; the halls were not short, and they followed the halls until they reached a set of narrow stairs.

The stairs were winding stairs, girded in the center by a stone pillar around which were engraved emblems of the god. The Priests led up those stairs, and the mages followed in single file. Rath brought up the rear, pausing to glance up toward the pillar's height where eagles were, indeed, in perpetual flight.

He approached those eagles as he climbed; the stairs, like the halls, were not short. Although halls branched from the spiral, they were not taken. Rath wondered why it was that even Priests loved the heights. Then again, this was their job, their place of employ; it was no doubt to entirely more humble—and thankfully less steep—stairs that they repaired at the end of their day's service.

But the stairs did end, and with them, the climb and the building ache they caused in the leg he favored. As Sigurne did not trouble to pause to catch breath, no one else could. Vanity was foolish that way, but it drove far greater men than Rath, and he acknowledged this with a wry smile.

The Priest noticed, of course. The one thing about Priests that made them so daunting was the utter lack of humor they indulged in while on duty. Not that humor on this particular day was required—but the lack of humor implied a certain self-importance that on the best of days annoyed Rath.

He let it go, and followed Sigurne down the hall. It was in all ways finer than the halls on the first floor, and windows graced it, colored light illuminating both walls and floors. Here, sun behind their insubstantial wings, eagles soared above both mountains and City, watching from a remove of flight, untroubled by the things that could not touch them.

And what, thought Rath, as he paused to watch their captured flight, *troubled gods?* Why, if they existed as they did, in their perfect distant lands, did they care about the fate of mortals, whose lives might end before they finished a thought?

He reached up with his right hand, and paused an inch from the surface of the window under the watchful eye of Sigurne, who had stopped and turned back. Embarassed, he lowered his hand. She simply waited, and her expression when he turned to meet her gaze reminded him, in ways that he could not define, of Cormaris, the god in whose service this entire cathedral had been built.

She held out her hand, command in the silent gesture, and after a moment he understood the grace she offered, and he extended his arm as naturally as if he had never left the patriciate for the hovels of his later homes in the holdings. She placed her hand upon that arm, and by simple presence, it steadied him. *What we ask for,* Rath thought, *and what we give. Both sustain us.* She smiled, as if she had heard the thought, and she inclined her head slightly.

Nor did Matteos resent his replacement; he simply fell into the position Rath had occupied, and continued to walk.

So it was that they came at last to the chambers in which the Exalted ruled the churches of Cormaris across the Empire. In the center of the chamber, in the center of a mosaic of stone, stood a throne. It was so tall in back that it seemed at first to be narrow; it was not. The rests were heavy and dark, and the seat itself could not be seen because it was occupied by the Exalted of Cormaris.

Robes of white and gold fell from his broad shoulders to the floor; his hair, in the light that streamed in from the ceiling, seemed pale, as gold was often pale, although it could have been brown, or even gray; the light was transforming. He wore a simple circlet, and it *was* simple, compared to the more complicated head-dress that was required by official functions outside of his own domain. His fingers were ringed, and he did, indeed, carry a rod, which lay now across that brilliant lap.

But it was his eyes that drew the attention, and his gaze that held it.

"Sigurne," he said, dispensing in a word with formality.

She was trusted, Rath thought, that much.

She bowed to the Exalted, as did Rath and Matteos; they held their bows longer, but some consideration was due her age and the rank granted her by the Order of Knowledge. And yet, in the eyes of the god-born son of Cormaris, there was no obvious acknowledgment of her power.

"Exalted," she said, as she rose. Rath smiled slightly; if informality had been offered, she had very politely rejected it. Nor did the son of Cormaris seem surprised or displeased.

"Have you come to have daggers reconsecrated?"

"No, Exalted. I have come to beg an audience with your father, if you deem it wise."

A pale brow rose in the light. "Speak plainly, Sigurne."

"I have received word from my associate of a dreaming Wyrd," she replied. "And it is significant, if indeed it *is* a Wyrd." She turned to Rath. "Ararath," she said quietly. "Tell the Exalted what you have told me, and let him judge."

Rath bowed to her. "With your permission, Exalted," he said quietly.

"Granted."

He told this man in his room of light and gold what he had told Sigurne in her room of magery and silence.

The Exalted of Cormaris was quiet when Rath at last finished speaking. He had interrupted Rath only a handful of times, and only for clarification or wording. Since the exact wording was in Rath's room in the thirty-fifth holding, this was frustrating; Rath seldom felt the awkward child, and it was not a reaction that he appreciated.

But the god-born did not seem to notice; he merely absorbed the information he had requested. Only when it was clear that Rath had come to the end of the words he knew how to offer did the Exalted leave his throne. He rose.

To the silent Priests who had led them this far, he now gestured.

They stepped forward, to either side of his throne, and uncovered small braziers that rested on stout legs against the tiling. These, they lit, and incense began to trail thin smoke toward the ceiling. Caught in beams of light, the smoke was striking; if the dead cast shadows, they would be these trails, these rising streams.

To the Priests, however, they signified little; once the braziers were lit, they walked to the doors, and these, with some obvious exertion, they closed.

Sigurne moved to stand closer to Rath. "I don't know if you've experienced this before," she said quietly. "But if you haven't: don't speak to the god until, or unless, he addresses you. Let the Exalted ask questions. If the Exalted asks a question, speak to him; the god will hear your answer." She smiled a small, weary smile. "I have been between worlds many times, but I admit I have never grown fond of it. There is something about it that is not quite comfortable."

As if she were talking about the ache damp weather caused. He could not help smiling at her. Even here.

But it was brief; he turned to watch the Exalted. His face was shorn of expression, but his eyes—his eyes had turned gold into something liquid that captured the essential nature of light. It was hard to look at him. It was impossible to look away.

Even when the mists began to roll in, in lazy, billowing clouds that, unlike normal mist, were neither damp nor wet, Rath could not look away. The floor vanished, the braziers disappeared, the throne wavered—but the man with shining eyes did not. He was the bridge between worlds.

God-born.

He had not raised his arms, had not lifted his face to the heavens where the gods were reputed to dwell. Nor had he raised his voice. He stood, and only when he slowly turned was Rath free—if a man could ever be said to be free in the presence of a god.

It was said that gods chose their forms when they appeared in the lands between. Without experience, Rath could not divine the truth in that belief. But the god appeared robed, much as his son was robed; he carried a rod in one hand, and in the other? A staff. His hair was gray, but not the gray of age; it was almost silver. His face? Neither young nor old, or perhaps all of these things, for his face was hard to look upon. It shifted, rippling constantly, as if it were the surface of a lake. On his left shoulder, an eagle sat, an eagle the color of mist, with blue eyes.

The god's eyes were all colors or no color, and in their way, they, too, were hard to look upon. But it was his voice that made the deepest impression: it was a chorus of voices, all speaking at the same time, and to the same beat, but all distinct enough that he could peel each back by layer—if he wanted to ignore the actual words.

It was, however, for those words that he'd come.

"Father," the Exalted said quietly.

Cormaris nodded. "Why have you summoned me?"

"We seek your counsel," was the soft reply. The Exalted then turned. "This is Sigurne Mellifas, and her two companions, Ararath of Handernesse and Matteos Corvel."

"Sigurne," the god said. He inclined his head, and the eagle spread its wings a moment before settling.

She inclined her own head in turn; bowing in these mists would have made her momentarily invisible. "It has been some time," she said softly.

"And yet, not enough time? Were it up to you, Sigurne, I believe you would gratefully never come to this place at all." He spoke, in all of his multiple voices, with affection.

"We seldom disturb the gods to share either peace or happiness."

"No. And I will not even call it selfish. What is of enough concern that you present yourself here?"

"A dreaming Wyrd," she replied. "Three dreams."

"Ah." He turned to his son. "Tell me of these dreams."

As Sigurne had predicted, the Exalted turned to Rath. "Tell me again," he said quietly, "the content of these Three Dreams. Precision and brevity are not required; the time in the between passes differently."

Rath did as the son of Cormaris requested.

The god listened, silent and impassive. Only when it was clear that Rath had finished did he speak. But he spoke to Rath.

"Ararath Handernesse," and if a multitude could speak quietly, this one did.

Rath inclined his head, although this took effort. Standing for a moment in the god's gaze, he felt the weight of it, as if all history had been—and even at this moment was—absorbed by the gods. He rarely felt insignificant when he did not desire it. He felt worse than that, now; he felt entirely exposed, and in a way that the lies and the elaborate fictions that he had often constructed for his personal use could not alleviate.

"Who was the dreamer?"

Silence.

The air grew colder, and the god's voice sharper. Rath felt Sigurne's hand on his arm; he could not look away to see it. "Who was the dreamer?"

"Ararath," the Exalted said. "Please answer the question."

"My apologies, Exalted," he said, because he could—barely—speak to the son of Cormaris. "But that is not information that I can freely divulge. Had I realized that I would be required to do so, I would not have approached Sigurne, and I would not have come to trouble you."

The eagle launched itself off the shoulder of the god, and Rath felt the beat of its wings. He closed his eyes as the eagle landed upon his shoulders, but he did not attempt to evade it.

Talons pierced robe, jacket, shirt, and skin.

Rath did not move.

But the god did. He covered the distance that separated them, marked by eddies in mist and gray. Some three feet away from Rath, he halted.

"This is not a game."

"No," Rath replied. "I have endeavored to overcome my caution and my personal scruples to deliver this information. The information itself is in no way filtered."

"Do you think you can protect her?" the god asked.

It was not the question Rath had expected. *Her.* That much, he had already divined. But he shrugged the shoulder that did not contain the weight of the eagle. "As I can, I have. And as I can, I will continue to do so."

"Is she seer-born?"

Rath was silent.

"They cannot hear your answers; they cannot hear my questions. This much, I am willing to cede you, in this place."

Rath glanced at the eagle, then. "Yes. She is seer-born." He almost asked why this was relevant; most of the Wyrd-driven dreams were not the dreams of seers. The seer-born were very, very rare. He stopped the words from leaving his mouth. Not even someone as jaded as Rath could argue niceties with a god.

"It is relevant," the god replied, "because what she sees, when she dreams, is not necessarily the Wyrd of the nameless god; it is a gift that resides in part within her own future. I would have you bring her here," he added, "But I will not demand it."

"She dreamed of gods."

"Yes." Cormaris frowned. "And it is troubling. What you say implies much."

"The god we do not name cannot be here."

"No. If he were in your 'here,' you would not question; you would *know*. But something is ... wrong. I am aware of Sigurne Mellifas, and her lifelong burden. If I am not mistaken, you are more intimately acquainted with the daggers blessed by ancient rites than even she."

Rath nodded.

"There are demons, here."

"There are demons," Rath replied, "in the City. What they seek, we do not know. But they kill for things ancient in our measure: old and broken artifacts. Ancient Weston writings." He paused, and then, meeting the endless gaze of Cormaris, asked, "What city lay here, before our founding?"

The god was silent for long enough that Rath thought he would not answer.

"There were three, but it is not of these that you speak. They were cities of men, and they rose and fell long after the gods last walked your world. But before that, this was home to The Shining Court, and it was part of the dominion of Allasakar. If the kin can delve there, there is a danger."

"They can," Rath replied.

This time, the god did not ask him for the details that he did not wish to divulge. "How long have the demons been present in the City?"

"At best guess? Thirty years. Perhaps more."

"And they have operated undetected until very recently."

Rath nodded.

"But the Kings have not fallen, nor have the Exalted. There has been no war, no obvious display of power."

Thinking about the burning brothel, Rath grimaced. "There have been no obvious contraventions of the Kings' Law. And without even one such incident, we cannot move forward."

"I understand the small political games men play in these times," the god replied. "But they do not understand their peril."

"Is there peril, in this?"

"Yes, although I do not fully apprehend their intent. There are things that lie beneath Averalaan that we do not wish disturbed." He frowned. "But if the Lord of the Hells delves there, it is not in his interests to disturb them either." He reached out and stroked the eagle's head. "You have not told Sigurne all of your intent," he added.

"No. I have not told anyone of what I intend, because if there is any other way, I will choose it. In my experience, the kin are not human—but they share some human frailties: greed, lust, desire for power. All of these things can be manipulated, with care. They need make only one mistake, if it is the right one, and we are free to act."

"And you can be certain that they will make such a mistake?"

"Nothing is certain," Rath replied bitterly. "And in truth, I delivered the information to Sigurne because I had hoped—"

"That I might supply her, or my son, with information that could be used to sway the Kings."

Rath nodded.

"Understand," Cormaris said, "that the gods are not of your world. We cannot directly affect events there except through our children; we are not omniscient, and we see what our children see, no more. What you see, and what you have seen, none of my followers has seen; if there have been deaths, and if the demons hunt in the City, they have taken care to kill where such deaths cannot be witnessed by *any* of the god-born. It is troubling," he added softly, "for such subtlety is the mark of the powerful and the ancient among their kind.

"Where we can aid, we will aid you," the god continued. "What will you do?"

"Die," Rath said, exhaling. He no longer felt the eagle's talons, although the eagle had not left his shoulder.

"And how will that serve your purpose?"

"I am brother to The Terafin," he replied. "Estranged, by my choice. It is our belief that one of the demon-kin has taken the form and shape of Lord Cordufar. If . . . my connection . . . to The Terafin is known, it might be a matter of ease for them to take my form and likeness."

"Estranged."

Rath nodded, but it was stiff and offered nothing.

And the god was merciful; he asked but one question. "And will your sister see you, if you choose to approach the seat of her power?"

"Yes," was the bitter, but certain, answer.

Cormaris grew silent; the mists rose and fell, as if they were attendants to the god's whim. His eyes were all colors and no colors as he held Rath's gaze. But in the end, he offered Rath little hope.

"I believe you are correct; they will go to The Terafin. If they approach The Terafin, and they are detected, the word *demon* will be on every powerful tongue before the day is out, and the interests of The Darias will not stand in Council against the anger of The Terafin."

Chapter Eight

JEWEL, HER LEGS DANGLING off the seawall, gazed across the bay to the looming square block that was Senniel College at a distance. From there, she looked to the cathedral towers, and the towers of *Avantari*, the palace from which the Twin Kings ruled the Empire. *Averalaan Aramarelas* had always seemed like a magical place to her—one she could see and could acknowledge, but one that remained forever out of reach.

But during the Festival of The Gathering, the Kings left their palace. Once a day, accompanied only by a small group of Swords, they came to one of the bridges that separated the Isle from the rest of the City. From her vantage on the seawall, she could see that bridge— and could see, as well, that both sides were crowded with Festival clutter and Festival celebrants. A Rath word, that. At this distance it wasn't possible to tell who was rich or who was poor by anything other than the side of the bridge upon which they gathered.

People were in the streets, as well; if you wanted to be alone, this was the wrong damn time of year to do it. There were extra stalls, set up nearest the bridge, where merchants sold food, drink, and the small bits of badly embroidered heraldry that were supposed to be

the Kings' crest. Sword crossing rod, at angles: One for
the Justice-born King, and one for the Wisdom-born;
swords to either side. The background was an odd blue,
rather than the richer color of the real thing, because
technically it wasn't a crest that could be worn by anyone but the Kings.

Besides the stalls were wagons, and counters behind
which people sat. They didn't ask for coin, and they offered food and drink as well; these counters were paid
for, and offered, by whichever one of The Ten it was
who claimed this day of The Gathering. You could see
them, because they always had a crowd, and the crowd
itself never seemed to thin or disperse.

Jewel sat alone.

Finch had arranged the daily outing to the Common.
She had heard the brief discussion from her room, and
she had done nothing to interrupt it; instead she waited
until the den had filed out of the apartment. Only then
had she come out of hiding. She had taken a few coins
from the iron box, and she had made her way here.
Where here was a section of the seawall at which no
business was done.

She pulled her knees up, tucked them beneath her
chin, and wrapped her arms around her legs.

Here, in the silence of waves, where the salt on
the cool breeze was the strongest, she could hear her
Oma's voice. It was not a voice she wanted to listen to,
not today, but the press of the other voices that usually
drowned it out were harder to hear. So she accepted,
with as much grace as she could muster, the shadows
of her Oma.

Oma, what is a ghost? She also exposed the shadows
of her younger self, speaking from a time in which the
world had been smaller and safer.

Well, if you listen to all these Northern Priests, her
Oma had replied, rolling up her sleeves and sitting at
the kitchen table because Work Did Not Wait and you
could do it while you talked, *ghosts don't exist.* She had
snorted when she said it, but that wasn't suprising; her
Oma had never cared for Northern gods.

Jewel had picked up a small knife, because if Oma worked, *everyone* had better be working. She could remember that knife now only as a sensation in her palm. It had been small enough that it was deemed safe to use, and sharp enough that safe-to-use came with harshly barked warnings to be careful.

But don't you let those Priests fill your head with clutter. The older woman had picked up a potato. It was fresh enough that they didn't need to peel skin; they could scratch it off with the knife's edge. *Ghosts,* she added, *exist where the wind exists.*

But what are they? The dead go to.... Even at that age—and Jewel could not quite remember what that age had been, it had receded so far in memory—she had known better than to finish that sentence. She could, if she tried, frame the incident and mathematically derive an age from the probable dates—but that wasn't the point of memory. No one was testing her, here.

She'd scraped the skin off potatoes alongside her grandmother.

The dead go where the dead go, her grandmother had said sharply. But her hands slowed their movement, and her expression lost its edges.

"A ghost," she told her granddaughter as she rose and walked to the shuttered windows, "is the spirit of a dead person, robbed of flesh and life."

"What do they want?"

"Hmmm?"

"What do ghosts want?"

The old woman had come away from the window slowly enough that Jewel could see the sun against the weathered, leathery wrinkles of her face and neck. Had she been anyone else—and Jewel could recognize this only in hindsight—she might have stayed there, anchored to the light. But she was Oma, and there was work to do.

She went back to the table, resumed her seat, picked up her much larger knife and the half-naked potato, and began to once again scrape it.

"Ghosts," she told her granddaughter, in a slightly different tone of voice, "are memories."

Jewel, who understood what a memory was, couldn't see how this was true. But she said nothing, skinning while she waited.

"They're a reminder," her Oma continued, "of things we would sometimes rather forget."

"I wouldn't," Jewel said quietly.

"Wouldn't what?"

"Want to forget."

Her Oma's laugh echoed down a decade; it was bitter, because her laughter so often was. "What could you want to forget at your age?"

Lots. But Jewel didn't say this. "If you died," Jewel told her, "I wouldn't *want* to forget you."

"And you'd want to be haunted by your Oma?"

"Yes. Because you'd still be here, then."

And after a long pause, a long stillness in which her hands and her knife were momentarily at rest, her Oma had exhaled heavily. "Aye," she said softly, "there's that." She looked at her granddaughter and added, "You just pray I'm not one of your ghosts, girl. I'm cranky enough alive."

But the thing is, Oma, you are.

Stronger than her father, whose voice was now so silent. Stronger by far than her mother. It was her Oma who chided her, berated her, and offered her whole new ways of looking at guilt.

Guilt.

She let her legs drop again, restless. She wanted to walk, and after a moment, she swung those legs round to the other side of the seawall and hopped down. She was so damn tired. Tired of waiting. Tired of watching. Tired of searching because they'd searched *everywhere,* for a whole damn week, skimping on laundry and everything that wasn't food or water.

She'd gone with them. She'd directed the searches. She'd helped with the ropes and the gaps. She'd carried waterskins, called stops, retreated in defeat, and returned the next morning after breakfast. Her den had followed in silence, and they'd broken the silence only to call his name: *Fisher*.

He hadn't answered. And the calls had gotten softer and more strained.

Jewel kicked the wall she was walking along in momentary fury. Helpless fury, but it was better than kicking an actual person.

What had Rath told her?

Leave the damn maze alone. Go *with* them, if you go.

And what the *Hells* had she been doing? Reading gods-cursed books and trying to add pointless numbers together. Or multiply them. Or divide them.

Fisher wasn't coming back. They talked with dwindling hope, they pointed out all the things that *could* have happened. But hope was never the same damn thing as belief, and they didn't believe any of it. They looked to *her*. They had *always* looked to her.

Hadn't she dreamed of Finch? Hadn't she saved Arann? Hadn't she found Teller? Yes, damn it.

Yes, she had done those things. And here, and now, in isolation under the relentless clarity of summer sky and the bright baubles, ribbons, and flowers of The Gathering, she accepted the bitter truth: she had failed them. Her gift had *failed* Fisher. She'd had no sign, no warning, no *feeling*. Nothing.

He had gone to the undercity to forage, and he had not come back.

She had never been one to cry in public, and she *could not* cry at home, because—because—

If she did, it meant he was gone.

And Fisher? He'd never spoken much. Ever. What words of his would come back to haunt her? What voice would invoke him when the memory of his taciturn face faded at last, submerged by numbers and daily necessity?

No, Oma, she told her dead grandmother. *I never want to forget.*

17th of Aeral, 410 AA
Twenty-fifth holding, Averalaan

It came back to money. It always had.

Jewel opened the iron box, and took just what was
needed for the early fall market, no more. But truthfully, there wasn't a lot more to take. In the two and
a half months since Fisher had disappeared, they had
used the money the last piece from the undercity had
brought in.

Arann and Angel worked Farmer Hanson's stall,
when he had work; that covered some—not all—of
their food. The farmer had introduced them to a few of
the other merchants who worked in the same section of
the Common, and they had picked up a day or two that
way, but the handful of days' work would not keep the
den going.

"Jay?" Finch poked her head around the door. The
sun wasn't high enough for encroaching rays to touch
her, but Jewel smiled anyway, because Finch was, in
some ways, like morning birds.

"Sorry," she said, rising from her crouch and shutting
the box firmly. "I was just thinking."

If sun couldn't touch Finch, shadow could; her expression lost some of its light. But she was kind—she
was almost always kind—and asked nothing. Instead
she waited, her own little imperative, until Jewel left the
room. She closed the door behind them.

She hadn't even finished buying winter clothing. She'd
started; over half the den would be fine. But Arann?
She grimaced. Angel? It was cooler now than it had
been, but it wasn't cold by a long stretch. And at least
Farmer Hanson had said he didn't think it would get really cold this year. No snow. If they were careful, maybe
they could sit the winter out.

Because they weren't burning wood, this year.

Farmer Hanson noticed, of course. Because she
bought less food. He said nothing, offered no advice

and no encouragement beyond his usual friendly hand-shake. But he had already started to worry.

Fair enough. So had she. She'd started worrying when Fisher vanished, and she'd never stopped. None of her den had gone back to the undercity. Duster wanted to, being Duster, but she hadn't put up much of a fight. If she was never going to be kind, she had curbed cruel just enough to sit on most of the words.

"How much do we have?" Angel asked quietly on the way home. He walked to her left; Duster, to her right.

Jewel didn't answer. She tried, but the words—which were going to be lies anyway—wouldn't leave her mouth; they sat there like ashes.

"Jay," Angel said, pressing the point. He could always just find out for himself; there was no real lock on that box, and she knew it. But she also knew that he wouldn't; that he would wait until she was too desperate for lies. For anything, she realized, but fear.

She turned to face him, and stopped walking. Around her, the den slowed, but the rest of the City streamed past.

"A week," she finally told him. "A week, maybe ten days if we're really, really lean."

Duster gestured to Carver, and Carver walked over to where she stood. They talked briefly, and only in den-sign. Duster kept her back to Jewel for the whole of the brief conversation. The others caught some of what was said, but not a single one of them interrupted. Instead, they glanced beyond Duster's shoulder, and when Jay began to walk, they followed her.

They didn't talk about the undercity. They didn't talk about foraging in the maze. That would have been easier, because they had signs for that.

But when Jay had pulled far enough ahead, Duster said, "You, me. Maybe Jester; he's never really said."

Carver nodded briefly. "Jester. You. Me. Jay won't like it."

Duster shrugged. "She met Rath because she'd cut his purse from his shoulder and run away. She knows what we need to do to survive. You think she'll try to stop us?"

Carver hesitated for a moment, and then shook his head. "Let's hope we're not as rusty as we probably are."

"We're not."

"You don't care, do you?"

Duster shrugged again. "Not really. What we had—it was good. But good things never last. That's why people like me exist in the world," she added, with just a touch of bitter pride. "Because good things *never* last.

"Rath taught us all how to pick locks, how to hide in plain sight, how to run the Hells away. You think he did that for nothing? He *knew* what we might have to do. And Jay learned," Duster added quietly, "because she knew it, too." She kicked a stray rock, and added, "She'll do it. She's practical."

And then, shoving hands into pockets, she added, "It's not that I didn't like those years. It's not that I won't miss them." She spoke softly, and in a voice that was almost entirely unlike her normal voice. "I was good enough for her, when things were good and she didn't need me. I was good enough to share everything else with. She didn't ask me to do anything—*anything*—that she wouldn't do. She won't ask now, either.

"But I don't *want* her to have to do them. It's stupid."

Carver said nothing, but it was a quiet, listening nothing.

"I hated her, when I first met her. I hated her even though she saved me, tried to set me free. I wanted to hate her," she said, speaking now to the cobbled streets, the yellow weeds growing between stones. "I just— wanted to hate her.

"But after Lord Waverly, I didn't want her to hate *me*."

Carver started to speak and Duster lifted a hand. Den-sign. *Shut up.*

"You're going to tell me I don't have to say any of this. I already know. Just save it.

"Most of the den?" She shrugged. "They weren't worth the time. I didn't hate 'em because they weren't worth it.

"I don't hate 'em now. Sometimes I remember why I used to. Sometimes I don't care. When we went back, when we went home that first night, I never thought I'd last. It's been more than three years, Carver, and I didn't think I'd last three weeks."

He didn't ask her what night she was talking about. He knew. Anyone who'd been there would.

"But I lasted. I made three weeks. And then four. And then five. Every damn week another struggle. Not to snap at Lefty. Not to smack Jester. Not to spit in Rath's face because he's so damn condescending. Not to take the damn money she leaves lying around by her bedroll and just run someplace where there weren't so damn many *rules*."

"I stayed for the winter. That's what I told myself. The first year," she added. "I didn't want to freeze my ass off in some broken-down hovel with three walls and half a roof while the rest of you were warm and fat."

"That's what you told the rest of us," Carver said, shrugging almost exactly as Duster had done.

"Yeah, well. You never called me on it."

"Not calling you on it now."

"Bullshit." She glanced at him. "When Carmenta had us boxed in, you could have run. He was after me."

Carver shrugged again.

"I never asked you why you didn't."

"You didn't need to."

"I need to now." She turned, shoulders hunched; she looked smaller than normal. Felt it, and hated it.

Carver was not big on fancy words or speeches. It was one of the reasons she could talk to him at all. "You're kin," he finally said. "I figured we'd see worse, sometime. I knew you could fight. I know I can. I knew we wouldn't have to stand for long."

He didn't ask her why she hadn't run. He wouldn't. That was the other reason she could talk to him.

"After that," she said, "it was easier. It was just easier. To be in that place, with everyone else. I can take care of myself," she added, trying to keep the defensive edge out of the words, trying to make them simple fact. Learning from Teller. Gods. "I always knew I could take care of myself.

"But sometimes I forget. Sometimes it's too easy, being there. I go out. I get into fights." She shrugged, trying to get out from under the weight of the words she hadn't yet said. "I tell myself I don't have to go back. But I do. I know everyone thinks it's because of her—it's just Jay.

"Sometimes," she added, "it is. But sometimes it's *more*. It wasn't Jay who stood at my back when Carmenta and his den cornered me. It was you. It wasn't Jay who talked me into coming back, that first night—it was Lander. It isn't Jay who cooks the damn meals or washes the damn clothes half the time—it's Finch or Teller. Jay's got no sense of humor. Jester can make me laugh. Or piss me off."

"Fisher isn't coming back."

Carver nodded.

"I thought that would break her," Duster told him, her voice rougher. "And I wanted that, once. Maybe I want it now. I don't know. *I don't know.*" She shoved her hands through her hair. "It hasn't. She's still Jay. She's still there. But this?" She swallowed. "I don't want her to do what I'm willing to do. Maybe—maybe I never did. I want her to be what she is. I think we *need* her to be what she *is*. She gets too far away from it, I don't know what she'll become. And if she changes, I don't know what we'll be either.

"She's so *goddamn* annoying."

Carver shrugged again. "We've got a week," he said. "Maybe ten days. We'll figure something out."

"What does she want from us, anyway?" Duster said, as she turned in the direction of home.

"Family," he replied.

"Family is supposed to make you worry this damn much?"

He shrugged. "I don't know what it's supposed to do. It's just what it is. And what it's going to be if Angel eats all the food again is violent."

Duster snorted, but they both sped up.

After dinner, though, the den *did* talk. Jay didn't call a meeting, but even without the formality of the kitchen table, they could still get things done. They sat on the floor, or lay across it. Lander and Lefty were against the window wall, side by side. They didn't talk much, not out loud, but their hands were flying.

Arann watched them from across the room. He was just outside the crushed circle the den made, against the wall. Lefty looked up, caught his eye, asked him if everything was okay. Arann, who didn't sign much, nodded.

But it wasn't, and they both knew it.

"A week," Jay said. She'd picked up a couple of slates, dropped one of them in Teller's lap and set the other in her own. Her hair, slightly red with the sun the way it always was at the end of the summer, she'd shoved off her forehead by tying a cloth band just beneath it. It wasn't holding. In the humidity of the warmer seasons, nothing kept that hair in place.

And even if it had, she'd have pulled it half out by shoving her hair out of her eyes. She always did, even if it wasn't in her eyes to start with.

"I can go down to the docks," Angel said.

Teller cringed slightly, but said nothing.

Jay even started to say no, but stopped herself. "For what?"

"Loading. Unloading. There's always work there, while the port's open."

"More work than at the Common?"

Angel nodded.

"What kind of work?"

"Moving boxes, mostly. Moving cargo."

"They don't have their own people for that?"

"On ship, they have some; they sometimes pick up hires to speed things up. It's busy, this time of year."

"Only lifting?"

"More or less."

Arann watched. Arann knew how her father had died. "I'll go," he said. "I'll go with Angel."

Angel said nothing, waiting. After a minute, Jay nodded. "Carver?"

He looked up. Shook his head.

"Not yet," she told him softly. "We're not that desperate yet."

"We will be," was his quiet counter. "A week, Jay. If we're smart, we won't touch what's there."

"We don't have a choice."

"It's not cold yet," he added, as if she hadn't spoken.

Even Lander and Lefty fell silent, hands dropping into their laps.

"But it will be. Having no money when it's warm isn't nearly as bad. Let me go back to some of my old haunts."

"No. You're not working this holding alone."

"I won't be alone. And it probably won't be in the twenty-fifth. This isn't where I camped, before."

She wanted to say no. Everything about her already did. But she held Carver's gaze, and he didn't look away. In the end, she did.

She nodded.

21st of Aeral, 410 AA
Twenty-fifth holding, Averalaan

Among the other things that came home with Carver and Duster on one of their foraging sprees was a deck of worn cards and four dice. "We left him his shoes," Carver added, when he emptied his satchel. "And his clothing."

If he meant this to be comforting, it wasn't. "Cards?" she asked.

He shrugged. Duster looked at him and snorted. "Wasn't my idea."

They did bring back money, though. It wasn't a large amount, but it would cover a day's worth of food.

The first night out, they'd come back with more, but Carver had also come back with bruises.

Angel and Arann came back with less, because even if the port was busy, it was still difficult to find people who would pay them. People who would agree to pay them once they'd done the work could be found—as they discovered to their great annoyance—with some ease. Getting the coin, however, was much harder. The Port Authority guards were not, after the fact, their friends.

Arann, however, was fascinated by the ships and their flags; he was fascinated by the Port Authority itself. He didn't care for the miles' worth of very tired and irritated people who often walked the docks on their way from those ships to the Authority building but, like Angel, he learned to stay out of their way. He was off in the corner now, talking to Lefty. Lefty, boxed in, was listening as Arann told him about the ships and asked him about ship words.

Which, of course, no one in the room actually knew. Not even Jay.

"We'll ask Rath," she told him, the third time he asked. "He'll probably know."

They were, by Teller's count, only a day and a half behind. Jay checked his numbers.

A week later, they were four days behind.

Two weeks later, and they were just barely even.

It was growing dark earlier, but the nights weren't cold; Jewel worked by magelight at the table, reading the same passages over and over again because she couldn't keep her mind on the words. Tomorrow, she thought, staring at Weston but seeing, instead, the blackened inside of an almost empty iron box.

She couldn't *do this*. She'd spent three years building a safe place, and it was going to crumble—was crumbling now.

For years, she'd been angry and upset at her father,

but she understood his death now. He *had* to work. Because if he didn't, this is what they would have faced.

This is what he would have faced, alone in the dark; he had no magestone, and every other form of light cost money. He hadn't believed her, when she'd warned him that he would never come back. But he hadn't wanted to believe either. Because if he failed to show up at work, they'd replace him, easily. And then he'd be *here*. With no money for rent. Or for food. And with a child who needed him to have both.

On the seventh day of Maran, the ninth month of the year, Jewel woke, went to the Common with what remained of their money, and then headed home in silence.

An hour later, she gathered her den, and in the same silence, the magestone in her pocket, they headed back to the undercity for the first time in months.

7th of Maran, 410 AA
Twenty-fifth holding, Averalaan

Angel and Arann went to the Port Authority. Carver and Duster went "out." Finch, Teller, Jester, Lefty, and Lander went with Jewel.

Duster made clear how much she hated this arrangement, and she and Jewel exchanged terse words, but in the end, Jewel wouldn't budge.

"We need what you bring in," she said, her voice flat. "Even if we find something, we won't have money from it for a week. Or two."

Carver had put his hand on Duster's shoulder. Duster shrugged it off. But she stopped speaking. "Take Angel," she finally said. "Or Arann. You'll find the cracks in the ground harder without 'em."

Jewel's brows had lifted in surprise. "I would," she finally said, "but we can't spare them. We need anything they can bring in, as well."

Duster stood, mute now. She was poised in the doorway, one foot over the threshold, frozen there; it was hard to tell, looking at her, whether she was coming or going. Had she been anyone else, Jewel would have hugged her. She was Duster. Jewel raised her hands, not to touch, and not to push, but instead, to sign.

Duster hesitated, and then said, "Don't lose them."

The den watched her leave in silence.

7th of Maran, 410 AA
Undercity, Averalaan

There was no sky in the undercity. No sea breeze, tasting, always, of salt. No moving maze of people. No light that wasn't theirs. Jewel held the magelight as they emerged into the streets. Familiar streets, opening up into the darkness of perpetual night.

They walked in a huddle, and this slowed their progress, but that was fine. The undercity had become strange with absence, and unknown with Fisher's loss. Everything—every step, every hushed word—was hesitant. Even Jewel's.

But the hesitance couldn't last.

With each step and each word, a little bit of confidence returned. Teller pointed at familiar facades, Lander and Lefty signed, poking each other when their gaze wandered from the moving flight of den-sign that was their hands.

"Where do you want to start?" Teller asked.

Jewel frowned. She didn't want to start exploring the uncharted areas of the undercity, but all the ones they knew had nothing to offer; they'd been over them, time and again. "Let's head to the center. We can decide from there."

The center of the undercity—which was, as far as Jewel could tell from her study of Rath's maps, an accurate description—was where the larger roads met. Some of those roads were wide, and buildings, stepped back from flat, smooth rock, girded their progress. She thought grass or flowers or even trees must have grown near the building fronts at some point, because there was dirt in evidence; none of the foliage remained. Some of those roads were impassable; bridges had fallen across them.

At least Rath had called them bridges; they were *also* stone, and Jewel couldn't understand why you'd build a stone bridge above the streets. But apparently, the people who lived here had thought it was a good idea to never touch the ground.

Teller knew more, because he asked more questions, and because Rath actually liked talking to him; he told Jewel and Finch that Rath thought the original buildings on some of these roads had been taller than *Avantari*, the palace of Kings. Taller, he added, than the Cathedrals. But wider. The bridges that had fallen had crossed from the heights of one structure to another.

Thinking about the number of steps you'd have to climb several times a day just to reach those heights made Jewel sneeze. She wondered if that's where the poorest of the people lived, way back. She'd asked Rath once and he'd laughed, which had set her teeth on edge. She'd been younger.

"No, Jay," he'd replied, using her preferred name the way he generally did when other members of the den were present. "I think we can safely assume that only the very, very wealthy, and the very, very powerful, lived at the heights of this city."

"But *why*? They want to run up and down a mile's worth of stairs every single time they need water or food?"

"I imagine," he replied dryly, "that they would pay other people money to do it for them."

"They'd have to come down sometime."

"Oh, indeed. But I think that's where the bridges would have been useful, or even necessary."

"How do you even *know* they're bridges?"

"I don't. But the maps that you found suggest levels to the city; they would either have to descend into basements, or climb. And some of the fallen stone is not architecturally consistent with the style of the facades of actual buildings. In my explorations," he added, which Jewel knew far outstripped her own, even three years later, "I've found nothing to suggest that basements were used as a tunnel system.

"There was wealth, in this city," he added softly, "and power. Never doubt that there was power."

Power enough, apparently, to build huge stone bridges that collapsed across buildings and roads, making them completely impassable. Jewel swore that if she ever possessed that elusive thing called power, she was *not* going to waste it on something so stupid.

"And what, then, would you waste it on?" Rath had asked, that annoying half smile on his face. It wasn't a smirk, or she wouldn't have answered.

"A bigger place for us," she replied. "Food. Clothing."

"Haval's expensive clothing?"

"No, *real* clothing. And good boots. And better daggers. Oh! And magestones. For everyone. And solarii for Farmer Hanson. And—"

He lifted a hand. "Enough, Jay. Enough. One day, you'll have those things, and you might—just might—be required to waste money on the things you don't want and think you don't need."

"Why?"

"Because to others, it will signify power. Your power," he added. "And they will therefore treat you with more care."

"Or try to kill you," Teller added.

They both turned to look at him. "Well," he added, "that's what always happens in your books."

Rath's smile had faded, although his expression hadn't changed. "Yes," he'd said softly.

Jewel avoided fallen bridges. She'd traveled to the center of this city often enough that she knew how to jog around the wide, main streets where the roads vanished beneath the weight of too many kinds of rock.

"There's more stone than there used to be here," Teller said quietly, when they'd made their second detour.

Jewel looked at the road. She couldn't see any difference. But she didn't *want* to see one either, and his words settled into her stomach like bad meat. "You're sure?"

He nodded. "And the cracks are wider in places as well."

Lefty snorted. "Tell me about it." And then fell silent. Lander touched his shoulder and Lefty looked automatically at his hands. The hands were still. After another quiet pause, Lefty nodded at Lander.

It reminded Jewel—as if she needed a reminder—why she loved these people. She smacked Lefty on the back of the head. "Let's go," she told him.

They reached the center of the city. It was obvious in part because the roads seemed to converge to meet here, and in part because of the statue. Well, what remained of a statue. Its base was large enough that the whole den could line up against one of its square sides, end to end, with plenty of room to the right and left. The statue's lower torso and legs were still attached to the base; Jewel had no idea how tall they were because they couldn't really climb the statue's base without a lot of effort; it was just too damn tall.

The remains of the upper half of the statue lay strewn along the ground for some distance. They examined every single piece, hoping for some gold leaf or gems they could pick out, but had no luck.

Mixed in with the slabs and chunks of broken stone was always a smattering of glass; it caught light, and the reflections glittered across the surface of otherwise dim and solid ground, hinting at riches and delivering small wounds, instead.

Teller looked at Jewel, and Jewel caught herself before she could shrug. People were tentative, now, and that was fair—she had to resist the urge to count them every time they stopped moving.

"Let's head this way." She started walking. Teller fell in to her right, and Finch to her left; Lander, Lefty, and Jester walked behind. Footsteps were like heartbeats, constant, steady, and slow. Where rock lay in their path, those steps stopped and shifted as the light shifted. Here and there, Jewel stopped when something glinted on the ground ahead. Glass or no, they couldn't afford not to look.

Whole days had been spent in this rhythm, hours in the darkness while streetside the sun slowly sank; whole days of work, knees against rubble and feet against rock, backs bent to move larger pieces to one side or the other. There was swearing because, inevitably, someone failed to move those larger pieces far enough to one side, and there was muted laughter or chuckling. Even Lander talked while they worked.

The den fanned out around the radius of light, kneeling, standing, moving a foot or two every few minutes, working carefully and deliberately.

"That's my spot."

"I was here first."

Jewel grimaced, but the grimace relaxed into a smile. She knew who'd spoken, but it didn't matter; echoes of the voices of every single one of her den could be heard in those words if you knew how to listen. She let them scuffle; as long as there was no actual shoving, it didn't matter.

They moved when she called a halt, heading slowly down the road. Most of the streets closest to the city center were covered in rubble. But not all; when the streets became smooth again, they could see facades of old buildings, most of which vanished because the light cast by the magestone couldn't chase them that far.

Buildings were often tricky, but this close to the center, the floors could generally be trusted not to buckle. Jewel whispered the light up, and walked, slowly, toward the nearest one.

It was fronted, as so many of them were, by the frame—the stone frame—of a door. Standing to either side of that frame, were statues. They were only as tall as Arann in height, which was taller than anyone present, and they stood on small, square pedestals. Teller walked closer to one, and reaching out, touched the cracks that had appeared in the rigid drape of long robes.

"You think this was a temple?" he asked quietly. He glanced at the face of the statue; it was a woman's face, her hair bound above her head. She looked neither down nor up, but instead, off into the distance, her expression the serene, empty expression of stone. Her arms were at her sides—the gown was sleeveless—and her palms were turned toward the den.

"I don't know. It's not the first place I've seen statues, but most of the outdoor ones are broken."

He nodded, and reached out to place his palm across her left hand.

Jewel caught his wrist before stone and skin made contact; he froze at once. This wasn't den-sign, but it was visceral.

"Jay?" Finch asked.

"Don't touch them," she said quietly.

Teller lowered his hand without flinching. "Magic?" he asked her.

"Maybe. I can't tell if it's the stone or the magelight, but there's something orange around her hands. I don't think it was there before you approached her." She no longer asked if the den saw what she saw; she knew. "Let's skip this one."

They nodded and withdrew, following Jay, although Teller cast a backward glance at the statue. They had always fascinated him; they were evidence of those who had long since abandoned this city, one way or the other. Carver had pointed out that everything was evidence—the buildings, the streets, the big damn piles of rubble—but Jewel understood why it wasn't the same. Carver didn't.

Carver wasn't here.

"Come on," she said. "There's another quarry ahead." It wasn't really a quarry, but that's what they often called the largest of the debris piles.

It had started so well.

She'd been so nervous, heading back into the darkness that had devoured Fisher whole. They had come down the chute so carefully, it almost felt like the first time—but the first time, she'd had Rath, and he *knew* the undercity.

She could remember that day so clearly, on this one. The first time she had touched the walls of the tunnels. The first time she had seen the stone walks that Rath said were probably the remnants of an old cloister or a courtyard. The Stone Garden. She didn't walk that path on the last day she would ever see the undercity.

She walked a path less traveled.

Her den was around her, or all of it that wasn't streetside, looking, in their own ways, for money. She watched them as she worked, moving stone with her feet while she held the magestone aloft. She heard their grunts, their whispers, the grind of stone against stone as they braced themselves on things that wouldn't quite bear their weight. She heard their calls for light, or for more light, and responded with the ease of long practice.

She felt, for a moment, at home again. This place had been theirs, and some part of it still was.

And she should have known, then.

She should have remembered that home is something to strive for, but nothing to rely on. Hadn't her mother, her Oma, and her father, gone, one person at a time, taking warmth and sound with them? In their wake, the familiar rooms, the old crates, even the walls, had moved beyond her, while she was standing in place. She should have known.

But she'd had warning, then, hadn't she?

Her mother's illness, her cough, her pale, sallow skin, her voice, harsh and quiet at the same time. Her Oma, in winter, still struggling to light her pipe, to sit in her chair, to be *of use* in the last hours remaining to them. And her father, who listened to responsibility and duty—who listened to his fear, for her, and for himself, in a city bereft of any other family.

She should have *known*.

Never trust the gods. Never trust a gift. Never trust a curse.

They worked, in the darkness. They chattered. They argued. They came up empty, but that had happened before, and when Jewel called a halt, they stretched, brushed stone dust off their clothing, and made their way to the exit, following the light she held. It took less time to leave than it had to find a site to search, but that was normal, too.

"We'll come back tomorrow," she told them, as they left the larger walks for the small tunnels and crawl spaces that led streetside.

She was wrong.

The tunnels narrowed. They always did, this close to the streets. The den walked single file, their words bouncing off cool stone, their hands brushing the same surface. Teller and Finch passed ahead of her so that the light could remain somewhere in the middle of the moving line.

But the light stopped as she did, shifting slightly as she turned to look back at the other three.

Lander. Jester. Lefty.

She forgot to breathe.

Lander. Jester.

They saw her face, her chin brightest because it was closest to the source of light. Everyone looked pale, in that light.

Jester saw her expression, and Jester turned first. Lander almost ran into her. But he saw what Jester had seen, and he turned as well.

No one was following them.

Her hand closed in a red fist. Jester and Lander flattened themselves against the nearest wall as she walked past them, smothering the light they all needed. She was breathing; she must have been breathing. But she couldn't feel air pass her lips. She couldn't feel anything except the silence. Not even her boots against cracked stone made enough noise to reach her ears. She walked, following the tunnel, aware, peripherally, of when it fell away and she stood on the border of the actual city proper.

Standing there, in the windless, sunless silence, she forced her fingers to uncurl. Light, then. Small, diffuse, insignificant light. All the shadows it might have cast were absorbed by the shadows that lived here.

She was dreaming. She must have been dreaming. And in the dream she could see, laid out against the impenetrable darkness of the undercity's sky, familiar ghosts: Lightning. The pause of storm. Thunder.

There were no clouds, here. No rain. No flash of the light that both illuminated and terrified. No sound at all.

No warning.

They came, then.

Finch. Teller. Jester. Lander.

They didn't touch her. They didn't speak. They stood almost as she was standing. Minutes passed. Jewel might have been a statue, much like the one she had told Teller not to touch, her arms locked in the habitual position that kept the magelight exposed. She couldn't breathe.

She didn't want to breathe.

Because if she did, if she *could,* she would have to talk.

And she knew, at this moment, in this darkness, that to get *to* words, she would have to get past what waited for breath, first: a scream. And if she started, here, it might never stop. It might go on and on and on, swallowing her words forever.

7th of Maran, 410 AA
Twenty-fifth holding, Averalaan

She screamed in the silence, waiting. In the apartment, sitting in her chair, the table flat beneath her forearms, her hair in her eyes. Shoulders slumped but tense, jaw locked. Waiting.

They had asked. She didn't remember the exact words because she didn't want to remember them. Lander had started forward into the darkness. Jewel had grabbed his shoulder, pulling him back. No words left her lips, but she lifted one hand, den-sign. *No.*

So many things she would never forget, and he added a new one: his face. His expression.

Lander, who loved sign, had picked up words instead, and they were wild, heavy words, carrying sudden and unexpected emotion into familiar channels: Confusion. Anger. Fear.

He had shouted at her, and she had stood, like stone, in the rain of words, watching him, pale, his body shaking with too many things. And still, one-handed, she signed, *no*.

He had *hit* her, shoved her, both hands palm out; he had grabbed the front of her shirt, jostling the magestone from the cup of her palm. It fell, rolling between her feet and beyond them, and she, who knew the importance of light in this place, had let it.

Finch had bent, retrieving it before it traveled on ahead.

Jewel said nothing. Just that silent *no*.

And Lander said everything that Jewel couldn't. Everything that she would have said, if she could. *We have to find Lefty! We have to go now! Don't you even care?* All words were scattered, lost, like beads when their necklace string has snapped; she'd find them again later, but finding them? They'd never be the same.

So she absorbed his words instead, and only his. No one else spoke.

Why didn't you warn *us? Why didn't you* see?

Flinching, as she had not flinched then, she lowered her head to her forearms, settling in to wait.

Because Arann would be home. Not soon, but it wasn't dark yet. He would walk through the door, with Angel in tow. He would walk into *this* room, into their home, and he would know, instantly, that *there was no Lefty*.

He would never say what Lander had said.

He would never raise his hand against her. He would ask her if they could go searching, as they'd searched for Fisher, and she would tell him no. And he would know that the person he cared most about in this godsdamned world was *gone*.

Lefty and Arann.

Arann and Lefty. The two boys that Farmer Hanson had worried about. The first of her den. The first to trust her. To help her. To bring people noises into the empty and silent life she'd led at Rath's.

Why had she brought them here?

Why had she promised she could keep them?

So that she could sit here, in the waning light, to tell Arann that he had trusted her with Lefty and she had utterly betrayed that trust?

What she had not been willing to do for Fisher, she did now, her face hidden by her sleeves and the distance the others kept. She wept. Because she had to be done with tears before Arann arrived; she had no *right* to them. Like anything else in life, they had to be *earned*.

Chapter Nine

R ATH SURVEYED THE CROWDED ROOMS
that had been opened, by Lord Cordufar, to his
various associates in the Merchant Authority, on one
pretext or another. The pretext itself? The presentation,
to the Averalaan patriciate, of Lord Cordufar's niece, a
young woman Rath had never seen, and had heard of
only when the announcement of this particular ball had
caused Haval several sleepless nights. Haval, aware of
Rath's interests, and aware, as well, of Rath's intent, had
seen fit to bring it to his attention.

"By all accounts," Haval had said, "Everyone who is
anyone will be in attendance."

"The Kings?"

Haval's frown was brief. "Not the Kings, of course, and
not The Ten, although I would be surprised if at least a few
of The Ten do not make an appearance. Lord Cordufar has
spared little expense, if gossip is to be believed."

"Do you believe it?"

"If one tenth can be believed, it is still impressive."

"I will have to inquire into this ball."

Haval, needle between his lips, had nodded and
reached for a bead.

* * *

Rath, true to his word, had begun his inquiries, but they were not expansive. Indeed, they started—and stopped—in the house of one man.

It was Lord Cordufar's duty as host to personally greet each of his many guests as they arrived. They were announced, as a matter of form, when they entered the exquisitely decorated grand foyer of the Cordufar manse. Some houses, built for entertainment in a bygone era, had been constructed with an eye to exactly that announcement and presentation, and new arrivals—the timing being specifically spaced—would be announced only once they had reached the height of either stairs or balcony.

The Cordufar manse did not boast either of these social niceties, and the balconies that did exist did not have the requisite stairs from which one might descend into the crowd. Here, the ballroom on the level with the dining chambers, the great room, and the well-oiled wood of the reception rooms, he was forced to make do.

He had done so flawlessly. He was not possessed of any notable charm; there was nothing light or socially assured in the way he gripped—or kissed—a hand. But he exuded the confidence of wealth, or more precisely, power, and this was seldom without its attraction.

He was a man of middle age, but it was an age that suggested that youth was callow and untried; his hair had not significantly paled with the passage of time, and the width of his heavy frame was girded entirely by muscle. To the eye.

His son at his side, and his guards—in gray livery—as attendants, he offered his thanks to each and every man, woman, and not-quite-child who crossed his threshold. This was, as Rath remembered from his youth, quite tedious. He approached Lord Cordufar quietly, in the midst of Hectore of Araven's many sisters, children, and grandchildren. Andrei was present as an attendant, and not as a guest; he was therefore free to observe, although his observation was, as expected, silent.

But Rath was not there as a servant; neither had

he come as one of Araven's extended family. When his name was announced, at the end of all of theirs, he stepped forward.

"Ararath of Handernesse," Lord Cordufar said, extending his hand.

Rath took it smoothly; it was adorned by rings, that would, on any other hand, seem a sign of vanity and ostentation. Rath noted them because he was used to noting objects of value.

"Lord Cordufar," he replied, offering an expert bow.

"Something about your House Name is familiar."

"Perhaps." Rath forced himself to smile. "I am frequently far from home, and I have just returned. My godfather seeks to indulge me and perhaps reacquaint me with the joy that is Averalaan society."

"A worthy man," Lord Cordufar replied, bowing in turn. When he rose, his eyes were narrow, and a flicker of darkness etched its way across the triangles of the whites.

"Indeed."

"If you come with his recommendation," Lord Cordufar added, "I will be duly impressed. Enjoy the hospitality of Cordufar. Perhaps if we make your stay worthwhile, we will have the pleasure of your company at a less . . . crowded event."

Rath was prepared for his smile, and did not react to it in any way. "I cannot say, for certain, how long I will remain in Averalaan, but perhaps I will accept your offer." His own smile, offered in precisely the same manner as Lord Cordufar's, accompanied his last words. "I believe we have much to discuss, you and I."

Lord Cordufar had attempted to use no magic. Had he, Rath would have known—Rath and everyone standing in the foyer. Andrei had insisted that Rath wear something protective; Rath had insisted that it was not required. Hectore, coming in midway, had insisted that Rath accommodate Andrei's request, even if he had failed to actually *hear* it.

If Rath had been a better man, he would have failed

to bring this to Andrei's attention; he was not. He was, however, a cautious man, and contented himself with one long glance and the lift of a single brow once they were quit of their host.

Andrei answered in kind, entirely unflustered. His expression suggested that the evening—which promised to be long—was not yet close to over.

Rath conceded the point with a grimace; half of the guests, if that, had arrived, and there would be a long and interminable reception for each and every one before dining and dancing were even considered.

The time he had spent in the past year at the side of Sigurne Mellifas often made him remember—and regret—the choices he had made in his angry youth. Occasions of this nature, however, merely reaffirmed them. Rath glanced once at the guards to either side of the large and open arch that led from the foyer into the great hall. From above, to the right and left, were shallow galleries, and beneath those, tapestries and paintings. The pillars that traversed the hall to the left had been adorned with sculptures that suggested that delicate, graceful stone hands held the roof above them. The roof itself? Rounded, corniced near the pillars.

The floors were not carpeted; they were a dark, stained wood. There was very little in this hall that muffled sound, and therefore, there was a good deal of it. Here, nestled against the walls, were long benches and chairs at which those weary of the standing crowds in the great chamber and the rooms beyond might sit a moment in privacy. They were not, now, in use, but they would be before the evening's end.

Rath paused in front of one painting, his hands behind his back.

"It's a Lauvelin," Hectore pointed out.

Rath nodded. "But an unusual subject, for Lauvelin."

"I think," Hectore added, coming close enough to touch the large stretch of canvas, "that this is one of his youthful pieces. It has, at any rate, that feel."

It did. Raw, red, ugly: Lauvelin's war. He had painted only a handful of such pieces that had escaped into the world; he was known for the quality of his use of both light and shadow, and very little of the former was in evidence here. Here, Rath thought, was the eye of a soldier, and indeed, the dead that littered the field as far as the eye could see had only the faintest hint of the markings that would have identified which banners they had come to the field under.

Cloth was stained, its color lost; arms, limbs, the unattached parts of the dead, had fallen in just such a way that they could almost entirely obscure crests. The standards flew, proclaiming the leadership of two armies, but they flew only over the dead, like carrion birds.

"He knew war," Rath said softly.

"Yes. But in the end he chose to make his name bringing to light the things that war does not touch. Beauty, in all its guises." Andrei's voice. "It is a lesson," he added quietly, "that we would do well to learn."

"And yet," Rath replied, knowing full well the range of Lauvelin's luminescent work: his children, his women, his young men bursting with pride or shadowed, a moment, with worry in the bustle of life; his flowers, his vases, the odd flash of flight in his birds and butterflies. "Much of that is also extinguished, in the end, by unchecked war."

"Yes. But in some small way, that is why we fight, even if we do not, in the end succeed."

"Fight? I think, rather, that is why *they* die."

"And is that different? They die, if you prefer, to preserve the things that they hope war will not touch."

"If they knew, for certain, that they would face death—and at that, an unpleasant, undignified, ugly death—they might never march at all."

"Perhaps. But if they knew, if they could know, that one life, or if you prefer, one death could turn the tide of the battle?"

Rath glanced at Andrei. His expression, his unblinking regard, was entirely unfamiliar.

"Come, Ararath, Hectore has already all but left us behind."

*   *   *

Rath stood by the long, open arch between the great room and the great hall, at the end of which, on a gleaming, dark stage, musicians played and sang. He recognized only one: the youngest master bard of Senniel College.

As the gathering was meant to impress the various Cordufar merchants and their associates, Lord Cordufar had extended the hospitality of his home in as wide a circle as a man of his rank could, with any dignity, do. Among the associates Cordufar claimed was one of The Ten: The Darias, otherwise known as Archon to those who held him in no high regard, holding court to the left of the stage. If Rath had still had a place among the patriciate, he would nonetheless have been unable to identify The Darias on sight; Handernesse had never been of enough consequence to merit visits to, or from, The Ten.

But he recognized The Darias from description, if nothing else: an autocratic man at the edge of his prime, gray streaks showing in the brown of his hair. Not more than six feet in height, he nonetheless dominated the small crowd that had gathered around him. He wore the muted colors of House Darias: russet, brown, and gold. They did not entirely suit his coloring.

"Ararath?" his companion said quietly.

Rath glanced at Hectore of Aravan. "I did not realize The Darias himself would be in attendance this eve. It must have been difficult indeed to arrange an invitation on my behalf."

Hectore smiled. "No. I am, after all, one of the merchant houses which Cordufar desires to impress. And he clearly desires to impress, this eve; The Darias is not the most significant of the luminaries you will see in attendance."

"Senniel's master bard?"

"Very good. But it is not the bard to whom I refer."

Rath raised a brow, and Hectore laughed again, pausing only to relieve an overburdened servant of both drink and food. The servant paused in front of Rath, and Rath shook his head slightly.

"Ararath," Hectore said, "the vintage is excellent. Even Andrei would approve."

"I note, however, that the inestimable Andrei is not partaking."

Hectore raised a brow. "He, like any good servant, does not drink while working."

Rath nodded, scanning the crowd. It spilled out into three or four rooms. His brows drew together slightly, which, in Rath, was as much an expression of surprise as he ever showed.

Hectore smiled, greatly pleased with himself. "You've seen Guildmaster Gilafas of the Makers' Guild."

"Indeed."

Gilafas ADelios was commonly referred to as the most powerful man—outside of the Kings and The Ten—in Averalaan. He was not particularly handsome, and neither young nor old; he was not particularly fit, but his body had not yet surrendered to age or gravity. He wore his hair, which was not yet white, in a long braid at his back. His clothing was very, very fine, and he wore it with the indifference—the casual indifference—that marked the very wealthy. Its colors were a rich, deep burgundy, with traces of gold and silver along the hems, but he had forgone jacket for the more stately robes of the elder gentleman.

As he was not a terribly forbidding man, he was surrounded by men and women whom Rath did not recognize. He did not look entirely *pleased* to have garnered this attention, but bore it well.

"I can count the number of times that Master Gilafas accepts invitations that require him to leave the guildhalls on one hand," Hectore added. "Lord Cordufar has outdone himself, this eve."

"As you say, Hectore."

The patris of Araven raised an iron brow. "Ararath, I have not asked you what your business here is, but conduct it less obviously."

Rath offered his godfather the lightest of smiles. "As you say. Will there be dancing, this eve?"

"No doubt," Hectore replied with a grimace. "Which

will please my wife and daughters to no end. And my granddaughters, if truth be told." He smiled, and added, "All but the youngest. You should spend some time with her, Ararath. She would meet with your approval, I've little doubt."

"I have the greatest of respect for all of your family."

"Yes, yes." He raised a hand before Rath's attempt at polite praise could leave his lips. "Don't overdo it. I'll leave you with Andrei," he added, "because I see my lovely wife's expression, and I believe it indicates that I am being neglectful."

"Take Andrei."

"No." He turned to his servant. "If Ararath desires trouble, make certain that he does not receive it at *this* event."

Andrei bowed. They watched in silence as Hectore made his way through the crowd, skirts parting and circling as women and girls moved to one side or another without pausing to see who had passed them.

"He is concerned for you," Andrei said quietly.

Rath nodded. "I would have spared him the worry."

"Indeed. It is perhaps one of the reasons why he still values you so highly. Ah," he added, seeing the waves of brightly colored cloth ripple as the crowd parted once more. "I forget myself."

Rath allowed himself a small smile of recognition as he saw who now approached. He bowed, and it was both perfect, formal, and exactly the correct gesture to offer the woman who appeared in the small gap left by two men.

"Member Mellifas."

She inclined her head, smiling. She walked with a cane in one hand, and it, like the woman whose hand rested upon its polished brass handle, was practical. No carvings adorned its length, and no jewels had been imbedded in metal and offered for the ostentation of such a fine gathering. Yet it was not poorly made, and the wood itself was dark and hard.

She would never have been one for the very fine, and very daring, court dresses whose styles changed,

314 ◆ Michelle West

year after year. Even in her youth, he could not imagine those dresses in her wardrobe, never mind on her person. No; she wore the gray robes of her chosen profession, and although they were of a fine cloth, they were edged in neither gold nor silver. She wore shoes that were not, perhaps, practical in the confines of a tower with narrow, winding steps as the only method of entrance—or exit—but these were the only obvious concession to the occasion.

Sigurne, like Master Gilafas ADelios, was not known for attendance at events of this nature. But unlike the Maker, Rath understood some part of why Sigurne chose to be present.

"Is Member APhaniel present?" he asked, as he rose from his bow.

"He is, indeed. I am not entirely sure where he has gone," she added, "but he is often like that at gatherings that seem official in nature."

"Meaning?"

"He chafes under their tedium."

Rath laughed, and the sound almost startled him. "I thought he might be here in attendance."

"Mine?" She shook her head. "Matteos is here. He has, however, gone in search of wine or sweet water, and I fear that he will have some difficulty locating me."

Rath, smiling, offered her his arm.

She accepted, of course. But as she did, she slid a hand into her robes—the advantage of such a volume of cloth being that they could both contain and hide much. "Come," she said. "Lord Cordufar has coaxed the youngest of Senniel's master bards out for the evening, and I would like to hear him sing."

"He can make himself heard to the Isle," Rath replied.

"Very well. I would like to *see* him sing, if that is possible in this crowd."

"It is, indeed, Member Mellifas. Very well. Let us go and stand in discreet awe of Senniel College." He turned to Andrei. "Will you accept the escort of Sigurne

Mellifas as a guaranty of my good behavior and return to my godfather's side?"

Andrei's smile was slight. "As you wish. But be cautious, Ararath, if that is in you this eve." Andrei knew well that were there to be trouble in the vicinity of any of the Magi, blame would be laid at the feet of the Order, regardless of who had actually started it.

"Cautious? We merely seek closer proximity to the master bard."

It was harder done than said.

Kallandras of Senniel was enormously popular with the young ladies. He was, however, enormously popular with the older ones as well, and if the young men who hoped to make an impression on either of these formidable groups resented the ease with which the bard commanded their regard, they were wise enough not to show it. The charm and the diffidence for which Kallandras was famed was turned wholly toward his music at the moment, although bards were seldom called upon to sing during either the dinner or the following dance itself.

And bards, unlike servants and guards, were expected to socialize when they were not singing; they were expected to eat, drink, and if the occasion called for it, dance.

Sigurne sighed a moment, and turned to her companion. "Have you seen Lord Cordufar's mistress?"

"No. She is striking enough that were you to see her, you would know."

Sigurne raised a delicate brow. "Will she be present?"

"I cannot say with certainty. But in a gathering of this size? I think it likely."

"She concerns you."

"At the moment," he said softly, "she concerns me less than Lord Cordufar, even given the dreams."

"You spoke with him."

"Briefly."

"Your impression?"

"He is dangerous." He gestured toward the stage. "I believe we might have an opening, if you still desire it." He offered her his arm, and she took it. "I admit I had not expected to see you here, this eve."

"I did not expect to accept the invitation," she replied carefully, "but given our current concerns, Member APhaniel wished to be in attendance. I believe," she added, "that he will be offending some minor noble in a corner somewhere; Meralonne is not easily confined in a setting of this nature."

Rath raised a brow.

"It is true. He is irritable, and often irritating, in equal measure. He is seldom as serious about titles and wealth as most of the patriciate require when they seek the service of a mage. He can be brusque beyond bearing, even among the mages." She stopped walking and turned to him. "But I admit that I have seldom seen him so focused or so driven as he has become in these last few weeks. He is almost a different man."

"Oh?"

"He reminds me of the Meralonne I met in my youth."

He remembered how they had met, and nodded. "If you fear—"

She glanced at his face, and then turned, quietly, in the direction of his gaze. A woman had entered the room. She was tall, for a woman, and clearly unconcerned with her height; she wore it in the bold and easy way the Northern men might. Her hair was one long drape of sleek black, straight from head to knees. She wore a deep blue gown, and it was edged in red and black; the gown was long, with a demitrain, and it was fitted as if it were skin. Her shoulders were exposed, and a thick gold chain circled her neck. But it was her eyes that caught, and held, attention; they were a brown so dark, they seemed all pupil.

"So," Sigurne said wearily.

Rath looked back to the head of the Order of Knowledge with some difficulty.

"Come, Ararath," the Magi said. "We would do well to be away."

He allowed himself to be led. "It is hard to believe," he told Sigurne, recovering his voice, "that such a woman could be hidden away at any man's pleasure."

"It is," was the quiet reply. "And yet, she was. She is not hidden now," Sigurne added.

"No. Perhaps she no longer feels she must be."

"Which tells us much, and none of it to my liking."

It was not to the liking of any woman present. Rath, well aware of the ways in which jealousy and envy could color a crowd, watched in quiet fascination as this woman—he could barely bring himself to think of her as a demon, although he knew it for truth—made her way through the great room, pausing a moment here or there to speak. He could not hear her voice at this remove, but he could *feel* it; had he still been young, he would have been drawn across the floor in fascination, like a moth to fire.

He grimaced. Were it not for Sigurne, he would, youth or no, be drawn to her regardless. Even knowing.

The men who did not, however, turned to her as she approached, even if she approached from behind; they were aware of her presence, and aware, as Rath was aware, of the promise implied by presence alone. The rest of the women, young and old, were aware of the sudden lack of their own. Talk shifted and died, souring in places as many of the younger women retreated.

"No," Rath said quietly. "If she has ever been frightened at the thought of discovery, she knows little fear now."

"She is bold, and I fear that it will not be to Lord Cordufar's liking."

"Perhaps. But in claiming her," Rath replied, scanning the crowd for some glimpse of said lord, "he will underline his own power and wealth. Ah. There he is. And I would say, Sigurne, that I owe you an apology. He is not well pleased by the presence of his mistress."

Lord Cordufar, trailing various guests, came to stand beside the tall, arresting woman. Rath did not think her beautiful, although in any natural sense of the word, she was. Commanding, striking, undeniably attractive, yes. But these were also accolades he might offer to the Generals of the Southern armies; there was something about that woman that reminded him of those men. She was—obviously—alive, but it was not life, in the end, that moved her.

Lord Cordufar, however, did. He caught her elbow firmly in his left hand, and the silk of her sleeve dimpled with the force of the grip, even at the distance that Rath had chosen to maintain. Or, if he were being entirely truthful, that Sigurne had chosen for him. He could not hear what passed between these two, but it was not short, and judging by expressions alone, it was not pleasant.

One or two of the men to whom she'd been speaking raised brows, and poured their own words into what was barely conversation. The woman glanced at them, and then at Lord Cordufar's hand. He removed it, but slowly, silk running through his fingers. She smiled, then, and the expression was exquisite. Reaching out, she cupped the cheek of one of the men who had so clearly interceded on her behalf. He was not by any means a young man, certainly old enough to know better, but regardless, his face flushed in the light, which produced another smile from her.

And another few words from Cordufar. Whatever he had chosen to say this time, she heeded, but it was not to her liking. She did not pout or flirt or play the fool— these things, Rath thought, were, and would remain, beneath her. But she bowed to them all, spoke again, and smiled with just a hint of regret, before she turned and joined her lord. It was a subtle regret—but even so, one that could be seen halfway across the room with ease.

Rath, who had never been possessed of Jewel's talent, nonetheless felt a momentary chill as he watched the man she had graced with the touch of her palm.

"Ararath?"

"I do not think that man will survive the evening," he said quietly. He folded his hands behind his back.

"Do not," she warned him, "draw those here."

"As you say, Sigurne." He forced his hands back to his sides. "But it is not clear to me, at this remove, who is lord here."

"No," she replied, "and that is interesting. But I confess some curiosity about the Cordufar family; I wonder if the picture galleries are open."

The picture gallery was, indeed, open. Of the varied galleries that framed the courtyard, it was the longest, and the windows were the most ornate; they balanced, in some ways, the visual pull of the framed portraits that ran the length of the hall. Between the larger windows were small, functional ones, and these were open; neither, at this time of night, provided illumination, and Rath regretted the hour of the day, because he thought the sunlight, seen through colored glass, would underscore both the colors of the house, and the gallery itself.

Still, in a mansion of this size, light could always be provided by other means. The wall sconces were decorative; the magelights were imbedded between the exposed beams of the ceiling above.

The gallery was by no means empty, but it was sparsely populated, and the conversations that the paintings invoked were muted.

Matteos Corvel had finally found Sigurne as she and Rath headed out of one set of open doors toward the gallery, and he joined them silently. Rath smiled, however, at his expression; he was clearly not a man who was comfortable in crowds of gaily dressed and well-decorated people. Rath surrendered Sigurne's arm with a pang of regret; Matteos Corvel assumed his position like a starving man who has just found food.

Rath noted, however, that he had failed to find water, and smiled.

Sigurne, therefore, led. It was almost comforting to follow her, in part because any conversation that was in any way delicate could be made inaudible to inconvenient eavesdroppers. There was enough base magic on the grounds in lights alone that the use of such minor magic itself would go unnoticed, and even if it did not, the magic was of a legal variety.

They walked the length of the hall, noting the artists where the artists were noteworthy, and noting the family resemblances where the artist was not. Sigurne paid particular attention to the portrait of the current Lord Cordufar's grandfather, standing in the midst of his sons. The sons, one of whom had reigned until he was almost eighty, were all dark-haired and dark-eyed, although the style of cut hair was outdated.

The son that had succeeded this man was represented by a portrait in which he stood alone, with no sons and no wife. "I think this is new," she said quietly.

"He was a striking man, in his prime." Rath noted the line of jaw, the prominence of brow, and the color of his eyes. "And his son is very much in the same mold."

"He is. The painting," she added softly, moving to the current Lord Cordufar, "does not do him justice."

"No. It captures likeness, however."

"It does. But his chin seems weaker, and the beard does not suit him."

"No, but he no longer has the beard."

"When was this painted, Ararath?"

Rath bent closer. "In 397."

"Which would be the year his father died."

Rath nodded. "What do you think, Sigurne?"

"I think you are correct in what you've surmised," she replied softly. "The man in this painting and the man in the great room? I think they look identical. But I would not be at all surprised if the current Lord Cordufar rose to the occasion of the title in a way that surprised almost everyone."

"He did," Rath said, staring at the portrait. Wondering, now, if the current lord's son was human.

As if she could hear the thought, Sigurne said, "but the heir is, at present, unpromising. Self-indulgent and wont to require money to resolve the issues that arise in his personal life."

"That," a familiar voice said, "is an unkind representation of my son."

Turning slightly, they saw that they had been joined by Lord Cordufar.

Sigurne had the grace to look embarrassed; she retreated into the posture of the old woman she claimed to be. But Rath saw her eyes, and the slight tightening of her lips, and he knew that she was now as watchful, or ready, as he had yet seen her. Matteos Corvel, however, looked as if he had turned to stone.

Lord Cordufar's smile was a work of art. It was genuine and it implied a softness or an amusement that, while it transformed his face, somehow failed to touch anything beyond it. "But perhaps it is true. Unkind words often are.

"The same, however, was said of me, in my youth, and I have, I think, disappointed my detractors."

Rath wondered, silently, how many of those detractors were now alive to regret their opinion. "Responsibility often transforms those who accept it," he said, instead.

"Oh, indeed. It transforms those who reject it as well." He turned to the portrait, standing in front of it as if it were a mirror. "Which of those, I wonder, are you, Ararath Handernesse?"

"Don't you know?" Rath replied.

"Based on your personal history, I would have assumed the latter." He glanced at Rath, and if the gesture itself was casual, the sudden sharpening of his eyes, the shift in expression, was not.

"It would be the safe assumption."

"No doubt," Lord Cordufar said. "And yet, here you are. I find it curious."

"Oh? What man would not wish to see Cordufar in all its glory? House Cordufar is not known for the frequency with which it opens its doors to society."

"Perhaps. Perhaps not. Times change, and people will change with them. Do you intend to return to your house?"

Rath, prepared for this, smiled. It was the practiced smile of the habitual liar, and it fit his face far more easily than Cordufar's attempt. "There are advantages," he said, "to be found in Handernesse at this time."

"There were advantages, surely, to be had in remaining with Handernesse, that you did not fully consider at the time."

"Perhaps. But Handernesse had not yet produced The Terafin. My sister and I," he added softly, allowing—forcing—truth to seep into his words, and losing, in the process, some of the finer control of his expression, "did not always see eye-to-eye, but we were close in our youth, and the estrangement, I regret to say, was, and has been, largely one-sided."

"Indeed? I regret that your sister did not see fit to accept our invitation."

"She is The Terafin. House Terafin is, as you are no doubt aware, the foremost of The Ten. Her duties seldom permit her the luxury of an evening such as this."

Lord Cordufar nodded. All pretense of the merely social had eroded; he was staring at Rath, as if by so doing, he could memorize every detail, every nuance. "And yet, you are here."

"I am not The Terafin, nor will I ever be. I have always been second to my sister in ambition, and I was content to live in her shadow."

"A long shadow."

"Indeed. Long and powerful. Even when she resided in Handernesse, and it was assumed she would take the reins of the House. But Handernesse is not Terafin, and its resources, not Terafin's."

"And you have approached your famed sister?"

"No."

"Ah." Lord Cordufar's smile was sharp edged and composed of teeth that were too white. "Perhaps you fear the estrangement is not as one-sided as you hope."

Rath frowned. It was a very slight frown, but it, too, was perfect. "Perhaps, in the upcoming months, you will discover the truth for yourself."

Lord Cordufar lifted a hand. "I mean no offense," he

said, the smile still curving his lips. "And hope that you will, when you visit your sister, remember the hospitality of this House."

"I am certain he will, my lord."

And there, at last, Lord Cordufar's mistress, a vision of blue, with streaks of red, black, and gold to lend color to the majesty of her skin. She walked like a conqueror, and she walked without fear.

Lord Cordufar's face lost the traces of smile, and he turned to look at the woman who had caused such a stir in the great room.

"Your pardon, my lord," she said, and she offered him a curtsy. It was not necessary, and might have been considered old-fashioned had it not been so deliberately provocative. "But you have spent much time in conversation, and your niece is waiting your announcement before your worthy guests can be seated for dinner."

"Indeed, I have been selfish," Lord Cordufar replied, "in my attempts to further the interests of this House."

"By talking?"

"Indeed." He turned to Rath. "Ararath Handernesse, may I introduce you to Sorna Shannen?"

She held out her hand, and Rath stared at it for a long moment. Then, reluctantly, he took it, and bent his head. He did not kiss the hand that was offered for just that purpose; the bow would have been considered enough, in most circles.

But her fingers tightened as he rose, and he felt the edge of nails press into his wrist before she released his hand. His hand was shaking at the contact, and if he could have ascribed the unsteadiness to something as simple as fear, he would have been comforted. It wasn't fear. He experienced, firsthand, what he had watched at a distance: the intoxication of her simple proximity.

"You are Ararath Handernesse?" she asked. Lord Cordufar came to stand by her side, but he did not touch her; he merely waited, watchful.

Rath nodded. After a moment—when he trusted his voice to convey words in a manner that did not reduce him in all eyes to a simpering boy—he spoke. "I am, and it is a pleasure to make your acquaintance." The words were as smooth and polished as Lord Cordufar's.

Sorna Shannen raised a soft brow. "You are gracious." Her voice was cool. But the smile that she allowed to change the shape of her mouth transformed her expression slowly. "And perhaps I see so little grace that I am unaccustomed to it. We can remedy this."

He bowed again, in part to force his eyes to leave her face. When he rose, he said, "I am not, unfortunately, as graceful as I should be. May I introduce my companions?"

Again her brow rippled. Lord Cordufar offered her his arm; she ignored it. "Please," she said coolly.

"This is Sigurne Mellifas. You may have heard of her."

"I don't believe I have."

"She is the titular head of the Order of Knowledge."

"I see." She did not look away from Rath. Rath, however, looked away from her. Sweat beaded his forehead, and he was afraid, for a moment, that the protections he wore against otherwise undetected use of magic would suddenly throw off both light and sound. They did not, and he took a steadying breath. "This is her aide, Matteos ACorvel. He is also a member in good standing of the Order."

He turned back to her, as if everything were entirely ordinary, or would be again. "It is very seldom that a mage of Sigurne's stature graces a purely social event; your lord is a very fortunate, and very influential ... patron."

"Oh, indeed." She smiled, and the smile was at once ice and fire.

"You are perhaps needed," Sigurne told Lord Cordufar. "I am an old woman, and I do not walk quickly, but we will of course return to the great room for your niece's presentation." She took the arm Rath offered. "Your niece, as your companion has pointed out, is waiting, as are your guests."

Sorna Shannen stood for a moment in the gallery,

the man to her side inconsequential. If Lord Cordufar had seemed forbidding—and he had, and dangerous as well—it was forgotten; she drew herself up to her full height, and her hair rippled down her thighs in a cascade that seemed to absorb both vision and light. Her skin was the white of a woman who has never known any labor not of her own choosing, but it was a white, as well, that suggested rage.

Rath thought she would speak, and she opened her mouth to do just that, but her jaws snapped shut. The sound was audible. She turned instead, her train swirling at the speed of the movement, and she stalked down the hall.

Even in the startling absence of grace or manners, Rath could not take his eyes off her until she had turned the corner and disappeared entirely from view.

Lord Cordufar's lips curled up in a smile that was, in its own fashion, as exquisite as Sorna Shannen's. He watched her leave, and then, turning to the Magi, bowed once, exactly. "I will, as you so gracefully remind me, return to my duties. Ararath," he added, "you are indeed an interesting man. I hope to see more of you in the near future."

Ararath bowed. It was not as smooth or precise a bow as he would have liked, for his gaze was still drawn to the now empty hall through which Sorna Shannen had walked. Lord Cordufar moved away, down the same hall.

Sigurne touched Rath's arm, then. "Ararath."

He shook himself and looked down at her.

"Be wary of her. It is as you surmised, I fear: she holds the reins here, even though Lord Cordufar is not human."

"What does that make her?"

"Among her kind? Powerful, if she can bind a demon who can assume and maintain the illusion of mortality. She is dangerous, and she is now aware—as is Lord Cordufar—of the opportunity you might afford them." She hesitated and then added, "I thought it was clumsily done, on your part."

He inclined his head in agreement.

"They are capable of subtlety, Ararath."

"They are. But they are capable of greed, as well. I do not think that I have harmed my cause, this eve; I think that I have furthered it."

"I think you have placed your life, and possibly the life of your godfather, in grave danger."

"There are," he replied, as he began to move, "worse ways to die, surely." His smile was slight and sardonic.

Hers was entirely absent.

Even before they had reached the great room, they became some part of it; the sound of speech, laughter, and the occasional unfortunate shout, carried into the gallery, surrounding them before they could see the crowd to which it belonged. Softening that noise was the sound of violins, or perhaps just one; the piece was difficult enough that it was hard, at first, to tell. It was, however, a modern piece; Rath did not recognize it. Was chagrined at the lack of recognition, and then at his reaction to his own ignorance.

"I admit," Sigurne said, in a louder voice than she would normally be forced to in quieter circumstances, "that I do not miss the crowds when I absent myself from such gatherings—but I regret the lack of music. The music," she added, "was one of the first things I discovered when I came to Averalaan. Meralonne invited me to attend Senniel's annual recital. I was not certain what to expect, and perhaps that was for the best.

"When I first began to study in the Order, I had enough time to frequent concerts, but I was not exposed to society in Averalaan until I rose in the ranks of the Magi. I was deemed suitably inoffensive, however, and when I had proven my worth—if such a proof can ever be accepted without constant testing by other members of the Order—I began to attend debuts such as this.

"They were like theater to me, then. Or perhaps spectacle. All of these men and women, dressed so very strangely, and at such obvious expense. We had nothing of this kind in my childhood, and looked for nothing of this kind when we were deemed adult.

"But in my early years as a mage, there were always stories, if one knew how to listen. There are stories here, tonight. There is no magic in them, but sometimes, faint and attenuated, the type of beauty which magic can never emulate." She smiled. "I feel my age."

Rath looked at the crowd that now surrounded them on all sides. He failed to see the beauty of which Sigurne spoke, but he had always failed to see it; even as a young boy, crouched between the banister rails at the side of his sister, Amarais, and stealing a glimpse of the glittering adult world, he had seen only the type of beauty that could be bought and put on display.

"Do you find her beautiful, Ararath?"

He glanced at Sigurne.

"Who?"

"Lord Cordufar's mistress."

He considered the question with far more care than he might have if the questioner had been any other woman. "I will answer," he said at last, "if you will also offer your opinion on the same matter."

She laughed then, and the sound of her laughter was so unexpected, it invoked an unfettered and entirely genuine smile in response. "My apologies, Ararath. I am not in my element in this particular arena, but I feel, given everything, that I *should* be. It makes me somewhat nervous, and in a First Circle mage, this is not considered a desirable state of mind.

"But I will answer. She is beautiful to my eye."

This surprised him.

"But, so, too, was the companion of the Ice Mage. It was not glamour and it was not enchantment; he was beautiful, and compelling. I remember him well." She listened as the strains of the violin song grew sharper and faster. "But in the North, at that time, beauty and deadliness were often wed. The white bears that hunted in the Northern snows were, in their fashion, beautiful. The economy with which they could kill, the speed at which they could move—we respected these things. We made warnings of our stories, and the unaccompanied songs we sang, but there was always some quiet admiration for the deadliest of things that nature had created in both.

"She is like that, to me. Compelling not in spite of the fact that she is *kialli*, but in part because of it."

"She is *kialli*?"

Sigurne glanced at his face, and then away. "I would say so. I cannot be certain without more of a confrontation than this crowd would survive."

And you? Rath thought. *Would you survive?* He did not ask.

Instead, he inclined his head slightly. "Yes, Sigurne, I find her beautiful. But it is, as you say, the sinuous beauty of the coiled snake, the delicate beauty of the poisonous spider's web; it is entirely what it is. There is no pity in her, and were I to be entirely smitten with her, I would expect to find none; there is no kindness, nothing that is not, in the end, about her own power. Love, if it were professed, would change nothing, acquire nothing.

"But in one guise or another, we are often attracted to power, and we are also often attracted to those who do not *fear* it."

"I have feared it," Sigurne said, as the last strains of music were buried beneath the constant rain of spoken words. "I have feared it for all, for almost all, of my life. Even when it is beautiful. Perhaps especially then.

"But encountering such beauty at the debut ball of a young girl is jarring. I wonder, at times, how Duvari endures it."

"Duvari?" Rath's eyes rounded slightly. "You speak of the head of the Astari?" The Astari were the men—and women—who stood in the Kings' shadows and protected them from assassination. Unfortunately for the patriciate, they were both thorough enough and paranoid enough that they could see the assassin's hand in anyone who had accumulated enough wealth or power.

"Indeed."

"You should abstain. It's rumored that any mention

of his name draws the full force of his attention." It was only half a joke.

"That," Sigurne replied dryly, "is hardly much incentive, given that the Magi are already blessed by the questionable benison of his suspicion. But he is a young man. Don't make that face, Ararath; it does not suit you. He is young, as you are young. And I appreciate him in exactly the same way that I can appreciate Sor Na Shannen."

Rath frowned. Her pronunciation of the name was slightly different than Lord Cordufar's had been.

"Perhaps I appreciate him more; I understand his goals, and I find them more personally acceptable. Come. There is Lord Cordufar, unfettered by his lovely companion. The girl by his side is his niece."

"About time," Matteos grumbled. When Sigurne frowned up at him, he added, "I'm hungry. I haven't eaten since breakfast."

Meralonne APhaniel joined them for dinner. The great hall had been suitably furnished, and the hundreds of guests likewise seated at rectangular tables across which fine linens had been draped. The table runners were a lace embroidered with the colors of Cordufar. The napkins were likewise embroidered, but the insignia on these was small and tasteful; the rest, Rath did not consider important enough to notice.

Nor did Meralonne APhaniel, although when he produced his pipe, Sigurne glared it into nonexistence. They sat in a silence accentuated by the quiet music of musicians whose task it was not to interrupt conversation.

"We did not see you in the great room," Sigurne said, engaging Meralonne when his hand strayed, again, to the folds of his robe.

He glanced at her. "I was much occupied with the somewhat confused architecture of this mansion, and eventually ended up in the wine cellars."

She raised a silver brow, and then, after a pause, she relented. "Wine cellars?"

"They are quite, quite good, even to my admittedly

jaundiced eye. And no, before you ask, I did not choose to test the vintages."

"Imagine my relief."

He raised a brow that was not dissimilar to her own. "You have obviously had a more interesting evening than I have managed."

"Indeed."

"However, I sensed no magic, and heard no raised alarm. I'm somewhat bored."

If Sigurne found his utter lack of conventional manners annoying, she hid the annoyance well. Rath wondered, and not for the first time, what a meeting of the Magi must be like. "Very well," Sigurne said. She slid her hand into her robe for a moment, and then withdrew it. "We may speak freely. We met, and spoke with, Sor Na Shannen, Lord Cordufar's mistress."

Meralonne raised a brow. "And?"

"She is kin."

"*Kialli*?" The single word sharpened syllables that should have been soft.

"I did not think to test her in a crowd of this size. I would appreciate it if you likewise refrained."

"What did you speak about?"

"Ararath of Handernesse."

Meralonne frowned. He reached for his pipe for a third time. It remained, unlit, in his hand. "You play a dangerous game," he said, speaking now to Rath.

"So I have been informed. If I am not mistaken, Member APhaniel, you yourself do likewise."

"In the cobwebs of a wine cellar?"

"Many a man considers the wine cellar the heart of his home."

Meralonne laughed. "And clearly, this is one such man." He set the pipe to one side on the table. "There is magic in the wine cellars of Cordufar, and it is not a magic that is easily tested; without care, I think it would pass undetected."

Sigurne, silent until that moment, froze in place.

"You expected no less." Meralonne spoke softly.

"You used Summer magic?"

He nodded.

Rath frowned. "Summer magic?"

"It is an old branch of magic, and one not studied now," Sigurne replied. "It is not forbidden, but in order to test its efficacy, one would require a practitioner of arts that *are* forbidden."

Rath did not ask how Meralonne had studied the school.

Instead, he examined an entirely internal map of the undercity, as Jewel called it. It was not a map in the way that the maps Jewel had saved from a burning building were. It was some part of his eleven years of experience in the silent dark: The feel of dirt beneath his feet as it gave way, by descent, into stone; the solid stone of the safe roads; the worn stone of stairs; the rough and sharp edges of cracked walls, cracked statues, cracked pillars and columns; the trembling edges of open crevices; the mustiness of air that was never disturbed; the sound of bats, like high-pitched thunder, when they took sudden flight.

He knew the width of most of the roads; he knew the shape of them, the way they turned in on themselves, the way they cut and bisected other roads. He knew that the undercity traveled for miles beneath Averalaan. He knew, as well, that some of the exits and entrances that he used opened up near the Merchant Authority, and in that section of town, real estate was costly. But not so costly as the Cordufar Estates; they were old.

How old?

"Ararath?" Sigurne said, and Rath shook his head slightly.

"My apologies, Sigurne. Meralonne, did you detect this magical disturbance only in the wine cellars?"

Meralonne watched Rath closely, his gray eyes narrowed. After a moment, he nodded.

"Near a trapdoor or some other method of descent?"

"A curious question."

Rath said nothing.

"This is not a game, scion of Handernesse."

Sigurne placed a hand on Meralonne's arm. He affected not to notice, and his eyes were shining slightly. The light and the color of those eyes made them seem, for a moment, like blade's edge.

"I don't know," Rath replied, meeting the gaze, and aware of how little corresponding light shone in his own eyes. "What lives do gods lead? They fear no death, they suffer no pain; what is left them, in the end, but the dalliance of long games?"

"They fear death," the Magi replied quietly. "But for the rest, I will concede your point, and will offer information I feel you already know: there is a concealment and a protection cast upon the floor of the farthest of the wine cellars. The concealment is a trivial magic; the protection, I fear, is not.

"Had I discovered the wine cellar first—had I been apprised of the import of descent—I might have been able to untangle the protections that lay upon it. As it was, I had a scant hour."

"An hour?" Sigurne asked.

"An hour, but . . . there was some surveillance, and in order to ward myself against detection, I had to move slowly, and within the sphere of the watcher."

"What spell?"

Meralonne glanced at her. "It was a simple spell," he said, grudging the admission, "but it covered the whole of the last two rooms."

"And you were not discovered?"

"No. But the wine cellar was visited."

"A servant?"

"No. You need not look at me in such an accusatory fashion, Guildmaster. There were no deaths, and no disincorporation."

"I feel less than entirely reassured."

"I could do neither, while I wished to avoid alerting the master of the house."

"What did you do?"

"I observed," he said coolly and with genuine distaste. "And while I fail to see the necessity for subtlety at this time, such subtlety was practiced at your request."

He turned, then, and glanced down the long hall, to the head table. There, in the center, was Lord Cordufar.

"He is not the master here," Rath found himself saying.

Meralonne glanced at Rath.

"She is," Rath added.

Into the hall, unescorted and unattended, strode Lord Cordufar's mistress, her blue dress swirling in a way that suggested thigh without exposing so much as an ankle. With all of the guests seated, she made a statement of her simple strides. Rath watched her until he found the watching uncomfortable and forced himself to look away.

To look at Meralonne.

There was no lust, no expression of desire, upon his face. The lights in the long hall paled his skin, and if time had etched lines there, they were gone. But there was a hunger in the way he watched her, and it reminded Rath of death.

Sigurne once again put her hand over Meralonne's wrist, and he shrugged and turned away, but his expression did not, and had not, changed.

Chapter Ten

DINNER PASSED. Rath ate and found, to his surprise, that he enjoyed the food; that he enjoyed the variety of small and elaborately prepared dishes. Soup, in shallow, slender bowls, water and wine in elegant cut crystal, partridge eggs, poached, tiny perfection, laid out against a bed of greens, with strips of smoked meat laid across them. He appreciated the baked cheese, in a deep pastry dish, and also the beef that followed, garnished by long, slender new beans.

He thought it a pity that Andrei could not, or would not, drink the wine, for it was a vintage worthy of the Araven wine cellars. Dessert, when it came, was a chilled custard.

During dinner, musicians played, and the sound of laughter, and the occasional raised voice, drifted across the great hall. When dinner drew, at last, to a close, Lord Cordufar's attendants rose to announce the opening of the ballroom, and the subsequent dance.

Meralonne grimaced, but did not speak. Rath privately doubted that words were necessary; the expression itself spoke volumes. The mage drew his pipe from its place on the table, and he took out leaf and began to line its bowl. Matteos looked both pained and annoyed, and he cast a furtive—and hopeful—glance at the reigning guildmaster. No rescue came from that quarter, and in any case, pipes were brought to the tables, and tobacco followed.

Rath, avoiding Matteos' gaze, took a pipe for himself, and when it was alight, he looked at Meralonne APhaniel. "Will you join the dance at all?"

"I am not much of a dancer," the mage replied dryly, "and as Member Mellifas is too kind to say, I can only afford to embarrass her order on a single front. As I have not yet done that this eve, I fear to waste the opportunity on the merely trivial."

"Meralonne."

"Sigurne herself does not often dance, although she occasionally likes to watch. Why," the Magi added, blowing a perfect ring from pursed lips, "I honestly do not know."

"Matteos?"

"I was not raised in Averalaan," Matteos replied. "And were I, it would not have been among the wealthy."

Rath nodded, and smoked for a while.

The music shifted in both tone and volume. "And will you brave the wine cellars again?"

"I may. The chance that I will see them again before the storm is upon us is slim. Lord Cordufar is much occupied, and I believe his mistress is now by his side. They will, in the custom of Averalaan, open the dance."

"I believe that Lord Cordufar will open the dance with his niece."

The correction was clearly too trivial for Meralonne APhaniel, who merely shrugged and rose. "I will, perhaps, see you later," he told them.

Sigurne watched him go. "He is right," she said quietly.

"He's just bored," Matteos told her. He had not touched pipe, and he had a nearly full glass of wine in front of him. "I told you not to bring him."

"I could hardly refuse his request. Not when he went through so much effort to make it politely." She rose as well. "Ararath?"

Ararath left his chair, taking only a moment to douse his pipe. "It would be my honor."

In Meralonne's absence, Rath and Sigurne drifted toward the dance. He had no intention of joining it, but found it oddly compelling. Jewel was not yet at an age where such a gathering could have been held in her honor, and even were she, she hadn't the station. But he smiled, briefly, as he thought of what Haval might do to prepare her for a night such as this.

And thinking it, his thoughts drifted, treacherously, to the night of Amarais' presentation. He could see her in the long, cream silks that she favored at that age, her hair beaded and flowered so heavily it was a wonder it hadn't overbalanced her. Just a fragment, a momentary image.

But with it, the other memories.

He had sat to one side of her bedchamber door, peering into a room that was a bustle of frenetic activity; he had watched her maids as they worked, brushing her hair, laying out her dress, her jewelry, her hair piece, and her combs. They had fussed over her fingers, her hands, her nails, they had polished her shoes, they had laid out so many small containers of powders and colors, each with several brushes of different length, width, and thickness, that they might have been artists.

She was their canvas, but she was, as she had always been, a fractious, difficult one. She did not stand long where they told her to stand, and sitting was worse. Nor did they take this in stride; they cajoled, commanded, pleaded, and nearly wept. His mother had been intelligent enough to avoid the unruly scene.

But Rath had watched, and admittedly, he had snickered. Amarais was composed, but not so perfectly that she hadn't taken the time to throw something at his head; it was a small purse of the kind that one would never wear to a social gathering. He'd kept it for three weeks, because she'd always had a good aim, and it had hit him square in the forehead.

He was not, of course, to be present for her presentation; he was too young. This had not stopped him from pleading for the privilege, and to his surprise, it had not stopped Amarais; they had had weeks between them to attempt to change his grandfather's mind.

His grandfather, however, had been resolute in his determination; he did not want his granddaughter distracted by her younger brother, and Ararath was not, in his grandfather's opinion, well enough behaved to be the adult that Handernesse expected.

But he was allowed to watch. So he had, taking up his position between the banister rails after he had changed. This was to be the first time he would watch alone. On every other occasion that he could remember—and at that age, he remembered much of the childhood his life had slowly eroded—he sat at his sister's side, often attempting to push her head out of the way, no matter where she placed it. He remembered, absurdly, that he'd believed that wherever she was was always the best place to be.

Not on this night. Wherever she was about to be was not the best place. He watched her silent progress down the stairs, her hand touching, but not clinging to, the rails. He watched the stiff angle of her chin, the rigid line of her neck, the perfect fall of her dress, and the powdered even quality of her complexion.

He watched her, and as he watched, she turned—carefully, as if motion would dislodge some vital component—to look at him. And he realized, then, that she was nervous. Amarais. Nervous.

At any other time, he would have laughed at her. He recalled wanting to laugh. But she was so *silent,* he couldn't. Because he knew, truly knew, that she would not throw anything at him; that she would not come thundering up the stairs to whack the side of his head; that she would not threaten to make him suffer later. There was *no* later. This was where she had to be, this silence, this poise. And those stairs?

Those were the path to them. It was like walking into a cage. But it was a cage, conversely, that she wanted. Every other person of power and significance in the Empire lived behind those bars.

He met her gaze, and then, hesitant, he smiled at her, nodding. Urging her to look away, to walk away, to become one with the intractable and frustratingly elusive adults at the bottom of those stairs. His parents were waiting. His father, his hands behind his back, his mother, her expression both strained and joyful. His grandfather, behind them all, serene and placid.

She smiled. Just that. Smiled, and turned, and concentrated on descent.

And he remembered it now, the last lonely vigil by the banister rails, his shadows part of the dim lights of the house in which the beautiful and the powerful were not welcome. He sat, he listened for her name. He listened for strains of music, and waited while Hectore of Araven—who should have known better, and probably did—slipped away from the crowd to bring him food and gossip, as he had done at every such ball in Rath's memory.

But the food and the gossip were wasted on Rath. Amarais had loved the talk; Amarais had peppered Hectore with questions; Amarais had held him at the curve of the rail until his wife had come, resigned but slightly impatient, to drag him away.

"You haven't lost her," Hectore told the much quieter Rath.

But Rath looked at the empty place by his side, and said nothing.

He looked, now, at the men and women in their expensive dress, their makeup slightly caked in the heat that any crowd produces. He heard the music, as he had heard it that last night, for he had never again gone to the rails to watch in fascination and boredom.

Amarais had never been nervous again. Not that way. Perhaps on other days, perhaps on the day she made the announcement of her adoption into House Terafin. But if she was, she didn't show it, didn't share it. She had become, in all things, the woman her grandfather had always claimed she would become. And she had broken his heart, for Terafin.

Perhaps, had he lived, he would have had that heart returned to him when his granddaughter ascended the Terafin seat, taking it in the midst of a brutal war, against all other claimants. But he had not lived.

Rath had.

"Ararath?" Sigurne touched his sleeve, and he turned, smoothing the lines of his face into a gentle smile. "I am worried about you," she told him gently, as if she were a grandmother or godmother.

He shook his head. "It has been a long, long time since I have attended a social function of this nature. I was merely reminiscing."

"And in the way of men, choosing only those recollections that are mournful or pensive in nature?"

He raised a brow, but his smile deepened. "Indeed, Sigurne. In the way of a man such as myself." He straightened, and bowed. "Will you join me?"

Matteos' brows disappeared into his hairline, and Rath laughed.

"I do not dance," Sigurne replied, with just a hint of an answering smile, which changed the lines of her face.

"But I do."

And there she was, unheralded and unheeded until this moment. *So,* Rath thought, *you are capable of subtlety when it suits you.*

"I am a guest of a guest," Rath replied, bowing slightly before her. "And I imagine that there are many, many men of import who would be grateful if you favored them with your time."

Her eyes glittered. She did not smile, and she did not command; she merely waited.

Waiting, she attracted attention, and it was the type of attention that draws moths to open fire and their own brief immolation. He could see it, in the men who circled her. Another woman might have found their presence and their barely concealed desire distasteful or even threatening. She was, Rath thought, the very fire: she neither noticed nor cared. They spoke and she replied, but her gaze never strayed far from Rath's face.

He noted, however, that every word she spoke was a refusal.

"If you are inclined to waste your time on one such as I, I would be honored." His voice. He was surprised by it.

He was not the only one. Sigurne's fingers tightened, briefly, on his sleeve. She withdrew the hand, but Sor Na Shannen had noticed; she noticed, Rath thought, everything. And responded to very little.

Rath offered Sor Na Shannen his arm, and her hands closed on it tightly. They were of a height, but had anyone asked, he would have proclaimed her the taller. She was bold, could be nothing but bold, and bold women often seemed, to his admittedly jaundiced eye, both delightful and graceless.

She was neither. She did not seem young, to the eye; there was about her a solid power, an utterly unselfconscious presence, that denied youth its vitality. But she walked with the music as if she were of it.

"I am not, I'm afraid, more than an indifferent dancer." It was a confession.

"No," she replied, as if it were insignificant. She met his eyes, then, and her gaze said, *I know that you know.*

He was not certain what his said in reply. Of the many things he had considered when he had approached Andrei with his request to be included in the Araven party, this was not one. He had assumed that he, like Meralonne, might be searching the grounds, with an eye to things belowground; that he, like Andrei, might be taking note of the servants—or guards—of the Cordufar manse with an eye to later investigation.

"I am not," she said, as the strains of music died and dancers left the floor, making room for those who would engage each other in the next set, "originally from the Empire. This," she added, lifting an arm to encompass the whole of the floor—and perhaps, as well, the mansion and everyone in it, "is difficult in its fashion. I have learned some of your dances."

"You speak like a native."

"Yes." She shrugged, as if speech itself were beneath

notice. "All of my people do." She held out her arms, and he placed one hand beneath hers, and one around her waist. Silk ceased to matter; he was touching her skin, and it was, for a brief moment, the only sensation he felt, and the only sensation that mattered.

This, too, she knew. There was power in it, and she was aware, in all things, of power. Of the necessity of it, the desire for it, the wielding of it. What form it took was inconsequential. Power implied weakness.

He had not lied; he was an indifferent dancer. Had he been more, he would still have failed to be other than indifferent. He would age, had aged, and she? Never. He saw that clearly: she would die, yes, if she was weak enough to be killed, but no other infirmity would touch her.

He wanted to.

But he had wanted many things in his life, and he smiled instead, accepting the weakness, allowing it play.

She raised a manicured brow. "You do not fear me?"

"I fear you," he replied, allowing that as well. "But in the manner that I fear storms at sea or earthquakes. Lady," he added, voice low, "you are what you are. You do not, and cannot change. I do, I can, I have."

This did not amuse her, but neither did it disgust her.

He danced with death, understood it, and found that he could not fear it; fear, if it came, would come later, with pain: moth and flame.

"Fear rules the world," she said, when he thought she would speak no more.

"Ah. And did it always rule yours?"

She stiffened; he felt the muscles shift slightly beneath his hands, heard the sharp intake of breath, saw the narrowing of eyes that eclipsed almost everything else. But she said, in a cool voice, "You are bold."

"It is a failing," he admitted. "But it is not always a failing; I have become adept at hiding over the years."

Her smile was astonishing and unpleasant; it was a potent combination. "And you do not seek to hide, now."

"I see little point in it."

"I see little point in your lives, they are over so quickly, but you guard them as you can." Her lips brushed his ear, and he almost stumbled; it amused her. "Do you desire me?" she whispered.

He laughed. "Does it matter?" he asked, moving to the music, leading in only the technical sense of the word. "Does it matter, in the end? You can kill me, I've no doubt, with your bare hands; what I desire, what I repulse, are inconsequential."

Her brow lifted again, and the expression that rippled across her perfect, hard features was almost—almost—confusion.

"You will not kill me *now*; for your own reasons, you and your confederates play a game—I think it a long game—and my death in the middle of this dance floor would necessitate a great many other deaths at a time and place not of your choosing."

"And this makes you feel safe?"

"No. You are only barely controlled, even knowing this. It is precisely because it is not safe that it is interesting at all."

She chuckled because this she understood well. But there was, again, a flicker that crossed her face, changing her countenance. "That is not all."

"It never is."

She lifted a hand from its place on his shoulder, and she ran one fingernail lightly across his cheek. He felt the sting of it; knew that it bled. He laughed again, and this drew attention from other dancers. But he had their attention, wanted or not, because of his partner.

He spun her, in time with the music.

"Do you think you love me?" she whispered.

So much, this eve, to make him laugh; so much that was unexpected. The laugh was bitter, but genuine; she'd surprised and amused him. Nor was she delighted to have done either.

"What, to your kin, is love, that you can even ask?"

"It is not what love is to me, but what it is to you: A lie, a thing you tell yourself to hide your ugly truths."

"Very well. I have ugly truths, and no great desire to

hide them, Lady. I find you fascinating; I would never claim to love you. But I admit I am now deeply curious. What *is* love, to you?"

She stiffened, at that, losing music, separating herself from both the rhythm of the song and the dance that it enveloped. She drew herself up, and in, acquiring height and radiating presence as if either were the plumes of a threatened peacock. For just a moment, Rath thought he would die, here.

If he did, however, with all of Averalaan society watching him, that would serve his purpose. That would be a death that he could, in some irony, live with.

But if he had spent much of life learning how to taunt or enrage his enemies, he had done so deliberately. And he was, at the moment, possessed of the almost physical memories of life in this society and on this floor. He offered her a half bow, as she stood in her towering, compelling rage. "Lady," he said, as he rose. "I mispoke. I did not mean to offend; I did not mean to accuse you of either weakness or the vulnerability of weakness."

"What do you—what *can* you—know of *love*?"

Sigurne had said, in a distant tower, on a night entirely bereft of music, light, and society, that demons could see a man's soul. And if this one could, what matter hiding? What pretense could he offer, what words could adorn and ultimately distract her from the shoddy state of the effects of this life?

He thought of Amarais. He thought of Jewel. He thought of the ways in which he had failed both. He accepted that love, his version of it, had always been flawed and narrow; it had always been selfish.

"Nothing," he whispered, offering her that much.

Even this was not mollifying; it was not enough. She reached out with both of her hands, cupped his face in either palm, held his gaze, although she would have held it, regardless. Music quelled around them; movement ceased. It would start again, soon, or it would never start.

Rath did not much care.

"I will kill you for this," she whispered. He felt her

344 ◆ Michelle West

nails against his skin, stroking it lightly, biting it on the edge of sensation that was not—quite—pain. "Will you not struggle? Will you not plead?"

"No." Silence, and then, softly, he said, "I have already said that I do not love you. What struggle and what plea could I therefore be moved to make?"

She withdrew her hands slowly as the music started. Some of the fire left her eyes, then. "You will understand, in time, the answer to your question. Even you will understand, who clings to a love that you do not even believe is of value."

He bowed to her, then, and he offered her his arm.

She stared at it, stared at him, and then glanced around the floor upon which men and women had begun their slow overtures. Wordless, she spun, and wordless, she parted the crowd in her wrath. The envy and the petty jealousy, the attraction and the heated desire, that she had spent the evening evoking at every opportunity, she left behind, as if seeing—as if reminded, by his careless words—how unworthy these merely mortal vessels were of such a benediction.

Sigurne was waiting at the edge of the floor, in silence. She glanced at his face, her eyes tracing the scratch across one cheek. "That was unwise," she told him, the words stiff with mingled disapproval and concern.

He bowed. "It was entirely unwise."

"If your intent was to anger her, you succeeded."

"I had no conscious intentions, Sigurne. I did attempt to gracefully refuse her, if you recall."

"Given the way you were dancing, I was not entirely certain that you did."

He chuckled, but he found himself glancing toward the great hall. "I understand," he said softly, "where the danger lies in those who are not mortal."

"I would have imagined you would understand it well, by now. You've met many who were not."

"Yes. And I killed them. But the purpose of those encounters was entirely death; there was no conversation, no exchange of information; I had no time to appreciate any nuance, any subtlety. And truthfully, it is neither of those things that I find compelling, in her; she is not particularly subtle."

Sigurne waited.

"She does not doubt. She does not fear. She scruples to hide what she is because it is necessary to achieve her goals—but it is only for that reason that she bothers. And even so, she does it poorly. She—" he shook his head. "I am not besotted, Sigurne; you needn't look at me like that."

"It is not some youthful fancy that I fear."

"She used no magic. Had she, the entire gathering would have known. But ... she requires none. She is compelling simply because she is strong."

"A very narrow definition of strength, I think."

"She is like your white bears," he replied, "but she can talk and think and feel." He turned away from the great hall, and toward his companion.

In the poor lighting, she seemed old and bent. Age of this type would never grace Sor Na Shannen; it would never diminish her fire. But it would also never lessen her pain or calm her anger.

"Ararath?"

It would never lend her wisdom. He smiled at Sigurne Mellifas, a woman who had, in spite of age and the vagaries of mortality, made power her study, her goal, and her responsibility. It was this last that defined her. Had it always defined her?

No. No, he thought. But in weakness, she had learned the core of what she required to be strong. And because she owned weakness, because she did not fear it, she could afford to be kind. "Yes," he said. "It is a narrow definition of strength. It is, perhaps, a younger man's definition of strength, and at heart, we are foolish enough to gloss over the misery and ignorance that was youth; we see only the things that burned, because we cling to their very odd, very painful beauty. Come. Let us repair to the great hall. I find myself thirsty."

He bowed, and then offered her his arm; let Matteos flounder. "Where," he asked, as they began their leisurely stroll toward the refreshments the great hall housed, "has Member APhaniel gone?"

They were almost upon the great tables at which food had been laid out when they had an answer, of sorts: The distant sound of thunder, and the sudden, sharp, shock that traveled through the mansion.

Sigurne grimaced, and caught Matteos' arm. "Wine," she told him, more command in the single word than she had used all evening. "Ararath." He had dropped his arm and spun, although the tremor was not directional. She lifted her arm, and that wordless gesture was also a command; he at once offered her the arm he had removed.

Matteos was grinding his teeth in frustration, but to Rath's eye, fear was in the mix. "I told you, Sigurne."

"Indeed you did. And next time, he will have to do far more than just ask politely."

"Are you so certain that it is Meralonne?" Rath asked softly.

Another shudder shook the floor.

Sigurne lifted a white brow; she did not otherwise dignify the question with a response. "Do you see Lord Cordufar?"

"Yes. He is standing by the musicians."

"Does he seem overly concerned?"

"Not at this distance."

"Good. Be visible, Ararath, and allow me to be visible as well. I believe that I see our young master bard, and I would very much like to have his attention *now*." She began to make her way through the crowd, to where said bard was flirting in a charming and entirely proper way with a number of young ladies.

Age, Rath thought, had its privileges. Sigurne was entirely polite in her approach, if one did not consider the audience that had already gathered around the bard.

The bard, however, understood the social standing that age granted women; he disengaged almost instantly, and he tendered Sigurne a very respectful bow. "Guildmaster," he said, as he rose, introducing her without the trouble of actually offering her the names of the young women surrounding him.

The young women were wise enough not to look displeased; they were aware enough, in fact, to look slightly troubled.

"Kallandras."

"If you will excuse me," he said to the four young women. His smile as he offered this apology was, to Rath's practiced eye, perfect; it implied regret at being forced to abandon their company due to the burden of the more onerous manners and attention expected by the elderly, without ever descending into actual words.

Sigurne, however, lifted a brow at the performance. Kallandras' smile deepened into something that was very wry. "Your pardon, Member Mellifas. I did not expect to have your company, and I have duties to Senniel."

"Visibility?"

"Indeed. Would you care to join me in the hall?"

"I would," she replied, "because if I am not mistaken, I will soon be approached by a somewhat angry Lord Cordufar."

Kallandras raised a brow. "You mean we will have excitement at this ball?"

"Beyond the excitement caused by his mistress?"

Kallandras laughed. "She is very striking."

"Oh, indeed. My companion was lucky enough to dance with her."

Ararath, who vastly preferred to be mere witness to the conversation, lifted a hand. "It was a single dance," he said, "And only a dance. We hardly exchanged a word."

"I see," the bard replied, and from the tone of his voice, he did. While Rath understood the value of the bards to both the Empire and the Kings, he found them disconcerting. "Pardon my manners. I am Kallandras of Senniel."

"I am Ararath of Handernesse."

"Handernesse?"

Rath nodded.

"Will you join us, Ararath?"

"He will," Sigurne replied. "I would like it to be noted that both he and I were present, and in your company."

"You expect a writ to be served." Kallandras' smile had lessened as they walked.

"I expect a writ to be served, or rather, I expect a writ of exemption to be demanded, and before you ask, no, I do not yet know on what grounds."

"And do you carry such a writ?"

"I would prefer not to speak about writs of exemption," she replied. "As they are exceedingly rare, and I am the guildmaster. I am old for this, Kallandras. It is a young man's game."

Kallandras, very wisely, chose to offer no opinion on this subject, but from that moment on, as he made his way through the small enclaves of Lord Cordufar's esteemed guests, he drew their attention, and made certain, both in subtle and less subtle ways, that their attention was also caught, for a moment, by Ararath, Sigurne, and even the taciturn Matteos.

Perhaps a quarter of an hour later, Lord Cordufar suddenly stiffened. Ararath, watching from the great hall with a lazy and suitable ennui, touched Sigurne's shoulder briefly. She did not speak a word; she was otherwise engaged in conversation with a middle-aged woman from Lessar, a merchant house that was neither as old nor as wealthy as Araven.

Rath turned to the conversation at hand as if it were suddenly of interest.

Lord Cordufar apparently thought it might be.

"Member Mellifas," he said, and she turned. Everyone did.

"Lord Cordufar," she replied. She inclined her head slightly; more was not required of a woman of her rank and her age.

"Ararath of Handernesse," Lord Cordufar continued. "I was not aware that you were an acquaintance of the guildmaster."

Rath raised a brow. "It is, of course, my privilege, but I was not aware that it would be of significance, here."

"One can hardly dally with a First Circle mage as a matter of happenstance."

"Ah, no. I have some well-known interest in the antiquities, and I have spent countless hours within the Order itself."

"And those interests would lead you to the woman who governs said Order?"

"Clearly," was the dry reply Rath offered. "She herself has no little knowledge of an area in which I had hoped to be considered an expert."

The silence was slight, but notable.

"Where, Member Mellifas, is your other companion?" She frowned. "Member APhaniel?"

"Indeed."

"Matteos, have you seen him recently? I must apologize," she added, in the sweetest and most conciliatory of tones, "but Member APhaniel is famed for his intense dislike of dancing. I confess I am not entirely certain *why* he should dislike it so; I myself do not attempt to dance, but find much of interest in merely observing."

Sigurne, Rath thought, was a marvel. Had he not known better, he would have said all of her words were entirely genuine.

"As an example," she continued, and Rath tensed, "your very lovely Sorna Shannen accepted Ararath's invitation to join him on the floor. Did you see them?"

Lord Cordufar looked at Rath. It was a look that hovered between glare and gaze, with the intensity of the former and the neutrality of the latter. "I was myself much occupied in my duties," he told Sigurne, although his eyes did not leave Rath's face. "But indeed, as you say, she is an elegant, powerful dancer."

Those eyes certainly noticed the scratch across Rath's face.

"If you would like to speak with Meralonne, we can attempt to find him. He favors his pipe after dinner," she added, "and it is likely that he will be outside, in the pavilion."

"I will search for him myself."

"Is there a problem or a concern?"

"Believe that if there is, Guildmaster, you will be among the first to know."

"My gratitude for your consideration."

He raised a brow and then his eyes narrowed, but she was hidden behind the mask of her face, and what was there beyond it, not even Rath could say. He wanted, briefly, to introduce Sigurne to Haval, just for the sheer joy of watching their conversation and their silences.

Lord Cordufar desired to say more; that much was clear. But he was aware of the presence of his guests, in particular the young master bard, and after a moment, he bowed curtly and made his retreat. It was a long retreat, and it carried him directly out of the great hall, through a door that led to the kitchens and the rooms beyond.

"Member Mellifas," Kallandras said, bowing. "Perhaps we should seek Meralonne APhaniel."

"He is not in a particularly social mood," she replied, "And I, for one, do not desire more of either his pipe or his complaints. You, however, are far more familiar with the patriciate than I; I was raised in a simple village in the North, and much of what occurs here is beyond my ken. If you think it wise, Kallandras, I will bow to your experience."

He offered her his arm, and she accepted the offer; the hall was quite warm, and the night, cooling in the light of the moons. Doors led from the ballroom itself onto large terraces; there were three. From the middle terrace, winding stairs led to a path that was three men wide; this path was lit, and led, in turn, toward a garden that even in the fading light was impressive, to Rath's view. The scent of rowan was strong, but mingled with the scent of lilac, and indeed, white lilac, and violet, grew near the path.

But as they descended, Kallandras said, "Be wary of the lord, Sigurne."

She raised a pale brow, and in turn offered the bard a weary smile. "I am wary, young man, of almost everyone."

"There is something . . . unusual . . . about his voice."
He glanced at her, as they reached the flat stones.

"Indeed?"

"And you are not surprised in the slightest to learn
of it."

She smiled. "I am flattered that you feel it is important enough to tell me, and I admit that you are charming enough that your concern pleases me."

"Which is entirely unlike surprise or fear."

"Believe that I am concerned, Kallandras."

"You are also adept at speaking with the bard-born."
He smiled. It was a smile made different by moonlight
and breeze from the smiles he had offered both Sigurne
and any other woman with whom he had spoken in the
hall.

"I am old," she replied. "At my age, dignity is possibly
the last bastion on which to shore up pride. I would like
to think that dignity requires an ability to choose what
is heard when one speaks."

"Many a man your age—or older—would let his
voice say more and care a great deal less."

"Oh, men."

He laughed. "As you say, Member Mellifas. I see the
pavilion, but I do not see your mage."

"No."

He glanced at her. "You are not worried about his
absence."

"I am. But I am not worried about his well-being.
And I do not miss his pipe. If it comforts you at all, I
am considering strangling him when he does choose to
show his face. If he does," she added.

The slight shift of expression across the bard's face
caught Rath by surprise. "He must be a brave man, indeed, if he is willing to risk your anger, here."

"I wish I could call it brave. At my age, brave and
reckless often seem the same, and regardless, he is not
a *young* man. He is not brave; he is merely bored." She
smiled. "And if I were this open in all of my discourse,
Master Bard, would it not in the end tell you far more
than you would want to know?"

He laughed. "No. There is music there, if one knows how to listen, and Sioban Glassen is my Master; I know how to listen. Lord Cordufar is not pleased, but his fear is not of you, not precisely. It is broader and deeper, and it is tinged by some constant malice and no little anger."

"You've met him before?"

"No. I have, of course, heard of him. But this is the first time that I have had any cause to speak with him personally."

"Surely he spoke to you when you agreed to grace his ball?"

"No. I am not entirely certain he appreciates the role of bards in Averalaan. But I would say he understands the unofficial ways in which the bards are beholden to the Twin Kings."

"If he does not appreciate bards, it is a wonder that Sioban acceded to the request at all."

"Ah," he said, smiling slightly. "The actual request did not come from Lord Cordufar. It was tendered to the bardmaster, in person, by The Darias."

"Personally?"

"Even so." He shrugged. "I am often on the road, and it is pleasant to play and converse this close to Senniel. But I will offer you this much; even at the insistence of The Darias, I do not think Lord Cordufar was pleased to have me in attendance."

"Oh?"

"His manners, where he must treat with his guests, are of course very fine. But the only time I have heard him speak more than a few words in my presence was when he spoke with you, and he spoke, I think, less guardedly there than he has all eve. He is aware of what I am," Kallandras added, "and he has not your practiced patience in speaking with the bard-born."

"But he is aware of the need for such practice."

"Even so. I believe that your presence, and the presence of your guest, has been noted."

Sigurne did not correct his misapprehension, and Rath, therefore, remained silent.

"I will now, if you will countenance my lack of manners,

go in search of your missing mage. I think any contest of wills between the Order and the Cordufar family would, in the end, go through The Darias, and therefore through the Council of The Ten, and I do not feel that such a confrontation would be in the interests of Averalaan."

She was silent for a long moment as she considered this. "Nor," she said quietly, "would it be in the interests of Senniel to be embroiled in the same contest."

"Sioban can barely control the bards as it is, and this is known."

"I have misgivings."

"Indeed, as a First Circle mage, you must. If you did not, you would not now live in the tower." He smiled, and the smile was slight. "Very well, Member Mellifas. If Sioban cannot control her bardmasters, I think it unlikely that the concerns of the Order could. The Order must, by necessity, keep those born without talent calm; in order to achieve this calm, they maintain decorum, and where possible, foster the public image of mages as dotty and obsessive individuals.

"The bardic colleges are seldom the focus of public fear or scrutiny. Our power is not your power, for good or ill. If The Darias or Lord Cordufar object, in Council, to any behavior of Senniel's, Sioban will, of course, hear it. But both House Darias and Cordufar will *also* hear, in response, the lyrics of Senniel brought to bear in the most public and amusing way possible.

"Those lyrics will be sung at every tavern and home in Averalaan before the month is out, and power, in society, is based in large part upon reputation." He bowed. But when he rose, he was looking at Rath, not Sigurne.

"You must forgive my boldness," he said, in a tone of voice entirely shorn of lilt or charm. "But you are of Handernesse?"

Rath knew that bards could watch a play once and recite almost all of the lines from memory thereafter; he therefore recognized the question as a polite overture. He nodded.

Kallandras studied him for a moment. "You did not arrive here with Sigurne's party."

"No. I arrived with Hectore of Araven, and if I have not offended him by evening's end, it is likely I will leave that way as well. Why?"

"I was asked, by an acquaintance, to deliver something to you, should you be in attendance this eve."

Had Kallandras not been a Senniel bard, Rath's confusion would have shaded instantly into suspicion. As it was, he still had to work to mute it. "An acquaintance we have in common?"

"I assumed as much; I failed to inquire further." His tone made clear that the failure was both desired and desirable, and Rath accepted this—with difficulty—and discarded his questions.

Kallandras then removed a small box from the folds of his jacket. It was the size, and shape, to hold a ring or small cuff links, and it was old and tarnished. Engraved into the surface of that slightly grayed silver, was a single initial, with its curls and heights so extremely overdecorated it was hard to read. He handed this to Rath.

Rath's hand closed around it. "Was there no message?"

"Given the nature of the delivery, I did not think to ask," Kallandras replied. He turned, and then turned back, as if drawn. "But given the acquaintance, Ararath, I will say this: I do not know where she leads you, or where she intends to lead you. But she offers nothing freely; the cost of her advice is high. What advice she has given me, I have followed; it has not yet killed me. But I've no doubt at all that it will.

"If she is not yet known to you, and she becomes so, bear only this in mind: she is without pity or mercy, and she will ask more of you than anyone you have met before or might meet in future. If, in the asking, she knows she will destroy you, your life, or those for whom you care, she will ask it, regardless."

He had seemed, to Rath, older and urbane. The careful manners, the carefully careless speech, the choice of the right word and the right gesture—all of these implied experience. But absent these, he was younger than he had first appeared.

Younger and infinitely more angry.

"Who is she?" Rath asked softly.

"Her name is Evayne." Kallandras turned away, and then paused, but did not turn back. "It may be, Ararath, that you will have no cause to meet her. What she sent may be enough." He left, then.

Sigurne watched his back. "That was both unexpected and interesting."

Rath, looking at the box he now held in his hands, merely nodded. He hesitated a moment before opening it.

Nested in a bed of blue velvet was a gold ring, a man's ring. He spared it a glance, no more, and looked up to see Kallandras vanishing in the crowd, as if the crowd were a forest, and he, a small, wild animal who wanted and needed no observers.

"Ararath?"

"It is the signet of Handernesse." His voice was cool; he could keep ice from it, with effort, and he made the effort.

"I . . . see."

"Forgive me, Sigurne, but I do not think you do." It was too much of an effort. He was shaking, slightly, with anger. The anger surprised him, but not enough that he could loose its grip. "If I am not mistaken, this ring is *the* signet of Handernesse; it is not a copy."

"But—"

"It went missing some years ago, much to the distress of my father. Another was made, and he wears it."

"You are certain?"

He swallowed the yes that had been forming, and said, instead, "Let me go to where the light is brighter."

She nodded. Most of the other mages of his acquaintance—not that they were many—would have merely gestured light into existence without a second thought. Sigurne? She used power for a purpose, and where there was an alternative, she used that, instead.

Light existed, encased in fine glass that had been blown into shapes appropriate for a garden's path. They darkened the path a moment by huddling closer to that light.

Bright, pale white made the tarnished box look infinitely more dingy. But the gold itself, noble metal, was unchanged. The crest of Handernesse was large; it was a ring that was meant to be noticed. There were rubies at the heights of each stylized section of the "H." Unlike the elegant and nearly unrecognizable scrawl upon the lid of the box, this letter was done in bold, simple lines.

He lifted the ring out of its blue bed, and held it up to the light. It was heavy, the way gold was heavy; heavy the way history was heavy. Between finger and thumb, it caught light. One of the rubies was cracked. "It is," he said quietly, "the Handernesse signet. You can see the cracked ruby, even in this light."

"When was it cracked?"

"In story? Hundreds of years ago, in one distinguishing battle or another. I asked, and I believe I received an answer, but I was a child. It was not the battle itself that was significant. It was the flaw," he added softly. "The flaw that was a matter of quiet pride."

Sigurne frowned. "Ararath."

He looked away from the ring.

Matteos Corvel glanced at Sigurne. Something about her expression changed the whole cast of his. "Sigurne?"

She lifted both of her hands, and spoke a single word, twisting her palms toward her body as she did. Her sleeves fell, drawn by gravity toward the carefully manicured grass that surrounded the standing lamp.

"Lift the box, please."

Rath did as she asked so quickly she might have been bard-born.

"Matteos?"

The mage was concentrating as well. "Yes, I see it. Whoever worked the spell upon that case was an adept. It hides—it mutes—everything. Even the magic upon the case itself is all but folded into the protection. With privacy stones and magestones in such common use, this would pass entirely undetected."

Sigurne nodded. All frailty and age had fallen away from her face, and only the lines remained, but they now appeared chiseled by a hand other than time's.

"The ring, Matteos?"

He frowned. "The ring seems, to my eye, to be a ring, no more. It is not ostentatious, but it would be noticed, if worn. What do you see, Sigurne?"

"Death," she replied. She gestured and the ring flew from Rath's hand and stopped two inches short of hers, suspended in midair.

Matteos frowned, his brow rippling as he examined the ring again. And again. After a third time, he grunted in frustration, which was almost as much expression as Rath had ever seen him show. "I do not see what you see."

"No. Damn him, where is Meralonne?"

"He is here."

She turned as Meralonne APhaniel approached them on the path. His cheek bore a slight scratch, and blood had beaded along its length; it was not deep. He bowed, slightly, after he had reached her side. "It is possible," he said, in a flat, neutral tone, "that a writ of exemption may—just may—be required."

"May?" Matteos spit the word out, as if it were something wholly unpleasant that he had just been fed.

Meralonne shrugged. "I feel that it is not in Cordufar's interest to make public any mild inconvenience I may have caused."

Sigurne gazed at him, but the outraged lecture that Rath expected failed to emerge. "The ring," she said quietly.

A platinum brow rose. He did not, however, argue. Nor did he lift hand or speak word; he merely looked. But his eyes widened almost imperceptibly.

"Where did you get this?" he asked her softly, his eyes still upon the ring that hovered above her hands in the air.

"I did not; it was given to Ararath."

"By?"

"Kallandras of Senniel College."

"Impossible."

"It is not hearsay, Meralonne," she replied, her voice as flat and even as his. "I myself witnessed it."

"You will excuse me while I attempt to locate the master bard."

"No, I will not."

"Sigurne—"

She lifted a hand, and Meralonne's eyes flashed, reflecting a brief burst of light that had not actually occurred. His hair rose slightly in the breeze. It was long; longer than Rath had realized.

The guildmaster, however, was unmoved and unimpressed. "I will deal with an angry Patris," she told him. "I will not deal with an angry Senniel College."

"I merely wish to ask him where he obtained this ring."

"No doubt. You will not, however, do so."

Rath now intervened. He had never seen Sigurne and Meralonne argue, and he had no intention of allowing them to do so here. "He was told by an acquaintance, possibly a mutual acquaintance, that I might be in attendance at the ball this evening. She asked him to deliver it to me, should we meet."

Meralonne looked at Rath. In the light, the gray of his eyes was the color of steel. "You expected this?"

"No."

"And it is of significance to you?"

"Yes. Given my life and the choices I've made to be where I am, it should have no significance at all—but yes. What did you see, when you looked at the ring?"

"Death," he replied. And then, as if questions were now to be traded, he added, "Was this acquaintance a woman named Evayne?"

"It was the name Kallandras was given. It is not, however, a name with which I'm familiar. And I admit that I would like a few words with her, myself."

"That is not always the wisest of courses," the mage replied. He was still for a long moment—utterly still—before he exhaled.

"What is the intent of the enchantment upon the ring?" Rath asked, for he was certain now that it was enchanted.

Meralonne glanced at Sigurne. She nodded.

"If it is a gift, it is a treacherous one." The mage lifted a hand, and the ring came to rest above it. "There is a magic upon it that I have not seen in a very, very long time. It is not a magic that is practiced in the Empire, and not a magic that can be easily contained."

"Is it forbidden?"

"It would be. If it had been studied and wielded in a way that the Order could see and understand, it would be. But the Order of Knowledge specializes in those magics that mortals wield; the other magics are less understood because they cannot be policed. This is Winter magic."

"But Sigurne noticed something."

"Sigurne has had an usual education, and she is adept. Matteos probably saw nothing."

Matteos frowned.

So did Meralonne, although he frowned at the ring; he hadn't bothered to give Matteos so much as a glance. "It is a death magic," he said at last. "A Winter magic. But it is subtle, Ararath. Of old, such gifts could be given to mortals—in crowns, rings, necklaces, but in other things as well: swords and armor."

"To kill them?"

"To kill them, yes, but at a moment of the giver's choosing, if they so chose. They were worn as a symbol of fealty."

"Of . . . fealty."

"Yes. If you had no intention of ever displeasing your lord, what harm in the wearing of such a trifle?" His smile was cool and unpleasant. "It depends on the lord, however, not being capricious. Given the nature of people, it is not an item I would ever choose to wear.

"But this is different."

"How?" Rath knew, or thought he knew.

Meralonne again looked at Sigurne, whose lips were a thin, white line. "APhaniel, where was this magic worked?" she asked, as if the effect of the enchantment itself were not of concern.

"I cannot say."

"Cannot, or will not?"

He did not answer. Instead, frowning, he looked at Rath. "The ring has no master," he said quietly. "It is death, and it is the type of death that only Winter can give so quickly. But it is not bound to any lord that I can see."

"What does that mean?"

"If I am not mistaken—and I am aware that it is not my own life in the balance, so I can afford to be mistaken—the ring allows its bearer to call his own death."

"There are many, many ways to cause one's own death. All of them would seem to be more convenient. Certainly less costly."

"And certainly more pleasant," Meralonne continued softly. "It is not a minor magic." He gestured, and the ring glided through the air to Rath.

"A question," Rath said, as he took it.

"Ask."

"What you detect, could it also be detected by the kin?"

"Yes. And no."

Rath frowned.

"They will see what I see," Sigurne told him. She glanced at Meralonne, who nodded.

"And why do you see it differently?"

"I would guess," Sigurne replied, when it became clear Meralonne would not, "that he knows who made this ring. Or rather," she added, as Rath opened his mouth to speak, "who bound it. What will you do, Ararath?"

He smiled. Taking the ring, he slid it over his left ring finger.

Chapter Eleven

4th of Scaral, 410 AA
Twenty-fifth holding, Averalaan

THREE TO FOUR. Not dark, not yet, but cold enough that breath was almost a thin mist in the air. Her breath. Carver's. Arann's.

Theirs: Carmenta's. Three of his people. She didn't know their names, but called them One-eye, Asshole, and Dog. They were armed. But so were Duster and Carver.

Duster glanced at Carver, a quick movement of eyes. He lifted a hand, signed: *wait.* Fair enough. Three to four were not *good* odds. She glanced at the geography. They could retreat into the short alley between two buildings; the buildings were tall, and had no obvious yards. No real way to back out or run, but no chance that someone could crawl up behind you either.

Or they could retreat—run—to the crossroads, where Quarry met up with Scaffold. There, the roads were wide, and if there wasn't a lot of traffic, there was an open tavern or two. It wouldn't be the first time the den had ducked into one to avoid trouble.

It would, on the other hand, be the first time that they had no money to spend to allay the annoyance of the tavern's owner.

And it might not come to that; three to four weren't

good odds—for them—but they weren't a guaranteed takedown for Carmenta either. They might get away with exchanging threats, and backing slowly down opposite ends of the narrow street.

Carver clearly had that in mind.

"We've been seeing too much of you," Carmenta said. His dagger caught magelight from its perch high above the night streets. Carmenta turned it. Duster almost snorted.

Carver shrugged. His dagger didn't move much. "Small holding," he replied. "Busy streets."

"Too damn busy." Carmenta shrugged as well, but it was a jerky motion. It was also some sort of signal; the three closed in, Asshole coming to stand by Carmenta. Duster called him Asshole because he wore an eye patch. One-eye didn't bother. Dog began to talk, and it became clear why she thought of him as one: he yapped. She ignored him. For the most part, so did the rest of Carmenta's den.

"You're not working our streets." Carmenta had to kick the yapper before he could deliver the statement. Like any good den leader, he didn't much care for interruptions.

"Look like we're working?"

Carmenta spit to the side. But he shrugged again. Odds in his favor, Duster thought, but he was still weighing them. She was looking at the road behind the rest of his den. And at his den, because she didn't do the talking when they ended up in the same square yards of street.

She never relaxed. She could tell, by the set of Carver's shoulders and jaw, when he did, and he was almost always right. But she was used to watching Carver; she was used to watching Carmenta's den. She was used to scanning the street, in small, brief glimpses, for more of his den because Carmenta knew how to stall. Give him that much; so did they.

She was *not* used to watching Arann.

Carmenta said, "I haven't seen the cripple in a month. Maybe you're finally smartening up—"

And then there was no more question about a double retreat with some name-calling and some lame threats. Because Arann—Arann who was slow and who hated to fight and who it was *safe to ignore,* went berserk.

Carver stood there. They *all* just stood there. For seconds. Even Duster was frozen, her arms locked in place, her mouth slightly open. Arann barreled into Carmenta. He was shouting, but it was a wordless scream of rage; there were no syllables. There was no threat.

There was blood; some of it was his, some of it, Carmenta's. Arann had drawn a dagger. Neither cut was deep. Didn't have to be.

Carver swore, and then Duster wasn't watching much of anything, anymore. They could retreat into the alley, but if they did, they'd have to leave Arann behind. He wouldn't move when they moved; he wasn't even aware of them, anymore.

Wasn't aware, Duster realized, as her gaze skirted him, of the spreading patch of red across his left forearm. She slid in to one side, kicked Asshole's knee, brought her fist up and into the underside of his chin.

"Arann!" Carver shouted.

She didn't bother. She'd seen violence like this before, and she understood it on a visceral level.

"Arann, Mother's blood!"

"He can't hear you!" She shouted, kicking again, holding the knife's edge, the knife's point, back. Not even sure why she was bothering. Dog was uncertain; Carmenta was fighting. But Arann had the reach and the bulk; he just didn't have the cunning.

And right now, he didn't need it. Duster had always said he'd be damn good muscle if he wanted to be. He took another cut, to his right arm, and he roared. The two looked connected; they weren't. She knew they weren't.

Carver tried to grab Arann.

Carver went flying.

No one tried to take advantage of it either.

"Arann!"

Carmenta went flying in the opposite direction.

Arann grabbed Dog, and pitched him across the road. He reached for One-eye, but One-eye jumped back. Arann started to walk across the road.

"Damn it, Duster—help me!"

"He'll take your head off—leave him alone!"

He looked at her, and then—stupid, stupid, fool—he ran after Arann.

When the door opened into the apartment, silence started and spread in a wave. Jewel heard it, and rose, leaving her table and its endless slates behind. She took one look at Arann, and then glanced at Carver and Duster, who were supporting him on either side.

Carver shook his head. "It's not bad," he told her. "It's better than it looks."

"But it's going to cause problems," Duster added.

"What happened?"

Arann looked at her, and then looked away.

"Carver?"

He shrugged. "We ran into Carmenta."

"His whole den?"

"No."

"One-eye, Asshole, and Dog," Duster said.

"And they attacked the three of you?"

"Not . . . exactly." Carver glanced at Arann.

Jewel looked at Arann. "Come in. Arann, sit down in the chair." She walked, stiffly, to her room. Picked up the bandages and the small jars that she had taken with her from Rath's, and headed back out. It was always bad when the den wasn't talking. It was worse when they weren't even signing.

She helped Arann out of his shirt; there were two gashes, both on his arms, and they weren't very deep. He sat there, shoulders slumped, staring at the hands in his lap as if he were surprised, somehow, that they belonged to him. Jewel set about cleaning and dressing the wounds he did have. Even if the bleeding wouldn't kill him, infection could.

He let her move his arms, let her lay them against the table beneath the glow of diffuse light, and didn't even

wince when she started to clean them. He said nothing,
did nothing; even his breath was quiet. If his eyes hadn't
been open, he might have been sleeping. They were, and
he wasn't. Nothing, in the end, was as easy as that.

Finch brought water and the scraps—the clean
ones—they used as towels. Jewel grimaced and added
Arann's shirt to the scrap pile. He had another, although it was smaller. *How much smaller?* It was money.
It always came back to money. To money and the lack
of an easy way beneath the streets. She finished binding
the cuts. Arann didn't move. After a moment, she did,
gesturing to Carver and Duster.

They went outside, into the hall. The bedroom door,
such as it was, couldn't even muffle the squeaks of mice.

"What happened?"

Duster and Carver exchanged a glance, and she tried
not to let this irritate her. When had she become the
person they had to hide things from?

"Carver?"

He shrugged. "Carmenta mentioned Lefty. Arann—"

She lifted a hand. "Never mind." She looked at the
closed door.

"Jay."

She didn't look at him. "What else can he do? He
can't shout at me. He can't hit *me*. He can't find Lefty,
and he can't bring him back." She turned to them both,
then, her hands shaking because she *could not* stop
them. "What can he say to me that will do him any
good? What can he say to me that I'm not *already* thinking? He knows," she added, shoving her hands back to
her sides, and turning away. "He knows, but it doesn't
help."

"Time will."

Jewel looked at Duster. They both seemed surprised
that Duster had spoken at all.

"Give him a couple of months. Give him something
to do."

Jewel said, "there's almost no work at the Port Authority, not even for Angel. There's no work in the Common. He can't steal for crap."

Duster shrugged. "He *can* fight, though." A lopsided grin turned her lips up at the left corner.

Jewel laughed. It was a little too loud, a little too hysterical. But better, in the end, than nothing.

12th of Scaral, 410 AA
The Common, Averalaan

Farmer Hanson stopped asking after Lefty when Arann was around. Jewel knew it was unfair, but she wished he would stop asking, period. It was hard to go to the Common, with what little money they could prize from pockets and purses. The only thing of value she had was the magestone, and she didn't trust herself to sell it.

But Rath was never home, and getting to his home, the hard way, was almost a full-den outing.

"Getting colder," Farmer Hanson said. He had taken to slipping extra food into the basket, and Jewel's pride wasn't up to the task of refusing. He said nothing when she thanked him, but his face was careworn.

"It's colder," Jewel told him. There was little chatter that wasn't teeth. "Is it—"

"No. It's going to be a mild Winter, this year." By which he meant no snow, and therefore none of the inevitable deaths that snow brought when it fell this far south. Her breath came out in a thin stream of mist as she exhaled.

He hesitated, started to speak, stopped himself. She let him. She had no words to offer that he'd believe, and she didn't feel like making the effort for so little return. But it was Farmer Hanson.

"It's been a tough autumn," she told him, meeting his worried gaze and holding it. "But we've all seen worse. We're okay. We'll be okay. The port's still open, and we've got some work there."

"And Arann?"

She sucked cold air between her teeth. "He's— you've seen him."

"Aye."

"He's been better, but he'll be okay." She didn't believe it, but that might be guilt talking. Guilt talked a lot, these days, albeit seldom with simple words.

Words you could fight. Or argue with.

"Take care of him, Jay," the farmer said quietly. Echo of older words, when she had been younger and she could believe, for weeks at a time, that things would work out *well*.

And they had. For a while, they had. She tried to remember this as they turned away from the stall, carrying baskets that were half the weight they had been scant months ago.

Carver and Duster joined them as they headed toward the gates, signing.

Money, Jewel thought. She nodded.

You do what you have to do, her Oma said quietly, and in that tone of voice that meant there was to be no back talk without pain. *You do what you have to do to keep your family going.*

She nodded to herself, and to her dead—all her dead—and she tried not to think of how the other people who now, because of Carver and Duster's successes, had less money than expected were going to make up for it; if they went hungry, or if their children did, in a holding very much like the twenty-fifth, but with different names across the streets.

And her Oma said, *It's a hard world. You do what you have to. You don't choose strangers over your own.*

She wanted to believe it. She must have, because she wasn't.

But it was bitter, this necessity. What she wanted to be, and what she was, were so far apart she had almost lost sight of the former. She struggled to hold it, somehow, even though she didn't deserve it, didn't deserve the hope and the belief that somehow, someway, she would get there.

But she watched their backs as they left the Common, seeing Angel's spiked head, and Carver's black hair, Duster's, braided because they didn't know when a

fight would be around the corner and they had no easy
way to dodge it anymore.

Duster had been right. Carmenta's den caused more
trouble. She understood why Arann had snapped; she
understood where the rage and the despair had come
from. Wasn't it her own? But it didn't matter why.
Carmenta knew two things: That the den was now picking through the streets, looking for the same things
Carmenta needed to survive, and they were there a lot
more often.

His den took to traveling the routes that Jewel's den
did, spoiling for trouble. Once or twice, they got it, and
Jewel got to see, firsthand, what Arann looked like in
a fight.

Except it wasn't a fight.

Yes, he used his fists, his hands, his head—but it
wasn't like watching Duster or Carver; there was no
thought behind it, no intent. If Rath had insisted on
training them—and he had, in the early years—he had
mostly given up on Arann and Arann's instincts, and
while he was frustrated with Arann, Jewel had always
privately thought he liked Arann the better for it.

But he would have been angry, had he seen Arann
like *this*. Angry, and silent, the way he was. Even knowing why. She couldn't be. But she was terrified, watching
him go away—or emerge. She wasn't sure what would
call him back.

Finch had, that time. Jewel didn't like to take Finch
with them, because Finch was too small, too slight, and
she didn't want Finch there if things went bad.

But there was something incandescent about Arann's
inarticulate fury; it burned them all, even Carmenta's
den. Carmenta? He was used to fighting—when the
odds favored them—like a jackal. He wasn't used to
fighting people who simply did not care about odds or
weapons or threats. Fighting between dens was almost
like courtship. There were rituals, words spoken, subtle
physical negotiations, before they closed. There was
warning.

With Arann, there was none. He snapped from one state to the other in an eye blink. He put them off their stride, but it put Jewel's den off theirs as well. And soon, if he did this enough, Carmenta's den would figure it out, and their fear, the shock of Arann's brief cry, wouldn't be enough to make them clumsy or stupid.

After the second such fight, Jewel left Arann at home with Teller and Finch. She had to; she wasn't willing to watch him die, and she knew where the fighting—the graceless surge of rage, shorn of anything that resembled thought—would lead. Rath had told her, time and again, that anger was not her friend. He had told them all, but he had never had such a striking example to offer.

She took Angel, Carver, and Duster everywhere she went, sometimes taking Lander and Jester, and sometimes leaving them with the others; on those days, Teller was to teach them more reading, and more writing. When she was in, they went out in groups of four. Duster chafed at the restrictions. No one else said a word.

Through it all, Arann said almost nothing.

She understood this, because she didn't either. Shock—the shock of seeing him for herself—did not yield, as it usually did, to anger. It led, instead, to guilt, and a slowly growing fear that was almost, but not quite, panic. She'd led them this far, but it had been easy. Now, faced with hard, she was failing them.

Because she had already failed, she had no words to offer. And no comfort either, and she wanted both.

Kalliaris, she thought, as she walked, or studied, or ate, or tried to sleep. *Kalliaris, smile.*

21st of Scaral, 410 AA
Thirty-fifth holding, Averalaan

Rath had, for years, prided himself on his ability to compose. To compose specifically with words. Spoken, or written, he could massage them and lay them out in exactly the right tone for his intended audience. He could feign ignorance, or knowledge, with the same ease, without—quite—lying. He could change the style of his writing script, from the precise and perfect letter forms the Order employed to a bold scrawl that traveled in slanted lines across the page.

But the letter that held his attention, now, was work. He labored over it. Scattered around the inkstand were various iterations, some three lines long, some almost a full page. It was difficult because there were two letters written, the obvious letter, and the subtle one. If the person for whom it was intended could find—and read—its contents, she would give it, in the end, to another, and it was the second reader that caused him so much grief. Amarais Handernesse ATerafin. The Terafin.

It had been years—decades—since he had corresponded in the Handernesse style. If he had found the den and their sign language amusing, he too had been young once, and impressed with his own cleverness. They had had no specific code for apologies; in the Handernesse household, apologies were given silently, if at all. Even had they, he would have gone out of his way to avoid them. Had, in fact, already done so, discarding anything that even faintly implied it. He did not, and could not grovel.

But it was hard.

Because on the other end of this letter was Jewel Markess. He had seen her, at a distance, over the past month. He had watched the den, and he was aware that Lefty no longer ventured out into the streets. That blow, he thought, might break her.

What he wanted for her was not complicated. Achieving it might be. It was not in his hands, now; it had never truly been in his hands. But he placed it in the hands of the sister he had not seen for decades.

He paused, rose, and stretched his shoulders, lengthening his arms to either side. He disposed of the failed attempts, burning them in the grate, one sheet at a time; watched paper curl in a dark lip over the background of words, before the words themselves were consumed.

If he were honest—and when had he last been an honest man?—he might admit that he labored over this letter, this last communication, because he feared to reach the end. Three days, four, it had taken him, and he was not yet done; he could not think of another letter that had occupied so much of his undivided attention. He returned to the desk, and the letter, and he resumed his seat. The light of the stone made the ring on his hand glow. He tried, and failed, to ignore it. It was not his ring to wear; it was not his ring to keep.

But he made no effort to arrange for its disposition, and that said much, both to and about himself. He took up quill again, and wrote. The absurd desire to explain his life came and went, like waves. This was the last thing that he would say to Jewel—and one of the few that he could say without any interruption, any diverting questions.

When he heard the creak of floorboards, it was almost a relief. It was also a threat, and he rose, quietly, turning as he did, the seat of his chair against his knees. He had heard no key, no movement beneath him, and he slid his hand across the hilt of a dagger that was only useful for fighting one type of opponent.

But his hand stilled, and he did not draw the dagger.

A few feet from the door—on the inside of a room—a figure stood. The light in the room was dim, but not so dim that it was incapable of casting shadow, and shadows darkened the floor beneath the draping fall of a cloak. Rath whispered the light to brightness; the figure did not move.

They stood in silence for a long moment, and then the figure reached up with both hands and drew back the folds of a hood. As it fell, it surrendered a face to the light; a woman's face. Her hair was darker than Duster's, except for one prominent streak of white, which reminded Rath, incongruously, of the marking on his favorite horse in the stables of Handernesse.

She was younger than he was, but not, he thought, by much; it was surprisingly hard to tell. Her lips were almost the same color as her face, both pale, adorned by

violet eyes; her hands were long and thin, and she wore
no rings, no bracelets.

"Can I assume," he said quietly, "that you are
Evayne?"

Her forehead briefly gathered in lines as her brows
rose; the lines faded as they fell. "I am," she replied.
"And you are Ararath Handernesse, forsworn."

"I am." He lifted his hand, catching the light that
shone on the desk below his shoulder.

She nodded. Waited. So, too, did Rath. The moment
stretched. Thinned. Broke when Rath decided that he
could not afford the time taken to win such a pointless
contest. He turned away from her, and toward the letter
across which ink had already dried.

"It is not often," he said, as he sat, "that I have visitors, and I'm afraid I will be a very poor host, this eve."

He heard the rustle of her robes as she moved, but he
did not turn. She was a danger. He knew it. But he did
not feel threatened by her.

She did not speak, but came to stand on the opposite
side of the table.

"Where," he asked, dipping quill into ink, "did you
get this ring?"

"From Handernesse," she replied.

He did not ask her how; if she could enter *his* home, a
manse the size of Handernesse, with its many entrances
and exits, would be no difficulty.

"You mistake me," she said.

He moved the quill so that it rested above a desk that
was already somewhat blotched with ink. "How so?"

"I did not steal the ring. I came to Handernesse, and
I was given it."

"Impossible."

"I will not say I am not a thief," she replied. "Nor
will I say that I will not be one again. I spoke with your
grandfather before his death."

"And he *gave* you the Handernesse crest?" It was
hard to keep scorn from the words, and Rath was famously lazy.

"He did. I told him why."

"Why?"

"Why it was needed. I told him for who."

"And he countenanced *this*?" Rath lifted his hand, sharply, in denial.

"He was an autocratic man." Evayne was still. "But he was not a cruel one. I understand that he valued your sister highly. But in his fashion, Ararath, he loved you. He knew that you would never again cross the threshold of Handernesse."

"You told him this?"

She nodded.

"But he knew, in the end, that the threshold you finally crossed in its stead would be the more difficult. He did not greet death with any great peace."

And there it was. Spoken by a stranger.

"He knew, as well, that you *would* cross it. He understood, in the end, the need, and understood that you would—against the bitter disappointment of his expectations—do what was necessary, at the right time. It had to be that ring. Because that ring, in the end, you would wear." she added softly.

"You could both be so certain of that?" It was a bitter question.

"He was."

Ararath looked at the stylized H, and remembered, briefly, the man who had worn it. And the boy who had watched him. Both were dead.

"I told him," she continued quietly, "how you would die, both with and without his . . . intervention."

He flinched. He had resigned himself to his fate. Once a night. Twice a night. On bad nights, several times in an hour. "And how," he asked, forcing a lightness to his voice that he would never feel again, "will I die?"

"With or without the ring?"

"Without it. Let's start with that."

"The kin," she replied.

"They have not managed to kill me yet."

"No. But they will kill you, and you will not fight it. What they do before they kill you, however, we cannot afford."

So. He sat heavily, and once again took to the quill.

"And the ring?"

Her robes suddenly twisted, tightening around her body until he could see the shape of her thighs. "It will grant you death," she replied.

"A good death?"

"No."

He frowned. "Why, then, would this be of use to me?"

"You have made yourself a target. Deliberately. You have aimed yourself at Terafin."

"I have not—"

"And they desire Terafin. But you do not understand the kin; they are not mortal, and they are not all of one thing or all of another. Lord Cordufar is *not* mortal."

Rath nodded.

"Nor is Sor Na Shannen. They serve Allasakar."

The name fell like doom, and silence eddied around it. Not even the Priests of the gods and goddesses who could be worshiped across the breadth of the Empire spoke that name.

Yet she did, and she did not flinch.

"They will not simply kill you. They will not kill you at all."

"How then could I be of use to them?"

"They will possess you, Ararath. A demon will be summoned, and he will have no flesh but yours. He will take your body, which is not a threat to any but The Terafin."

Rath waited. This time, he won the round.

"If he takes your living body, they will have access to everything—everything—that you now know. They will know, not only about the undercity, but about Jewel Markess."

He stiffened at her use of the name, half-rising from his chair.

But she lifted a hand. "I mean her no harm, Ararath. But I know of her, and I know what she is."

He forced himself to return to his chair, to lift his quill. This woman had, through one of the most famous bards of Senniel College, returned the crest of Handernesse. She was not—could not—be normal.

"They will know about the letter you choose to leave her; they will know where you live, and when you hunt. They will know *all that you know,* and they will control what is left; you will be present, and you will see every action your body takes, without the ability to control—or stop—it."

"If they can do this—"

"They cannot do it easily, and they cannot do it often. It is far better to take shape and form flesh; to hide behind illusion. But illusion will not give them what they need to know."

He wrote a sentence, and then another, before he again looked up. "The ring," he said, "will destroy me."

She did not look away, and did not blink. "The magic is a Winter magic, Ararath. To use it, you bind your soul to the Winter road. It will devour you entirely. Some pieces of mind and memory will remain if you do not call it quickly. But you will die, and they will have shards, no more, on which to act."

"And if I am dead?"

"They will have perhaps two days. The demon will still live within your flesh, and he will expend magics to ensure that that flesh does not wither or decay, but he will have a corpse, and not even preservation magics— and they are not adept at those—will disguise that fact for long. They will have to act, immediately, upon their desires. They will have to choose caution or boldness."

"You favor bold."

"They are becoming bold even as we speak. Yes." She looked at the letter. "They will not be able to prevent the use of that ring. When they see it, and they detect the magics upon it, they will assume that you are the pawn of an ancient enemy; this will explain much to them, for that enemy will be in their minds. They will do what they can to prevent that enemy from seeing or knowing of their existence, and this close to Scarran, they can achieve that. It will be an expenditure of power that they feel they can afford, but it will hurt them.

"It will not occur to them until far too late that the ring is bound to you, and only to you. They may never realize the truth."

"And your role, Lady?"

"To guide." A flicker of expression crossed her face, as if it were a trick of the light.

"And when will you guide me to this death?"

"Tonight, Ararath. I would not have come, but you have stayed here these past four nights, writing and rewriting the same letter." As she spoke, she drew from the folds of the midnight-blue robe a small sphere.

It was as if legends walked, in that small and dingy room with its lack of natural light. The globe shone more brightly than the magestone in its stand, but unlike the stone, with its flat, gray surface, the globe was almost alive. Clouds whirled in it, blown by some internal wind that could not be felt, and every swirl, every movement, was like the beat of a heart.

A seer's crystal. A myth.

He wrote. Not of the crystal, and not of the seer; not, in the end, of the demons, or of the god they worshiped. Not of the hopes that he had for Jewel, in a future he would never see, not directly. But hope was there.

He set the quill down, but did not rise.

"It is almost too late."

He glanced up at her face, and saw, in the violet of her eyes, some dark reflection that the moving roil of clouds hid from his view. "If you know the future," he began, as he at last vacated his chair, "why did you not seek out someone with the power to prevent what has happened?"

Her expression stiffened, as if cold had leeched the warmth from muscle. He thought she would not answer, and he busied himself, curling the letter, which ran several pages, into a tube. This, he carried to the bedpost, and, after fussing with the top knob, inserted it into its hiding place.

"When you deal with gods, and you are not one, it is difficult."

He raised a brow, exchanging one jacket for another.

"A better question would be: How is it that we can expect to have any hope at all of thwarting the will of a god?"

"They are not here," he replied. "And they care little for what occurs upon this plane."

"You don't believe that."

He shrugged. "You don't. Or perhaps you do. What I know is this: If you are to be believed—and I believe you—you spoke to my grandfather and he gave you the symbol of his *House*. If you could convince my grandfather of the truth of this, you could convince anyone. You could bespeak the Kings themselves, and they would listen. You could intercede with The Ten—" He paused, and grimaced. "Perhaps that is stretching things too far; The Ten are fractious and very little occurs that is not to the benefit of one or another member."

"I could," she agreed. "If I were given that choice."

He frowned. "And you are not?"

The bitterness of her expression robbed her face of years. He revised his estimate of her age down, for in the elderly, expressions of this nature often added them.

"I cannot speak of it," she said at length, "but the answer is no. I walk where I walk, but between one moment and another, I am not certain where I will appear, or who I will see when I do. I did not know for certain that I would speak with you this eve."

"You suspected you might."

She nodded.

"And if it were your choice?"

"Were it my choice, Ararath Handernesse, I would not be here at all. It is not a great pleasure to lead men to their deaths, however necessary those deaths might be." She stopped speaking a moment, and when she resumed, her voice was softer, her expression more careworn. "And that is unfair. I understand that in your fashion you gift me with your reserve. You do not burden me with your fear or your desperation, and you do not plead with me to change what I cannot change."

"I do not waste words," he said, "when it serves no

purpose. If I did those things, it would not change anything."

"It would hurt me," she replied, in a tone of voice that made her seem invulnerable to the pain she described.

"And that would avail me nothing." He set aside all but the oldest of his daggers; those and the ones that had come from Sigurne. He whispered the light to shadow, but before it dimmed entirely, he turned to face her, and he smiled. "But I would ask a boon, if you could grant it."

"Ask. But be aware that I can grant little."

"I will ask much. Are we walking?"

She nodded.

"Through the undercity, Lady, or upon the open streets?"

She hesitated, at that. "The undercity, as you call it, is not safe. Not this eve."

"Safety is, it appears, beyond me."

She nodded.

"It is not—yet—beyond the ken of those who live, work, and walk in the streets above."

"No."

"Then if there is to be death, let us avoid bringing it to those who are innocent. In a manner of speaking. When the kin hunt, men and women die. Children die," he added, bitterly. "If it might protect them, we will take the safer route."

She shook her head. "They will face far worse than this before the end. But you are right. Let them face it later, rather than sooner."

"Why did you not just tell them where I live? I understand that you have said you cannot choose where you arrive, but as you are now *here,* would it not have been a simple matter of a message?"

"I have no manner of sending them such a message, or I might have."

He raised a brow. "I would appreciate it if you did not attempt to lie to me in my own home." He was surprised at the slight blush in her cheeks; he would have thought her beyond it.

But he would have thought himself far beyond anything that had happened in his home this eve. He led her to the supply room, and to the basement, but he did not lower ladder or shoulder the backpack with the rope that the undercity often required. He began to, and she gestured; light filled the darkness. It was magelight, but it was not contained by something as small and simple as a stone.

"We descend?" she asked.

He nodded, although he thought it obvious, and she gestured again. Midnight blue billowed at her back, and her hood rose slightly, as if at a strong wind. He felt his feet leave the flooring, and drew one sharp breath as she carried them both to the ground below, light surrounding her as if she were stone. But once they landed, she waited, and he took the lead.

"Jewel," he said, as he walked, his hand tracing the gradual changes of the tunnel wall as if they were all the map he needed.

She said nothing.

"You mentioned Jewel Markess."

"I did."

"Tell me, will she receive the letter that I've labored over for such an unseemly length of time?" He struggled for, and abandoned casual; the words were right, the tone was wrong.

Evayne hesitated for long enough that Rath turned. But the hesitation was linguistic; her expression was seamless, shuttered. "She will find it."

"Will she take it where it needs to be taken?"

"She will."

He nodded, and continued to walk. "Have you been here before?"

"Yes." The word was like a wall. Tonight, however, walls didn't matter.

She fell in beside him, light following her. He almost told her to dampen it, because he was unaccustomed to walking with so much illumination among these broken cloisters and sunless galleries. The stone walls, height to floor, broken and cracked faces, were almost white; light made them unfamiliar. "What was this place?"

"It was called Vexusa, before its fall."

Vexusa. The word felt vaguely familiar, but the memory evaded him, like the flicker of dim starlight, glimpsed out of the corner of an eye, that cannot be clearly seen when confronted.

"It was like, and unlike, the Cities of Man." Her voice was soft enough that he slowed to catch it, and as he did, he noticed that she looked to the heights; what she saw, he could only guess. "But there was power here, and it did not hide itself. We will never see the like of such a city again."

"If we're lucky?"

She grimaced then. "I speak, often, to myself," she told him, with just the vague hint of embarrassment. "But yes; there is beauty in power. There has always been beauty in it, but it is not a delicate beauty, and it leaves room for very little else."

"What follows in the wake of power," he replied, thinking briefly of a single dance in a mansion that seemed a world away, "is often ugly."

"By our standards, yes. But by theirs? No. It's just another facet of power, the shadows beauty casts. Power doesn't exist in isolation; it exists in a hierarchy."

"A point. This way."

She frowned, but the frown cleared.

"Will Jewel survive?"

"Ararath, I am not a device to be pointed."

"No, Lady. But she is much in my thoughts."

Silence, and then, "Yes, she would be. But it is not fear for her own survival which drives her."

He raised a brow. "Have you met?"

Evayne did not answer. When she did, it was not the question he asked, or knew to ask. "The last time you spoke to her is not the final time you will see her."

He stopped walking, and she touched his sleeve. "No, you will not see her tonight, and you will not see her in Averalaan again. She will not be in the danger you are in.

"But if you can, remember this: You will speak one final time. I do not know what she will say to you, nor, in the end, what you will have—if anything—to say to her. That is all I can offer you, Ararath. I am not known for either my kindness or my mercy, with reason."

Ararath Handernesse did not leave the maze again.

He thought it fitting, in the end, although he did not expect it.

He walked the streets of the undercity in the glow of Evayne's light. Magelight, when carried by hand the way Rath carried his, was an individual illumination, and it required proximity to reveal the things that otherwise lay under the blanket of absolute night. Evayne's light was true magery; it was like the glow of dawn, before the sun has fully crested the horizon, and it opened the streets up, depriving them, momentarily, of familiarity. Familiarity returned as he walked; he felt the same solid ground beneath the slightly worn heels of his boots; saw the passing crevices and the cracked stones, and knew them as they approached. She did not once leave his side as he walked, although he had expected her to lead. Minutes passed. Perhaps an hour. Something was wrong.

His smile was a bitter twist of lips. Of course something was wrong. But he needed to quantify it, pinpoint it, understand it. That had always been his way, and the night's journey only sharpened the need. It took him some moments to understand what elusive thing had caught and worried away at the edges of his attention.

It was Evayne, of course. Not the woman herself, not even her light, but the way her light cast shadows. His own, he knew, and he expected; they were an ephemeral but constant part of the geography of this maze beneath the City of the living. Hers? They were too long for her height, and too wide for her style of dress, and as he walked beside her midnight form, he fancied he could hear whispers just beneath the sounds made by their footfalls, hissing and struggling to be heard.

He glanced at the shadows she cast perhaps once too

often, and she flinched. "It is Scarran eve, the night before the darkest night of the year, when the Old Roads are open, and the host is hunting." She shivered as she said it, and drew the folds of her cloak more tightly around her shoulders. "I should not be here."

He caught a glimpse of silver at her neck, some hint of pendant or necklace; she touched it, briefly, before it was lost to a surge of blue light. Her robes twisted free of her hands. The shadows in the folds of fabric grew, and as they did he heard, for a moment, the distant call of horns, and he felt the chill of a Winter so cold it existed only in imagination.

He heard her cursing, the flat neutrality of her syllables broken by brief, harsh sounds. The light which had shone so brightly around her *shattered* into a spray of colors, sharp and harsh, that might in a different sky, in a different place, have resembled a rainbow.

Before they faded, he drew his magestone from his pocket, whispering it to a brightness that now looked dim. The shadows across the ground, stretching now like a slender path, groped toward him, devouring the steady, gentle glow. Winds howled, here, and he felt them as a stinging caress on his cheeks; he lifted his arm to protect his face. It didn't help. There had never been even a breeze in the maze; the velvet silence of an empty, ruined city had been so much a part of its character he had almost failed to recognize it until it was broken.

But this darkness, he had never seen in his life. He felt it now, and he knew it was as much a threat to life in this city as the demons he had played his deadly games with in the streets above. And as if it *were* demonic, he reached for the hilt of a dagger, drew it, and held it.

In the dim light, the blade was glowing, the runes, carved and enchanted by some magic he did not understand, searing their way into his vision. "Evayne!" He lifted the dagger, edge toward her, and the gale broke against it. But the runes dimmed as it did, and he understood that the Summer magic which could devour a demon whole would fade and diminish here against merely the wind.

Evayne's eyes, as she turned to look at him, were all of black, as if she had swallowed shadow and it had filled her. She did not speak, but lifted her hand, her fingers shaking, trembling. In the mound of her palm, the seer's crystal rested, and the light it shed was striated, broken. He remembered his legends: the crystals were some part of the Seer's Soul, extracted and bound. By who, or what, those legends did not say; nor, at this particular moment, did he care.

She spoke, struggling with words.

"Ararath! Come, stand beside me!"

He took one step, one slow step, and then another; but it was hard; instinct told him to flee into a familiar darkness that was in every way a comfort in comparison. Horns sounded again, closer, clearer.

"Evayne—"

"Don't touch me!" She cursed again, softly. "I should have known," her voice was the bitter chill of the Winter that kills. The instincts that had preserved his life for long enough that he could be called Old Rath screamed as he took each slow step. He fought them; what did it matter, now?

The line of her jaw whitened. Her hand became a fist around the crystal, and her robes billowed, flying higher and higher as she stood her ground. He did not want to stand beside her while cloth flew in that wind, because the twisting of cloth suggested life where life shouldn't be. But that was fear, and fear could feed either caution or hysteria. Rath had never had any use or respect for hysteria.

"Whatever lives in the undercity," she told him, "will hear those horns. Hold your dagger," she added, "and wait; we will not, now, travel to Cordufar."

"Evayne—"

"We will not, now, have any reason to do so."

As he listened, he heard one note above the horns; it was not a horn call, but sounded instead like the low peal of a great bell. And in the distance, against the fallen walls and the standing facades, he saw a flicker of red that suggested fire.

Chapter Twelve

THIS HAD BEEN A CITY OF GHOSTS, of things dead and absent, the detritus of history preserved beneath ignorant streets above. It had suggested, the way a dignified age suggests, the passage of a beauty that, at its height, must have caused men to stand for a moment, awestruck and shorn of words, because words would never be equal to the task of describing what was seen and felt.

Rath had never paused to imagine what might have dwelled here, because he assumed that he knew: it was a city, and a city meant a press of huddled people, some too poor to survive long, and some too wealthy to fall. He had imagined, in the shadows of privacy and the almost smug sense of ownership he had felt in the undercity, how those distant—and long-dead—people had lived, where they might have worked, what they might have eaten. He had guessed, haphazardly, at who they might have worshiped, assuming in the end that that worship would involve the gods in their Weston guises. It made sense, after all; the written language that was left along the base of pedestals, broken walls, and the small bowls and household items that occasionally remained was the precursor of the Weston that traveled through the city's halls, high and low.

But he knew, as the flicker of distant red grew longer and deeper, that he had been wrong. What had walked these streets, when the city was open to sky and knew sun and rain and sea squall, had not been some simple variant of what walked above them now.

"Ararath, stand." Evayne gestured, and light, a pale blue strand in the shadows, scrawled a brief, hasty circle across the ground; it encompassed both of them. "Stay your ground for as long as you can."

"Lady." He watched light grow in the streets, red light, dim and visceral, like a heart exposed to sun while flesh still clings in places. "Against what comes, I do not think I will stand for long."

"Against what comes," she replied, "you will not stand at all, but it is not, in the end, for you that they come. You will see Dukes, here, Ararath, and a brief, brief glimpse of the whole of Winter.

"They will be weakened by this," she continued. "They will be weakened enough that we will still have time." But the words lent her no hope, and no peace; her lips were a thin, white line.

Who are you, Lady? He did not speak her name because of a sudden the syllables seemed too insignificant to contain her.

"Evayne," she whispered, indicating that he must have spoken aloud. "But I know the old and hidden ways, and some part of the Winter Road is in me. Some part, as well, of the Summer Road, but it has not been traveled for millennia, and even were it, it is not to be feared. Hold your dagger, and if the light gutters, wield the other. Do not touch me, or I will devour you, and we will fail."

Snow came from the shadows. Snow and silvered light. What it touched, it transformed, briefly, in his vision; he saw forest, trees as thick as columns rising, black, into the sky, branches splayed like gnarled, ancient fingers. Nothing grew on those trees but ice; nothing sheltered beneath them.

But through them? The notes of the horns, louder now than wind, but wilder in their keening.

Snow lay like a shroud across the stone of the undercity, piling in drifts, but its reach was not the storm's reach; it was bisected by a single line, invisible but present. On one side, forest continued to unfold, and on the other? The familiar: the columns and walls, the facades, the fallen rock. But these, too, were transformed by burning light. Not Summer light to Winter, but fire to ice.

Out of the fire came living flame. Tall as the buildings from which it seemed to emerge, it gestured and wings rose, pinions stretching between facades, which crumbled at the casual contact. The air around its body eddied as it moved. Rath did not step back, but it took effort. This death was not the death he sought, and it *was* death. No weapon—no meager dagger with its engraved, pale runes—could touch the creature that stepped through these streets, dragging in its wake the smaller and paler demons that had, until this moment, been the whole of his experience.

But he came to the snow, to the sharp edge of it, drifts piling against unseen wall, and he gazed across it to where Rath stood. If he noticed Rath at all, he gave no sign; he noticed, instead, Evayne. He stepped across the snow line and raised his arms, dropping them suddenly as if tearing at the very air. Snow evaporated, rising from his feet as sudden clouds of steam. Where he walked, snow melted, and if he did not walk quickly, it mattered little.

"Stand," Evayne commanded again. She lifted her arms, crossed them above her face, and spoke three sharp words. The texture of those syllables hung in the air, but Rath could not grasp them, could not even repeat them seconds after they left her lips.

"Do you—do you know this creature?"

"Yes. I saw him once, when I was younger. We will not defeat him tonight."

Fire flew through the air, like the lash of whip; it banked the moment it hit Evayne's arms; she did not even tremble at the impact. Fire struck again, and again, it fizzled.

The demon—and the word felt wrong to Rath, because it felt too small—roared. It was not rage; it was laughter. It was brief, savage joy wrapped in the crackle of heat and power.

Evayne's arms came down in that instant, and light flared in her empty palms, traveling the length of the snow-strewn street. It struck creatures too small and too slight, and the laughter was joined, for a moment, by twin cries of pain. Creatures such as Patris AMatie, creatures who might have been twin to Lord Cordufar, strode the ground by the winged demon's feet in the wake of a fire that did not burn them. They were not human in seeming, but taller, darker, possessed of arms that glistened like polished obsidian; some had jaws the width of a shark's, and some, eyes the size of fists. They walked on two legs, or four, or more, and they carried no weapons; nor did they require them.

The winged creature barely seemed to notice them. For a third time, fire raced above the snow, and for a third time, it faltered.

There was no fourth.

The demon paused, and snow melted beneath his feet, turning to ice at the edges of his steps' imprint. He lifted one arm, and he spoke a single word; the earth rumbled with the resonance of that voice, and the winds banked, for just a moment, as a shield came to his left arm, and a sword to his right. The sword was red, and long, its hilt obsidian. The shield, glowing red, was rimmed with runes that were the color of Evayne's eyes.

"Karathis, Duke of the Hells," Evayne said, and her voice was carried by the wind, strengthened by it. "You are far from home."

He raised the sword.

But horns sounded again, and they came not from the light that had birthed this living fire, but rather from behind the seer, and this time—this time the notes were accompanied by the sound of light hooves, the clatter of armor.

In the light of silver moon—a moon that could not shine, *did not* shine here, but was nonetheless evident by the artifacts of light—the Wild Hunt rode into the streets of the undercity. They rode past Evayne, streaming out of the shadows beneath her cloak to the right of where she stood; to the left stood Rath. He noted that nothing touched the circle she had sketched in the ground; they moved to one side of it, although some leaped above its arc. But they rode through the snow, and above it, weightless and terrifying.

Armor gleamed in the impossible light; helms, with long, narrow visors, pauldrons rising in exaggerated domes. Falling away from the shoulders, lamés narrowed to stylized points that echoed the rise of the helms. The riders bore spears and lances, slender and thin. They did not ride horses; they rode great stags, tines gleaming at the height of antlers that seemed like crowns.

But one rider stopped a moment, by Evayne's side, and she raised the visor of her helm, for they were all helmed. Her hair spilled down her back, silver in the moonlight; her skin was the color of snow. Rath, who had danced with Sor Na Shannen, fell into a silence that was not interrupted by something as petty as breath: He had never seen, and would never again see, a woman so beautiful.

A woman so beautiful, and so cold.

"Little sister," she said quietly. "How long will the road last?"

"Not long," Evayne replied, although she did not look up, did not meet the rider's gaze.

"Then we will ride while we can." She lowered the visor, and from no sheath that Rath could see, she drew a blade. It was blue, a thing of cold, cold light.

"Karathis!" she cried, and the demon of fire and flame turned in that instant toward her. "Have you slipped your leash?"

He hissed, and he spoke, but the words, harsh and guttural, were not in a language that Rath understood.

The Winter Queen laughed. Her answer was the cold tinkle of bells, and just as unintelligible to his ears. She rode toward the Duke of the Hells, then. Toward, and not away. She was not half his height, but Rath understood, as they closed, that here height did not define power; the snow followed in her wake like a cape.

He watched in silence as the woman suddenly vaulted off the back of her mount. The mount reared, leaped, avoided the downward arc of the great, red sword. Ice cracked beneath its blade.

The Winter Queen did not land; instead, she rose, and the air held her, buoyed her. Her hair flew back, against the wind; her cape, which was silver and black, flew with it, as if it were the only standard she required.

And thus, Rath thought, the answer to the question the heights that this city had once possessed posed. What need had they of something so trifling as stairs? The wind obeyed her.

To her side, left and right, the riders crested the surface of drifts, and where they met demons, they clashed; blood fell, darkening snow and freezing against it.

But Rath, who had seen battles large and small, watched in a silence of snow and wind and fire, seeing the undercity, for the first time, as it might once have been when gods walked the world. He did not flinch when riders fell, or demons lost limbs; there was, about the fighting, an orchestration, a choreography, that none of his battles had ever had. Nor would they; he fought like men fought: to survive. If it was graceless, if it was lucky, if it was underhand—in the end, what mattered was that he walked away.

But to the riders, to the demons, the simple consideration of *life* seemed no part of the engagement, no part of the swift and elegant dance.

"Ararath!"

He could not look away, but nodded.

"Ararath, they will close the road. Not all of the *kialli* here fight. Look."

He forced himself to look beyond the body of the fighting; to look beyond the armored Winter Queen and her clash with the creature that Evayne had called a Duke of the Hells.

There, in the open and empty streets, two demons stood. One, he did not recognize, and one he did: Sor

Na Shannen. Lightning struck from above, shattering stone.

"Fools!" Sor Na Shannen cried, and even at this distance, he saw the flash of her eyes, the moving strands of her midnight hair. "Do not die on the road! Do not give them that purchase!" She lifted her arms in a wide sweep, and threw not light, not fire, but shadow.

Evayne lifted her hands and caught it between her palms, staggering at the contact.

"Run," she told Rath.

He understood, as she struggled to straighten her arms, that she spoke without thought; that she intended to stand, and fight. It almost made him smile. But he turned again to the streets of a city made forever alien, and he bore witness. It was all he could do; the demons and the riders were well beyond him, and he did not think the dagger that he held, runes dark and almost sullen, would be of use should he choose to abandon Evayne's side.

Blue sword clashed with red above; below, blood spread as the cold yielded to heat.

Rath was beneath their notice, beneath their contempt. Whatever existed in the streets and the mansions of Averalaan, whatever plots or councils Sor Na Shannen took with her allies, had ceased to exist *now*. The kin—the *kialli*—could fight like this for eternity; if the world died around them, they might not even notice.

They would certainly not notice the deaths of tens of thousands of people whose lives, measured in a handful of years, would amount to nothing. This was how beauty was defined in this place. *This* was what they faced. The wild, inhuman creatures fought, Rath thought, as if this might be their last chance *to* fight; as if this dance, this death, was all of their desire.

Sor Na Shannen shouted again, raising her voice above the gale. She strode across the cracked stone, toward the border beyond which Winter ruled.

At her back, a lone demon stood. He might have been a man, a slender, tall one. He might have been a rider. The form and shape the other demons took in their graceful savagery was not his. He might have been, as Rath was, a forgotten, inconsequential observer; he even lifted a hand to his chin, resting his elbow upon his palm.

And then he smiled. He did not stride toward the snow. Instead, he bent to ground as casually as a man might who has dropped an item of little significance. But instead of straightening again, he placed one palm against the surface of the stone causeway. He spoke no words, made no gestures, but he lifted his head, hand still splayed against ground, and his eyes traveled past the battles, large and small, to rest a moment upon Evayne.

"Evayne, be wary," Rath said.

Evayne glanced at him, and he lifted an arm.

She frowned, a counterpoint to the *kialli* smile, and then her eyes widened.

"Ararath!"

He saw her double over. The robes that had billowed above her like a standard in a gale fell suddenly, heavily, toward the ground.

"Ariane!" she shouted, as she lifted her head and her arms in one sharp, jerk of motion. Her hands were entwined in shadow that writhed even as it coalesced.

The Winter Queen danced back a step in the air and turned slightly to see the woman who had called her name. Evayne, still crouched upon the ground, pulled her arms back awkwardly against her chest. Her brow creased and her eyes narrowed; she threw her hands forward. Shadow leaped from them toward Ariane, the Winter Queen.

The Queen of the Wild Hunt. Legend, Rath thought. Of course.

Ariane threw back her head and laughed as the darkness swirled around her, melting into the gleam of her perfect armor.

Evayne stood, staggered forward a step—and vanished.

With her went the snow, the trees, the moon's light—
and the riders.

But Ariane remained.

She did not stay to fight, although it was clear to Rath
she desired as much. Instead, still carried by a wind
that no longer howled, she swooped toward the ground,
and toward Rath. He had not, until that moment, been
certain she had been aware of him at all. Her gauntlets
upon his arm, however, were proof, if it were needed.

He had no time to brace himself, no time to speak;
cold, metal fingers closed round that arm and bore him
up, where he dangled like a mouse in a hawk's beak.
Fire singed his cloak, and a roar of fury followed them.
So, too, did flame; the *kialli's* wings were not decorative.
But he was hampered in this wind; it was hers.

"Come, mortal. We have the gift of my sister's
shadow, but it is fleeting. Let us see what she hoped we
would see ere it passes and the Winter Road is closed
once again."

She flew through the city as if she knew its streets.
Rath fumbled with his magestone, but she seemed to
require no light by which to navigate, and if he was not
a graceful burden, he hit no walls, no outcroppings, no
broken remnant of bridges. Nor did he fall.

But she came to rest, at last, upon the steps of what,
to Rath's eyes, seemed an open coliseum. He could
not be certain, and he whispered light to its brightest.
The steps formed benches where he stood; they both
ascended and descended. She alighted beside him, and
drew blade. It shone far brighter than the light in his
hand, but conversely, it did not illuminate.

"So," she said, softly, and leaped. She did not take
to air again, although he thought she tried. There was
no wind at all in this place, and very little sound. The
magelight had difficulty piercing the darkness, and he
unsheathed the second of the two daggers that Sigurne
had given him.

There would be no report tendered her, for these.

He followed the Winter Queen down the steps;

heard, at his back, the cries and commands of those demons who had not been slain by her riders. But the cries themselves failed to move him here.

She ran across the even floor of the coliseum; he hesitated at the last stair, remembering the glory of her aerial battle. Aware of how little he might add to it, or to her.

But she stopped; in the distance, which was not so very large, he could see her by the glint of armor and the blue light of the sword she carried. She drew no shield, but stood a moment, and he chanced death, leaving the dubious safety of this final ring of stone. Beneath his feet, where dirt should have been, the ground was hard and smooth, and it glinted as if it were polished. He cursed, and whispered light from stone—but this time, the light did not come; whatever magic the stone contained was not equal to this place. He knelt briefly and saw that he stood upon a smoky, marble floor of a kind that might be seen in ornate temples and grand foyers.

He glanced back, and saw the concentric ovals in which spectators might sit, and frowned. The magelight illuminated them faintly; it provided nothing for what lay upon the ground in their center. This was—or had been—an arena; of that, he felt certain. And Ariane stood at its center.

As he approached her, light held, he saw what she faced, and he froze.

An arch stood at the midpoint of the arena floor, within a circle traced by carved runes into which shadows spilled. They were large, these runes, and he did not recognize even the shape of the letters, if indeed they were letters at all. Two columns rose from the floor, and above those two, cut stones rested together to form an arch. The keystone rose above them, and it was the keystone that caught his attention, because engraved in that single stone was a lone rune that glowed. The light was not bright, and it was not lovely; it seemed almost sickly in color, some mix of gray and green that pulsed as he watched.

Ariane surveyed the runes upon the floor before she

leaped up and across them, landing heavily—landing loudly—against marble. She did not turn to see if he followed. She was not, he thought, aware of him at all; all of her attention was held by the arch. By what lay, suspended, within it.

He had thought it an odd structure, a freestanding arch with no walls, no room, no building to surround it. But he realized, as he watched it, that he could not see clear to the other side. Something lay contained within the frame of the arch itself. Something moved within it.

He froze then.

Ariane did not. She lifted her sword in both hands, and with a single, angry cry, she brought it down, into the marble upon which the arch now stood. Both hands were upon the hilt, and one remained there as she rose. With the other, she removed her helm and tossed it aside, where its clatter joined the sudden lap of fire.

Rath rolled across the ground, out of its reach.

The fire engulfed her where she stood. Her hair flew up in a wild, platinum wind, but it did not scorch or singe or burn; nor did she. If she felt the fire at all, Winter's Queen, she did not deign to acknowledge it.

She spoke, hand on sword, hair framing her as it rippled across her cloak and her armor. She gestured, sharply, lifting her head as she did; her voice above the roar of fire and the urgent cries of demons was a song.

And by the golden light that enveloped her, Rath understood what she did. It was a Summer song. How she could sing it, he didn't know, for she was Winter's creature. But here, for just this moment, he saw the Summer in her, and at Winter's height, it was still glorious; he could not breathe for the sheer beauty of it.

Power, he thought. Beauty. He understood why they had once been considered the same.

He heard the demon's roar at his back, but did not, and could not, turn. He understood, somehow, that her song had weakened the edifice within which darkness resided.

The arch trembled; the ground beneath the sword fissured. And in the center of the arch, the shadows roiled, and the shadows spoke her name.

"Ariane, I will destroy you for this when I arrive."

She pulled her sword from the cracked, broken stone, and lifted it. "It will not be the first time you have tried, and the last time you failed, you had followers, and you walked upon the plane. Now, you have the dead to do your bidding, no more. And I, Lord of the Hells, have the Hidden Court and the Old paths, and they were never your dominion.

"The world is not what it was when last you walked here, if you can truly walk here at all. Come, if you can. We will be waiting."

She sheathed her sword, and as she did, Rath felt a cold gust of clear wind. She turned to glance at him, and then she began to fade, growing slowly translucent in the dim light until she was gone from sight.

Lord of the Hells.

Rath stood upon the marble floor of the arena, his hand around the hilt of a dagger, gazing at the arch. He did not—could not—speak the god's name, although he knew it.

He had played his games, scavenging like a carrion creature through the vast empty space of this buried city, with no understanding at all of the stakes. He now understood the interest of Patris AMatie completely.

They attempted to bring a god to the world.

The god was not yet here, and Ariane's brief song proved that the passage was vulnerable; what might the god-born do here, what might Kings achieve, if they came at last in force? It was to hide this arch, this god, and his imminent arrival, that Patris AMatie had undertaken to remove *anyone* who might have some knowledge of what lay beneath Averalaan.

And people played out their shallow drama in the streets above, cozened and ignorant, as he had been cozened and ignorant. The voices of the demons grew louder at his back. Still, he could not turn. Nor did he attempt to run. Instead, he waited, the hair on the back of his neck rising.

She came to him while he stood thus, and paused at his side.

Sor Na Shannen was capable of doing what fire and the tremble of earth could not; she demanded enough of his attention that he could pry his gaze from the formless, dense shadow that spoke with the voice of a god. He turned to face her, and she looked pointedly at the dagger he held in his hand.

He could, he thought, stab her. But he sheathed the dagger instead. Wondered, as he did, how much of the impulse was his own, and how much could be laid at her feet.

"You serve the Winter Queen," Sor Na Shannen said, when the dagger's light no longer shone.

"No, Lady."

"You wear her binding."

He frowned, and then realized that she spoke of the ring.

"But she will not save you, now. She cannot."

"She would not even try," Rath replied. "What could I be to her—to any one of you—that it would be worth the effort?"

A brow rose over her perfect eyes. Instead of answering, she turned to look at the arch, and he saw her expression, made opaque by the turn of her profile, as it changed her face. "You do not fear me, Ararath."

"I do, Lady."

"No. I am *Kialli*, and I am kin; I sense fear, and you have none to offer me this eve." It was not, from her tone, to her liking, but it did not anger her.

He bowed. He would not argue with her. There was a quiet about her that hinted at awe. He had always desired the quiet places.

"What is love?" she asked him softly, placing a hand upon his shoulder to hold him fast.

It was a rhetorical question; he did not seek to answer.

"What is love?" she asked again, still gazing at the

arch as his eyes sought to map the half of her face he could see: the long, unbroken nose, the high cheeks, the full lips and the almost delicate turn of chin. Her hair, long and black, was like silk in its fall; it did not tangle.

"Sor Na Shannen," another voice said.

"I have him. Summon; he will not escape," she replied, although she did not look away from the arch or in any other way acknowledge the speaker. What she did not do, Rath would not. He found her beauty compelling, and he desired what sight of it she would grant before the end.

"What is love, that you seek it?" Still, she stared straight ahead. But her hand tightened, and he felt her nails pierce his shoulder. He should have been surprised that they traveled so easily through so many layers of fabric. He was not.

"What is love," she continued, "that mortal men and women, through all the long ages, have sacrificed, plotted, and died in its name?"

"Lady—"

"You asked what love was to me," she told him, her voice too low to be husky. "What do you see when you gaze upon the answer?"

This time he did turn, to gaze in the direction that she herself was gazing. "I see only shadow," he whispered. "Endless shadow, endless darkness, endless night."

"You see no form?"

"No, Lady."

"A pity. When I was counted one of the least of his servants, I served my Lord. He was beautiful, Ararath. He *is* beautiful."

"I am mortal," he replied, as if it were a failing.

She nodded. "We followed Allasakar," she said. "We will always follow Allasakar. When the gods agreed to the binding Covenant, we were given the choice: to remain in the world or forsake it to follow him.

"We followed." Her voice was so soft, he had to lean toward her to catch the words. "We followed, and we were betrayed.

"But even betrayed," she continued, "even then,

were we given a choice, we would follow. What is love," she asked again, "but pain? What is love but ballast? What is love but the greatest of lies, the most effective of weapons we give to our enemies to use against us? We cannot cast it off. We cannot deny it. We can hate it. We can be destroyed by its imperative. We can rail against it, but even were we to become the most powerful of the kin, we cannot escape its grasp.

"What love do you feel, that brings anything but the darkness?" She turned to face him then.

He might have answered. He meant to; he opened his mouth to offer her the words that she clearly desired. And she *did* desire them; he did not know why. But he hesitated, and in hesitation, lost the moment.

"Sor Na Shannen, we are ready."

"Very well."

Her hand tightened, and this time he felt pain as the nails bit deep. He grunted at it, saw the pale blush rise in her cheeks. She pulled her hand back; his blood reddened her nails.

"The Winter Queen has cost us. If you can take satisfaction from that, take it." She stepped back, and then nodded, her gaze flickering past his shoulder. "It is all you will have, in the end."

His shoulder began to burn, and that fire spread through his body as if it were liquid. He bit his lip, grunting; his knees buckled beneath him. But she held his gaze; he could not look away.

When the fire began to speak to him, he knew. He *felt* the voice. He struggled a moment against its imperative, but it rolled over him, ignoring his will as if his will were inconsequential. He opened his mouth to scream, but sound was denied him. His knees straightened, his hands unfolded. He turned—without volition, without will—to Sor Na Shannen, whose lips, full and red, lifted in a cold smile.

"You will help us now," she said softly, and she reached out to caress his cheek.

Ararath Handernesse, the voice inside him said, *you are mine.*

He could not think for the pain, but he *did* think. Of the undercity. Of his sister. Of Jewel.

No—

Everything you have ever been is mine.

He tried to move his hands, and failed. He would have stabbed himself with the consecrated dagger, but it was beyond his reach although it rested in safety against his body.

Evayne, he thought. *Your gift—*

He understood it. He understood why it was a benison. He understood all: the reason for it, the reason for the ring. A moment. A *choice.* His memories unfolded even in that instant, and were he not in so much pain he might have smiled.

But without smile, he called the ring's gift, and was answered.

Death came, then; he heard it in a sudden scream of surprise and rage. But the pain didn't end.

Chapter Thirteen

THERE WAS VERY LITTLE IN THE WAY of heat in the apartment, and Jewel suspected that most of it came from the floor below, where one or two of the tenants had had a better season than the den. This year, unlike the previous two, they didn't have wood for the woodstove. If Farmer Hanson proved wrong about the mildness of the winter, they'd be sleeping in the same room, pressed together so tightly they couldn't move without waking the rest of the den, because they *still* wouldn't have wood; they'd barely have food.

They had blankets; they had bedrolls. Those didn't wear out at the same rate that clothing did. And clothing was going to be a problem, because even with half the food, the den kept *growing*.

She glanced at the shuttered window; she could see the hint of moonlight between the warped slats. Carver, Lander, Duster, and Angel had gone on a foraging run, out by the taverns where people were less likely to be careful, on account of alcohol. She didn't expect them home any time soon; drinking apparently took a good deal of time. They'd camp out someplace and wait for the tavern to empty.

Jewel sat in her chair by the kitchen table, burning a

candle. There were two left, and she was almost look-ing forward to having none, because when she did, she would have to sleep with the rest of the den until Carver came home. Even though they didn't use the maze, he still took the magestone with him when they went to work; she let him because his work was still the more dangerous.

Her fingers drummed the top of the table as she added and subtracted numbers on the slate in front of her hands.

This was where she worked, when she wasn't out in the streets like the others, winding her way through anonymous crowds, cutting their purses, if they were fool enough to carry them on slender thongs around wrist or shoulder. This was where she sat, the detritus of these nightly attempts at maintaining even the most pathetic grip on hope spread out across a kitchen table that was used for almost nothing else.

It was the last night that she would do this.

21st of Scaral 410 AA
Thirty-second holding, Averalaan

Duster glanced at the moon and the magelights of the open streets. People were slowly hauling their butts out of taverns, stumbling in the doors and careening around the light posts. Carver and Lander pulled up the rear; Angel had her left, and the wall of the third building west of the tavern had her right. She carried a dagger; no one else did. They weren't here to fight; they were here to rob some drunken, careless idiot, empty his pockets, and hightail it back home.

This was familiar to Duster; it was what she knew. Living with the den for three years had made it pointless—but she hadn't forgotten anything. Neither had Carver. Lander was predictably silent. Angel was grim. She'd never quite gotten the hang of him. He was good in a fight. She knew enough about fighting to know that. But he didn't like it. It didn't prove anything to him. He hated the thieving as well, but never argued; he did his job. Farm boy, she thought. He'd said he was a farm boy. How many drunks did you roll on a *farm*?

But if you were going to lie, "farm boy" was a stupid lie. She gestured, den-sign, in the brief light. Carver nodded, started to break off, and froze. Angel froze as well; she could see his back stiffen. Couldn't see past it. Didn't have to see to hear.

"Well, well, well, look who's come crawling out of the twenty-fifth."

Carmenta.

Duster started to move, then. Carver's left hand rose; his fingers twisting in the air. *Ten.* Shit. Ten. He'd dragged out his whole damn den.

"We're not hunting on your turf," Carver said. "Unless you've branched out to the thirty-second." He didn't lower his hand. Instead, he motioned again. *One minute. Run. Split up.*

Duster hesitated, and then sheathed the knife. You didn't run with a knife you didn't want to lose, and she was *never* going to lose this one.

"You ain't ever hunting there again." She couldn't see what Carmenta was doing; wanted to look. Didn't. Instead, she watched Carver's single lifted hand.

They had no signs for names. *Meet back home.* Didn't need 'em.

Duster glanced behind her, turning to face the streets. Carmenta was still Carmenta; he had all of his ten practically standing on his own damn feet. None of 'em behind her; if he'd tried to box them in, it would have been bad, although they could still hit the river.

Lander was close to Carver; Lander lifted a hand.

Angel took one step back, spun.

Carmenta snarled something. Laughed.

They ran.

Duster and Angel took the first left that opened up, heading away from the river. Carver and Lander? They headed farther down the road; she glanced back once, saw them disappearing. Carmenta's den broke, depending on whom they were following, and she heard Carmenta shouting like a rabid freaking dog.

Angel signed something; hard to see and run.

She started to tell him as much, heard shouting come closer, and shut her damn mouth. *Move, move.*

But she knew where they were going. Taverns weren't closing yet, not tonight, and they still had one it was safe to duck into. They didn't hang outside Taverson's, picking off drunks; Jay wouldn't let them. She liked the man and his wife, and she wanted to hit outsiders first, if they had to hit anyone.

If they'd had time, Duster would have stayed in the thirty-second, because Carmenta was risking his den there. Yes, he wanted to take them out—but doing it, full den, in another den's turf was just *asking* for trouble. Maybe not right away, maybe in an hour or two if they took that damn long. But word was sure to get out to whomever now claimed the thirty-second, and they'd come hunting Carmenta.

But . . . she didn't know the thirty-second. And with maybe a minute's head start, they could dead-end in the wrong damn alley or the wrong backyard, and then it was over. The impulse to see Carmenta crushed by his own stupid mistake warred with the imperative to cut risks wherever possible, but it was close. Angel would follow her; they wouldn't split up again.

She could think and run.

Yeah. Think. Run. Carver had Lander. Lander wasn't good in a fight; didn't like 'em. He could stand shoulder to shoulder with the rest of the den—he could do that; could make himself *look* useful. But he couldn't fight. And if the odds were bad, he'd spook. Didn't scream, though. Didn't make much noise at all.

Damn it.

She hit the long road that led to the twenty-fifth; it wasn't empty, never was. But nothing between them and Carmenta's gang was going to be much help; there were no magisterians in the thirty-second anymore. If she and Angel were lucky, they'd hit a place to lose the gang before they reached Taverson's. If they weren't, they'd get in before Carmenta's boys. She tried to count steps; too many. Four. Five. But she hadn't heard Carmenta's ugly howl since they'd split up.

Probably meant Carver had him.

She took another corner, skidding on purpose to make the turn faster. Soon, they'd hit the stretch of alleys and yards that they knew well enough; they'd hit the obstacle course and keep going. Angel was better than anyone at it; taller, for one. But Duster was good.

Had to be good.

Because—

Jay needed her. Jay needed them all, now. Even Lander, who didn't talk much and couldn't fight. Fisher had hit her, hard. But Lefty? Lefty, crippled, terrified Lefty, had gutted the den. Arann was still lost in silence and rage. Finch and Teller barely took their eyes off the damn door. Jester had gotten damn quiet the past few weeks. Lander's hands were mostly still in his lap, and he'd never talked out loud much. All of them.

Even Duster. Damn it. Even her. How many times— she cornered by a building, this time, her palms losing skin to some of the only brick wall at the crossroads— had she wished he'd just *go the Hells away*? She'd never been good at numbers, and couldn't count that damn high. He'd bugged her. His cringing. His hiding behind Arann or *Finch*. His stupid humor, when he bothered to try. Would have said she almost hated him, if anyone had asked.

So now, *now,* the little rabbit was *gone*. Finally gone. And she *hated* it.

She hated it. Everyone else was lost, wandering around the hole he'd made in the den. She would've expected that. She would *never* have expected to be so damn lost *with* them. It made *no sense*.

There, Felstone Ave. Small alley between the standing buildings; gap in fence and a run-up you could use to get over it. They'd gain minutes there, if they were lucky.

She liked to think she'd never been lucky. But she was still here. Fisher was gone. Lefty was gone. No one knew where, no one knew how. If she died here, if Angel did, at least they'd know. Carmenta would probably leave their bodies in the middle of the damn street as a warning or a boast, or both.

But it'd break Jay. It'd break what was left.

Why do you care? she snarled at herself, drawing breath, feeling the dry walls of her throat try to stick together. Her hand fell to her dagger, as if it were an answer. Maybe it was. Maybe it was all the answer she could carry.

Jay should have let her slit Carmenta's damn throat. She'd *asked*. She'd asked a hundred times. He was a danger. Duster'd always known it: Carmenta was *what she knew*.

But it wasn't the only thing she knew, not anymore. She knew that they couldn't get caught, couldn't die. Not her—but also: Not Angel. Not Carver, not Lander. For Jay's sake. For the rest of them. Because if losing Lefty hurt—and it hurt *her,* and she *hated it*—what would losing anyone else be like?

Worse. So much worse. She'd killed her uncle. She'd been savagely, fiercely, exultant. She'd left her kin, not that they cared. She'd never had anything to lose before.

How was this supposed to be *better*?

Duster and Angel came in, opening the door into the flickering light of a candle. They hesitated there, and Jewel glanced up; saw them looking, not at her, but at the floor, as if they were counting.

Chalk snapped in her fingers as her hand tightened; it wasn't a loud sound, but they both looked up.

She asked the only questions that mattered. "Where's Carver? Where's Lander?"

They glanced at each other. She saw the bare hint of fear cross Duster's face. Angel's was shuttered tightly. Neither Duster nor Angel answered her question, and she pushed herself out of her chair. The chair toppled, the clatter followed by a silence that contained no breathing but her own.

No one was sleeping anymore.

"You were *supposed* to stay together!"

Angel met her gaze, held it a moment, and then looked away.

Duster bridled. "Carmenta had his entire gang out by the river. We ran into them. We ran." She shrugged, but it was a stiff, jerky motion, no grace in it. "We split up. We thought Carver and Lander'd come back here."

It had been a long damn time since Jewel had had to work so hard to keep her mouth shut. She did the work because the words that wanted out would be said to wound, and it would just be a transfer of pain and fear; it would do no damn good. In silence, she turned her back, took a breath, and picked up her chair. She pushed it halfway under the table, and then thought better of it, and pulled it out again.

When she could trust her voice again, she said, "Which way did they run?"

Angel answered. "We went to Taverson's. They went in the direction of Fennel's warehouse. We said we'd meet back here."

Arann rose, shedding bedroll and the one thin blanket he often used as a pillow when it wasn't too damn cold. "I'll go."

"No," Jewel told him, struggling, still struggling, to keep the heat out of her voice.

He started to speak, and she lifted a hand, den-sign. "Carver could outrun Carmenta in his sleep. He knows the holdings," she added.

"Lander—"

"Lander's with Carver."

"We could all go."

Jewel looked at Teller. He had come out of the bedroom fully dressed, but that wasn't surprising; he often didn't sleep until she did.

"Go where?" she demanded.

"Fennel's?"

"Carver's not stupid enough to get boxed in there."

"Duster said Carmenta had his whole den lying in wait. He might have no choice. We can all go."

What good will you be in a fight? She didn't ask. He heard it anyway.

And she hated that he did; hated that it seemed to be coming down to this, more and more: Worth was defined by the streets, and by what you could beat, or terrify. That wasn't why she loved Teller. It wasn't why she loved Finch.

As if all thoughts were shouts, Finch stepped quietly out of the bedroom as well, glancing at Duster. After a brief pause, Finch squared her shoulders and headed to the kitchen. Clinking plates were, for a few minutes, the only sound in the room. They were oddly comforting, even given the lack of substantial food to put on them.

Finch came back bearing that insignificant food to Duster and Angel, neither of whom had eaten. Angel, who ate anything, took the plate in silence. Duster stared straight through hers as if it were invisible.

"We're not going out," Jewel told them all. "We won't find them."

"You're sure?" Teller asked.

Jewel nodded, because she suddenly was. It was not a happy feeling. "Duster," she added, her voice lower, and wearier, "eat."

Duster took the plate from Finch's hand; Finch, knowing Duster, hadn't moved it far. The cat came out of the bedroom as if aware that there was a very real possibility that Duster would simply drop the plate on the floor. Duster glared at the cat; Teller came and picked her up.

"We don't eat Duster's food," he said softly.

Duster snorted and looked at the plate. But she didn't eat, not yet. Instead she drew one sharp breath. "Jay—"

"No. You were right. Splitting up was smart. I'd've done it, if there were only four of us and his entire damn den was out. Eat," she said again. "We can't afford to waste the food, and we can't afford for you to go hungry. We need you to be as sharp as you can be, especially now."

Mollified, Duster leaned back against the hall wall and then slid down its surface to the ground. But she was quiet, for Duster, as if she'd been winded. Her anger was

almost a legend in the den, but tonight it was brittle and
easily broken. Not, Jewel noted, by hunger; Duster was
pushing the food around her plate. Easy to notice, when
there was so little of it.

"He'll be back," Jewel added.

Hours later, he was.

He opened the door into an apartment that was,
as usual, carpeted with the sleeping; Arann, closest by
far to the door, with a gap between him and anyone
else who might be unlucky enough to roll over in their
sleep. Keeping Arann off the streets had put an end to
his sudden, terrifying rages—but if they'd ever thought
he'd woken up badly before Lefty's disappearance, they
knew now just how wrong they were.

She'd heard the door; you couldn't be awake in the
den's space without hearing it. Working at the table,
working in the mess of candle wax with its flickering
light, she listened for the sound of the floorboards'
creak. She heard Carver's breathing, and she did not
want to look up.

Because she *only* heard Carver.

And she *knew*, sitting in this not-quite-dark, that she
could listen until Moorelas rode again, and she would
only hear Carver.

Something broke in her. It didn't feel strange, and it
didn't feel new; hadn't she broken this way three times
now?

She knew what Carver would say, and she made him
say it *anyway*. She needed to let him talk; if she spoke
first, she wouldn't hold on to her words or her fury or
her fear, and she knew they'd be aimed at him.

But she also let him talk because she wanted him to
tell her that Carmenta had caught them, or had caught
Lander. Because if he could say that, she'd believe him.
And if she believed him, they could find what was left
of Lander, and they could bring him home.

She asked him questions and he answered, but she
didn't really hear his words, and didn't really hear her
own, although she knew some of them were bad. She

knew what Lander and Carver had done. She *knew*. But she made him tell her *anyway,* because even knowing it, she could try to lie to herself; she could try to pretend.

But Carver didn't lie to her.

Carmenta's den *had* boxed them in at Fennel's. He and Lander had gone to ground in the maze.

And only Carver had emerged.

She slapped him. She didn't even realize she'd raised her hand before her palm was stinging. He made no move to stop her or block her—and he could have easily done either. She stopped herself from hitting him again, but she didn't know how, and she almost didn't know *why* anymore.

But she understood Arann's rage, his uncontrollable fury: it was, for a moment, her own. And she *could not* take it out on Carver. She couldn't.

His eyes were already filmed with tears and certainty.

Gods, Duster had been *right*. They should have killed Carmenta ages ago. They'd had the chance, more than once, and it would only have taken *once*. Without Carmenta, Lander would be home.

She told herself that, and she believed it.

And she would make him pay.

22nd of Scaral, 410 AA
Twenty-fifth holding, Averalaan

She woke up the next morning. The money hadn't, thanks to Carmenta, increased. The night had been cold enough that the coins—the few that were there—hurt to touch for long. Hurt for other reasons, as well. Those, she kept to herself.

She led the den to the market and led them home in a grim silence. Everyone knew that Lander, like Lefty and Fisher before him, would not be coming back. They might have grieved openly, had Jewel given them time for more than a painful, painful silence—but she didn't. Her anger was bright and hot and focused—and she hid behind it, holding onto it as tightly as she could. She'd lost *three*. She'd promised them some kind of home. She'd promised them some kind of safety.

And she'd failed. She'd failed them, and they were gone. Dead, she thought, and finally *knew* it. But the rest? She would *never* let go of them. She would never let them disappear again. She was going to talk to Rath, the minute she could get food home, and she was going to demand the answers she should have demanded when Fisher had first disappeared.

She was going to make him tell her everything he knew about the maze and she was going to make certain that whoever had taken her den-kin would never be in a position to do it again.

How? How will you do that? Her voice. Her Oma's voice. Both bitter and slightly sarcastic.

I don't know, she replied. *Doesn't matter how. I can't fail them again. I can't. I get to be the next person who dies. Just me.*

As if it were a privilege, to die first. But wasn't it? Wasn't it better than being—than always being—the one left behind?

No one else, *Kalliaris*. If she had to lead them to the Free Towns as farm laborers, she would do that instead.

She took Carver and Duster with her; left everyone else in the apartment. Finch was talking quietly to Arann, but Lander wasn't Arann's problem in the same way that Lefty had been. Lander had been Duster's. Jewel considered, briefly, leaving Duster behind—but Duster had never been a berserker. She had a foul temper, and a tongue to match, but she wanted, first and foremost, to *live*. She wasn't stupid enough to start a fight she couldn't win. She could be vicious; she'd probably be *more* vicious, if there was opportunity for it.

But today? Jewel wasn't certain she'd even try to stop her. She wanted—they *both* wanted—someone to suffer for this loss.

And Jewel needed her. If Carmenta was out on the streets—and this was early, for his den—she needed Duster beside her. Duster and Carver.

"Angel?" Carver asked, but she shook her head.

"I want him here."

"Why?"

"Because if anything happens here, he can think on his feet."

"You're expecting something to happen *here*?"

"No."

But Duster and Carver looked at her, and so did the others, or at least the ones who'd heard.

"Jay?" Angel said quietly.

She shook her head. "I don't know," she finally told him. "I'm not—I'm not certain. I don't *know*. But—I don't have a good feeling."

That was enough for Carver.

It was enough for the rest of the den, as well. They were silent, but they would have been silent anyway; Lander was gone. She knew they were looking at each other and trying to memorize everything, because they didn't know who would be *next*. But so far, everything had happened out *there*. This was a safe place.

No, this *had been* a safe place.

"Just—be ready for trouble," she told them. It was lame, but Angel nodded.

They didn't have a lot of stuff here, but it would hurt to lose the bulky things: the bedrolls, the blankets. On impulse, she pocketed the magestone.

She glanced briefly at Arann, and Carver nodded. They left the apartment and took to the streets, blending in with the crowd. If Carver and Duster took the opportunity to rifle a few pockets, so much the better—for a twisted meaning of the word better—but she didn't slow down much.

Duster walked the cobbled streets as if her footsteps could crack stone. Or as if she wanted to, and she did. She didn't talk much, because there wasn't much point. Jay was closed up like a bank, and Carver wasn't a whole lot better.

Lander was gone.

Lander was dead. Jay hadn't said it, but Duster knew

her well enough to read it off her expression, to read it off the things she *didn't* say. She was angry, and Duster understood anger. What Duster didn't understand was how to let it go. How to bleed its edge. Lander was gone.

Lander, who she'd promised Waverly's death. Lander, who had told her to do what Jay asked—to kill him quickly and cleanly—and *come home*. Lander who had been the *only* reason she had learned the stupid densign, because if not for his silence, it would have been a kid's game, and Duster had never been a child. But Lander wouldn't talk any other way at the beginning, and besides Jay, he'd been the only person she cared enough about to make an effort. Lander had suffered almost exactly what she had suffered. It had nearly broken him.

The others—Arann, Lefty, Teller, Carver, Angel—they'd come from different places.

But it was Fisher and Lander that Duster grieved for, and the only safe way to express that grief was to walk as if she could shatter the street. *This* was what caring for people got you. Pain. Loss. She wanted to punch something, or to stab it, over and over again, because maybe if she caused enough pain to someone *else,* hers would leave her the Hells alone.

She should have known better. Life hurt you, it always hurt you, if it thought it could get away with it.

No more, she thought. *No more.*

The thirty-fifth holding was one of the worst holdings in the old City, and of course, that's where Rath lived. Jay took a few detours, and Carver and Duster followed, wordless, as she did. She had that look on her face and she didn't slow down for a second.

Carver glanced at Duster once or twice, and Duster forced herself to shrug. But she was uneasy; they both were. Jay wasn't even paying attention to the streets anymore. Duster had started off angry, and that was fine, but somewhere in between home and here, anger had been edged out by something like fear: Jay was in a hurry.

You couldn't argue with Jay when she was in a hurry, and Jay in a hurry was always a bad sign. Something was coming. There were three of them. Jay wasn't bad in a fight, but she wasn't Carver or Duster.

But nothing came. No Carmenta. No other nameless, faceless den intent on carving its rule in their flesh. The air was stale, breath was too damn short. Lander was dead.

They reached Rath's, and Carver headed up the steps to the main entrance, but Jay caught his arm, shook her head. They went down the steps, instead, to the old door that led directly into Rath's place. He never used it. Hells, *they'd* never used it. Carver glanced at Duster again, and he muttered something about knocking; Duster kicked him before he'd finished.

Jay opened the door, and it scraped along the frame as she dragged it.

Jay went straight to Rath's room. Carver split off to search one room, and Duster, the other. They didn't expect to find anything, although if they'd tripped over Rath's corpse, it wouldn't have surprised Duster much; Jay was that damn tense. Jay had told them to search the apartment, and Duster suspected this was an ill-thought attempt to get them out of the way while she rifled through Rath's real room.

Duster briefly glanced into the kitchen, and then made her way to the room that she had shared with Jay, Finch, and sometimes Teller. She entered the room; it was now mostly storage, and even then, mostly empty. There wasn't much here to steal, and if there had been, she wouldn't have bothered. This wasn't home anymore, but it had been, and while Rath had never liked her much, he'd let her stay.

Because of Jay.

She walked farther into the room and crouched by the wall, touching the floorboards.

This was where she had lain the first night she'd come to the den. That night, hand on her dagger, she'd pretended to be asleep, evening out her breathing, thinking of stealing the money Jay left lying around in her unlocked iron box and making a run for it. Wanting it, Duster thought, but never enough to *do* it. Jay had known, and Jay hadn't cared much. *Now,* Jay said, *is all we have.*

And what if what you wanted was more than now?

She closed her eyes for a minute; leaned her forehead against the wall. It was cold. *Lander. You wanted this, for us. For me. I never asked you why.*

And never would. Even if he were still here, she knew she wouldn't. Wasn't in her. Never had been. But here, in this empty, quiet room where everything had started, she wanted to know. She wanted, for a minute, to be the kind of stupid person that could care enough to ask.

The floor creaked, and she rose, hand dropping to dagger as she turned.

Rath stood in the door, watching her. His eyes were dark and cold, and his lips were turned up in a half smile that seemed oddly—wrongly—familiar. Something about it. He was still tall, but his expression, even with that cool smile, was so remote and so watchful she froze.

"What are you doing here?" he asked softly.

She shrugged. "We let ourselves in. You were out," she added.

"Obviously. You're not here alone."

She shrugged again, and this time, his eyes narrowed as he stepped into the room. He caught her arm—her dagger arm—and his fingers were tight enough to bruise. The hair on the back of her neck rose; she almost tried to break free.

But she didn't. Rath was clearly in a mood, and only Jay could fix that.

They found Carver first. Rath was even less amused to see Carver in the drill room than he had been to find Duster. He grabbed Carver with his free hand, and dragged him out. The two of them trailed in his wake as he walked down the hall to the rooms that had always been off-limits to anyone but Jay, and sometimes Teller.

"I guess you can't go home," Carver said, with a grimace.

Duster said nothing, but she noted, with grim satisfaction, that it was Carver Rath released in order to open the door.

"Jay," Duster said softly as they were more or less pushed, by the shoulders, into Rath's room. It was as much of a warning as she could offer. Jay, back to the door, didn't take it.

"What's the problem?" Jay touched the papers on Rath's table. Duster remembered that he'd worked there, rather than at the desk.

"I was hoping you could answer that," Rath said, pulling whatever conversation there was out of Duster's hands. "What are you doing in my place?"

Jay froze for a second. Then, lowering her arms and taking her hands away from Rath's precious letters, she turned, slowly, to face him. To face all of them. Four people in the enclosed space made the room feel smaller than it ever had.

Jay must have felt it, too. She folded her arms tightly across her chest, planting her feet across the floor as if she expected to be hit, and needed the balance. "Came to talk to you." Duster glanced at Carver, but Carver, brow furrowed slightly, was watching Jay.

"And it was so important you had to pick the lock instead of waiting?"

"Yeah."

"And these two?"

"Look, you know the situation with the maze. I had to come here *on foot*. I don't do the thirty-fifth on my own. No one smart does." She looked as if she might say more. Didn't. This time, when Duster glanced at Carver, he glanced back. Lifted his hand in a brief flutter of fingers. *Jay's worried. Something's wrong.*

Yes.

"What was so important?"

Jay flinched. "Lander's gone as well."

Rath didn't look surprised. He didn't look anything but pissed off. "When?"

"Yesterday. Early evening."

"And?"

"We—we think he was followed into the maze. Carmenta's gang."

"I see. Were you there?"

"No. Carver was."

Duster glanced at Carver as Rath removed his hands from their shoulders. Duster's fell to her dagger. The gift she hadn't wanted. The gift she wouldn't let go of, ever. They'd all been there then: Fisher, Lefty, Lander. Watching while she swore. Waiting for her to come back after she'd stormed out. They'd known. And this wasn't some cheap, rusty castoff. It was a damn good knife. It had cost them. If they'd never bought the knife, they'd've had a few more weeks. But they wanted *her* to have it.

She wanted it now, as well.

Rath turned to Carver. "Carmenta's den is?"

But Jay answered instead. Her voice was clear, and it was like ice; it made Duster frown. Then again, sunlight on the wrong day could make Duster frown. It just didn't make her cold. "Twenty-sixth holding. They nest above Melissa's place, near the Corkscrew."

"There's no maze door near the Corkscrew," Rath said quietly. His eyes were narrowed, and nothing that had happened so far had taken the edge off his expression. Duster had always known he was dangerous. But this danger felt different.

She glanced at Jay; Jay wasn't looking at anyone but Rath, and her expression made clear that she saw—or felt—what Duster did.

"You'd know," Jay told him as she shrugged. Stiff shrug. "But it doesn't matter. If they know about the maze, they'll be in it like a pack of rats. We'll lose our advantage. And you know Carmenta. Word of the maze'll hit the streets like rain in a sea storm." She tightened her arms across her chest and watched him.

Duster watched her, and kept her expression as flat and neutral as she could. What the *Hells* was Jay talking about?

"I see," Rath finally said, after a long, cold minute. He lifted a hand to his eyes, pressing his fingers against his lids. His arms were stiff, rigid. When he lowered them, he exhaled, and his expression was different. Less cold, Duster thought. But not kinder. "Go home, Jewel. I've kept out of the maze for long enough now. I'll find Lander for you. If he's injured somewhere in the maze, he'll have left some sort of trail. If there's something there . . ." He turned to Carver. "Where did you say you entered the tunnels?"

He hadn't.

Duster couldn't keep the frown off her face. This was *wrong*. The whole conversation was wrong. Jay's anger, Jay's fury—it was gone. And what was left felt a whole lot like fear. But Jay held it down.

Whatever was frightening Jewel hadn't taken hold of Carver. He shrugged. "Fennel's old space. At the edge of the holding."

"The warehouse?"

"Whatever. It's not used for much right now."

"Good. Ladies, gentleman. If you'd care to depart?" He pointed to the door of his room, which was slightly ajar.

"What?" Duster said softly.

"Get lost."

They all converged on that door as if they could fit three people through its frame at once. Duster's breath was short and shallow; Jay didn't seem to be breathing at all. Carver glanced at both of them, and signed, but Duster missed it, the gesture was so fast and so understated. They walked down the hall to the familiar, bolted door; Carver reached above Jay's head and pushed the bolts open.

"Where are you going?"

They all started. Jay turned as Rath walked toward them.

"You told us to get lost," Duster replied, hand on the knob of the apartment door.

"Use the underground."

No one moved.

"Well?"

The silence lasted for a minute. They let Jay break it, because it was Rath. "We don't use the maze," Jewel told him quietly. Her hands were by her side, and she signed: *Get ready to run.* But she was still and she sounded calm.

"I'm not telling you to go very deeply into the maze. Jewel, don't let the events of the last two weeks turn you into a frightened child. The tunnels are the safest way through the holding. Use them."

Duster took a step forward; Carver grabbed her arm. With his free hand he signed a simple *no,* and since there was no way to sign *Who the Hells does he think he is?* Or *He can't talk to Jay like that,* her own hands were motionless in reply.

"No," Jay said again. "Carmenta's gang is probably wandering around all through it. I won't risk it. And I won't risk any more of my den-kin to it either."

Rath stared at her—glared, really. "Carmenta's gang doesn't know about the maze."

She met that glare and held her ground. "They don't have to to get lucky. Seems like they already have," she added bitterly.

He looked as if he wanted to say more. Hells, he looked as if he wanted to kill someone—and wasn't particular at the moment about who. But he didn't try, didn't move. After a long damn minute, he said "I'll meet you back at your den, either with Lander, or with news of him. Don't get yourself killed on the way back."

"Thanks, Rath."

They spilled out of the apartment door, and pushed the boundary between a walk and run in their haste to leave the building. No one spoke a word. The front door of the building itself wasn't locked at this time of the day, and had it been, it was a crappy lock that even Teller could pick, given enough time. Carver pushed the door open, and Duster, hand dropping to the comfort and familiarity of her dagger hilt, stepped into the streets of the thirty-fifth. Carver followed.

Jay waited until they were clear, and then she closed the door behind her and leaned back into it for a minute. It was only a minute; she straightened, plastered a really fake smile across her face, and began to stride down the streets. She wasn't being careful either; it was as if the thirty-fifth no longer held much fear for her.

Since it held the same people, more or less, that they'd taken detours to avoid, this said something. Duster didn't wait to find out what the something was; she'd never been much for subtlety.

"What was that about? Carmenta hasn't come anywhere near the maze." She walked to Jay's left, taking up her usual position; she also glared at an alley or two as they walked past the openings.

"Carver," Jay asked, instead of answering Duster's question, "are we being followed?"

Carver shrugged, and said something random. He repeated the phrase, and then laughed; Jay laughed as well. Duster understood what they were doing, but didn't join them. Then again, she didn't usually join them when the laughter was genuine either.

They followed the streets, Duster wincing at Jay's expression, which was so fake it was practically its own sign. But after a couple of blocks, each of which took them closer to the end of this godsforsaken holding, Carver signed, *Yes. Followed.*

"Who?" Jay said, voice low.

Carver hesitated for a moment, and then shrugged. "Old Rath."

"*Kalliaris.*" Jay stumbled. Duster grabbed her arm before she could take a spill onto the cracked cobbles, and held her up until she found her feet again. She was white, and she was shaking. "Smile. Smile on us, Lady."

Carver and Duster exchanged one long glance. They

all prayed to Kalliaris at one time or another; gambling, thieving, taking a risk. All of them. But they almost never prayed out loud, and if they did, it was bad.

How bad? Duster thought. She opened her mouth to ask. Closed it. Felt Jay's fear invade her, as if it were a disease.

Jay didn't hear the question, because Duster didn't ask it—but she answered it anyway, in her fashion. She was walking, but she was walking badly, the way she did when she'd woken in the night because of a nightmare. "Duster, go home. Now. Take a route so twisted even your shadow couldn't follow you. Get everyone out."

"But—"

"Don't argue with me!" Jay took a deep breath. Held it for a second, and spit it out, wrapped around more words. "Get everyone out! Take the iron box and leave *everything* else. Find a place out of the holding to hunker down, and then send a message to us. *Send* it. Don't come yourself."

The silence fell like night. Duster struggled with it. Struggled with the trembling in her arms, in her chest, the certainty of danger. Not starvation. Not cold. Worse. She wanted to tell Jay to send Carver, but she couldn't force the words out.

Don't trust me with this. Don't trust me with them, Jay. What she said, instead, was:

"Where?"

"The trough." Taverson's place was one of the few watering holes the den felt at home in. It didn't deserve the nickname they used. Nicknames were like that. "If we're not there, or you don't hear from us again, the den is yours—and it's your responsibility to keep it safe. Stay out of the maze; *never* use it again."

"This have something to do with Rath?"

"Yeah." Jay brought her hands to her face, and rubbed the sides of her cheeks. "I don't know who that was back here, but I do know it wasn't Rath."

"What?"

"Rath's dead. Now go, Duster, or we'll all end up that way as well."

*   *   *

Rath—or whoever it was that looked so much like him—followed Jay and Carver when Duster split off. But he'd glanced at her as she did; it was a quick glance, and in it, she felt herself weighed, as if the single look was a scale. He hadn't hesitated, and he'd barely paused, but he'd noted her, noted where she took off running.

He hadn't followed.

He hadn't had time to make sure someone *else* did. She clung to this as she began to make her way home. She didn't go straight, but she didn't take as long and twisted a route as Jewel had demanded; she didn't have the *time*.

The one thing Rath had taught them all was this: the ability to travel, quickly, while being tailed. He'd also taught them to notice tails, to watch for them, by pointing out the little things that were often wrong. The man who smelled like a bar but who seemed too alert and aware. The woman who lingered in doorways in clothes that advertised availability, but who somehow failed to engage a customer.

Duster had paid attention while pretending to ignore him. She cursed herself for her need to impress him by her display of obvious boredom, because she wasn't completely certain that she'd learned *enough*. Wasn't certain that she wouldn't have learned more if she'd just given him the whole of her attention.

Gods, she could be so damn *stupid*.

Carver should have done this. The den—they all knew Carver, and they all *trusted* Carver. She'd done damn little to earn their trust—what would they say when she burst into the room and told them all to clear the Hells out? To follow *her*?

Her hand fell to her dagger. It was a comfort, its pommel warm with sunlight. She could threaten them all, round them up. If Arann stayed sane, it would work. Or she could just tell them that Jay had sent her—but would they believe her?

She used everything Rath had ever taught her, now—because she was afraid. That was the truth, beginning and end. She had *never* seen Jay look like that before, and even if she wasn't blessed with Jay's vision, she *knew* what it meant.

She glanced over her shoulder. The streets seemed like streets; she'd crossed the boundary of the thirty-fifth on her way to the twenty-fifth, cutting corners around the thirty-second to do so. In all of this, ducking across yards, where they existed, and around stalls and shops where they didn't, she wondered if she'd seen enough. If she'd avoided enough.

She hated it. The worry. The fear. It was all wrong.

What the Hells was she doing, anyway? Why was she running *to* the den, when something this big was up? She didn't even *understand* it. Rath was dead. Jay had said Rath was dead.

But Duster, thanks to Haval, knew enough about makeup and pretend to know that the man who'd plucked her out of her old bedroom *was* Rath. It wasn't makeup. It wasn't just clothing and dye. The only thing it could be—if Jay was right—was magic.

Magic could kill. It could kill them all, yes.

But it could kill *her*.

She slowed her stride, hands shaking as she made her way up Wright Street. She cornered it cautiously, and avoided one teetering wagon that was dangerously close to the building fronts. She stopped as the shadow of the wheels rolled past, long and crenellated against the uneven stones of the street.

There, in the shadows cast by wagon and by the un-known, Duster finally admitted the truth: She had wanted the den. She had wanted a home. She deserved *neither*.

Maybe this was her punishment: to have it only so she could lose it. Because she knew, and Jay knew, it was gone. Maybe it had vanished with Fisher, and they'd all been too damn stupid to acknowledge it. When had she gotten so stupid? She could run home—but all she'd be doing would be clearing it. Scaring people out into the streets who didn't have the brains to survive there.

She shouldn't go.

She'd only have to leave one way or the other, and

this way, she'd be safe. Her hand hit her dagger hilt almost reflexively, and paused there. She didn't look down at it; she didn't have to. A birthday gift. Her only birthday gift. She'd *hated* it. And wanted it. That was her life. It was never just one thing, never just the other; it was always dumb, always complicated.

She turned; the wagon was long gone, and the streets were full of people. None of them seemed to notice her, much.

Godsdamnit.

She started to run.

She didn't stop until she reached familiar turf, and even then, she slowed just enough to catch breath. Carmenta and his den weren't ranging the streets—not that she could see, and given their den, you could see them swaggering a mile away—and she made the front door without pause. She slid into the familiar daytime darkness of the stairwell, and then bounded up those stairs, too numb to pray. Even if she'd been able, she wouldn't have been certain what she would be praying *for*.

But the door was still shut, and when she swung it open and staggered into the familiar large room, with its spread collection of bedrolls, blankets, plates, and crumbs, she saw the den look up. Everyone except Jester, who was talking to Arann and Angel while lying against the window-side wall.

Teller, sitting in front of the slates, his hand white with chalk, looked up. Finch was seated to one side of him; she rose.

"Duster?" Finch said, her brow furrowing and her dark eyes narrowing in concern.

Duster took a breath. "We need to move," she told them. "Jester, shut the Hells up!"

Jester, who had failed to look up when she entered, looked up then. "What's up?"

But Angel, seeing her expression, vacated the floor. He was, she noted, already wearing his boots, and she could see the hilts of daggers butting against the underside of his tunic.

"You. Or you'd better be. Get your shoes on. Everyone, shoes. Now."

Arann rose as well, kicking off the blankets that were lying across his legs. "Duster?"

Teller stood. He started to stack the slates.

"Don't bother with those," Duster snapped. "Just go and grab the iron box. We need to get out of here."

Silence. It was the silence she'd feared. She started to speak again, but Teller lifted his hands. It took her a moment to realize that he was signing with them. It was stupid.

But her own hands rose in response. *Danger. Now. Run.* Speaking their language as easily as if it were her own. *Jay said run.*

Teller and Finch exchanged a brief glance, and then he did as she'd ordered; he left the slates and the chalk, and ran—ran—to the bedroom. He came out with his boots and the box. Arann was already tying laces, and Finch rushed past Teller to grab her boots and do the same. Jester grabbed his boots as well; the laces were knotted. Angel snorted, and bent to help him undo the knots. Some days she *really* wanted to smack Jester.

But they were moving.

"Duster," Arann said, when he'd finished. "Where are we going?"

"Someplace else. Here's not safe now."

"What happened?"

She grimaced. Started to tell him to shut up, and bit it back. "I don't know," she said, her voice low.

As if he understood what it cost her to admit that much, he simply nodded. He glanced at Angel. "I'll take the lead."

Angel nodded. "I'll pull up the rear."

Duster inserted herself between Arann and Finch; she was willing to let Arann lead, because she did her best work from the side or the back, and she didn't have his obvious strength.

They made it as far as the street. It was the usual crowded daytime street, with the usual children, the usual grandparents, the usual pedestrians walking toward the Common or the well. It was even the usual cold but sunny of a Scaral day. But their shadows seemed longer, and without clouds, the sun's light was too damn bright. No place to hide, here.

Duster watched the road. Glanced briefly at the people passing by on either side; she never looked at one thing for long, bouncing instead between different objects: alleys, wagons, stray dogs, Arann's broad back. Everything was in motion now. Every motion had a natural rhythm. Rath had taught her that, as well. Look for the false step. Look for the inconsistent movement.

What she hadn't been looking for was a total lack of movement, but it caught her eye, and this time, her glance was riveted. A man stood dead center in the street, as if he were a large rock in a moving stream. He was dressed for the weather, and had he been walking, she might not have noticed him—he was too old to be part of a den, and too poorly dressed to be important; he didn't carry an obvious weapon and wore no uniform that could attach him to the magisterians. His hair was a short, cropped brown, his jaw was slightly square. He was of medium height, although he was broad around the shoulders and chest. His eyes were brown.

Brown or something darker.

But he just didn't *move*. He didn't swing his hands, didn't flex his fingers, didn't speak or tap his feet or shift his position at all.

People flowed around him to the left or right, some cursing him—at a safe distance. He didn't appear to care.

Kalliaris.

Duster reached out and tapped Arann's shoulder, but Arann had noticed as well. He slowed. Behind him, Duster signed, her hands at her sides, her fingers leaving the hilt of her dagger to do so. She hated its absence, and she was terse, to the point. She saw Finch and Teller stop, heard Angel's single word to Jester as she found her dagger again.

Arann attempted to go to the left, because that's

what Arann did. He never tried to push his way through an obstacle of any kind if he could avoid it. Duster watched, moving behind him at a slower pace, slipping into some of the crowd that wasn't her den to get a slightly different view.

It was enough.

As Arann went left, the man moved for the first time: he turned. She saw his face in three-quarter profile, and she saw his *smile*.

She almost froze, then, because she recognized the smile. Not the face that wore it; that was still nondescript. It made the smile that much worse, because it didn't belong on his face. But there it was.

She'd seen it before. Before she'd met Jay. Before she'd met Finch, although only by a handful of days. Before the den, when all of her life had been bitter pain, degradation, and—yes—fear. She'd seen it in the shadow of Lord Waverly, in the wake of his passing.

And she'd seen it in the mirror. That's what they were, after all: mirrors. They saw in her what they were. They'd told her as much.

She *knew* what he was. The knowledge almost paralyzed her.

But Arann kept moving.

Arann, Finch, Teller, Jester. Angel, pulling up the rear, as he'd promised. She saw them, and saw the man turn again, and then he began to walk through the crowd. He knocked four people over without rushing them; he just walked, slowly and inexorably.

This was it. The den. The demon. Jay hadn't believed in demons.

Jay had believed in *Duster*. What Jay had seen, the demons couldn't, or didn't want, to see. Duster hadn't either. She hadn't believed in it. Not until Lord Waverly, and even then, it had been *so damn hard*.

Her hand closed in a fist around the dagger's hilt. It was not the right grip for the weapon.

Duster hadn't believed in what Jay had seen, but she'd *wanted* it anyway. She almost couldn't remember why. What had she said? She wouldn't cook or clean or run errands for Jay or her den because she wasn't *good at that*. She was only good at one damn thing.

One. Damn. Thing.

That had been enough, for Jay.

Watching the den, the people she hadn't obeyed, hadn't served and hadn't deferred to, she realized that it had *also* been enough for them. She'd come on as muscle because it was the only thing she had to offer. And Finch in her kitchen, Teller at his slates, Angel at Jay's side, Carver, Arann, even Jester with his stupid, stupid jokes—it had been enough for *them*. She hadn't cooked, or cleaned, or washed the clothing. She *had* faced Carmenta down. She *had* kept the others safe when the streets got too crowded or too rough.

And Jay had told her to keep the den *safe*. Her order. Jay was the only living person that Duster took orders from, ever. She hadn't had any doubts that Duster *could* do it; she hadn't told Carver to come. She'd sent Duster.

She sent me.

"Arann!"

Arann turned at the sound of her voice, and the demon stepped forward and hit him, twice, in rapid succession. He carried no weapon—no dagger, no sword—he'd hit Arann in the side with his fists, one-two. Arann's eyes widened and he buckled. She couldn't be certain, but she thought she had heard the telltale crunch of bone. Broken ribs, maybe worse. Just like that. Arann looked up, and the man hit him hard across the face, twice; he went down.

She came in at the side and she slammed his knee as hard as she could. He shifted his stance, not quite staggering as she drew her dagger.

"Arann!"

Finch and Teller were at his side, grabbing his arms, trying to add their pathetic weight to his attempt to get the Hells up. He staggered, the way the demon hadn't. The way, she knew, the demon wouldn't. Arann's forehead was bleeding; something had broken skin, and it was deep enough to weep blood.

Oh, she *knew*.

"Go to the trough! Go now, damn it—run! Angel!"

He'd lined up behind the demon as the demon turned, at last, to face her, his mouth split in a hideous grin. Her dagger had cleared them some space in the streets; Angel's dagger had cleared some more. Neither of them were the danger that this man was.

Time slowed. She'd heard that it did that sometimes. This was the first time she'd experienced it.

She'd never gotten the hang of Angel—but she knew he meant to fight here. To join her, the way Carver would have joined her. He'd seen what had just happened to Arann, and it didn't matter.

He'd try to fight. He'd fall. And then—then it would all be over.

Run, she thought. She had to run. He'd fight; she'd make it out alive. She'd make it out.

And she would have nothing, again. There would be no den. There would be *no den*.

"No! Angel! Trough! Damn you, *leave me and go*!"

Angel shook his head, and she spit, leaping out of the way, into the crowd, under the demon's unblinking gaze. "*He's not human!* Run!" To prove her point, she drew her other dagger and she threw it. She was a better throw than anyone in the den but Carver.

The dagger bounced. It bounced off a plain tunic, and clattered to the cobbles.

Angel hesitated, and then he met her eyes, and she saw the shadow in them, not of fear, but of something like recognition. He nodded once—that was all she had time for—and then he hurried over to Arann, who had gained his feet. Angel's hands flew. Just his hands, but the den started to run.

She wondered if they'd be stupid enough to look back over their shoulders, to argue with each other. If they were—if they did, and she somehow survived—she'd kill 'em herself.

But right *now,* she was in the street alone, in a widening circle of people who knew enough now to be afraid. She took a breath, and it was a clean breath, an easy one. *Jay,* she thought. *Jay, I get it. I get it.*

Did she love them? She couldn't say no. She wanted to say yes. She had no answer: She was Duster.

She had no idea how long she would last. But she laughed in his face. "Do you recognize *me*?" she said, her voice low and guttural. "Were you there?"

"One mortal is the same as another," he replied. "But you are almost kin."

She spit then. Maybe. Maybe she was. Maybe she'd just done the same thing with the den that she'd done for Finch—got them away because it would cost the demons. She felt that triumph now, and it was the same triumph saving Finch had given her.

What had she said to Jay? Saving Finch had been the only *good* thing she'd ever done. The only thing she'd ever gotten right. Even if she'd done it to strike out at her tormenters.

But . . . it didn't *matter why*. Jay had said that: It didn't matter. What mattered, in the end, was what you *did*.

And this had to count, didn't it? This had to count for something. She backed him up, trying to lead him down the street.

She didn't stand a chance.

She'd hate them, for running. She'd hate herself for letting them run. She knew it. Pain and fear did that, to her. But right now she felt as close to peace as she ever got. There was a fight. There was a death. It was all so close to the bone it was clean.

And she wouldn't be the one looking at the empty spot in the room, and waiting for a voice or a gesture that never came.

Chapter Fourteen

ANGEL HELPED ARANN; he was the only per-son there who had the mass to do it. But it was hard to drag Arann away. He'd gained his feet, confused and in pain; when he spoke, blood trickled out of the corners of his mouth. But he made it half the block and staggered to a stop in the lee of the tall, narrow build-ings that housed so many people in the twenty-fifth. "Where's Duster?"

Angel shook his head.

Arann met his eyes, and then tried to turn. To go back. Angel grabbed his shirt and his shoulder, turning him around again.

Arann's expression made Angel look away, to warped wood and cracked cobbles and the damn weeds that even the cold didn't kill; to the green and the gray of something that seemed normal. Arann knew.

"Arann," Angel said, voice low, "we need to get Finch and Teller out of here. We need to get them to safety."

"We can't abandon Duster—"

Angel flinched. This time, he didn't look away. Shadows passed them, colorful shadows that indicated people walking by, minding their own business. "We're not. She's holding him off. Arann, *she chose*. Don't waste that." He glanced down the street, at the distant crossroad. They could clear that distance in a minute or two, and this was costing them time they didn't have.

"But—"

"She's twice the fighter *I* am. She's ten times the fighter you are—more, in your shape. If she can't take him, *none* of us can. We've got to *go*. Finch!" He gestured with his dagger.

Arann hesitated. Blood reddened his lips and his teeth; it darkened his brows, sticky and wet across his forehead. He turned, once, to look back through the streets. Duster's name left his lips in a whisper that was, in its own way, almost a scream.

"Arann," Finch said, taking his sleeve in one hand and looking at his face; it was white, except for the gash along his forehead, and those lips, that trickle of his own blood. "Arann, *please*." Some of it dripped onto the shoulders of his shirt. She pulled at the sleeve, and he looked down at her, his eyes narrowing as if he found it hard to focus. He wanted to say no. They all saw that.

Finch said quietly, "I won't go if you won't."

He closed his eyes for a few seconds, and then he nodded and followed, stumbling over the larger gaps between stones that were so common in this holding. And in the next two, truth be told—but they were staying in the twenty-fifth. Jay was still here.

The den turned at the crossroads.

They ran, but it was hard; Arann was slow and in obvious pain. Something was wrong with his breathing; Finch asked Angel, and Angel, remembering his father's words, said nothing. "Just get him to the trough," he told Finch, trying to keep grim out of his voice. "Get him to Jay. We can figure out where we go from there."

The unspoken *nowhere* hung in the air.

Arann had taken no obvious life-threatening wounds; the man had held no knife. The gash across Arann's forehead, while it might scar, wasn't going to kill him. But wounds or no, it was obvious that he was in pain, and it was not the type of pain that sleeping for a day would cure. It was the type of pain that cried *doctor,* or worse, *healer,* and they didn't have enough money to eat, let alone pay for either.

"Duster said he wasn't human," Finch whispered to Angel, when they turned a corner and almost collided with the stream of people moving toward the Common. They were heading toward the river, and they were moving against the crowd. Running wouldn't be a problem—if they didn't have Arann.

Arann stumbled; Angel caught him and they both almost went down. "Angel," Arann said, wheezing, "leave me. I'll catch up. I'll be right behind you. Get the others to Jay."

But if Angel had seen the wisdom of leaving Duster behind, he *would not* leave Arann.

Arann knew. "You left her," he whispered, "because she had to stay. Leave me."

Finch shook her head, almost mute.

"It'll kill Jay," Angel told Arann. "I won't do that to her. We *all* go, from here on in."

"You think losing Duster won't hurt her?" He coughed, choking on the last word.

"Yes. It'll hurt. But Duster did this so the rest of us could escape. We owe it to Duster. *You* owe it to her. Come on. We can see the river," Angel added, his tone as encouraging as he could make it.

Jester was watching the streets; Teller was standing beside Finch, clutching the iron box to his chest. It made a *lot* of noise when he moved. Angel almost told him to drop the damn thing; there wasn't all that much in it anyway.

But it was all they had, and if Arann needed anything—anything at all—the scant hope of its contents couldn't be abandoned.

"Break's over," Angel's voice, terse. Steady. "Jester?"

"We're clear." Jester hesitated. "From what I can see, we're clear. You should be watching the back."

"I—" He broke off, nodded. He'd trained with Carver and Duster at Rath's. Jester hadn't, much. *Carver, damn it.*

Arann coughed, straightened. He glanced at Angel

and said, with a grimace that was only part pain, "I'll take the lead."

"I'll pull up the rear."

The river had never seemed so far away. Not even on days when Angel was on laundry duty and had to lug a basket full of clothing from the apartment to the water, which wasn't hard, and back, which was, because it was all wet.

He walked alongside the den, close to Jester, who walked behind Finch and Teller. Jester had given him point, but he helped where he could; they ran in spurts because that was all Arann could handle, but they took advantage of the breaks to scan the street. It was messy. If anyone was following them carefully, neither Angel nor Jester was going to catch them. Duster would have.

Duster.

Angel swallowed. Straightened. This wasn't the first time that he'd let someone else do the fighting; it wasn't the first time that that someone else had died because of it. He'd never expected to be faced with the same damn choice in the City of Averalaan. Dens, yes. Street fights, yes. But those weren't the same.

This was like Evanston.

Angel shoved the thought as far out of his mind as he could when Arann rose and began to move again. He kept his eye on the crowds, looking for the sudden moving ripple that would speak of pursuit. Watching, and dreading it. Because if he didn't see it, it meant that there was still some hope for Duster.

Hope? he thought bitterly, as Arann staggered and coughed. Her dagger had *bounced*.

Angel, grim, straightened his shoulders. One way or the other, they were going to make it to Jay. That was what Duster had stayed for, and that was the only thing he could do for her now.

It had been the only thing he could do for his parents: survive, when they hadn't. Help the others survive. It was what they'd wanted; the last thing they'd probably even thought. It was also the only thing that his Free

Town parents and the volatile, violent Duster had in common: They'd paid the price for his passage.

The den made it to the river, and then, along the riverside to the magelights that girded the river side of the street on their thick poles. It was cold enough that no one was playing in the water; it wasn't cold enough that people weren't trying to wash things at its banks.

They stopped just to one side of Taverson's. "Arann," Angel said quietly, "go in. Find Jay; ask her what she wants us to do."

Arann hesitated, and Angel added, "I'll keep watch out here. One of us has to."

"Send Teller."

Angel shook his head. "Go. If we have to, the rest of us can scatter."

"And you can run faster without me." No question there. Arann took a breath, wincing, his hands holding his side.

Angel kicked the door open, and Arann moved just enough to catch it before it slammed back on its hinges. Angel watched him leave, and then turned his gaze to the streets, his hand on his dagger, just as Duster's often was.

No one spoke. Jester scanned the street as well; Finch and Teller huddled together, Teller's arms clutching that damn box as if it were a baby. He'd taken it; he'd left the cat. Judging from the look on his face, he'd actually had the time to make that choice. Angel touched his shoulder briefly.

"Where will we go?" Finch asked. It wasn't directed at Angel; it wasn't really directed at all.

"Let's see what Jay says. If she's still here."

Finch nodded. After a pause, she said, "This is where Jay found me. Taverson's. I was running. That way." She lifted a slender arm, and pointed more or less into the middle of the busy street.

"It saved your life," Angel replied, for he'd heard the story before. "Let's hope we get lucky twice."

The tavern door swung open, and Carver stood in

its frame. He glanced at them all. "Duster?" he asked Angel. His gaze skirted the streets, and the people moving through them.

Angel shook his head, realized that Carver wasn't looking at him and couldn't see the gesture, and spoke instead. "She's not coming. Is Jay—"

Carver swore. Two brief words. "Get in," he told them. "Now." He turned on his heel and vanished back into the tavern.

Angel held the door just long enough for Finch, Teller, and Jester to slip inside, and he followed them, wondering who—or what—Carver had seen.

Jay stood to one side of Arann, or they would have missed seeing her at all. Arann turned as they pressed around; he was white, and the single gash was livid; his eyes were also bruising. Carver glanced at Arann, but otherwise ignored him; his lips were thinned, and he spoke tersely.

"Jay, we've got to run."

Jay forced herself to look away from Arann. "I know. Did any of you bring the box?"

Teller stepped around Arann, and lifted his arms; the box was still nestled there, and it clinked as he shook it slightly. He was rewarded by the sharp exhalation of her relief; she had no joy to offer any of them.

"Good. We're going to need it. We've got to get a carriage."

Angel's eyes widened—and they weren't the only ones. Jay and her den didn't *do* carriages; no one who lived in the twenty-fifth holding did. Carriages did pass through, although they weren't as common as wagons, and Angel knew that some of the older people did call them and did climb into their cramped, odd cabins; none of those people had ever been den.

No one, however, said this.

Jay turned to Arann, her voice dropping. "Arann, can you run?"

"Yeah."

"Good."

They turned to head out into the streets. They stopped before they'd gone five feet.

Standing in the door, blocking all light—or perhaps absorbing it—stood a man that Angel recognized. Old Rath. His gaze scanned the crowd—and for midday in the holding, it *was* crowded—before settling on Jay. On the den.

Jay did not, by any stretch of the imagination, look happy or relieved to see him.

She cursed under her breath, which was all the breath she spared for useless words. Her hands went to the daggers she hardly ever used. She squared shoulders and took a step to the side, her gaze never leaving Rath's face. Angel drew a dagger, motioning Finch and Teller to someplace behind Jay. Jester went as well, shadowing Finch, as he often did when there was trouble.

"Carver," Jay said grimly, "get going."

Her grim was not a match for Carver's. "No."

"I said, get going. I'll take care of this."

"*No.* Duster couldn't do it. You can't."

Unspoken truth, there: Duster had *always* been their best in a fight. Always. Carver? Second best, by a notable margin. Angel was almost Carver's equal, although they had different styles of fighting.

Carver, therefore, drew a dagger. The innkeeper, who wasn't Taverson at this time of day, hadn't noticed yet; he would soon. This much steel? But Jay came here often, and they knew her well enough not to actually pay much attention until there was a real fight.

Carver stepped in front of her, aiming himself at Rath; he didn't run to him, and didn't otherwise move, but his intention was clear. Angel looked at Arann, at Jay, at the rest of the den. At Carver.

Time, he thought, *to stop running.* He lined up behind Carver, and Jay grabbed his arm, pushing him to the side. He stumbled; Teller caught his sleeve, drew him back, almost dropping the box in the process.

Jay opened her mouth. "Fire! FIRE IN THE KITCHEN!" Her voice was high and clear, the syllables knotted by the very obvious fear she felt. Using the fear, fanning a different fear in the men and women who might have been onlookers, and who, by her words, became instant participants.

Angel winced. They were so screwed if the innkeeper caught them.

But if that occurred to Jay at all, it didn't slow her down; she reached out, kicked the side of Carver's knees hard enough to make him stumble, and dragged him around, holding him as people began to look for smoke. The more timorous of the inn's occupants didn't bother with looking; they leaped from their seats, and began to stream toward the entrance.

Toward Old Rath. They were a moving wall, and they weren't a particularly peaceful one either; everyone knew what a fire could do in this part of town, and they knew how *damn fast* it could do it.

Carver righted himself, and looked at Jay; his ferocious focus broke into a very slight grin. He nodded. "Back alley?"

She shook her head. "They're not stupid. Come on."

She led them—quickly—through the kitchen and up the back stairs that Taverson's maids and wife used. Above the tavern were a few rooms that could, and did, double as guest rooms if people were willing to pay for them; she hadn't gone that route. Instead, she'd pushed herself through the doors and up the much less accommodating stairs toward the small rooms in which Taverson, his wife, and their children sometimes lived.

"Roof?" Carver asked.

Angel had never been up this way, and judging from other expressions, neither had most of the den.

Jay nodded. "We can climb down from there, if we have to." She didn't point out that the alley was a bad place to be caught, if a pursuer was too damn close. They all knew it.

Carver glanced at Arann, and lifted his hand in brief den-sign.

Jay didn't reply. She didn't need to.

But Angel signed to Carver, and Carver nodded; they looked at Arann, and said nothing.

They came up a very narrow set of stairs, through a door that barely looked like it was built for one—but it opened, as Jay and Carver had said, onto the roof. The roof itself was mostly flat; it sloped very gently to the streetside and the back road. Water pooled unevenly along the edges to either side, an artifact of the time of year. Eaves lined the roof, and creepers twined around them, climbing from unseen cracks in the stones across the face of brick and wood.

Carver flattened himself against the roof, and inched his way across it until he could see over the edge, alley-side. He lifted his hands; signed, *Pursuit* and pulled back much faster. *It's Rath,* he mouthed.

Angel crouched; he didn't drop, didn't flatten himself out. Couldn't fight on his stomach, and didn't relish the thought that he'd be caught out that way. But he listened. Someone was climbing the wall.

Rath?

Angel glanced at Jay; she was utterly still, and her face was winter white. She didn't say a word; she barely seemed to breathe.

Carver leaned out over the alley-side edge of the roof, drew a dagger. Angel started to shout, stopped; it was too late. The dagger flew from Carver's hand.

"Cartanis' blood." Carver pulled back again; his hand, empty now, was shaking. He was about the same color as Jay—and it suited neither of them.

"It's him," Jay whispered. "It's Rath."

"The knife. It—it *bounced.*"

Her breath was so sharp it cut. "Everybody, north side. *Now.*"

If the roof had been a ship, Angel though, it would have teetered with the sudden redistribution of weight. Jester looked at the eaves, the trellises, the lips of the windows that the creepers crossed. He glanced at Jay; she nodded. Jester wasn't the one who was afraid of heights. The tavern was only two stories tall, and they could drop from one full story without breaking anything. He went over the edge.

Finch hesitated as she watched him climb; Jay said *nothing,* but it was a loud, desperate nothing. Angel stepped in front of Finch, sheathing his dagger for the climb; he motioned Teller over to Finch's side as well. "Step where I step," he told her. "Unless I fall." He grinned.

Her grin was a faded, nervous echo; Teller's was sharper; he clung to the iron box until Carver reached over and plucked it from his hands. But he led, and they followed; they moved as quickly as they could. He looked up halfway down, to see Arann struggling with the same climb. Arann's body was shaking with effort or pain. Probably both. Angel flinched as Arann missed a hold twice, but he managed—barely—to keep himself from falling. He had Carver just above him, and Carver could climb these walls in his sleep; he could climb them one-handed, and he more or less did, juggling the iron box between the two.

So could Angel; it was possibly the only thing that Angel had over Carver in terms of raw skill. But Angel was with Finch and Teller. Carver spoke to Arann; the sense of syllables drifted down, but the talk and the sound of street noises drifted up, canceling them.

Jay was still at the top of the roof, looking down, when Carver was halfway home. He looked up at her, lifted his hands—both of his damn hands, the bloody show-off—and signed.

She signed back, but her hands were shaking enough that Angel couldn't read them. *Come on, Jay,* he thought, as he jumped the last eight feet to the ground. *You can make it. Come on.* Teller and Finch were already down when she started to climb, and they were pressed against the wall, looking up—at Arann. Their arms were raised, hands open, and Angel joined them; he didn't tell Arann to jump or let go, because in Arann's case the landing would hurt him.

Jay headed down while they huddled near Arann. Her arms were stiff as boards, legs trembling as she moved them to place her feet. She missed more often than Arann, but like Arann, she didn't fall.

And just before she let go and leaped down the last few feet, she shouted in frenzied relief, and pointed.

A carriage—significantly, an empty carriage—was pulled into view by two horses that looked like they'd seen better years. Jester ran to flag it down, while Jay shouted.

It was a good thing Jay, Finch, and Teller were so damn small, because the cabin of a carriage wasn't *meant* to have this many people cramming themselves into its small doors. The driver opened his mouth to say as much, but the den moved *fast*.

Jay plucked the box from whoever now held it—in the press of bodies, it was kind of hard to tell—and she flipped the lid wide, scattering the coins beneath the driver. "It's yours. It's yours," she added, glancing out the window, "if you move *now*."

The gods knew there wasn't much *in* the box; they also knew it was enough for one damn carriage ride to anywhere. Apparently so did the driver. He nodded, looking none too pleased.

"But pick 'em up."

Jay did that, and the den—well, Finch and Teller, because they could reach more easily—helped.

"Where are you going?"

She swallowed, and ran her hand along the folds of her sleeves. They sounded like paper to Angel. "To the estates of Terafin." She looked at Arann, then.

Angel and Carver looked out the windows; the carriage hadn't started to roll yet.

But they saw two things. The first: that their pursuer had gained the height of the roof, and stood there looking out. Looking down.

The second: he jumped. He didn't bother with the climb; it would have only slowed him down.

But everyone heard the landing; it sounded like it had just cracked the stones that were road in these parts.

The driver, apparently, heard this kind of noise all the time; he shook the reins and the horses began to move. It wasn't a smooth damn ride, and it wasn't a fast one. Rath—or whoever it was—unfolded, stood, and began to run after the carriage.

He ran damn fast.

"Jay, we've got a problem," Angel told her.

"On it," she muttered. She slammed her fist into the roof of the cabin, and, holding onto the edge of the window, leaned out and shouted. "You've got to go *faster*. What kind of lousy horses *are* these? Look—a man on foot can keep up!"

"Don't get cheeky with me."

Jay pointed in the direction of the road, and in the direction of the man who, on foot, and only barely bothering to avoid pedestrians, was *gaining*. Easily.

The carriage picked up speed, then. Whatever cheek Jay had offered the driver had stung his pride as well. Rath fell behind.

And behind, and behind.

They weren't really thinking of where they were going; they were thinking, instead, of the fact that they'd escaped. The entire cabin erupted in shouts and high, clear laughter. It was the wrong kind of laughter to Angel, but it didn't matter. They weren't dead.

They weren't all dead.

But one of them didn't join in the noise, and didn't seem to notice the cause for celebration.

"Arann, are you all right?" Jay's voice was louder than it would have been anywhere else; the wheels made a lot of noise, and if they hadn't, the horses and their driver would have.

"I'm fine." He looked at her. Looked at all of them. His eyes were almost like window glass. You could see through them. You couldn't see much of Arann.

Jay flinched. She touched his face. Reached out, and wiped away the trickle of blood that was falling from the corners of his lips. The carriage ride was *not* gentle.

"Tell me if it gets to be too much."

"I will."

*   *   *

Angel had never been across this bridge. None of the den had.

They quieted as they approached it, as if silence was a better bet. Which was stupid; you couldn't hide this many people in a carriage. Or at all, really. The driver slowed as the bridge guards signaled.

Angel and Carver bracketed the windows, and they listened to the brief and cursory exchange of words, followed by an equally brief and cursory exchange of money. The tolls.

But if there *were* laws that prohibited the poor from seeking access to the streets of the Isle, the guards seemed to be ignoring them today. They asked the driver where the carriage was bound, and they nodded when he answered.

Jay was as tense as the rest of them, but most of her attention was now turned inward, and it extended as far as Arann. Her hand stroked his brow and brushed sticky strands from his forehead; they touched the darkening bruises around his left eye; they lingered, briefly, beneath his jaw, where the pulse—when it existed—could be found. All this, in silence, as if silence would stop the rest of the den from worrying.

Angel glanced at them from time to time. He felt almost guilty, but he couldn't keep his eyes off the passing streets. Here, on the Isle, the very richest of the nobles lived. On the Isle, the Guild of Makers worked, and the mages toiled in the Order of Knowledge. On the Isle, the Exalted lived, speaking to their parents: Cormaris, Reymaris, and the Mother.

And on the Isle, the Twin Kings ruled from *Avantari*.

Golden-eyed, all, beloved of the gods. Angel wondered what it was like.

There was no answer, but as they drove, the spires of the three cathedrals came into view against the cool of azure. Flags rippled from the tower heights, and gold caught sunlight, brightening it.

There were fine carriages and armored guards in the streets, but very few pedestrians—at least compared to the Common and the streets of the holdings with which Angel was familiar. There were buildings behind fences, here. They were not as large as some of the estates the carriage had passed on the mainland, and Angel didn't know enough about city versions of gardens to judge whether or not the smaller grounds were somehow finer.

But he knew that, among all the nobles, The Ten lived here. Their lands were their own, and not leased from the Kings or the Crown Estates; they were guaranteed a home upon the Isle. Rath said the rest of the patriciate was not so lucky; for the rest, it was only money or political power that mattered.

Jay explained only a little of what had happened with Rath. Where a little was a curt, "He's dead" and not a lot else. But that was enough, for Angel. Teller wanted to ask questions; he could see that clearly. But Teller was good at silence, good at waiting. Both were needed here.

Duster. Angel glanced toward the mainland, although it couldn't be seen; here the buildings were tall, and they weren't sparse. He must have said her name out loud; he hadn't intended it.

But Jay said quietly, "She's dead." Just that. It was enough. He closed his eyes.

"Here it is." The carriage slowed. The streets on the Isle were smooth, the stones large and flat; the journey from the bridge on had been less jarring and far less uncomfortable than the wild, careening ride that had led to it. "Home of The Terafin. You want me to wait?" Angel couldn't see the driver's expression, but he knew curiosity when he heard it. He could sympathize.

"No. We'll be fine from here," Jay told him curtly. She'd opened the door, and now stepped out, her knees folding slightly at the unexpected boon of solid ground beneath her feet. She took a breath, held it for a moment, and then looked across at the manse.

Coming to House Terafin had been no part of their morning's plan. No part of their life's plan, if it came to that. But the den looked up, now, to the gates that surrounded the property. Those gates were thick brass, the ends ornamented with tines that rose like solid spears into the heights. There was a guardhouse, of the type that existed in stories, and it was manned.

The den gazed at the building beyond these gates, at the small front grounds and the road that bisected the lawns, surrounded on either side by rows of flowers that Angel couldn't name; they would never have grown them in the Free Towns.

Angel looked at the manse for different reasons than the rest of the den, emerging as they had into the streets, sunlight, and the lack of moving wheels. His father, Garroc, had served The Kalakar, one of The Ten. He had found distinction in service to the House, but in the end, he had left it, seeking the freedom and the quiet of the Free Towns in which to live out the remainder of his life. Short life, Angel thought, with a momentary bitterness, a clean resentment.

Angel now stood in the lee of the Terafin manse, before the guards who served the most powerful woman in the patriciate. Possibly one of the most powerful in the Empire. Here, so close to her presence, he could not help think of Terrick, of Weyrdon, and of his father's isolated quest.

He glanced at Carver, and from there, to Jay. Jay was looking toward the carriage. She cursed, and Angel let go of the remnants of his old life in time to turn and see Arann, slumped partway out of the cabin. Caught, facedown, in the doors.

"Shit," Carver said. "Angel, get off your backside and help me move him." Carver went for Arann's left; Angel crossed over and reached for his shoulder on the right. Arann was damn big, and he was unconscious. Moving him without killing him was going to take more than the two of them.

Finch and Teller moved in to try to help as well.

But Jay watched, her face graying in the bright sunlight.

"What's wrong with him, Jay? Why are you looking like that?" Carver grunted as they managed to heave

Arann into an upright position. He and Angel immediately slid under his shoulders before he could fall forward again, while Teller and Finch tried to brace him. They did their best not to touch his ribs, not to add any weight to them.

"It's nothing."

"Jay?" Teller looked at Arann's face. It was gray. It was the color that Jay's was slowly shading. After a pause in which no one spoke, Teller said, in the same quiet voice, "He's dying, isn't he?"

"Shut up, Teller."

Angel and Carver exchanged one glance. Jay told them to shut up frequently. It was a daily occurrence. But Teller? Almost never. Never, in fact, that Angel could at this moment recall. "Just shut up."

This is what Angel knew: You don't get miracles. You can pray for them. You can wait for them. If you wait, life passes you by. You *don't* get miracles. If you're lucky, you get your life.

But only, he thought, looking grimly back at Arann, *your* life. He glanced at Jay, but it was hard to look at her face. She had banked her life on being a miracle, and for a while, it had worked. Now? Fisher, Lefty, Lander, and Duster were gone; Arann teetered on the edge of joining them.

He looked at Arann, thinking over the last few weeks. Wondering if it wouldn't, in the end, be a kindness. After all, the dead waited by the bridge that led to Mandaros, and Lefty was certain to be there, hovering nervously, and looking for Arann's shadow to stand in when he at last approached the Lord of Judgment.

But Jay didn't want to let him go. She wouldn't—he saw this as clearly as he had ever seen it—let *any* of them go without a fight. Arann—unlike Fisher, Lefty, Lander, or Duster—she had some hope of holding on to, and it was a fool's hope. An act of desperation. Her face was white with it. And open, for a moment, with the fear of, the certainty of, failure.

We followed you, Angel thought, without recrimination or anger. *And we're still following, Jay. Where have you led us?*

Carver tapped her shoulder, and her expression shuttered. Her shoulders were so stiff they didn't relax, but she schooled everything else, and she turned to face two guards, who watched them without apparent curiosity.

"What's your business with The Terafin?"

The guards, Angel thought, were good. They asked the question as if it *had* an answer. Angel leaned in slightly to catch it.

"I've been sent to deliver a message." Jay spoke clearly, but nervously, at least if you knew her; her voice was a little too high. Angel wanted to stand beside her—or at least behind her, and ready—but he and Carver were all that was stopping Arann from plummeting face first into the ground.

The guard glanced at Arann. It was the only sign of inattentiveness toward Jay that he showed. "You can leave it with us; we'll see that she gets it."

"I was told to deliver the message to The Terafin herself."

"You aren't ATerafin," the guard said, as if that fact weren't obvious.

"No," Jay replied, as if she knew it was. Yes, she was nervous.

"Well, then you probably don't understand the rules of the House. The Terafin's day is governed by strict schedule; if your message is a matter of emergency, you may deliver it to her right-kin, and he will see that she receives it."

Right-kin? Angel glanced at Carver, and Carver shrugged. He didn't sign, which was their preferred method of speaking about an ongoing discussion in which they weren't even peripherally involved, but Arann was both heavy and difficult to hold up.

"We can't. Look—I've been told to tell you that the message is from—is from Ararath Handernesse. But I can't tell you any more than that. You just go and tell her—and see if she won't see us."

Angel winced. Carver grimaced. Finch and Teller said nothing; they didn't move. Even Jester, who never seemed capable of understanding the words "shut up," was silent.

The guard stared down at her impassively, but his glance flickered again to Arann, and it stayed there for a minute. Something in his expression shifted; whether it was a good shift, or a bad one, Angel couldn't tell.

But he felt that, in different circumstances, he could trust this man.

As he had trusted Terrick, knowing so little about him.

"I'm afraid," he told her, as he looked away from Arann and the den-kin who were holding him up, "that the most I can do is carry your message to Gabriel ATerafin. Who did you say sent you?"

"Ararath," Jay replied. "Ararath Handernesse. Look—if you don't carry the message to The Terafin, you'll regret it. She'll want to hear it, and she'll be very angry—"

The guard almost winced, it was that bad. Angel wanted to tell her—but said nothing, did nothing. *Jay, don't push him.* "What is your name?"

"Jewel," she said. "Jewel Markess."

"But everyone calls her Jay," Finch added, from over her left shoulder, carefully not looking at either Carver or Angel, both of whom were rolling their eyes.

"Jewel, I am Torvan ATerafin. The Terafin personally chooses the guards who answer the gates of her manor on the Isle. She knows me by name, and I have some knowledge of her; she is the lord that I serve.

"If I choose not to deliver this message in the fashion you demand, it is unlikely to cost me much. There is trust between my lord and me."

Jay's shoulders fell, and her head went with them for a moment. Angel could only see her back, but he understood, then, why she was so awkward, so unlike herself. He looked at Arann. Mouthed the word *pulse* at Carver. Carver grunted, but lifted a hand, listening with the tips of his fingers. He nodded, but it was a brief nod, and it held no hope at all.

Jay still held all the hope they could spare, and it was eating at her.

They had time; Arann had next to none.

But the guard, this Torvan ATerafin who had the House Name, even though he worked here on the outside, looked at Arann as well; he looked at the den. Angel met his gaze and held it. What the guard saw in the den, what he saw in Arann, Angel couldn't say. But his jaw tightened slightly, and he glanced, for the first time, at the second guard, who had remained silent.

Something passed between them; it was not den-sign, but they didn't need it. The other guard nodded in silence, and Torvan turned back to Jay.

"Wait here, Jewel Markess. I'll return."

"I'll wait," she replied.

He turned, then, and he walked—quickly—toward the manse, looking neither left nor right. The doors swallowed him, and left the den in a tense silence. Arann gurgled again. He wasn't conscious, not exactly. Angel wondered how much he was aware of, if he was aware at all.

Jay turned at the sound of his voice, and she bit her lip. Lifted a hand to his neck, and let it linger there before she closed her eyes.

"He's still alive," Carver told her.

"I can't find—"

"He's still alive. Jay."

She swallowed, and her eyes were a shiny blur, but she didn't cry. Wouldn't, Angel knew, even if Arann died right now. He wanted to tell her that this wasn't her fault; that it wasn't even her doing. But he knew how much comfort she'd take from the words: none. He didn't offer them.

The wait was hard.

Jewel kept glancing at the single guard Torvan had left by the gate, as if she wanted to ask him if this was a game. Carver stepped on her foot, and she kept her mouth in the same, thin line that was her silence.

"Jay." Angel touched her elbow to get her attention; she allowed it. "He'll come back."

One dark brow rose, and she grimaced. "That obvious?"

Angel shrugged, falling back on Carver's most familiar gesture. His father, back in the day, would have smacked him for its constant use, and you had to love a man to miss him, even knowing this.

"We don't have time," she whispered.

Angel said, again, "He'll come back. If he didn't intend to do something, he would have sent us on our way."

"You're so sure?"

"You're not?"

It was the wrong thing to say, but he couldn't unsay it. He didn't try.

"I'm sure of death, right now. Rath's. Duster's. Lander, Fisher, Lefty. I'm sure of death, Angel. Anything that's not death?" She spread her hands, palms out.

"There he is."

She looked up, then. Torvan ATerafin walked—almost jogged, clanking loudly, his shadow rippling over grass and flower beds—toward the gate. He spoke quickly, in a voice too low to be heard as more than background murmur, and the gates swung open.

"Jewel Markess. The Terafin has requested your presence. Please follow me."

Jay hesitated. She stared up at the man, who wasn't small, and her knees locked. She moved just enough to glance at her den; they were, to a person, waiting patiently for her word.

Except for one.

"Arann?"

Carver nodded grimly. Angel grimaced, and braced himself for the forward movement of this much dead weight. They staggered as they began to walk, trying to keep away from his ribs, his sides. There was no way they could move quickly.

The guard watched them, silent. Not impassive, but as if he were assessing the situation. As if the situation meant something to him.

Teller leaned toward Arann's white face, listened there a moment, and then looked up at Jewel.

"He's . . . breathing."

He was dying.

Jay reached out and touched Arann's face. "Arann?"

There was no answer but the silence of her den. Angel knew, hearing the single word, that had *he* been Arann, and in any place other than Mandaros' Hall, he would have walked, danced, and sung just to ease what he heard there. They all would have.

But Arann couldn't, didn't, hear, and maybe that was a mercy.

"C'mon, Carver, Angel. Let's get him in. We can't leave him here."

Finch was pale, and she fluttered like her namesake between them all, returning time and again to Arann's limp head, his slack face. Teller shored up Carver's side, inasmuch as he could, because Carver was on the side that the stranger *hadn't* hit.

Jester walked behind them, and more useful, directly behind Arann's back. Once or twice, he'd braced himself, holding out both hands to take some of Arann's weight when either Angel or Carver was overbalanced.

They made maybe ten feet—the distance between their initial huddle and the now open gate—in five minutes. They would have taken the time if it had been five hours, but they knew, because it was so damn clear on Jay's face you could almost read it word for word, that the time would kill him. It was already killing him, and Angel had a suspicion that their jostling and their handholds weren't helping either.

But they had no stretchers, not even the makeshift ones that had been called into service after the raiders had done their grisly work in Evanston. Angel looked at the guard. He wanted to ask if they had such a thing in the manse—but the manse, with its broad, perfect, and forbidding wings, spoke of a station in life that was so far above him he couldn't even figure out how to *approach* it.

Throughout it all, Jay walked backward, watching them. Pointing out steps, slight turns, the proximity of the gate. Telling Angel when to adjust his awkward grip.

"Here, Markess," Torvan ATerafin said gruffly. "Let me help you."

They all turned to stare at him, surprised that he had spoken. Surprised that when he had, it was to offer aid. Jay didn't speak. She just stared at him as if his words weren't Weston—or the Torra she loved to use in a foul mood—and she was still trying to figure out what he'd actually said.

He pushed her firmly to one side, stared down at Teller until the boy got out of his way, and then caught Arann under the arms and legs as the two who had been shouldering his burden stepped away at the quiet directive of their leader.

He strained as he lifted him, but he lifted him.

Torvan ATerafin carried Arann, which in theory freed up the rest of the den to pay attention to the manse through which they walked. Angel did. Carver did. Jester may have been—with Jester it was hard to tell. But Jay? No. And Finch and Teller were walking to either side of her, as if they thought she might need their literal support at any minute.

The place was *huge*.

The front doors weren't adorned with House Guards, but a man in clothing so impeccable it might as well have been armor greeted them as they entered. Or he started to; Torvan brushed him aside, with a grunted apology for the lack of time, and the man hesitated for just a moment before nodding and getting the Hells out of the way.

Torvan led. Jay kept pace with him, walking to the right and five feet behind where Arann's head dangled.

She walked through the long, rectangular arch that separated a huge gallery from the main foyer, her feet brushing the colors of discrete rugs, stretched end to end with a break for benches between each, as if she were walking on cobbles.

Against the gallery walls, paintings alternated with long, long tapestries; the stitching in some were so fine, if it weren't for the fall of the light against cloth, they might have been painted. Nobles were there, in the coalescence of disparate, long threads, but so, too, Kings and gods. Angel recognized them, and wondered what their import to the House was.

He had no time to ask, and no real time to follow the unfolding story—besides which, given the direction they were walking in, he'd seen the ending first.

Jay didn't notice them.

Angel felt guilty about doing so when she couldn't, but took comfort from the fact that Carver was doing the same. Carver, whose lips were pursed, probably to stop a whistle from escaping, was cataloging the things he recognized—the silver, the magestones, the vases— all things that would make life much, much easier in the holdings, once they were palmed and sold.

Fair enough. None of them had any idea why Jay had dragged them here, spending the last of their money on a one-way carriage ride. But they'd all heard her claim to carry a message of import to The Terafin, and frankly, if any of them had been skeptical, they were *in* now. Maybe she thought The Terafin would reward them somehow for whatever it was Jay meant to tell her.

Because they weren't eating tomorrow—or most of this week—if she didn't. And Duster, along with Carver, had been pulling in most of the coins they'd been spending so carefully until today.

But, damn, this hall was long.

Angel glanced at Arann, or at what he could see of Arann from around Torvan ATerafin's broad back.

If the long hall was unadorned by guards, the smaller halls through which Torvan led them were not. He struggled with Arann's weight, and when Jay asked him if he could hurry, he failed to hear her. If Arann was heavy—and he was—Torvan ATerafin didn't pause, and didn't put him down. He asked for, and took, no rest.

Jay would normally have seen that.

Today was so far from normal she could be forgiven much. Angel winced once or twice, and Finch's expression rippled with obvious concern. No one else said a word. Jay led, trailing in Torvan's wake until they reached a set of large, closed doors.

These doors were girded, on either side, by guards in long surcoats and armor that literally gleamed in the magelight. They were rectangular doors, but they were wide and tall, and a symbol, surrounded by a single golden circle, crossed the seams between them.

As Torvan approached, Arann in his arms, the guards raised swords, crossing them to bar entrance, as if the closed doors didn't already have that effect.

Jay stepped in front of Torvan ATerafin, shielding Arann with her body. It wasn't effective. "We're here to see The Terafin. It's urgent. We've got to—"

"Marave." Torvan spoke, literally, over her head. "We're here by The Terafin's command."

The female guard, who had failed to hear Jay, glanced at Torvan and the burden he carried. She nodded, a short, smart motion. "You may pass."

Her sword fell in unison with the raised sword of the bearded, fair-haired man who stood directly opposite her. "You may pass."

The den fell in behind, glancing at the swords of the House Guards, or their reflections in those swords. For Angel, it was the former; he knew enough about blades to recognize the quality of these at a glance. Still, the muted and often mismatched colors that were den clothing passed across the sheen of the flats like ripples or waves. It was comforting.

They entered the chambers beyond those large, solid doors, and saw four more guards; these men stood with swords sheathed, along either wall. The room itself was large, but it had none of the colorful finery that the galleries boasted. There were shelves on the far wall, to either side of a fireplace mantel that was dark and oiled; those shelves carried books in larger numbers than Angel thought he could count without a slate. In one half of the room was a grand, but severe looking desk, behind which was one empty chair.

Torvan passed between the guards, and came to a halt in front of a lone woman, who stood, rather than taking one of the many chairs that were placed along the floor in the back of the room. Tables joined those chairs in a sparse arrangement that implied an equally spare welcome.

Torvan ATerafin started to bend, and Angel darted forward to help with Arann. But the woman spoke, and Torvan froze.

"Don't stand on ceremony. I do not require you to kneel, Torvan."

And so it was that Angel a'Garroc first laid eyes on The Terafin.

Her hair was dark, where it touched her forehead, but it was bound back behind her ears, and held in place by a very delicate net. In that net, something sparkled, a hint of the finery that the manse displayed openly. At this distance, Angel couldn't tell what caused the sharp little twinkles of light as she turned her head. She wasn't tall. Taller than Jay, Finch, and Teller, yes—but she was at most of medium height, for a woman.

And she looked, to Angel, like the exposed blade of a sword, a Northern weapon. She was pale, but in a way that implied light on steel and not something softer or more feminine, and she wore a pale blue drape that suggested clear winter sky. In his days on the docks, Angel had seen all manner of current Imperial fashion, as well as the fashions of other nations; she bowed, in the end, to none. The dress was almost a simple shift, and it fell unimpeded by something as restrictive as a belt.

As if aware of his regard, she glanced at him, and her eyes, dark as her hair, narrowed slightly. He offered an awkward half-bow in response and acknowledgment. This woman, he thought, was the leader of her House, not only in name, but in fact.

He remembered, again, the task set for his father, Garroc of Weyrdon, a task that he had, in the end failed. The duty of its completion, the redemption of Garroc's life—and death—now rested with Angel.

And what, in the end, was the geas laid upon him? That he find, and serve, a worthy leader.

But to do that, he had to have something to offer; he was aware, as he stood in this room, that he had nothing at all that she could not easily find elsewhere. Elsewhere in men like Torvan ATerafin, whom she clearly trusted.

"I believe that you have a message for me?" The Terafin spoke to Jay.

Jay nodded. Angel felt that this was smart, given the difference in their ranks, and their relative power.

"Then I would have you deliver it."

Jay nodded again. But this time she unfastened her left sleeve, and from it, withdrew several curled papers that had obviously been half-wrapped around the length of her forearm.

Carver lifted his hand in den-sign, but his fingers froze; Jay jumped forward, and grabbed, of all things, a lamp that rested on one of the tables. By its flickering, Angel knew it contained not an expensive magestone, but rather, simple oil.

Fire, he thought, almost numb, which was now held in one hand below the curled paper.

"Jewel," Torvan said, his voice hard. "You don't have to do this."

"This is it," she said, ignoring him as she waved the rolled vellum above the burning flame. "This is the last message from Ararath."

"What are you doing, child?" The Terafin took a step. A single step. Then she held her ground as Jay spoke again.

"Stay right where you are." Jay's voice was wild, almost broken; it was a desperate thing. Shorn of the control and the wisdom with which she had kept her den safe all these years, Jay sounded like . . . a child. A child upon whom their entire future depended.

Had she always been this small?

"Who are you?" The Terafin asked.

"I'm—I'm Jewel Markess. I'm the den leader here."

"And you've come to my House in order to extort something from me?" She was cold, this woman, and what little friendliness she had displayed—and by Angel's lights, there had been little enough of it—guttered. "I don't know how you found out about Ararath, but—"

"He taught me." Jay waved the papers over the fire. "He taught me about all of this. I—" she shook her head. "I don't want to do this. But you've got something I need."

"And that is?"

"Money."

"You do realize that there are a roomful of guards in the antechamber?"

Jay nodded. Her face was so pale, their skin—the woman's and hers, leader of the most powerful of The Ten, and leader of a small den from the twenty-fifth holding—were almost of a color.

"Vellum burns poorly. I dare say that they'll have you in hand before even one of the scrolls that you carry are lost."

"Just try it," Jay replied, but her voice was thin, and her words held no strength. What The Terafin said was true.

"Shall I call the guards?" The Terafin took a step forward, and this time, Jay did nothing.

"We used all our money to come here," she murmured, so quietly it was hard to hear her. "And even if we hadn't, we'd never have had enough for a healer." Then she turned to look at Arann's body, and she lost her voice.

For the first time, The Terafin looked at Arann. "I see," she said. "And this money—you want it for him?"

Jay nodded. "He's my den-kin," she said.

"And what would you do for it, if I had it to give you?"

"Anything," Jewel replied, straightening up and lifting her chin. "I'll steal for you, if that's what you need done. I'll spy for you. I'll kill for you. I'll even—"

The Terafin lifted a ringless hand. "Enough." She walked to the fireplace and pressed her hand against a square of the stone wall just above it. She looked at Jay very carefully before walking back to her desk. This time, she sat behind it, signaling a more formal interview. "Tell me about Ararath."

Jay swallowed and looked, again, at Arann. She struggled with words—and Jay never had to struggle with anything but keeping them on the inside of her mouth. "I—we didn't call him that. We called him Old Rath. He lives in the thirty-fifth. He's a . . ." She took a single, deep breath, and straightened her shoulders, gaining an inch or two of height. It shouldn't have been impressive

But to Angel, it was. Because he knew that it would never, ever have occurred to Jay to ask for *anything* but Arann's life. And she knew, now, that answering The Terafin's questions as cleanly—and quickly—as possible was now the only hope she had. "He was a thief there. The best. He was good with a sword—that's why he lived to be old. He knew how to read and write and speak like a gentleman.

"He didn't much care for the patriciate. He didn't much care for commoners either, when it comes down to it. But he was a good friend."

"Was?"

"We . . . think he's dead." She looked at the letter she had claimed came from Rath, and Angel saw her expression stiffen, as if she was now holding its lines as rigidly as possible. She surrendered completely, then, and set the lamp safely down upon the floor by her feet, putting her life—no, putting a life she cared far, far more about—squarely into The Terafin's hands.

Chapter Fifteen

THE TERAFIN GLANCED AT TORVAN ATera-
fin, and nodded. It was a short, graceful dip of the
head, and although it was offered in silence, it had the
force of words behind it.

Torvan ATerafin knelt carefully—and in that much
armor, with Arann as a burden, it was an impressively
supple motion—and laid Arann gently on the floor. He
nodded once to his lord, and then he stood and withdrew; he did not, however, leave the room. Instead, he
took his place by the wall to the den's left, his hands by
his sides.

Teller approached Arann first, and knelt to one side
of his white, motionless face. He bent, slowly and hesitantly, to listen a moment, and then moved, and placed
the side of his face against Arann's chest.

"Jay, I don't think he's . . . "

"Arann!" Jay shoved Teller to one side, and Finch
stepped in to catch him before he fell flat on his butt
in front of possibly the most powerful woman in the
Empire.

"Arann, come on. We're safe now." She lifted his
face in her hands and shook him, but not hard. "Please.
Arann, please."

"Jay?" Finch approached her with care, her eyes turning down at the corners the way they did when she was in pain and she couldn't decide for who. But she was smart enough, especially here, not to touch Jay.

The only sign Jay gave of hearing her name was a fierce shake of her head. She didn't move. Finch lifted a hand, and Angel caught it. Neither of them spoke.

But Torvan did.

"Jewel, come. There's nothing you can do now." He didn't know her; he didn't know better then to touch her. "Jewel. Come."

Angel knew she wouldn't turn, and she wouldn't rise, and he even knew why. Jay didn't cry in public.

"Torvan, that's not necessary."

All of the den looked up at the sound of this new voice; all of them but Jay, who was huddled beside Arann's chest, her shoulders curving toward him, her neck stretching as her head bent.

A man had, silently, entered the room. He was old. Older, Angel thought, than anyone he'd met in the Free Towns, and older than anyone he knew in Averalaan, although the latter wasn't hard. But his age didn't quite make him frail.

It wasn't his age that caused a ripple of silence, an exhange of glances, and the lifting of hands in the comfort of familiar den-sign. It wasn't his robes, which were all of white, except for golden embroidery at the hems; it wasn't his odd, white hair, or the odd blue of his eyes. It was the pendant he wore on a heavy golden chain around his slightly bent neck. Two hands. Two exposed palms.

Healer-born.

Breathing almost stopped as he approached Jay, and approached, by so doing, the person over whom Jay crouched, defensive, and almost broken.

Like Torvan, he didn't know better than to touch Jay. But she made no attempt to shrug him off when he laid one hand on top of hers.

The other hand, he laid against the center of Arann's

chest, where blood had fallen from his forehead or his lips, and dried in a red-brown crust.

"I'm Alowan," the man said. His voice was a whisper, but it was a whisper with the subtle strength of louder speech; it carried, filling the silence.

"I'm Jay." She glanced up at him, then, and her gaze drifted down the sleeve of the hand he had rested so gently upon Arann. She fell silent when she realized that he wasn't speaking to her. He was speaking to Arann, who lay well beyond hearing.

Moments passed, the silence swallowing Alowan's gentle words. Jay's eyes were red, yes, but she'd done with pride for the moment; she looked at the old man's face, his hair, the veined, lined thinness of eyelids. Angel knew the moment her eyes drifted down from his face to the pendant he wore; he heard her breath catch, and he saw her turn her face away again.

Hope was like that, when it came unexpected. It cut.

Silence. Minutes stretching into nothing.

They wanted to ask this man if it was too late.

They wanted to preserve hope, who had almost none. If Duster had been here, *she* would have talked, because Duster was afraid of hope.

Duster wasn't here. Would never be here again. Teller lifted his head, swallowed, and opened his mouth. Before he could speak, Alowan did.

"Come, Arann. Come home. I am Alowan. Follow me. No, do not be frightened. It is safe. Come."

Silence fell once again, but it fell deeper this time. No one opened their mouths to speak, to ask, or to give voice to the hope that was so much like fear it was impossible to tell them apart.

Instead, they listened to the old man. He spoke seldom, and when he did, he spoke some variant of the same words, calling to Arann, wherever Arann might be. They knew, in this hush, that Arann was not—quite— here, but neither was he entirely gone.

Silence. Words. Silence. Words.

And then the words ceased entirely, and the old man withdrew the hand he had laid against Arann's chest.

"Welcome back, boy," he said. He rose, and then realized that Jay's hands were still sandwiched around his.

"Jay, you must release my hand now. It isn't safe for the healer and the healed to be too long joined."

She looked confused, but she did as he asked. Anyone would have, really.

Arann's eyelids began to flicker. It was ever so slight, and nothing else about his face had changed, but they noticed it anyway. They watched, bore witness, captive still to the beginning of hope, and anxious to see its fruition. He drew a sharp, audible breath, and they all breathed then, as if they were one person.

But he drew breath to moan. It was not a scream, but it was unmistakably a cry of pain. He was still for another moment, and then he opened his eyes. His tears caught the light of the lamp that Jay had set on the floor.

"Arann?" Jay spoke. She spoke for all of them.

"Jay?" He reached out for her as if she were his mother. She froze for an instant, stiff as his arms encircled her neck and shoulders, and then she hugged him back. Hiding her face.

Teller came first, and quietly; Finch came last, and hesitantly. In between, Carver and Angel joined her at Arann's side. Jester rolled his eyes in mock contempt, grinning broadly and tapping his left foot as if to a tune.

Arguably the most powerful woman in the Empire stood, to one side of her desk, and observed. She was utterly silent; she might have been a wallflower at a great ball, seeing all and interacting with nothing.

The message that Ararath Handernesse had purportedly penned lay on the ground, forgotten. It had, she thought, served the girl's purpose. And if the girl had been foolish—and she had—she had not lied; the cause for that folly was written clearly both upon her and each of the young men, and the young woman, who attended her.

She had called herself the den leader, and it was clear that these were her den.

The Terafin glanced across the room at Torvan, and

he, accustomed to her, lifted his head and met her gaze. He lifted a brow in question; she raised two fingers in reply. It was not a deliberate language; she was long past the age in which she required the delight of a hard code by which to communicate. But he understood what she meant, and he nodded.

The Terafin watched this den. She gave them the time to touch their fallen giant, and they did; his face, his hands, his shoulders. As if they couldn't believe he was alive, as if they had never thought to touch anything of him again but his corpse.

Then, when she judged the impulse satisfied, she looked at the boy himself. He was pale, and his face, tear-stained. His forehead would not scar, but Alowan had used as little of his power as it was possible to use in a healing of this nature.

She was not, had not, been kind to Alowan, this day.

Alowan was watching her.

And he was, of course, watching the boy, the den. His expression as he did was not an old man's expression, and the smile on his lips, if weary and pained, also held a very surprising joy in great measure. He was, indeed, happy. For them.

Which told her much. The rest, she now desired to learn. She lifted a hand. Not a single one of the strangers noticed, but all five of her Chosen did.

"Torvan, escort Alowan and the boy—Arann?—to the healerie. If our visitors are concerned, take one of them with you. Any," she added, "save the leader."

"Lord." He stepped forward.

"Carver." The young woman spoke a single name without looking at anyone but The Terafin. There was, in the girl's face, both gratitude and the weary reassumption of command. Had the circumstances been different, The Terafin might have taken the time to ask for the story behind their situation, for if it was true that many sought—and frequently attempted to demand—her attention, it was also true that they seldom came with companions who were literally at death's door.

She had known, of course. She had seen death before, much of it in this house. At least one death in this room.

"Me?" The young man, with his ludicrous but strangely appropriate mane of hair, said, denying her the perfect obedience that the patriciate itself was accustomed to. "But—"

"Go." Jewel Markess did not seem to be embarrassed by this denial; she didn't seem surprised by it either.

"Yessir."

The Terafin stepped forward and held out a hand. "Now," she said quietly, "you will deliver your message without further delay."

The girl nodded firmly, and opened her mouth as if to speak. She snapped it shut again, showing more judgment, and far more control, than she had in her wild and desperate attempt to somehow save the boy's life.

And who, The Terafin thought wryly, *am I to judge?* It had worked, after all. Whatever it was that Torvan had seen in this slight and silently angry girl that had caused him to speak for her, and further, to carry the dying down the length of the long halls that led to The Terafin's day office, The Terafin could not entirely discern.

But she could not dismiss it; she saw something in the girl herself.

Perhaps, in the end, she saw Ararath. It did not occur to her to doubt that Jewel Markess spoke truth: that she knew Ararath, and he knew her. Ararath would guess that he might send Jewel to House Terafin, at least once. What she might buy here, with her presence, he could never be certain. But that he had been willing to send her at all?

Her hands closed upon the letter; it ran several pages. She glanced, briefly, at the shape of the writing, at its orderly, neat lines, its cramped and entirely recognizable style. After all these years, his hand had not changed so very much.

She stilled a moment, seeing in the shape of words, and the choice of them, one other thing that had not changed. It surprised her. The language of Handernesse, one of their chief delights in their early years, was here. She turned from Jewel, and spoke to her guard.

"Tell the secretary to continue without me for the moment; I can be found in my chambers if matters of import arise."

To Jewel, granting her only the sight of profile, she added, "Please wait for me in the antechamber."

She kept Jewel Markess waiting.

It did not take her long to read the letter, but she read it more than once, in the presence of Morretz, her domicis, and no one else. She had repaired to her rooms and the much larger office they contained, not because she required the space—although the letter was laid out, sheet by sheet, against the perfect sheen of her desk—but because she desired privacy.

In rooms that were easily accessible to the public, privacy was never guaranteed. She seldom needed it.

Morretz was, of course, utterly silent. He was not still, but even his movements failed to create a sense of noise, or destroy the questionable peace in this room. Here, her history lay, hidden to those who had not also experienced it. She knew the stories told about her rise to power in House Terafin, because she had helped to spread them, in her fashion. She did not stoop to lie, of course; a lie was not effective, and it was easily revealed.

And only those who felt threatened, only those who felt their position was untenable, resorted to that tactic. No, instead, she selected a few truths from among all of her truths, and she allowed those few to travel unimpeded.

She did not, of course, choose to speak of Handernesse directly. On those occasions when she did, she spoke with modulated respect for the House of her birth, and with guarded affection for her grandfather, whose distant words and dismissive anger had placed her squarely upon the path that she had traveled.

In happier times, before the shadow of Terafin

loomed, she had adored him. She adored little, now. It wasn't safe.

She glanced again at the letter. She had loved Ararath. Ararath, the child, Ararath the frustrating and taunting boy, Ararath the feckless and slightly idealistic youth. But she had left him, to Handernesse.

She drew breath; it was sharp.

We think he's dead.

She had accepted his anger. She had even understood that she would face it, although its breadth and depth had astonished her. This was where worship led, for he had worshiped her. Perhaps, had she waited a few years, perhaps had she made clear the ways in which she had stumbled in her slow walk toward House Terafin, he might have ceased to worship her at all; he had not quite begun his own road to understanding, and his own idealism had blinded him.

She had been perfect, to him.

The perfect future. The perfect older sister. He had been *so proud* of her.

But he had also shown a more bitter pride, in his fashion. He had left Handernesse, in his fury, and he had never again returned. She knew, of course. She knew, as well, that Hectore of Araven still heard from Ararath on occasion. More than that, she did not trouble to discover—but it had been difficult.

Still, if she had been a woman to give way easily to impulse, she would not now be The Terafin.

So she returned, again, to a letter whose authenticity was beyond doubt.

Jewel Markess was seer-born. Ararath was certain of it. He did not detail how; the language of their youthful devising was not a complicated language. But more was here, between those words, and all of it—if true, and if she indeed remembered what the code was—was grim.

Reading between the lines—the ones he had written for Jewel's eyes, and the ones he had written for Amarais, his lost sister—she understood that he not only valued Jewel, but loved her. He did not, of course, reveal this; no more did he reveal his regret or his apology for the past.

To do either was to expose some part of himself to the sister who had hurt him so badly, and Ararath had never been a boy to forgive and forget. But neither had be been a boy who was easily charmed or addled by youth or beauty. What he valued in Jewel Markess, she could guess at: her concern for Arann, the dying boy. The way she held her den. Her sense of duty to those she had made her responsibility.

What surprised Amarais, as she sat, considering the information, was that he had allowed this one girl—and by extension all of the others—into his life at all. Yet clearly, he had, and just as clearly, he now attempted to take responsibility for her future.

We think he's dead.

But this was, of course, his way. To accept and surrender when facing death. And only then. He had placed Jewel Markess, seer-born, and therefore of incalculable value to the House, in her hands. And he had stepped back. How far back, she could not yet be certain.

But the girl was not a gift to Terafin.

She was, Amarais thought, a plea, and delivered in the only way that Ararath was capable of; disguised as something other, something that might be tempting to a woman of power. She could have told him, absent as he was, that she owed him nothing.

But lies were a tool of the weak. She made her decision, and she looked up at her domicis.

"Among the domicis, Terafin retains the service of three."

Morretz was the fourth, but he served her personally; his contract was not with the House. Of the four, Morretz was therefore the most valuable to The Terafin. She watched him, aware at this moment of all the changes in her life from its beginning to the present—and aware, as well, that he had not seen the girl she had been when Ararath had been of Handernesse.

Lines had been etched around Morretz's eyes and

the corners of his lips with the passage of time, although they were not in evidence at the moment; it was rare that he either smiled or frowned. Consummate care in his chosen profession forbade either. And yet, of the men and women whose service she had taken, he understood her perhaps better than any.

Ironic, that the two men who best did had not chosen to take the House Name. Morretz, because he was of the Guild of the Domicis, and until he chose to leave it, could not take another title or rank, and Alowan, for his own reasons, some of which she understood, and some of which she did not.

She waited for Morretz to speak, but he merely nodded at her simple statement of a fact they both knew well.

"If you were to place an untried and ill-mannered young woman with one of those three, whom would you choose?"

And there it was: a momentary frown. It was seldom that she could coax that much expression out of his watchful face. "Is the young woman to remain here under your permanent protection?"

Yes, he knew her well—and this was as close as he could come to asking her openly what she intended. "Perhaps." She watched him. If he knew her, she also understood his measure, and it was pleasing, and even soothing, to know that in the silence of thought, his calculations and his eventual reply would tally so closely with her own. Nor did he disappoint her, for when he lifted his head, he simply shook it. None.

"It is as I thought as well." She glanced, again, at the vellum that lay, like her palms, across the surface of her desk.

"To whom," he asked softly, although by now he knew the answer, "do you wish a domicis assigned?"

"The street child and her kin."

She had succeeded in nudging a frown from his lips, be it brief, and now succeeded further: he raised a bronze brow. It, like his hair, had weathered the passage of years ungrayed. But although his eyes were the same brown, the same warm dark, they had changed much in the intervening years—inevitable, given what they had seen.

"I do not think there is one among the whole of the guild who would willingly take such a lord."

"If I guess correctly, Morretz, she will be a lord whose origins belie her import to this House."

"And your guess would be worth much. But I still cannot think of one—"

She waited, patient now. He had never failed in any task she assigned him, and while this was in part because she did not assign tasks to those who were incapable of carrying them out, it was also in part the nature of the man.

"Ellerson."

She raised a brow in reply.

"Not a name you would know, Terafin. Not a man who has served, in any capacity, for many years. But I believe that he might be persuaded to take this service, at least on a contract basis."

It piqued her curiosity, this stranger with his unfamiliar name. But she had always been, as her grandfather had said in his early affectionate indulgence, a curious child. It was clear that Morretz thought highly of this Ellerson, whoever he was.

"When can you have an answer?"

"When the offer is tendered. I will speak with the guildmaster immediately." He hesitated for a fraction of a moment, and then said, "You realize that word of this is bound to travel?"

"I have considered it, yes."

"You realize that the House Council members do not retain the services of a domicis at Terafin's expense?"

"I know what it will mean, Morretz." She rose. "But in this case, the risk is justified. Do not question me."

"Terafin."

Ellerson of the Guild of the Domicis was not a young man.

Neither, in common parlance, was Morretz—but

Morretz was in his prime. Ellerson approached the Terafin manse at the side of the younger domicis.

"I am not entirely certain," he told Morretz, "why I let you talk me into this."

Morretz offered Ellerson an unfettered smile, which robbed his face of years and the gravitas required of a man who served such a powerful lord. "It is my belief," he replied gravely, "that you were bored."

"Teaching is seldom boring. Frustrating beyond all possible measure, yes. You might recall," Ellerson added, "as you were one of those frustrations in your time."

"And look where it's taken me. House Terafin, and The Terafin."

Ellerson nodded. "You've done well here. Not beyond expectation, but well. She is an acceptable lord?" He had the pleasure of seeing Morretz look slightly affronted, but the affront was buried quickly.

"She is. She is more than that. I admire her, and her service is what I might have aspired to in idealistic ignorance when I first came to the guild."

"I admit my curiosity. It's seldom that a woman of The Terafin's power sends her personal domicis to the guild to negotiate for the services required to bring a handful of street urchins into line with Terafin itself."

The quality of Morretz's silence told him much.

"How much do you know of these urchins, as you call them?"

"Very little. They have been observed—discreetly— for at most a handful of hours. But the leader of this den is unusual. And their arrival, unusual as well." He hesitated; Ellerson marked it. "One of the den was dying when they arrived. I believe he now resides in Alowan's healerie; you might meet with him if you choose."

Ellerson shook his head. "I understand the way responsibilities for a House are carved up. Show me to my wing, and introduce me to the man or woman in charge of the servants there. The boy will come to my domain in his own time." But he paused, then. "Alowan?"

Morretz nodded.

"He is healer-born?"

Another nod.

"Then she was generous beyond measure, your lord."

"She is seldom generous without cause."

"She could not be, and be The Terafin. I believe you are right," he added, as they made their way past the gates and the House guards. "I have been perhaps a little wearied by the constant routine. I believe I shall find the challenge you have set me of interest, Morretz."

The den arrived—if such a hesitant and suspicious state could be called arrival—in Ellerson's domain in the presence of no less than six of the House Guards. No less, Ellerson thought, than six of The Terafin's personal guards—her Chosen. That was interesting. He watched from the relative obscurity of an antechamber as the doors to the wing opened.

He had been some hours within, closeted with the head of the household staff, a grim and dour woman who clearly had some opinions about these new guests which she was well enough trained to keep—barely—to herself. Regardless, they had discussed the needs of the young men and women, as well as the probability of their relative knowledge, before the rooms had been set in something resembling order.

There were, to Ellerson's knowledge, seven. Seven occupants: two young women and five young men. The wing itself was easily large enough to house them all; seven of the bedrooms had been opened, and linens and towels had been brought, as well as sheets, and clothing of the loose and draping style chosen when one is not entirely familiar with exact size.

Some inquiry into the state of their clothing—and the expense of its replacement—had been made; clearly, their clothing was as much an affront to the head of the household staff as their possible origins. The dining rooms had been cleared, one for breakfast and the lunch hours, and the more formal room for the dinner hours; the kitchen itself had been scrupulously cleaned, and the head of the household staff, who by this point had graciously acknowledged that her name was Margaret Emile ATerafin, had suggested a budget from which a cook, and his various assistants, might be hired.

This, in Ellerson's opinion, was putting the cart before the horse, but he wisely refrained from any argument or dissent.

Nor did he inquire about their personal requirements when it came to the style of their lodgings. At this point, Ellerson understood the unspoken burden placed upon his tenure: they were to adapt to Terafin; Terafin was not to adapt to *them*. In Ellerson's experience, such a one-way interchange was seldom the rule, but his experience also made clear that argument with the head of the household on this particular score would be fruitless, at best.

He inquired of Margaret about the availability of tutors, and the suitability of the same, and at this, she shrugged slightly. "That," she told him firmly, "is the least of my problems. It is not, in fact, *my* problem at all."

"May I then assume it is mine?"

"You're the domicis," she replied curtly.

"Very well." It was not something he could arrange on short notice, and as he was aware that this group of unruly almost-children were probably closeted in a room with guards and their own anxieties, he judged the facilities in a state of suitable readiness for his new masters.

Word was sent, and Margaret vacated the wing, along with the men and women who had come to carry out her commands in the most scrupulous, tidy, and speedy way possible. Ellerson was, for the moment, alone.

But not for long. His arms ached slightly; the damp had been bitter, and he felt the sting of it in his bones. He had not lied to Morretz; he was not a young man.

But Morretz had made clear the unusual nature of the position, and after some careful thought, Ellerson could come up with no likely candidate within the guild itself. He had therefore approached the guildmaster and requested a leave of absence from his teaching duties, not to exceed two years, while he settled these strangers into their possible long-term routine within House Terafin.

Nor was the guildmaster happy to see him go, but she did accede.

He watched in silence as the den was ushered into the sitting rooms, and the rooms in which visitors would customarily be greeted.

Two young women. He was surprised at just *how* young they both looked. They could be as old as eighteen; they could be, in his opinion, as young as twelve. The one girl, with her auburn hair and her tense and watchful face, was no doubt the leader of whom Morretz had spoken. He saw this not so much by her own stance or words, but rather by the furtive glances that the other five cast in her direction.

The other girl was the shortest and slimmest of the bunch, and she kept her hands by her sides or clasped behind her back; her gaze wandered across the whole of the single room as if she were in either shock or awe, and could not quite decide whether to be delighted or terrified.

One of the Chosen now bowed to the leader.

"I am Arrendas ATerafin," he said gravely, offering her his name. The girl did not seem to understand that this was significant. "We leave you now, but if you feel the need for guards while you are under The Terafin's protection, don't hesitate to request them."

"Uh, right," the girl replied. Ellerson winced, but did not otherwise speak or move.

The guard lifted his hand in an open palm salute that was meant to convey respect, rather than obedience. It was clear to Ellerson that the girl wasn't aware of what it meant either. Nor did the Terafin Chosen seem to be offended by her. But when he turned to leave, she shouted, "Wait!"

He stopped instantly, and turned to face her. "Yes?"

"If I—if we—need guards, who do we ask for?"

The man nodded slightly. "Arrendas or Torvan." He waited for a moment, but the answer had satisfied her, and at length he left them entirely unescorted in the meeting rooms of the West Wing.

Only when the doors had once again closed did this motley group of youths relax. Ellerson waited, observing them. They were very poorly clothed, and the clothing itself followed neither current fashion trends nor the bare rudiments of good taste; the colors, for one thing, were horribly mismatched. But the clothing itself was in good repair, and it was clean, for a value of clean that belonged in the holdings. They all had shoes, or boots, as well.

The red-haired boy whistled loudly and the smaller girl began to move from the first room through the large arch into the second. She threw up her arms and shouted, "Look at us! Look at this!" She ran over to the west wall of the sitting room, and lifted—ah, a small magestone, often used for reading. It was framed in gold and brass, and it sat upon a side table. "If we took this with us, we'd have it made. This is worth a fortune!"

"Indeed it is," Ellerson told her, for he felt this was the correct—or necessary—time to intervene.

She shrieked and dropped it, and everyone else jumped and turned.

He watched them, waiting for them to speak; they watched him, dumbfounded. This was, he thought, going to be interesting. It was perhaps not going to be *easy*.

"I am Ellerson. I am the keeper of these rooms; if you will permit me to ask you a few questions, I shall see that your needs are fulfilled while you reside within them. I am called the domicis."

"Does everyone have to talk like that?" the red-headed boy muttered.

Ellerson chose not to hear the question, and was aware that for the first few weeks, he would have to cultivate very selective hearing. What he wondered, watching them now, was what they meant to The Terafin, and whether or not they would be worthy of her.

"Well," their leader finally said, "we want food."

"It has already been laid out, and is waiting for you in the dining room."

"Great!" One of the taller boys, with hair that looked like a work of art, albeit one left out too long near the dusty road, said. "Just lead us there and let us at it."

Ellerson pinched the bridge of his nose. "Follow me, sir."

He led them, slowly, from the sitting rooms into the part of the wing that would be their personal quarters, wondering when it was that they'd last eaten. It did not, however, matter. It was best to begin as they were meant to continue.

He led them to the baths. "These are the towels. Soap is with the bath, in the silver dishes beside the scrubbing brushes. Those are pitchers and small basins, and there are two boys who will help you with your bathing needs."

They all stared at the simple walls of the largely unfurnished room, at the light slanting in from high windows, which brought out the luster of the marble floor.

"But we're hungry," the boy with odd hair began.

His leader stepped, hard, on his foot. Not a bad sign, really.

"Of course, sir," Ellerson replied, as if it weren't in doubt. "And after the traditional bath, you will be seated in all haste. Unless you'd prefer the barbarian custom of coming to a table in your . . . current state."

The auburn-haired girl shoved curls of hair out of her eyes. "Bath first," she told her den.

"But, Jay—"

"Now."

Torvan ATerafin led them to the healerie. Everything in the manse seemed to be so large, Carver thought walking from the kitchen to the dining room would take forever; his stomach reminded him that kitchen to dining room would be better.

The Terafin clearly liked light, and the galleries possessed large windows, some mosaics of multihued glass, and some as plain as open shutters. These, more than the paintings and the statues, caught his attention as they walked.

Torvan and the healer obviously found them unremarkable. Must be nice. But the long halls led, eventually, to shorter ones, although the ceilings still seemed tall and light. When Torvan reached a plain, closed door, he stopped.

"This," he told Arann and Carver, "is as far as I go. If you need anything while you're staying with Alowan, he'll either send for it, or send for someone who will be able to help." He started to speak, stopped himself, and glanced at Arann. "Your den leader is an interesting girl," he said at last.

Carver nodded, because it seemed self-evident to him; Arann said nothing at all.

Torvan turned on his heel and vanished back the way he'd come, his boots making more noise against the floor than simple conversation in the hall would have. As if aware of this, Alowan waited until the steps had receded before he spoke.

"The Chosen seldom enter the healerie, except on stretchers," Alowan said quietly. He opened the door, which appeared to be unlocked, and then stopped in its frame.

"Arann, Carver, you will note the large box on the wall to the right of the door. It is most of the reason the Chosen seldom visit."

Arann looked at the box, but the glance was muted, almost uninterested. Carver looked because it was large, and about two feet off the ground. Not the normal adornment in a hallway, and certainly not halls as fine as the ones they'd passed on the way here.

"Leave your weapons in the box," he told them both.

Arann had already removed his daggers. Carver stared at him, but his gaze seemed to pass either around or through Arann, because Arann didn't respond.

"This is the healerie," Alowan continued, "and it is my space. I will not have weapons beyond my door." He waited.

Arann deposited his daggers in the box. The unlocked, unguarded box. Carver stared at him. And then stared at his own knives. If even the Chosen were supposed to strip themselves of weapons here, it was no damn wonder they didn't visit often.

Arann lifted his hands, and signaled, *It's safe,* in den-sign.

Carver wanted to ask him how he was certain, but didn't, because the old man had watched Arann's den-sign, and he clearly understood what it meant. Which was disturbing.

But Arann was almost never wrong. Grinding his teeth, Carver removed his daggers, lifted the simple wooden lid, and dropped them into the box. He felt naked.

Alowan, however, appeared entirely unconcerned. Carver had a suspicion that the old man would have waited all damn day beside the door, calmly barring his entrance. Now, however, as if capitulation had never been in doubt, the old man turned and and touched the door. "Welcome," he said softly, "to my healerie."

The door opened into sunlight and greenery as far as the eye could see—which, given the profusion of plants, was about as far as the fountain whose water trickled—from a grail, held by an arm that rose out of the water itself—into a small, shallow pool, girded by a solid, gray stone that was wide enough to sit on. Around that fountain, leaves of many different kinds trailed; some stood, as tall as his chest, single fronds that came to white points.

All of these plants were dappled by light that fell from windows—glass—in the round dome of the ceiling above. If it weren't for the lack of breeze, Carver might have believed that the door he'd entered had been an exit. But there was no breeze, here; the plants only moved when they were touched.

He'd never cared much for plants—at least not the nonedible ones—but Alowan obviously did. The healer left them standing quietly in the door to tend them, or rather, to *speak* to them. Arann glanced at Carver, but

Carver was, for the moment, speechless. The old man appeared to be *apologizing* for neglecting them.

Alowan paused, as if suddenly realizing he had visitors, shook his head and stopped his one-sided conversation. "My apologies," he said quietly, this time not to the leaves.

They followed the old man into another room.

The room itself was, or seemed to be, round. The floors were tiled in what looked like marble, but it was a pale, smoky marble, with hints of jade. Trellises lined the walls at different heights, and pots of all sizes housed the plants whose creepers were entwined around them. They produced flowers, as well, white, pink, and a deep, deep purple. Carver sneezed as he passed them.

"Ah, Marla," Alowan said.

A woman appeared from around the plants. "Alowan?" She was older than Carver and Arann, but not by much. Hazel eyes were narrowed in obvious concern. "Why did The Terafin summon you?"

"Marla," Alowan replied, "we have guests. One visitor, and one patient. It is necessary, for the moment, that I leave the patient in your hands."

Her eyes widened slightly, and then she nodded and turned. She looked at both of them—Arann and Carver—but Arann was still wearing the blood-splotched clothing.

"Come with me," she told him gently.

He nodded, and allowed himself to be led from the round room into the room that lay beyond it. It was a good deal larger, and although plants also grew in pots around this room, they occupied only small tables.

"Wait outside a moment," Marla told Carver.

But Arann shook his head. "He's seen me in a lot less clothing."

She nodded, letting the patient lead. She was brisk and efficient when it came to the removal of the pile of clothing, and he had a long, plain robe around his shoulders before he'd stepped out of his pants and his shoes. She held his tunic dubiously between two fingers. "I'm not sure this is worth laundering," she said, although the words rose slightly as if it were a question.

"It can be cleaned and repaired; it wasn't cut or torn," Arann told her. He slid into the bed she indicated with a nod of her head.

"It might be washable, but it can't magically be made larger. That's the problem with mages—they so rarely do anything *practical*."

"It's all I have, at the moment."

She looked as if she would like to argue further, but she didn't. "Are you hungry at all?"

Arann shook his head, as if the defense of his clothing had sapped what little remained of his strength.

"No, you wouldn't be," she said, after a pause. Her whole expression softened, and her eyes were narrow again, the lines of brow folding in almost the exact same way they had when she'd first seen Alowan.

"I'd like a word or two with your friend, and then I'll leave you both alone." Her concern evaporated like summer rain when she glanced at Carver. "Follow, please."

She led him back into the room with the fountain, and asked him to wait. He sat on the fountain's edge and, after a little while, turned and began to trail his fingers across the surface of the falling water, adding ripples that clashed with the spill of water from the stone grail.

But he stopped when he heard steps across the marble, and when he turned and straightened, he faced Alowan, the healer.

He started to rise, but Alowan waved a hand, dismissing the possible politeness Carver was about to offer. "Don't bow here," Alowan told him quietly. "It makes me feel that I am not at home." He paused, and then sat a third of the way around the fountain from Carver, staring not at the water, but at the foliage. It was both quiet and peaceful, and Carver glanced toward the room with the beds, where Arann now lay alone.

"What do you know about the healer-born?" Alowan asked.

Carver shrugged. "They're expensive."

This evoked a very wry smile. "Beyond that?"

He shrugged again. Alowan was healer-born, and even if Carver hadn't known that for a fact, his clothing and his age made the difference in their relative stations clear. Carver had no desire to offend the old man; he just wasn't completely certain what might *cause* offense in this strange place. Besides daggers. "They can heal anything, if they choose. Anything but death."

Alowan nodded. "Anything but death. And yet they seldom choose to heal the dying."

Carver stopped himself from shrugging for a third time. "Why?"

"Because to heal the dying, a healer must almost die himself. Or herself."

Carver was silent, waiting. He knew how to wait.

But Alowan had patience and age on his side, and after a few minutes, Carver said, "Why?"

Alowan's smile was slight, but it was surprisingly warm.

"Because they are almost across the bridge, the dying. Short of a healer's intervention, nothing will prevent the crossing. Healers are not beloved of Mandaros for this reason," he added, "and Mandaros is reputed to have stern words with them when they come, at last, to his Halls."

This surprised Carver. Until this moment, it hadn't occurred to him that anyone could dislike the healer-born.

"I get ahead of myself. We must approach the bridge across which the dead travel to reach the Halls of Mandaros, and we must call the dying back before they cross it. It is often a close-run thing.

"We must call the dying," he added. "And we must hold them; we offer them the promise of life, and safety—and the safety, at least, is a lie. An illusion. What we touch when we are there is all that they are—or were. And what they see in *us* is similar. It exposes us; it reveals all strengths, but also all weaknesses.

"There is love, of a type, in that call. And need. And fear of its loss." He glanced at Carver. "I am old.

Arann is not. I have lost, and I have survived loss, in my time."

"So has he."

Alowan closed his eyes. "You speak of Lefty?"

Carver's eyes widened.

"I told you," the old man said gently, "that the healer must know the healed when they are called back from death's edge. I know of Lefty, and I know what he meant to Arann. I know you, as well. You can't cook, for instance."

Carver's grimace was brief.

"And I know Finch, Teller, Jester, Angel. I know your Jay. Jewel Markess. She is at an age where she dislikes her name."

He had never really thought of Jay as young, before now.

"I know what she sees, when vision strikes her," Alowan continued softly. "And I know what she's done with that vision. She saved Arann's life, the day they first met; she saved it again, later."

Carver nodded.

"He came when I called, but only barely." Alowan's eyes closed. "I did not expect him to be what he was. I think I did not expect your entire den. I certainly did not expect its leader. I will speak with Arann in a few days."

"Speak to him now, if you want."

Alowan shook his head. "It would hurt him."

"Why?"

"The distance is too great between us, who existed, for long moments in the lee of Mandaros' Hall, as one. He desires to cling to that communion. And in truth, so do I. It is difficult. Death is to be avoided, and possibly to be feared—but there is *peace* there, Carver. It is hard to return to a life that has so little of it.

"The healer-born offer the dying some of that peace—possibly in order to tempt them. It is not deliberately malicious. It is just the nature of the healer. We heal. We defy death until death, at last, takes us."

Alowan rose. "I will let you return to his side. Arann will not speak much, but I don't believe he was ever one who did. Do not leave him alone more often than The Terafin's service requires."

"We're not in her service," Carver replied.

"No. Not yet. I forget myself." He began to walk away, in the opposite direction from the room with the beds. But he paused. "She is a worthy lord, The Terafin. And Jewel Markess is a worthy den leader.

"I think you will find that there *is* a place for you in House Terafin, if, in the end, you desire it. Do not tell her that, if you feel it unwise. Jewel Markess is not a young woman who trusts either comfort or ease; she will earn her place here, or she will fail.

"But for my part, you are welcome in my healerie. Your daggers, as you are aware, are not. Bring Finch, bring Teller. I think I would like to meet them."

"Now?"

"I forget myself. Not now, not yet. But in a day or two."

"I'm not sure where we'll be in a day or two."

"I, however, am certain where Arann will be. The Terafin is powerful, and she is wealthy. I think it unlikely that she will return you to the streets before I judge your den-kin capable of surviving in them. You will be within the Terafin manse for at least as long as Arann is." He turned again. "I am weary, and I, too, must seek what peace can be gathered in a place that offers death and violence to the young as casually as the sun rises at dawn."

He hesitated, as if he would say more, and then he shook his head and left Carver beside the fountain.

Arann didn't speak much. And while it was true that he wasn't chatty—which, given the rest of the den, was probably a good thing—this silence was leaden, heavy, almost painful. Carver tried to break it, because Carver was not by nature as quiet or reticent as Arann. But it was hard to shoulder a conversation entirely on one's own, and in the end, even Carver fell into uncharacteristic silence.

He did not, however, leave. He stood once, to stretch

his legs, and Arann watched, his silence unbroken, his expression so openly desolate, it was a shock.

He was therefore seated, in that uncomfortable silence, when Jay came to the healerie. The healerie was so quiet and so lulling, she managed to knock Carver off his chair by simply touching his shoulder; he hadn't even heard her approach.

She came without daggers, and she looked tired and stretched, her face pinched by an anxiety that abated only when she saw that Arann was alive. As if the healing might have been a dream, or the part of nightmare that gives hope before it crushes it entirely, she stood at the edge of the bed, gathering her thoughts.

"It's fine. Everything's all right," she told Carver, taking the seat that he'd tumbled from. "There's someone outside the door for you. Tell him you're part of my den; he'll take you to where there's food. More food than a den full of Angels could eat."

They'd been hungry, these past few weeks; not starving, because they made enough in the streets to survive—but never full. Never full enough. He crossed his arms over his chest, however, and shook his head. "I'll wait." He nodded to Arann.

"No, you'll eat."

"I—"

"That's an order, Carver, not a request. Do it."

He hesitated for a long, long minute, and then he snapped a very sarcastic salute—a perfect mimicry of the same salute that Torvan ATerafin had offered his lord.

Jay, adept at ignoring sarcasm, failed to notice. Or perhaps it wasn't deliberate. Her eyes were focused on Arann, and on Arann's face. He had started, in the broken silence, to cry; the tears were utterly silent.

Carver started to speak, stopped, and quietly headed toward the arboretum. But he hesitated on the threshold, and turned back, watching at a safe distance.

"Are you still in pain?" Jay asked softly.

Arann's nod was slight, and he tried to smile. It was

a miserable failure. "But not the side, not the ribs. It's—the healer. He's—he's gone."

"Arann? What do you mean?"

Carver could have told her. But he waited for Arann.

Arann reached out and grabbed Jay's hand, holding it tightly enough that his knuckles whitened.

"Arann, I want to talk to someone. I promise," she added, extracting her hand, "that I'll be right back."

Time, Carver thought, to go. He vanished, rustling leaves without, by some miracle, breaking stems, in his haste to reach the door before she saw him.

More food than a den full of Angels could eat was a *lot* of damn food. And, to be fair, Angel had *tried*. But even trying—and he was now leaning back on a chair that was tilted on two legs in the cavernous room—he had been forced to leave half of what had been prepared, and it was there waiting for Carver when he was led to the wing by the servant that had, as Jay had told him, been waiting for him.

They had all eaten, and they all watched Carver sit down and dig in. While he ate, they peppered him with questions about Arann, and about Alowan's healerie; he answered them between mouthfuls. Well, mostly. None of the food fell out, which was good enough.

There was a moment of awkwardness when a stiff, almost starched old man appeared in the doors of what he termed the lunch rooms, and Finch rose to introduce him.

"This is Ellerson," she told him, with just an edge of warning in her tone, "and Ellerson, this is Carver. You've only one more of us to meet, and he's still in the healerie. Alowan told Carver he'd be there for at least another two days."

Ellerson nodded crisply enough that you could almost *hear* it. Carver lifted his hands in den-sign, and Angel signed back, *Yes, real*.

"Will your duties to your den-kin take you back to the healerie, sir?"

Carver signed, Y*ou're sure,* and Angel replied, Y*es.* So he swallowed, and said, "Yeah."

Ellerson's expression didn't change, but it now radiated a mild disapproval. The way snow radiated mild cold.

Seeing his expression, Finch said—quickly— "Ellerson is here to, ummm, help us adjust to House Terafin."

"And feed us," Jester added, burping.

Winter in Averalaan had never had quite the precise ice that now settled into Ellerson's pained expression. Teller glanced at Jester, and then, looking at Ellerson, shrugged almost apologetically.

Carver, however, ate. And he ate as if this might be the last real meal they'd have in months—because if they didn't come up with a way to steal *something* from this place, and given the guards and Arann's dependence on the healerie, it was going to be hard on all fronts, it would be.

Only when he finished did he ask, "Did Jay eat?"

Teller looked across the table, which was a fair distance, and said, "What do you think?"

"I think," Carver replied, standing and grabbing a plate, "that we should probably save her something."

"That will not be necessary," Ellerson told him.

They all looked at the old man, who had not moved.

"The kitchen staff will prepare food when she has the time to eat it."

"But what happens to *this* food?"

Ellerson did not reply.

But he did watch. He could watch in invisible silence, and sometimes he did; he could clear his throat and remind them of his presence when it seemed germane. For the most part, their manners were *appalling,* but he had expected that, and while he showed some disapproval for the most egregious of mannerly sins, in reality it was mild.

What he did not show, although he felt it more strongly, was the surprise they evoked in him. He did not comment when they stuffed food into the folds of their clothing, although he did wonder, if this was their normal behavior, how it was that their clothing remained even passably clean.

He understood, within the first ten minutes of the meal, that Finch and Teller were probably the people to whom he would speak, and from whom he would gain any useful information. He discovered that most of this den could read and write—although Teller hesitantly admitted that Jester was not perhaps the most legible writer.

He discovered, through this, that Jewel Markess had taught them. And that she was not perhaps the most patient of teachers.

He understood that what he would learn in the future—near or far—would be deeper, and it would answer some questions that he held in abeyance. He was willing to wait.

Now, he watched and listened to this den interact. The sign language they used frequently amused Ellerson. It was simple, and accompanied by facial expressions rather than words, it was not hard to figure out. But there seemed to be no malice at all in either these signals or their spoken words, and the concern that they showed for the absent was real.

They reminded him more of family than of people who had banded together out of mutual self-interest, and the puzzle at the heart of that was Jewel Markess.

It was a long, slow meal, and he allowed it to continue well past the end of late lunch; he was about to signal an end, for the sake of the servants, when a servant with whom he was not yet familiar came into the wing, walking with the crisp speed that implied that the news he carried was important.

Ellerson headed him off, which was acceptable.

"I've been asked to deliver a message to Carver," the servant said briskly.

Ellerson took the message, frowned for just a moment, and then delivered it to Carver.

"Your pardon, sir," he said, bowing stiffly and properly at the middle, "but Torvan ATerafin is waiting at the doors to the West Wing."

Carver, pockets half full, stood.

"I believe the food will not be of use to you," Ellerson added severely.

Carver grimaced and flattened his pockets by removing the food; Ellerson had been half afraid he would simply crush them into shape.

"What does he want?" Carver asked; the conversation had completely died around the table.

"He wishes, I believe, to convey happy news to you."

"Oh?" Instant wariness sharpened the line of the boy's jaw, and narrowed the edges of his eyes.

"He says that you appear to have been mistaken. Ararath Handernesse is not, as you feared, dead; he is, at the moment, in the waiting rooms of the manse itself."

Chapter Sixteen

THE SILENCE THAT GREETED THESE words was profound. It was not, however, lengthy. Densign flashed around the table at a speed that made it indecipherable to the older domicis who watched. He understood two things, however. The news was not happy news because this group of urchins somehow knew that it was not true, and *somehow*, in this case, was the absent Jewel Markess.

Carver rose. Angel and Finch rose as well, but he waved them down curtly. "Torvan came for me," he told them all, "I'll go get Jay."

"What are you going to tell him?"

"Don't know. I'll think of something." He turned to Ellerson the way a condemned man might turn to the guards who were to convey him to his execution.

Ellerson bowed. "Follow me, sir."

Torvan ATerafin was indeed waiting for Carver at the doors of the wing, although there were a number of doors to pass through before they reached them. He nodded to Ellerson, who returned this nod with an almost staccato bow.

Carver squared shoulders, and brushed the hair out

of his eyes. This was a habit he'd picked up from years of watching Jay, and the end result was pretty much the same for him as it was for her—all the hair fell back down again almost instantly.

"You received my news?" Torvan asked. He did not ask it in a friendly fashion; the man who had carried Arann from the road into the Terafin's office was somehow buried beneath the exterior of an intimidating senior House Guard. What had Alowan called him? Chosen.

Carver nodded. "I'd like to deliver the news to Jay—to Jewel. Markess. In the healerie."

Torvan watched Carver's expression for a long moment. To Carver's surprise—and relief—he finally nodded. It was not, again, a friendly nod. "I thought you might."

When they arrived in the healerie, Marla took one look at them—or, more accurately, at Torvan—and her jaw tightened. He failed to meet her gaze, and he failed to leave his sword in the box at the door. Carver, however, did not fail to leave his dagger.

"What's happened?" Marla asked Torvan sharply.

"We have news for the young woman who sits with the healer's patient. It will not wait."

"They don't make the Chosen messengers," she replied curtly. "And news won't account for a sword here."

"We'll be brief." He was entirely impassive, and she hesitated; Carver knew she was trying to decide whether or not to go fetch Alowan. In the end, Torvan took the decision out of her hands while she wrestled with it. He stepped past her, and toward the beds, and Carver followed at his heels.

Jay was in the room, sitting beside Arann, who was sleeping. In sleep, he was clutching her hand, and she in turn had placed her other hand over the top of his. Leaning forward, she watched him, sitting so still Carver thought she might also be dozing.

Carver passed Torvan and cleared his throat, in warning; she looked up, met his gaze, and then pried her hand free. Arann's grip tightened, but he didn't wake.

"What's up?" Edge, in those words. She was tired. Carver, who'd eaten enough for days, was not. Even had he had no food, he would have been awake.

"It's—it's—"

"What the young man is trying to say," Torvan said, executing a very stiff half bow without extending his palm, "is that we have good news for you."

She met Torvan's gaze, and Carver knew she was wondering what the healer's assistant had wondered: How often did the House Guard get sent on errands? She didn't ask, however; she owed Torvan ATerafin, and Jay had *always* been mindful of debt.

"Good news?" Jay glanced at Carver. He lifted his hands to sign, but didn't hold her attention for long enough.

"It appears that your friend, Ararath Handernesse, is not, as you feared, dead."

Whatever color there was in her face—and it was scant to begin with—deserted her entirely as his words sunk in. "W-what do you mean?"

"He's in Gabriel ATerafin's office, waiting for the opportunity to make an appointment to speak with The Terafin."

Torvan ATerafin watched her very, very carefully. He had not, as he had heavily implied to Ellerson, been sent to convey this news. He had been made aware of it, no more. But he had taken the measure of this girl, and her den, in the moments before he had decided to speak for her.

The appearance of Ararath Handernesse, on the heels of the almost dead boy, had cast a shadow on that decision. He did not—yet—regret it. But the girl had been so certain, and he was enough a judge of character to understand that the grief buried in her words was genuine.

She showed no joy at all, now. And this lack did not surprise him; perhaps it should have. But the Chosen operated in part on instinct, and he was willing to see how that instinct played out. No, not willing. Driven.

"*Kalliaris'* curse," Jewel whispered. She turned away from him, but only as far as her sleeping kin; she took the boy's hand in her own, and leaned over to kiss his forehead, as if she were either mother or sister, or in some fashion, both. It was not the gesture of a leader.

And yet, they followed.

When she rose, she turned to face him, folding her arms across her chest. Her color did not return, and her breath was a little too shallow; she was afraid. "That's impossible." There was no doubt at all in her words; they were flat and surprisingly even.

"What's impossible?"

"Ararath Handernesse isn't in Gabriel ATerafin's office. It's not possible."

"Oh, isn't it?"

She shook her head.

"Jewel—Jay, if you prefer—it can't be impossible. I led him there myself, at Gabriel's direct request." After which he had gone straight to the West Wing of the manse, to deliver the news.

"That's—that's not Ararath." Again, the words were flat and certain. She wasn't nervous. Not yet.

"And how do you know this?"

"Because I—I know he's dead."

Carver's hands rose, and his fingers danced a moment in his palms, but her hands did not rise in like fashion. Whatever message the boy had conveyed—to Torvan's admittedly jaundiced eye, it appeared to be a warning—she had chosen to ignore or dismiss it.

"Interesting. You didn't mention this in your interview with The Terafin."

"No." She glanced away. It was the first time she had chosen to evade his gaze.

"Jewel, if you're playing some kind of game, end it now. You weren't lying there—she would have known it—but I see now that you weren't telling the whole of the truth." He shaded the words with more force than he felt; no one in that room had expected that a thief from the holdings would *ever* speak the whole of the truth.

But she was young, and she showed her age; the tone of the words, and the force with which they were spoken, unnerved her. She was not, he thought, a very accomplished liar. This suprised him, but only slightly.

"Torvan," she said, spreading her hands, exposing her empty palms, "you *have to* believe me."

"Make me believe you," he replied, speaking with the same force, but shading it now with anger, with demand. He was not bard-born; the compulsion of his next words existed only within her. "Tell me the truth."

What she said next should have surprised him. But he had not come to the West Wing without cause. He trusted his instincts.

"All right! But—but you've got to get help, and you've got to get it now. Call all your guards, get them together, have them ready, please."

"Why?" He was already assembling the House Guard, and the Chosen, in his thoughts.

"Because I *know* Old Rath is dead! No, I didn't see the body—and I couldn't tell you where it is—but the creature that looks like Rath and calls himself Rath is what killed him.

"Old Rath—that's what we called him—he made me promise never to tell."

Carver touched her shoulder in warning. He didn't speak. Torvan noted both, but he waited in a grim silence that was no longer entirely an act. He believed her. He believed a thief from the holdings. It was why, in the end, he had chosen to deliver his happy news.

"I get these—these feelings. And whenever I get them, they're always right. They're *always* true. They've always been like that."

The shock of those words held him silent.

If what she was saying was true—and in the end, he could not doubt it, although he was wise enough to make the attempt—she was talent-born. And born, as well, to a talent that existed almost entirely in myth or legend.

She mistook his silence, and he allowed it, gathering—marshaling—his thoughts.

"I don't know how," she continued, her voice losing vehemence and strength until it was almost a whisper, "but Rath is dead. And if we don't stop whatever it is that's pretending to be Rath, The Terafin—and the rest of us—will die as well."

"Feelings? What do you mean? Instinct? Hunch?"

"No—stronger than that. I *know* when something's true, but I can't control the knowledge. I can't listen to you and tell you when you're lying or telling the truth—it's not some sort of market trick. It's just—just feeling." She paled, and after a moment's silence, asked, "Did you—did you tell him we were here?"

He watched her for a moment, and then said, "No."

"No? Why not?"

"Instinct." With that word, he offered her a very slight smile, and he allowed the distance that had masked his expression to lessen.

"Can I say something?" Carver broke in.

"What?" They both turned to face him, the single word a blend of different tones.

"You might want to point out that *this* Old Rath jumped off a three-story building and left a hole in the cobblestones, and then chased us down the streets and kept pace with a set of horses at a gallop."

"You might want to say that indeed." Torvan turned to Carver, and he spoke quietly, intently. "What else can you tell me? Be quick about it—we don't have much time."

"No," Jewel said. The sound of her voice made Torvan turn to look at her. She was staring into the distance just beyond his shoulder, and what she saw, he couldn't discern. "We don't."

Torvan led them to the chambers of the Chosen. It was in some ways a breach of etiquette, for to these chambers, not even the House Guards or the members of Terafin who were not Chosen came. But the Chosen were expected to exercise discretion, and in emergency, liberties were taken. Jewel Markess and Carver followed in his wake; he walked quickly.

He glanced once at Carver when they reached the outer chamber, and saw that the boy had drawn a dagger. It was a small knife, given his size, and to Torvan's eye, it was not a particularly *good* one, but he did not tell the boy to sheathe it. Instead, he said, "Have either of you any experience with real weapons?"

Carver understood the criticism implied by the question, but he was tense enough to take no offense. "Some," Carver replied. "Not much."

Torvan nodded, unsurprised. Jewel merely shook her head.

"Follow." He led them quickly past the tapestried walls and the standing weapon racks of the outer chamber and into a room that housed six of his companions.

"Torvan?" Alayra, the Captain of the Chosen, rose from the chair she had occupied. Her expression shaded from curious to the quiet of worry before she had finished speaking his name.

He snapped a salute that was in every way the equal of the salute he offered his lord.

It offered her no comfort. "What is it? What brings you here?"

"We have a hostile mage on the grounds. In Gabriel ATerafin's office."

Jay looked up as he spoke. Carver saw her face pale—and he knew that whatever she said next would be two things: bad, and true. "Torvan?" Her voice was soft, and broke between syllables.

"What?"

"He's—he's with her."

The other five Chosen rose at once, joining Alayra.

"He's with The Terafin?"

"Yes."

"Let me pass, Primus Alayra," Torvan told his commander.

Her face was now almost the color of Jay's, which made the scar down the left of her forehead stand out.

"And what will you do?" she asked, although it was clear she knew what the answer would be.

"I'm going to summon the mage."

"On your head, then."

"On my head alone." But he caught Jay by the hand, and he dragged her past the assembled Chosen and into the final chamber.

This room, unlike the previous two, was unadorned by paintings, weapon racks, or armor; it likewise had no tables or chairs. It was not a small room, but it was empty, if you didn't count the bronze brazier that burned in its center.

The three doorless walls framed that brazier; torches, in sconces, burned against those walls. There were no magestones here; the light was flickering and uneven. But had it not been for that light, they would have been in utter darkness.

As it was, it took Carver's eyes a few minutes to adjust to the lesser light. When they did, he saw that the walls were not blank, as he'd first thought: they were carved, in slight relief. Each wall contained a single arch, with fine, tall pillars and elaborate keystones. Beneath those arches? Stone. Just stone. It was a very strange room.

Torvan, however, wasn't concerned. He told them to stay put, and then began to walk, three times, around the burning brazier. At the end of the third small circuit, he raised his hand, drew a small knife, and cut his palm. His fingers wide, he let blood drip into the fire, and as it did, it sizzled, and the smoke the brazier emitted grew black.

Torvan ATerafin then turned toward one wall.

22nd of Scaral, 410 AA
The Order of Knowledge, Averalaan Aramarelas

Meralonne APhaniel sat in the tower rooms he occupied. In his hand was the bowl of his favorite pipe, but although he had taken the time to line its bed with the

finest of leaf, he had yet to light it. This was not because
he did not wish to smoke; he did. But he knew, from
hard experience, that the moment he lit the pipe, someone would knock at his door, and the promise of that
lined bowl would be ash—and not through any enjoy-
ment on his part.

He rose, and walked the short distance to the tower
windows that overlooked the Isle, and beyond it, the
stretch of endless sea, whose color did not shift or
change for simple things like weather. Storms came,
and the port closed for days or weeks, but that was all.
He watched the waves strike the seawall, and he turned
away; he was restless. A storm was in the air, although it
was not carried by cloud.

This morning, he had been summoned to the Chamber of the Magi, in which Sigurne sat unattended by any
save Matteos Corvel. She had looked up as he entered
the room, and then had simply waved Matteos aside.
Matteos did not care for Meralonne, which bothered
neither man overmuch, but inasmuch as he trusted
any of the First Circle mages, he was willing to trust
Meralonne, and he had retreated without comment.

Matteos was just the type of starched and well-
behaved individual who was highly unlikely to satisfy
his curiosity by eavesdropping; it was one of the more
annoying things about him. But Matteos, this morning,
was not a concern.

Sigurne looked both delicate and weary. Only one
of these things was accurate. Meralonne tendered her a
bow; it was not a formal bow, as befit rank; it was, however, not an affectionate gesture. It was a test. Sigurne
disliked formality.

But she failed to note—or comment—upon the
gesture, and Meralonne understood in that instant the
information she wished to impart to him. Saw, from the
slight rise of her brow, that she suspected he now knew.
She had always been—even as a young woman barely
over the threshold of adulthood—canny.

"Ararath failed to report last night."

Ararath Handernesse seldom ventured into the

Order of Knowledge, and the manner in which he made these reports was unknown to Meralonne APhaniel. But he did not doubt her words; nor did he doubt the significance of them.

Meralonne nodded. "I will repair to my quarters," he told her. "There, I will prepare."

She lifted a pale jade-veined hand. "It would not be the first time that he has failed to report."

"This close to Scarran, Sigurne?"

Her eyes were enormous and unblinking, an owl's eyes. But after a moment, she nodded. She did not look away; she did not lift hand to eyes or face. Her expression rippled briefly as if at familiar and unwelcome pain, no more. "That was my thought. Very well."

"If he was correct in his assumptions, and if he played his game *well*, we will have our answer."

"Too many 'ifs' for my liking. Too much risk. I dislike the Winter Solstice."

"With cause, Sigurne. I will wait in my quarters."

She nodded and he turned toward the doors, but paused before they opened. "I will wait two full days. If it is at all possible, I would like to be uninterrupted."

"It is not, as you well know, possible," she replied grimly.

He shrugged.

But he had, of course, been less than entirely truthful. He had been prepared for many days now. The preparations themselves had required thought and planning; they had also required the subtle and deep use of magic and the contingency theories so beloved of the academically inclined Magi. These men—and women—would remain in ignorance of his work. So, too, would those rare members of the Order of Knowledge who were also members of House Terafin, for it was within the walls of the Terafin manse that he had labored, waiting Ararath's final move.

Sigurne grieved.

Meralonne did not. He thought instead. Until the enemy was exposed, their allies could remain hidden.

And while it was not explicitly stated in his discussions with Sigurne, it was clear, to him and the woman who ruled the Order of Knowledge, that mages of some power were no doubt involved with the demon-kin.

It angered Sigurne; it was one of the few things that still had the power to do so. She had gained wisdom in her tenure, first as student, then as master, and wisdom had dulled almost all of her youthful edges. Not that one, however. It would be blunted with her death, and little else.

Meralonne was neither angered nor outraged. Men of power sought power, consorted with power, and hoped to gain advantage from it, regardless of the form the power took. It had been true for the whole of his life; it would no doubt be true long after. He did not have a high opinion of human nature, and because he did not, he was seldom disappointed.

He was, however, careful. Once, in his own youth, he would not have been; then, power only needed to be hidden if one was weak. Now? Power required subtlety if one was *lazy*.

He glanced at his pipe, and then, with reluctance, set it to one side. The chair in front of the desk was cluttered with books and papers; the chair behind it was empty. The former was meant to be a strong hint to those who might come to visit—and thankfully, they were few—but the latter was for his use. Taking that chair, he now began to sort through the papers that lined the surface of his desk. Some were old enough that they radiated magic; in no other way would they have weathered the centuries.

But that magic, and the magic that began to fill the room, were not the same. He smiled for a moment as he glanced at the color of the light that was apparent to his eyes; it bore his signature, folded among the lattice of white and gray.

"What now?" he said, as the power grew stronger. "I'm a busy man, and I don't have time for insignificant interruptions. I've students, patricians, and merchants clamoring for attention; you'd best set yourself apart from them very quickly."

The voice that replied caused him to lift his head; it was a young voice; too young for The Terafin's Chosen. "We need your help," it said. "The Terafin is about to be—"

"We call upon you," an older, and male voice broke in. "To fulfill your bond. I am Torvan of the Chosen, and I summon you to The Terafin's side."

At last.

He let curiosity about the girl's voice dissipate, and he lifted his face so that he could see, in the lines above his desk, the face of the man who now summoned him. He recognized him as Torvan ATerafin, although he had not troubled to hide his identity.

With a simple gesture, he changed his robes from the plain and unremarkable robes of the Order to robes that shifted in light, gray and white and all colors in between.

"Torvan, what is the danger that you perceive?"

Torvan, however, did not answer the question, not directly. Instead, he turned and spoke a single word. "Jewel."

"My lord," the girl said, and as she spoke, the vision shifted to frame her face. She was young; by Averalaan standards, not quite adult, although she hovered at its edge. Her eyes were dark, and her hair a brown that suggested auburn; his magic did not convey such nuances well.

"We—I—there is an—an assassin on the grounds. He looks like a friend, but he—but he's not human."

Obviously the girl was not accustomed to speaking in public. Or to speaking clearly at all. In spite of this, Meralonne was curious; it was to this girl that Torvan of the Chosen had deferred.

"Not human? What is he?"

"I don't know. But he—he jumped off the top of a three-story building and made a hole in the road."

"I see. I take it he then continued to move?"

She nodded.

He lifted a hand, and he gestured; along the relay he had placed just the hint of compulsion. It was not, strictly speaking, legal. Nor did the lack of legality trouble him; the girl was clearly unlearned and not therefore adept at maneuvering the nicety of Imperial Law. "You will wait until our business is done, for I wish to speak with you further."

She nodded, silent, and then, to his surprise, she broke from his gaze and turned to look off to one side. To Torvan.

"I will come," Meralonne told them both. "Step back."

And so, he thought, rising from his desk and arming himself, it begins. At last.

My thanks, scion of Handernesse.

22nd of Scaral 410 AA
Terafin Manse, Averalaan Aramarelas

Carver watched as the wall burned. White flames, with hearts of orange and gold, scoured stone engravings clean. It should have been impossible, but the man who now stepped *through* that solid rock surface was a mage, and mages defied the possible. He wore robes that looked as if they were made of fine, fine steel, and when the last of those robes cleared the wall, the rock cracked and settled at his back.

While he watched, Jay grim and silent by his side, Torvan shouted orders. This room, the one he had led them to, was filled only by guards. By, Torvan had said, the Chosen.

Those guards now obeyed his commands, but they weren't wordless.

"You'd better be right about this," a tall and grim-faced woman said. She was older than Torvan, and shorter, but her shoulders were broad and her arms suggested that the weight of armor meant less to her than cotton gauze would have to Carver. She wore a sword at her hip, and she carried a helm in the crook of her left arm.

Torvan said quietly, "I know." He meant to say more;

Carver saw that, and it made him wonder who this woman was.

But the mage clearly didn't give a damn. "Where is your intruder?" His voice was cool, clipped; Carver would have said he was irritated or annoyed, but something about his eyes were wrong for that. They were gray, those eyes, and right now they glimmered like steel reflecting light.

Torvan, however, didn't find the interruption offputting. "We believe that he is either with, or on his way, to The Terafin."

"Then let us repair to her quarters in haste."

The guards nodded, and Carver tried to find the tail of their six-man escort, so that he and Jay could slip behind them and follow. But the mage walked only as far as the wall opposite the one his arrival had seemed to destroy.

"What is he doing?" Jay asked Torvan, in something close to a whisper.

"He made this room, these walls, and these arches. That wall, the one that he's standing in front of, leads through the fireplace into The Terafin's audience chambers. We must follow; wait for us here."

She glanced, briefly, at the third wall with its stylized engravings, but she didn't have the courage to ask what it was for. Not now, and maybe not ever. Carver nodded, but he knew she had no intention of being left behind; if it came to that, neither did he.

Of course, he was stupid. Jay had no excuse.

The mage touched the wall, and the stone beneath the carved arch began to lose the consistency of rock. Carver had seen it happen once already, but it was still jarring to watch stone fade into something that resembled gray-and-white mist.

Through those mists, pale and insubstantial at first, Carver could see the unmistakable figure of The Terafin. She was not seated; she stood.

He had thought she might be in the room they had first entered, but the room the mist slowly parted to reveal was grander and larger, with paintings, and small statues in recessed alcoves in the wall, adorned on either side by glassed cases. She appeared to be alone.

But she looked up, and her eyes widened slightly as she saw who sought entry into her room, and why. "What is this?"

Torvan did not reply; instead, led by the mage, he entered the room, along with the other Chosen, Jay and Carver himself, who almost thought the better of it when he saw the expression on the face of the woman who ruled this House.

But he followed, and before anyone could answer her question—and Carver could understand why no one wanted to—he froze.

Standing between the Chosen and The Terafin, well-dressed, clean-shaven, and unarmed, was Old Rath.

The Terafin stood, silent, Ararath before her, and behind him, outlined by the wavering shape of an entirely magical arch, her Chosen, the mage whose services Terafin retained, and, all but hidden by both, two of the street children that she had chosen—for her own reasons—to take into her House. Only one of these people was welcome, had been welcome, even if that welcome had been fraught. Not even Morretz was in this room, because Amarais had some dignity, and she had been surprisingly uncertain how this interview would go.

She had not seen her brother for years. For decades. At one point in time, she could number the days. Nor had she expected to see him again. She saw him now, older and careworn; the streets had not been as kind to Ararath, in the end, as the House had been to her. When she had received word of his probable death, she had felt—carefully—nothing.

When she had received word of his *presence,* that nothing had crumbled, like an ancient and poorly kept wall—but what it would reveal, not even she could be certain. And yet, uncertain, she had agreed—in haste—to meet with him, choosing the function rooms that only the most important of her visitors might see.

She had thought to preserve privacy. To preserve the

part of the past that she, foolish in ways that years had not completely eradicated, had both hidden and, in the end, cherished.

Yet he had not spoken four words, and those a stiff and formal greeting, before she had seen the wall, and the great mantel that was the centerpiece of this room, shiver and become translucent, as if made of glass and smoke.

Her own words, she was now forced to choose with care. "Gentlemen," she said, each syllable as sharp as any harsh word she had ever spoken, "while it's been a pleasure to have your company, unless we can come to an understanding of circumstance, I will be forced to ask you to leave."

The Chosen were inscrutable. But she saw the flicker of her captain's eyes as Alayra's gaze brushed Torvan's profile. Her own glance strayed to Ararath; he had not moved.

She forced her hands not to gather in fists at her sides. "I have, as you can see, a visitor who arranged to speak with me."

That visitor now frowned. "If I've come at an inopportune moment, I can return at another time."

And would he? He had not come when she had been granted the Terafin name; he had not come while she had struggled to survive the war that had led, in the end, to the Terafin Seat upon the High Council in *Avantari*, the Palace of Kings. If she let him go, now, all of her words and all of his would remain unspoken. She could barely believe he had come at all. He would vanish; the streets would once again swallow him.

"No." She turned to look at her Chosen; she could not keep the ice from her voice, and no longer bothered to try. What her expression told them, she did not know, and did not, at this particular moment, care. "Gentlemen?"

They offered no answer.

But Ararath said, in a sharper voice, "What are you doing?"

The Terafin glanced briefly at the painting that

rested, in a gold frame, above the mantel. It was not merely decorative, although it was pleasant enough; a seaside painting, with brief sand dunes broken by waves and two large, standing stones. The sky in the painting, however, paled or deepened in the presence of magic.

The sky was, at this moment, the color of storm to her eye.

"Meralonne." The word was just short of command. Meralonne APhaniel was, as most of the Magi, fractious and difficult. He was not, however, like many, overfocused and under-sensitive. He could choose to offend, if it took his fancy; he could choose to charm in equal measure.

But he seldom chose magery as a greeting.

"Please explain your presence here *at once*." But even asking, she knew. She knew, and she, who had risen to power by trusting her instinct and her knowledge, chose to glance away from it now. It was bitter; she was no longer a child, and even as a child she had seldom been one who preferred not to see, not to hear, not to know.

But life taught, always.

"I am here," he replied, "at the behest of your Chosen." He stepped forward, standing neither in the room nor beyond it, interposed as he was across the mantel itself. She remembered—it was ludicrous, but memory was often like that—the argument she had had about the mantel and its value when he had proposed this strange security measure.

She had thought it odd, then.

She understood, now, that it had been deliberate. *This* was what he had built for. This moment.

And she wondered if she would ever forgive him for it. "Obviously."

He stepped forward, now, into the room; the Chosen followed him like a moving, metallic wall. They knew her anger, and they moved anyway.

"Please accept my apologies for the unannounced use of magecraft in your presence. And you, sir, if you would accept my most humble apologies."

"For what?" Ararath replied, but his expression was once again smooth and slightly weary.

"Indeed, Meralonne," The Terafin said, the cold in the words like a winter storm. "For what?" Because she could not, not quite, let go.

She had chosen the men and women who now accompanied the mage because she could trust them. It took effort, to remember that now.

"I merely attempted to negate any . . . illusion that might have been present."

"Illusion?" His voice was so familiar. Even changed by decades, the surprise and incredulity was entirely his. "Are you saying that I'm a mage?"

"Please accept my apologies. Terafin, it appears that I have been summoned in error."

She wanted to believe this. "Who summoned you?"

"I did." Torvan ATerafin stepped forward, and lowered himself to one knee, his helmed head bowed before her.

Torvan. She bowed her head in turn. "We will speak of this later."

"Lord."

As one man, the Chosen turned to leave. They passed through the arch, and returned to their chamber, sparing a glance for the two urchins who had waited in safety within.

But the mage left last, and she saw, with a pang, that it was not yet over. She glanced at her brother, at her brother's face, and she examined her desire as dispassionately as she could.

Ararath, she thought, but she did not speak, did not gesture; instead she moved, changing in unnoticeable ways not her posture, but her position.

When Meralonne APhaniel turned at the edge of the arch, she was not surprised.

"I will take my leave," he said.

She nodded, miming permission. Aware, as she met the steel of his bright gaze that he was not yet done. Aware, as well, that Ararath had already dismissed them all from his thoughts.

"But I think that I have not been summoned without cause."

He lifted one slender hand, and gestured. No fire left his fingers, no lightning, no sign of violent magic. Instead, for just a moment, the room was suffused with the fragrance of summer on the Isle. Of summer, she thought, in Handernesse, when the garden was in full bloom, a riot of scent and color, attended by bees and small birds, by men and women, and by her inquisitive, annoying, adoring younger brother.

She watched Ararath; even before the scream of pain and surprise left his lips, she saw the widening of recognition in his eyes. Saw, as well, the sudden narrowing of the same eyes, as pain was transformed by some emotional alchemy into rage, and a fury that she had never, ever seen on her brother's face.

Hope was foolish. Longing, foolish. Sentiment, expensive in the extreme. She paid the price for these, now. Ararath was, as Jewel Markess had so strongly implied, dead.

Her face was a mask. There was no numbness in her, and what care she could take was turned outward, not in.

"My lord," he said, turning toward her, his palms spread, "You can see that this—this mage," he spit out the word as he turned toward Meralonne, who had not moved once since he had made his single, his singular, gesture, "bears me malice for reasons I cannot begin to—"

And then he stiffened. Amarais understood this as well; he had seen, at last, Jewel Markess and her den-kin.

The wall exploded.

Amarais stood unharmed by the fragments of stone and wood debris that flew out from the wall. Meralonne APhaniel, who stood at the center of the blast, was likewise unharmed; the same could not, however, be said of the mantel, which had been—moments before—priceless and irreplaceable.

Unseen by either the mage or the man who was not,

and perhaps had never been, her brother, the painting of idyllic seashore had blackened to ash.

She looked past the shoulder of the Magi, to where Torvan now stood, and she offered him something akin to a smile. "I chose well, when I chose you."

He wouldn't hear her, of course; he would hear nothing but his own fear, his own concern for her safety. He had taken the risk of summoning the mage on nothing more than hunch, and Amarais knew well whose hunch it had been: Jewel Markess. The girl was white and silent; she and Carver all but clung to each other, although they did not actually touch.

Amarais should have felt fear; she felt none. Instead, something cold and sharp, a fury that she had thought long left behind in the streets of the holdings, in a childhood that she had stepped out of long before her debut, almost consumed her. What had she exposed, to be hunted in this fashion? What vulnerability had she revealed, that a powerful stranger might seek this audience, so certain that she would grant it, and alone?

It was the type of risk she *did not take,* and she had taken it for the sake of her past, and the younger brother she had once adored.

They would *pay*.

"Old man, do you think you are a match for me? Do you think that your magics and your pathetic human power will outlast *mine*? You've had decades, and I, eternity. But I will see you suffer before this is done."

The gods were kind to the woman who was now The Terafin; the voice no longer resembled Ararath's voice. The expression—what she could see of it, for the face was mostly turned from her—was not his. She could hone her anger at the masquerade because it was now so pathetically clear.

The imposter's shoulders tensed, and his hands flexed, and once again, the room was bathed in the harsh glare of magical fire. She felt its heat across her exposed cheeks, her throat, the backs of the hands she kept idle by her sides. She heard, as if at a distance, the crack and the tinkle of glass.

"Well, well, well," Meralonne replied, his lips turned in a half smile. "It *has* been rather a long time, and I do admit I'm rusty." He took a step forward, and cleared the arch completely.

Amarais saw that Torvan was a step behind him—a step and an invisible wall; she heard the crash of his armor and saw him bounce; saw the brief agony of his expression, the widening of eyes, the turn of head as the Chosen understood that they *could not* follow the Magi. The Terafin was on one side of the divide that they had *trusted* the mage to build; they were on the other side, the wrong side.

She had lost some of her most trusted guards in the fight for the House. She had accepted their deaths, just as she had accepted that her own might occur at any time. But she had grieved.

Here, now, she understood that Meralonne APhaniel kept them out of the storm of magery. She understood, as well, that the imposter was trapped in this room. The only way out was through the mage.

Interesting.

The imposter stared through the transparent wall behind the mage, and then he spoke. "You have caused me trouble, little urchin. My war is with you."

Jewel Markess was pale but resolute—either that or certain of the strength of the barrier that kept the Chosen out. She said nothing, and did nothing, but her hands clenched in the fists that Amarais herself avoided by dint of experience.

"Where is the real Ararath?" she asked. It was a mistake, and she knew it. It was a mistake, and it was hope. Hope was often just pain in another guise.

"He is our prisoner," the imposter replied, turning, wearing Ararath's face as if it were almost his own. "But if I do not return in safety, he will be a corpse within the day."

"He's lying!" Jewel shouted.

Amarais turned to look at the girl. "How is he lying?"

"Old Rath's dead."

"He will be," the imposter said coolly. "But he is not dead yet. Do you think we would destroy so useful a bargaining tool, Terafin? This—" and he snarled as he gestured at Jewel, "has cost us much. We had hoped to take your house from within; it appears that we will have to accept destroying its leader."

"A poor consolation." But Amarais did not look at the imposter; she had not taken her gaze from the street child's pale, determined face. Torvan had stepped behind the girl, had placed one mailed hand on her shoulder to steady her.

Jewel Markess. Ararath had loved her. Amarais knew it, and even thought she might understand why, one day; she thought to keep the girl until the moment that she did. For she saw a very real grief—and a very deep loss—in the girl's stark expression, and it was a grief that she herself *could not* show. Not now, and perhaps not ever.

Grieve for us, then, Jewel. Grieve as you must. Only we two are left who will, and only one of us can ever do so openly. Be what I can no longer be, for a little while.

"Master APhaniel," she said, cold now, "Who—or what—is this caricature?"

"I am your death," the imposter replied, and there was a very real anger in the threat. Clearly he was not a man who was used to being disregarded. He lifted a hand again, and gestured, and she felt the ground shake beneath her feet; she saw, briefly, a shadow limned in blue light, as it struck at her, and passed around.

Whatever power the Magi had put into preserving her life held.

Perhaps, she thought, as she finally turned, caught by some shift in color, some strangeness in the imposter's posture, he was not a man at all. In silence, she watched as the skin across his face stretched, thinned, and ruptured. Blood flew, and bits of flesh, as the creature discarded both the face—perhaps the literal face—of her brother, and the appearance of mortality, in one gesture.

His face stretched, his jaws lengthening until they

were almost as long as her forearms. His teeth elongated and sharpened, his eyes grew longer and narrower, sliding to the sides of an almost reptilian head. His skin was ebon, in the lights of this room, and he looked as if he belonged in the wreckage.

He opened his mouth, and he *roared*. Dragons, if they had ever existed, must have sounded like this, and she felt the earth shake at the sound. But the roar stretched, thinned, and broke, shifting over seconds into a sound of pain. He spoke, now, in a language that Amarais had never heard, and gods willing, might never hear again.

"Master APhaniel," she said, both sharply and loudly, "Cease this! We need information!"

"I'm trying," the Member of the Order of Knowledge said, through gritted teeth.

So, she thought. The imposter served a different master, and that master was not interested in offering any information to either House Terafin or the Order of Knowledge. The creature's screams grew louder, and the sound of syllables, less, until all that existed was pain.

She stood, she bore witness. She might have paled, but she did not otherwise flinch or move.

Across the divide, Jewel Markess did not fare as well. She was young, and untried, and she cried out in the end, in pain, in compassion, and in horror. Horror for the creature who had, no doubt, been the death of the Ararath they had both known.

Learn to hide, Jewel Markess. Learn to hide pain, or your enemies will seek it, and you will pay.

Having learned this lesson years in the distant past, she watched as Meralonne APhaniel struggled, not to defend himself, but to hold what remained of the creature. His hands shone, gold and bright, and that light enveloped his face and his chest; beads of sweat formed across his brow as he labored while the creature screamed. Shadows and darkness grew around the creature, some counterpoint to the light of the Magi, but it grew, to Amarais' eyes, more quickly, and it felt more solid.

In the end, Jewel Markess screamed as well; her companion was rigid and utterly silent, although he had long since ceased to watch.

And in the end, Meralonne APhaniel snarled and staggered, and the light in his hands lessened and dimmed as the creature, surrounded by shadow, dimmed—and faded from sight.

"Jewel," The Terafin said.

Jewel Markess blinked at the sound of her name, but her gaze did not travel to the woman who had called her back. Amarais watched her, and for the moment, only her. She knew that the girl's slow gaze would travel across the wreck of the mantel, its sharp splinters and broken boards pale where the dark, gleaming surface had been broken by a single blast.

She would look at the carpet, and at the walls; she would look, in the end, at what remained in the room's center: blood, scraps of skin, discarded flesh.

Ararath's flesh.

Morretz will be angry, The Terafin thought. She glanced at her hands and noticed that they were bleeding. Noticed, as well, that the fall of light against the floor had changed. The windows, she thought. So much power.

And yet a few men with hammers might accomplish the same goal, without the conceit of magic.

Jewel.

The girl turned, and was sick.

The mage was unconcerned; Amarais thought he had not noticed. He stepped into the room's center, and into the spread remnants of what might have been a corpse. Only when he moved did Alayra and Torvan follow, and they passed him as he bent, their footfalls absorbed by the ruins of carpet, flesh, and stone dust.

Amarais nodded to Alayra, but it was a brief, almost cursory gesture. She watched Jewel until the girl had straightened. Her den-kin came to stand by her side; he was pale, but not notably more so than her own Chosen.

Alayra did not return the nod with a salute; she did not mar the silence with words. Words were not needed here. They were aware of the risk that the mage had taken, and they were also aware—and would always be aware—that they had not occupied *these* positions when the creature masquerading as Ararath had decided to attack.

But they would be aware, just as she was aware, that had it been entirely in her hands, they—and the mage, whose presence had proved so necessary—would not have been here at all.

Amarais walked over to where the mage now crouched. "Is this human?"

He did not fail to understand the question. "Yes. These remains are human."

She nodded; it was the answer, in the end, that she had expected. It was not, of course, the answer she wanted. There were other questions to ask. She might start with: *What was that?* She might start with: *Why was he here?* She might demand the whole of the truth: *Whose flesh? Whose human flesh?*

She did none of these things. Instead, she turned from his side, and she walked between Alayra and Torvan as if they were pillars or columns, and not witnesses.

She needed, and wanted, none. "Leave me."

"Terafin—" Alayra began.

"That was not a request." The hands that she had managed to keep at her sides bunched, at last, into reflexive fists. Ararath, had he been alive, would have recognized the posture.

Ararath.

Rath.

"Leave me. All of you." She looked out of the window, and the ruins of the beveled glass, with its missing panes, its twisted lead, seemed the perfect frame for her, at this moment.

She heard their retreating steps; they were slow. Only one man approached her, and she knew who it must be; she did not even spare him a glance; the sky held her gaze.

"Terafin, I will repair to the Order and begin my report. On the morrow, I shall deliver it to you."

Enough of this game had been played at the mage's behest. "You may return this eve, after the late dinner hour." It was not a request.

Nor was he foolish enough to interpret it as such. He did not argue; he did not offer excuses. Instead, he bowed; she saw the shift of his robes out of the corner of her eye.

"Jewel. After the middle dinner hour, I would appreciate your company. I will send someone for you in your quarters. Please be there." She turned, then, from the window, and she met the girl's dark eyes.

Her face was still pale, still white with distress; she was still sickened, but she did not attempt to hide it, or otherwise acknowledge it. Her eyes were, even at the distance that separated them, reddened.

He was my baby brother.

But she did not say the words aloud. She said nothing at all, but offered Jewel Markess, and only Jewel, a glimpse of her unmasked and unguarded expression. She could not say why.

Jewel in turn offered what anyone else in this manse offered: obedience and silence.

Morretz came an hour later. She had not moved anything but her hands; they were clasped, loosely, behind her back.

He came to her carrying a cloak, and in truth she felt chilled; the air of Scaral was cold, and the windows did not deny it passage; nor did fire burn in the grate, to otherwise warm the room.

She had not summoned him. But she did not order him to leave her either; she acknowledged his presence, his singular presence, by a simple lack of such words. In the years that he had served her as domicis, she had exposed far more than this.

And what had he taken from that exposure?

He draped the cloak around her shoulders, and she let him, moving her hands at last; feeling her fingers tingle as she stretched them and lifted them to the clasp at the cloak's neck. There, in raised relief, she felt the solitary H of Handernesse.

In its day, this had been a truly fine cloak, and only one man had worn it; only one man would ever wear it.

But she gathered its folds around her now, seeking comfort from them.

"Terafin—"

"Jewel Markess will join me after the middle dinner hour."

He did not ask her if she would eat. He had brought her grandfather's cloak, and she wore it. He understood what that meant.

She did not order him to leave her; he did not require the command. He knew that she would stay some time yet in this room, and perhaps he even understood why.

But she waited until he left her; she heard the click of the door at her back. She knew he would wait just beyond those closed doors until the moment she chose to vacate this room. And she would.

First, however, she walked, encircled by the cloak the lion of Handernesse had worn when she had been his adored granddaughter and the hope of his House. She reached the ruined center of the room. The flesh and the skin, the scorched hair, the small, blunt teeth, remained where they had been discarded.

She was not sentimental or foolish enough to attempt to gather them. Instead, she knelt, and among these things, she found the one glimmer of light. She bent, and her fingers closed over the stretched, soft gold of a ring's back. Turning it, she saw the crest of Handernesse, and she lifted it, for a moment, to her lips.

More than that, she could not in safety do. She was The Terafin, and she had given up the luxury of tears and open grief when she had taken that title. She had given up more.

She regretted both, briefly and fiercely, here, where it was safe to do so.

Chapter Seventeen

22nd of Scaral, 410 AA
Order of Knowledge, Averalaan Aramarelas

SIGURNE MELLIFAS STOOD ALONE in her Tower room, her hands on drawn curtains, her eyes avoiding the reflection the night cast back at her. Meralonne APhaniel had sent word, but it was brief; he was to join her in her Tower. She waited. Decades, she had honed the art of waiting—and it was an art, one driven by necessity—but sometimes the ability failed her, like any hard-won skill. She let the curtains fall, and stepped away from the window, blind for the moment to what occurred in the distant streets below. It was dark, yes, but in Scaral, on this night, the darkness fell early.

She could not, of course, command Meralonne to tender an immediate report. So much of their work was shadowed and hidden, which was its own bitter irony. Even had he used magic this day—and he must have—no writ of exemption would be necessary unless The Terafin herself demanded it.

Amarais.

When the knock came, she walked to the door and opened it quietly. Meralonne APhaniel stood in the door's frame, wearing an ancient emerald robe and holding a guttered pipe. She stepped aside in silence, and he entered the same way.

"Well?" she asked him.

"Sit, Sigurne. I cannot sit if you do not, and I am weary."

She did not wish to be confined by the arms of a chair and the bulk of weathered desk. But she did not say this; instead, she sat upon the corner of that desk, and waited.

He frowned, but understood what she did not say; he was not a man who liked to be confined. And yet, she thought, staring at his shadowed gray eyes, he was. He was confined in the Order, and in his study, and in his role as Magi. He was confined by the First Circle, by the edicts of the Order, and by the Kings' Laws concerning the use of open magery in the streets of the City. He was confined by their need for secrecy, and their need for subtlety. He bore it, and he endured.

She did not tell him not to smoke; the friendly bickering and her genuine distaste for the smell of burning tobacco belonged in a different space, a different meeting. It would have been easier to demand he not bleed or breathe, and that thought made her smile, although the smile was slight and grim.

He sat; he filled, slowly and methodically, the bowl of his pipe. She did not hurry him, because she was tired enough, old enough, to want to delay his words, even for a few minutes. There was comfort in the familiarity of his actions; comfort in the ghost of the irritation they often produced.

What did she know of this man?

He aged little.

He had come upon her in the Tower of the Ice Mage, and he alone among the Magi had urged that she be adopted, rather than destroyed, for her part in the forbidden arts practiced in the cold of the distant North. The Order of Knowledge had acceded to his request— and at the time, it had seemed very much a request, and at that, a quiet one. But she had not taken his full measure. Not then; she had been young, and hollow with the death of both her childhood and the master she had willingly betrayed. She had expected to die.

Instead, she had been accepted, slowly, into the Order of Knowledge, her talent as mage-born acknowledged. Meralonne, among others, had seen to her teaching, and she had impressed the more suspicious members of the Order with her focus, her dedication. She had grown. At some point, growth became age. But Meralonne?

She shook her head.

"Sigurne?"

"I am feeling my age."

"And not mine?" His eyes were clear, his expression remote. Fire found the bowl of his pipe without so much as a flicker of his eye.

"No, Master APhaniel, not yours." She clasped her hands loosely in her lap. More than this, she did not—had never openly—said. "What news?" she asked softly, as a thin stream of smoke at last left his lips.

"You were fond of Ararath," was the quiet reply.

"I am." *Ah.* "Yes. I was." She was silent for a moment. "Tell me," she finally said. She thought the better of her refusal to sit in her chair; the armrests, if confining, were also supporting. So much was.

"What he saw, Sigurne, he saw clearly. The game he played, he won."

And this, she thought bitterly, was victory. She felt the emptiness of his absence, but if it was sharp, it was, like many jagged wounds, one that would be slow to heal.

She glanced up at the almost invisible wards that rested above her doors; they were nascent. Often, in the last few months, they would color, briefly, as if on fire, and she would rise and make her way to the more formal meeting rooms at her disposal as the Order's titular head. There, Rath would remove the dull, flat blades of consecrated daggers, returning them, by that silent gesture, to her keeping. She would tend his injuries, when he would allow it—which was seldom—and she would keep her own counsel. Only twice had she attempted to dissuade him from his chosen course, and in the end, she had done it to still her own uneasy conscience, for she knew he would not be moved.

But in truth, had she thought to have success, would she have tried? For she needed him to be where he was, to return the information he returned, and to leave as he left. She needed his fire, and she saw his hatred as the tool it was. Familiar tool; had it not driven her in all of her decades in the Order?

Her silence continued.

What might Ararath have achieved, had he turned that burning, focused ambition upon the fortunes of the House to which he'd been born? Handernesse might once again have risen on the shoulders of its son.

Pipe smoke eddied in the air between them, in a growing cloud of wisp and scent. "I was summoned, as you are aware, to House Terafin this afternoon. I was summoned in haste, and the contingencies that were laid against such a summoning were used. I am not certain that I will have the liberty to cast such spells again; they were costly, and I will be watched now."

"You were watched, regardless."

He shrugged.

"Why were you called, Meralonne?"

"The Terafin was in danger." He ran a hand over his eyes. It was a very rare gesture of fatigue. "She had received a visitor."

"Through irregular channels."

"No. The visitor came, as per House customs to the right-kin, and he was conveyed—in some haste—into the presence of The Terafin. He was conveyed alone," the mage added. "She had divested herself of all of her guards, and even her domicis was not in attendance."

"So she had some reason to trust the visitor."

"I think it not quite that simple. The visitor, of course, was Ararath."

"Ararath in the flesh, or illusion?"

"There is enough contingency magic in the room that the substantial magic required to sustain an illusion would likely set off some of the more visible alarms. Although the most cunning of those was destroyed. No. He was present, in the flesh."

Sigurne paled. This, this is what she had feared.

Meralonne lifted his pipe; smoke eddied, following the rise of his hand in a thin, downward stream that spread. "If you can, be comforted, Sigurne.

"Ararath was dead. He must have died last night, and it forced the hands of our enemies; they would not have had much time in which to attempt to contact The Terafin through this particular avenue. I attempted to preserve the body—and the demon that wore it—but I was . . . frustrated in that attempt. What remains is scattered across the room used for official meetings of import in the manse."

"So." She rose. Nor could she take her chair; she paced the room—which, in the end, was not large—like a caged beast. "In all suppositions, Ararath was correct—and at cost."

"We have," he replied, "proof, should The Terafin make the incident public. To attempt either the assassination of The Terafin, in the best possible scenario, or the impersonation, the assumption of her living form, in the most likely one, is not the act of a single rogue mage."

"No. We have not recently been operating under that assumption. Had they succeeded—and without your intervention, there is every probability they would have done so, what would the cost to the Empire be? That is the question—the first of many—that must be posed to the Kings."

Meralonne was silent, and it was not a silence to Sigurne's liking.

"You . . . do not think she will do so."

"She was, I think, attached to her brother, even given his abandonment. She was not greatly pleased at my intervention."

"Not initially," Sigurne replied, with a slight smile. There was no answering smile in return.

"Nor afterward. Pleased is not a word that would describe any part of her reaction; if I looked closely, I might see gratitude, although it would be slight. She is a woman who has wielded the power of a great House for many years, and if I do not trifle with politics, I can understand why she has held it: she was silent. Thoughtful. What she felt, she kept to herself; nor did she appear on the verge of panic. If I were to guess, I would say she was considering many things. The long list of her enemies, and the long list of those who are not actively seeking her destruction, but who would take advantage of any weakness shown. What *we* desire, what we *require* for the safety of the Empire, is not—yet—part of her planning.

"I believe in time she will forgive me for the destruction of her mantel."

Sigurne shook herself as the last sentence penetrated the worry all of the previous observations had accreted. "Pardon?"

"The creature was not a significant one. He did, however, have some amount of the power that might grace a lesser mage, and some . . . damage was done."

"Which room was this?"

"I told you—"

Sigurne winced, and as this was a more practical matter, which merely involved more money than the Order easily had available for what was only trivial if you were not The Terafin, she once again sat, this time pulling her chair toward the surface of her desk. She selected a thick, bound volume and laid it open, glancing up at Meralonne. "You recognized the maker of that mantel, surely? You are generally more aware of the art of the maker-born than most of our colleagues."

"I did not think it was of more value than her life."

Sigurne pursed her lips. "You did not think of it at all."

He shrugged, restless. "No, to be truthful, I did not; it is a mantel; it holds fripperies and girds fire; it is decorative but not in a way that inspires. The creature wore the ring," he added.

"You sensed it."

"No. I saw it, but it was a ring, no more."

She closed her eyes, her palms across an open page of accounts, the numbers now hidden from view by thin, veined lids.

"The spell was invoked, Sigurne. If you can, take comfort from that. I do not know how much the demons learned from Ararath before he invoked it, but he chose his death, and his death served his purpose. We have, now, the proof we need, if she can be brought to *use* it."

This, she thought, as she examined the fine veins in still hands, was triumph. This was victory. This hollowness, this loss. There would be no more reports, no more consecrated daggers—not from Ararath. His anger, his guilt, and his determination had, like the fires they were, consumed him. She bowed her head. But Meralonne had not yet finished.

"I believe I now know who his informant was."

"His informant?"

"Yes. The seer to whom he would never introduce us."

Sigurne was watchful. "This informant was at House Terafin?"

"Oh, yes. And I am certain that the demon had encountered her before; The Terafin, however, was not open to questions. Nor were her Chosen."

"How are you so certain?"

"She was there. She was the reason that the Chosen summoned me, and if not for her intervention, it is my suspicion that we would no longer have this particular Terafin lord at the House.

"She is young, Sigurne. She is young."

"But seer-born?"

"I cannot—yet—be certain of that."

"Be careful, Meralonne."

"I am always careful."

"You always survive; it is not the same thing."

"If she is a seer, she will also survive." He rose. "I have been given permission to return to The Terafin, with my report, at the late dinner hour. If you desire it, accompany me."

Sigurne was aware that the word permission, when used in this context, was inaccurate. "I . . . am not, tonight, up to such a difficult meeting, Meralonne. I trust

that you will curb your tongue and your temper suffi-
ciently that we will not lose the only essential ally that
we have at the moment."

He shrugged, his hair sliding over his shoulder and
down his back as he reached for an ashtray that over-
hung the edge of one of Sigurne's many shelves. Tapping the pipe empty, he said, "I am still retained by The
House; I have been neither replaced nor relieved. Nor
do I expect to be.

"I will speak with The Terafin, and I will report to
you." He rose then; his eyes were gray and dark; he was
restless, and the whole of their conversation had not
quieted him at all. He made the door, and then paused
there, turning.

"It is not my way," he said quietly, as if bowing with
great effort to hers, "to mourn as you mourn, Sigurne.
Ararath Handernesse saw clearly, and he did what he
felt necessary. His life, and his death, were his to choose.
Very few can say that, in the end, and I envy it—I do
not grieve for it."

She nodded. There was nothing else to say. She was
not Meralonne. She could send a man to his death; she
could, in fact, lift hand to kill one if it was required. In
the end, there was no functional difference between the
two of them.

But she yearned for Meralonne's certainty. She
yearned for his lack of sorrow, his lack of guilt, his lack
of questions; they did not stop her, but they plagued her
nonetheless, demanding their due.

And what due could she offer? In the end, his death
was to be unremarked, and unremarkable; The Terafin
would not expose her House in so public a fashion; nor
would she subject Handernesse to the gawking and the
curiosity of the idle. What remained of Ararath was scattered bits of flesh—or less, given Meralonne's imprecise
description of the magics used and encountered—
within one room in the Terafin manse, and given the
army of servants that any large House required, those
would be cleaned up, disposed of as unnecessary and
unwanted detritus.

That left memory.

There was no one to share that memory with; there would be no funeral, she thought. She could not suggest it to The Terafin without exposing her own hand in Ararath's death, and even were she so inclined, she could not expose that without exposing far too much of the Order's work to a woman who ruled. She rose.

The human need to share experience to give grief meaning was profound. It was twin to the need to share joy, as if by sharing either, they became real, as if they required more than one person to anchor them. She was long past the age where joy—or sorrow—could be shared in such an unfettered way, but she remembered, standing alone in the Tower she had made her life, the singular joy of one day in the North, in a land of snow made water by fire and flame, made red by blood and black by ash. It came to her, as a ghost and a reminder: the young woman trapped within the form and shape of the older one.

She lifted hands that were now wrinkled and pale, and as she did, she saw the grim final moments of the man who had taken her from her village, her family, and everything she had ever loved. They had called him the Ice Mage; they might have called him anything else, but it was a simple, declarative description for a stark people. He ruled; they could not bring themselves to call him Lord. Only Sigurne had debased herself enough to do that, and only when she had become a fixture within his abode: his apprentice. There were costs to defiance, and she had not—yet—become so bitter that life was worthless.

He had summoned the kin. He had trapped them with words and power, as he had trapped her with death and power, enslaving them both. And in her captivity she had spoken long, and late, with the most significant of her fellow captives, nursing her hatred, her anger exposing her fear and hiding all else.

It was forbidden, of course, this speech, this learning the education she'd been given—the only education she had been allowed. How she had hated it: the books and the slates and the inks and the precise alignment of geometric figures in the unyielding stone. But she had learned. Then, and later, she had *learned*.

The Ice Mage, in his arrogance, had assumed that he would be her only teacher.

Sigurne had summoned the Southern Magi, with the aid and the deception of the lone, bound *kialli* lord. They had come.

Watch, Sigurne. Watch. You will be the only witness, in the end, of any worth, for you have seen and you have understood enough to give this battle context. Watch it, for I suspect you will see an echo of the ancient days in its unfolding.

Survive.

Survive.

She, who now knew the danger that the *kialli* posed, had nodded, grim and dark and pale. She did not ask what would become of the *kialli* lord; could not bring herself to ask it, although she suspected it would have exposed nothing; he was—gods, he was—perceptive, cunning, treacherous. Had he used her? Yes. And she, him. Because their ends were the same.

I am summoned, little one. We will not speak again. Not now, and not after; I will go to the Hells, and you? You will wither and die, and where you go, we cannot see. He had turned from her then.

He had turned, walked, his pace quickening, toward where the Ice Mage now gathered the whole of his forces: men in glinting armor, men in chain and fur, men with pikes and axes and swords; demon-kin, the lesser, and the great, their armor a natural part of the form the world imposed upon them when they returned to its folds. Only the *kialli* lord had enough control, enough will, to force his form to conform to *his* desire; he looked almost human.

Sigurne, the Ice Mage did not summon; instead, he shut her in the height of his Tower, where the magical wards were the strongest, and windows that protected her from the wail of wind and the bite of winter death, lined the walls. She looked; she looked down.

The Ice Mage had his kin. He had his *kialli*. They were, for that moment, his.

In the distance, fighting the drifts that were so high, and the ice that was often shining and thin, she saw a like army, but it contained no demon-kin, none of the strange and fearsome shapes of their limbs, their heads, their elongated faces. No: these distant men, who struggled against the simple fact of the cold that could kill, wore armor—or less—as they approached.

She held breath, then and now, against hope. Against its bitter breaking—for how could it stand? Men, against the forces that the Ice Mage now arrayed, had fallen before. Some quickly, if they were lucky, and some over the course of three long days, in which their screams and their cries broke against the stone of the Tower.

But she saw one, clothed in blue fire and blue light, rising into the pale azure of the perfect, and perfectly clear, sky. She saw the white of his hair—even at the marked distance of the Tower's height—and she thought, although it was and must be the fancy of hope, she saw his expression, his exultation. She did not think, on that day, that he was human.

She did not think it now.

What had she thought he was, in that distant past? An Avatar. Angelae. Servant of the gods. He flew, and where he flew, there was death and a savage, cold joy: Meralonne APhaniel was a thing of the Northern Wastes, and yet . . . the kin died.

He came, at last, to the *kialli*, and the *kialli* lord bowed to him. It was not a bow demanded by the man who held his name; it was offered, a gesture of respect a glimmer of . . . familiarity. And in his turn, the white-haired mage had bowed as well, and a red sword, a red shield had formed in the hands of the *kialli*.

They fought, these two. Even the Ice Mage seemed momentarily forgotten, and Sigurne heard the demon roar his *name* above the din of endless wind, and she felt the name, and knew it. It was not a gift; it was a challenge, and the mage met it in perfect silence, with his blue blade, his wild, wild joy.

The *kialli* died.

The Ice Mage died.

Sigurne?

She wept. She wept when her master's head left his shoulders and his fires guttered and his creatures turned to ash that the winds would disperse until only story remained. She wept for her life, for what she had lost, and what she had gained, for *this* was victory: he had died. She would die, and she did not care, not then: the day was so clear and so bright and so beautiful, and everything she had *ever* wanted felt as though it had come to her in that moment.

She wept now.

Because it had not ended, not then, and it might never end while she lived. And because the joy of that day still lived, within her, the only bridge between her age and her youth, the fire that she touched when the days were shortest, the nights as dark and threatening as this one. She had lost family and friends and the whole of a life, before.

She had lost one friend today.

But he fought, as Meralonne said, and if death was victory—and she had faced that death, that certainty of death assuming it was *exactly* that—he had won an important battle. Not the war; not the whole of the war; that was in her hands, now, and in the hands of Meralonne APhaniel; it was in the hands, Sigurne thought, of a girl barely adult, and a woman who ruled the most powerful House in the Empire.

And it would be in the hands of the Kings.

She wanted to do something for Ararath. The best thing she could do for her family, in the end, had been to come South, to avoid the stigma of her shame shadowing her family's name and life.

And the only thing she could do for Ararath now was to find the source of the demonic magic that threatened the City, and eliminate it. Convenient, she thought, turning at last back to the center of her small room. Convenient gift, which would be given regardless.

23rd of Scaral, 410 AA
The Common, Averalaan

The Common in Scaral was at its least crowded, but even so, it was busy. Commerce of a certain sort did not stop for simple things like lessening daylight hours or inclement weather; nor did it apparently stop for loud, screaming arguments, although the foot traffic did as people formed semicircles at what they felt was a safe distance in order to watch.

Watching was, in its own way, an art, and many people who did choose to watch nonetheless observed very little; it was one of Haval's chief complaints about a so-called audience, although if he were fair, it was also one of the things he most relied on. He glanced at the windows themselves, and from there, through the letters, laid backward so that customers might read the words on the outside. Many of the merchants who owned such storefronts in the Common rented them out. Haval had taken advantage of this, for he did not own this building, much to his regret. He had, however, been installed behind its well-kept facade for many years. His sign, *Elemental Fashion,* was still bold and still perfect, although that was more due to magery than his own care.

Hannerle had disliked the name, of course. She had desired to see *Haval's House of Fashion* or something equally pretentious—and equally nondescript, in the end—and it was only the reminder that Haval did not wish to ever be known by name that had dissuaded her from this choice. She still did not like the alternative, however.

He frowned, although his hands still held needle and thread steady; he was beading, but the beadwork was both dark and minimal. Many of the current fashions adored by the young were lamentably spare, and while he appreciated the look, he did not appreciate the comparative lack of time and money it took to achieve it.

The needle stopped, although Haval's posture did not change.

In the crowd that had gathered, men and women who were clearly actually busy enough that an argument—admittedly a colorful one on the edge of violence—could not hold their interest, were threading their way through the less-busy spectators. One of those men, Havel recognized instantly, even at this distance.

Haval did not stand or otherwise draw attention to himself, but he was now aware of every movement that man made. It was not difficult; there were very few men who wore their hair in an unfettered drape of that length. The Northerners often wore theirs braided. Not so Meralonne APhaniel.

He moved with relative ease through the gathering; his presence was such that people stepped out of his way, many of them without noticing that they'd done so *only* for the mage, and had, in fact, required a good deal of jostling for much larger and more annoyed men.

What surprised Haval enough that he did not ask Hannerle to hang the "closed" sign quickly and furtively on the front door, was the man's companion, for he recognized the girl. Jewel Markess. Her lamentable flyaway hair was caught and tied back—as much as it ever remained tied back—and its auburn curls seemed to have collected dirt. Not dust, but actual, damp earth. So, from this distance, had her clothing, but she did not look bruised or injured; this detritus was not the aftereffects of a fight. Had Meralonne APhaniel not turned to speak to her, Haval might have assumed he had mistaken their association, although Haval very rarely made that kind of sloppy observational error.

Jewel was caught in the mage's wake, or so it first appeared, but as Haval watched, he realized there was some verbal struggle between the two: the man with his obvious power and his intimidating talent, and the girl with her dirty clothing, her dirty hands, and her sudden, tight jaw. If she feared the mage at all, her temper had gotten the better of her.

The mage, however, did not seem to notice enough to take offense.

Haval raised a brow, and then set the beadwork aside. Jewel Markess, he thought, had come here deliberately; she was not merely following the casual yet decisive lead of Meralonne APhaniel. He hoped, briefly but fiercely, that Member APhaniel would remain outside—and was slightly surprised when *Kalliaris* deigned to smile.

He was also instantly suspicious, but Haval had made a life of the game of suspicion; the goddess would surely overlook this. "Hannerle," he said, raising his voice. "I have a visitor, if you will watch the storefront."

The sound of his wife's energetic and quick movements momentarily occurred at his back, and the quality of those sounds told him that she was not—yet—annoyed. She came into the store's front room, removing her apron and fussing with her hair, just as Jewel did, albeit only Jewel's entry caused the bells to clamor in their high, tinkling voices.

Haval made no pretense of sewing or work as he stood to greet her. She made no sound at all. But she looked at him, her face pale beneath what look like suspiciously new trails of dirt. Her eyes were also the dark that comes with lack of sleep. "I can't stay long," she said, casting a glance through the window, where Meralonne APhaniel was now *leaning* against the glass and filling his pipe.

"I would offer you some method of escape," Haval surprised them both by saying, "but I fear that if Member APhaniel was the one hunting you, you would not get far. Are you well?"

She didn't answer. This was not—he saw this clearly—because she wished to keep secrets. But she couldn't grope her way to words; she struggled in silence, and he came quietly to her rescue. Silence could be so awkward when it was unlooked for and unwanted. "If you have a few moments, perhaps we might step into the back?"

She glanced, again, at her companion, and then her lips pursed as she made—in her characteristically obvious way—a decision. She nodded and he led her to a room that was meant, in its fashion, to offer comfort. He gave her moments of peace and privacy as he set about clearing space in which they could both sit. "If you are not staying long, I will not offer you tea or general hospitality."

"I'd stay," she finally said, "if I could. But . . . "

"Understood," he said quietly, although this was not entirely the case. "Sit, Jewel. Sit, and tell me what brings you to my store."

She sat as if the only thing that had been holding her up was the lack of a chair; it was a graceless, exhausted motion. As she often did, she sat sideways, with one arm—her left—draped across the back of the chair. This time, however, she drew her knees up to her chest. It was a shocking display of vulnerability, or rather, the awareness of same.

"Jewel. Jay."

She looked up at him, and the dark circles beneath her eyes seemed to swallow them. "It's Rath."

He turned from her then, but only for a moment. "Tell me," he said. He did not take his own empty chair; instead, he crouched by her feet, his arms folded across his bent knees.

She did not meet his gaze. Her chin drifted toward her knees, and she spoke into them, her voice slightly muffled. "I don't know his friends," she told Haval. "I don't know all of them. The ones I know—like you—I'm trying to speak with. But I—"

He held up a hand. "Do not explain more than you need. If you are asking me to take word to his friends, I will do so, Jay. Not for your sake, nor in the end for his, but for theirs.

"Ararath disliked complications and ties; his friends are scattered, and they are few. If you cannot make time to see the others that you knew of, rest easy. I know where word must be sent, and I know those to whom it will be less than safe to send it."

She turned her face, and her brown eyes met Haval's. What she saw, he knew—because he schooled his expression, changing the line of his shoulders as he did, drawing his height in and away, and offering her the sympathy of vulnerability. If she was aware that this was deliberate, her expression didn't shift or change.

Her words were unexpected.

"You know."

They were also so certain, Haval did not trouble himself with a lie. "Yes," he said quietly. "I know." Before she could speak, he added, "I did not know until you entered my store, Jewel. But when you did, I knew what you had come to tell me."

She relaxed, then, turning her face back to her knees, and wrapping her arms around her shins. She rocked slightly back and forth on the chair in silence. He did not touch her. Had she been another child, he might have, but this one required space. He now gave her what she required, standing and stretching his legs.

He busied himself tidying the back room. "Ararath—Rath—chose this course. I tried to talk him out of it, but he is not—and was never—a man who listened to the counsel of others when he had already made his choice.

"You have not failed him, Jay."

She looked up, again. He saw her eyes; they were reddened, but she was not weeping. That, he knew, took effort. "That obvious?" she whispered.

He smiled. "I am an observant man, and I have spent many hours in your company. Yes, to me, it is obvious."

"Did you know who he was?"

Dangerous question. Dangerous ground. Haval looked at it dispassionately, surrounded by the chaos of a shopkeeper's life. He, like Rath, had no distaste for, or compunction, about lying; it was an art, like any other. But lies served purpose, if they were used by an expert. Staring at this almost-woman, he could not discern or divine a good purpose for them. Not yet.

But she had come in the wake of Meralonne APhaniel, she had demanded, more or less, that she be allowed a few minutes to visit this one store, and in the end, it was Meralonne APhaniel who now stood outside of the closed shop door. Haval was not a young man, anymore. He had, with some regret—but with more determination—left the foibles and the trappings of his youth behind. He had married Hannerle; he had rented this storefront, and he had indulged in his obvious talent for clothing—the outer layer by which most of society judged either man or woman.

Jewel's question hung in the air for a long moment, and in the end, he chose to answer it honestly. "Yes. I knew who he was." He did not ask her what she knew, or how, although he was curious.

"I don't know when he died." She finally used the word.

"You found him?"

She lifted her head again, and this time, she unwrapped her arms, lowered her legs, and turned to face him. "He found us," she whispered. "What was left of him. He—he sent me to House Terafin. He sent me to speak with his sister.

"And his corpse followed us."

There was a story here. Haval knew that it was not a story it was safe to hear—but so many of the stories he knew weren't, and he had accepted them all, looking at their edges and their colors and the ways in which they might unexpectedly overlap. If Hannerle had been in the room, she would have cheerfully strangled him. The fact that he had done nothing to encourage the telling of this particular tale would have earned him no mercy at all.

But then again, Hannerle understood him as well as anyone living could. "Where are you staying, Jewel?"

She hesitated.

"If you have been asked—or ordered—not to reveal that information, I do not require it."

"I wasn't. Ordered. Or asked. It's just—it's strange, and it's scary. I'm working for The Terafin now, because of Rath. I *want* it. And I wish you could have told me how to earn it, Haval. I wish I'd learned more from you. I wish I'd asked you to tell me how to look smarter, how to sound more educated, how to command attention or respect when I *need* it."

He raised a brow at the heat of the words. This girl, this was the girl he had observed with so much concern. This was the girl he had sent to Lord Waverly, now dead these past several years.

"Why do you need it?" he asked in reply. He folded his arms across his chest while he waited for her response.

She didn't answer the question he'd asked. Instead, she said, "Duster's dead."

Haval disliked surprises. He disliked, in particular, to *be* surprised. Jewel Markess' expression was normally so open one had to work carefully not to read it. Now? Expression had drained from her face, with color, as if for the moment she had been reduced to bare fact. Duster was the only other member of her den that Haval had trained. Duster, in almost any way that mattered, was Jewel's opposite. And yet, in the end, Jewel had undertaken her role in the Waverly affair for Duster's sake.

"How?" His voice was harder than hers.

"Demons."

He did not turn away. He gave her nothing; no mockery, no disbelief, no horror. Haval had always told her that faces were masks, that expressions were, like anything else, best manufactured with truth, or as much of it as you could find. He had not told her that expressions were also like armor, and sometimes you gave *nothing* away. It was a lesson, and a free one.

But if it was, she did not appreciate the gift; did not, in fact, appear to notice it at all. "Lander's gone. Lefty. Fisher. Duster. They're dead," she added, staring into the space past his left shoulder as if he were no longer in the room. "Don't tell me I didn't fail *them*. Rath chose what he chose. I can accept that—because I *tried,* Haval. I tried, with him. He *wouldn't listen*.

"Rath was a friend. I trusted him. But he was never one of mine.

"The others *were*. Even Duster. They were all mine. The only choice they made was to *follow me*." She looked at him then, her eyes dry, her voice flat and hard. She offered him no excuses, and he knew it was because she'd tried them all, and they offered her nothing. "I almost lost Arann," she continued, when he failed to speak. "I almost lost him. He was dying. He was so far gone——" and at this, she did stop, her eyes closed, and she lost words.

He would not have been surprised had she left in silence after this. But she struggled with breath, forcing it from its uneven thinness to something steadier. "The Terafin saved him. Because The Terafin *could*. I promised I'd work for her, if she gave him back to me. It was the only thing I wanted.

"That was then. Yesterday." She spoke the last word as if it were a year. "But House Terafin has *everything*. Money. Guards. Mages. It has everything, Haval. And I'm living there, right now."

"In the manse?" he asked softly.

She nodded. "They've got a lot of room. I think most of the manse must be empty. We have a——a domicis. I think that's what he's called. And servants, apparently. I don't know for how long." She looked straight at him, then. "I don't know for how long.

"But I think——if I work things *right*——I can make it as long as we need."

He said nothing. He did not tell her that it was very, *very* unusual for her den to be given rooms within the manse itself; that The Terafin had hired a domicis for her was unheard of. Most members of House Terafin itself did not reside upon the Isle, and many, many men and women would have paid much for the privilege. That that privilege had been, however temporarily, given to an orphan from the poorer holdings would be noted by anyone who had not been given similar privileges in the past——but it would also be marked and noted by anyone who had, and this, in Haval's opinion, was worse.

He watched her bleak, desperate expression, and he almost told her to moderate it; to hide it. But that was not what she had come for, in the end, and she was likely to misinterpret the criticism. *Aie, Jewel.* And then, *Did you expect this, Ararath? Did you expect that Amarais would give this child what you yourself could never guarantee?*

And did you expect that she would return to me, now of all times? Do you think that your death will mark me enough that I will give her the lessons she needs, that I will support her in this?

"I can't—I can't bring anyone else back. I can't even go out and find their bodies. If I weren't with Meralonne APhaniel, I don't think I would have dared to come here at all." She stood. "But I won't fail them again. I won't lose another person. Whatever I need to do here, I'll do."

"You intend to remain in House Terafin?"

"I intend," she said quietly and grimly, "to *be* ATerafin." She ran a rough hand over her eyes; it smeared dirt across her face, but there were no mirrors here in which she might have seen it.

He saw it. He saw the set of her pale jaw, the dark circles that dirt didn't explain beneath the width of her eyes, the way her feet were planted against the floor as if she expected to be hit, and was willing to stand her ground anyway. He heard the anger in her voice, understood that it was aimed, almost in its entirety, at herself, and he let it be. She was Jewel Markess, and he had taken her measure years ago.

He nodded, his face still expressionless. "Many women, and many men, desire the imprimatur of a great House. They will work years, even decades, for the privilege, and in many cases, their motivations and yours will not be entirely dissimilar."

She did not disappoint him; she did not look crestfallen. There was no give in her at all, and he understood, watching the hard, harsh lines of her youthful face, that the whole of her life was defined by what she had chosen to serve—to serve, to protect, and in her fashion, to love. For herself, she might experience fear and the usual insecurities that plagued the youthful, but those fears were dwarfed by the realities of the failures she had already faced. Haval himself had not been immune to either the fear—or the costs.

But Haval had not undertaken the responsibility of building family the way Jewel Markess had. And Haval was not seer-born. He understood where Jewel's value to the House—to any House of her choice—might lie, and he wondered, briefly, if Ararath had mentioned this to his sister. Or if he had communicated with her at all. Had he been a betting man, he would have bet against it, at any odds.

But Ararath, in his fashion, had made Jewel Markess the only family he cared to own, and for family—for this one girl—he might have. Haval could not clearly say. He measured her, aware of the passage of time, and aware of the patience of Meralonne APhaniel. "If you do not waver, you will find what you need," he said at last.

She nodded and turned toward the arch that led to the front of the store.

But Haval had not yet finished. He knew he should be done. He knew. "And if you do, indeed, gain what you seek for the good of your den and its future, come to see me. For one, I would appreciate your custom, since you will not be able to function in the manse in the clothing you currently own." He smiled; she did not. "Jewel. Jay. You see The Terafin. You see the manse. You see the guards and the mage and the obvious wealth she has at her disposal. You see the signs of power, and you think that in power there is safety. It is a thought that many have, but that is the dream of the idle and those who will *never* attain power.

"Nor do I tell you that power is what you *must* attain. But to be in Terafin at all, to remain there safely given who and what you are, you will require some understanding of power. You will need to see that, in the end, the play of power among those who are educated, monied, and ambitious is a variant of the same moves used by those who have none of these advantages.

"You understand those, at base. You will need to understand them in future."

"And you can explain them to me." No question in the words. She was tired, now.

"I can. It will not greatly please my wife, for reasons that are too boring and too personal to explain, but I can. I do not know how easy it will be for you to visit me; if you require it, I can visit you, although not without obvious pretext."

She frowned.

"Fittings." He wanted to say more. But the door to the shop opened; he could hear the bells toll the end of this conversation, the end of more than this conversation.

"Haval—"

"I am not Ararath," he said gently. "And I will never replace him. But allow it, and I will be what I can. I believe that your companion has now reached the end of his patience. I am surprised that he lasted this long; he is famed for its lack."

"You know him?"

Haval allowed himself a chuckle; it was genuine. "I know of him, let us just say. Enough of him that I feel it best that we not meet at this time."

She didn't ask him why. He wasn't certain, given the stoop of her shoulders and the sunken line of her neck—both at odds with the set of her jaw—that it had even occurred to her. He let her leave, and waited until he heard the door chime again. He might have waited longer, but Hannerle's raised voice pronounced the shop empty.

He went to the desk at which he habitually sat, and found his wife waiting. She opened her mouth, but the words bled into silence before she uttered them. "Haval?"

He nodded, and managed a smile. It was an easy smile, because Haval's expressions always were. Hannerle, however, listened and watched in other ways, in part because she knew how little information his stance or his face would give, and in part because she knew that his use of either meant he felt the need to hide. Haval was adept at hiding in the open. He watched his wife's glance; it went to the window, and the faceless, moving crowd, before coming back to rest on him.

"Rath?" she asked quietly. His name had long produced much less quiet.

He nodded.

"She brought word?"

"She did." He walked past his wife, seated himself on the stool behind the counter, and picked up both his jeweler's glass and the fabric into which he had been stitching beads.

"Haval."

He lifted the small lid of the box into which he wove pins before he glanced at his wife. Everything that she did not say hung in the air between them. "We were friends. I was not a terribly *good* friend, and I was not interested in many of the things that interested Ararath." He took some of the pins out of the box, considered holding them between his lips as a way of stilling unwanted conversation. "But yes, Hannerle, Rath is dead. He is not the only person Jewel has lost recently; I believe he is only the most recent."

"How?"

"I am not entirely certain she knows."

"And does she fail to notice that her *current* companion is a member of the Order of Knowledge?"

He winced at his wife's tone. "I highly doubt, given the member in question, that that's possible, even for one who has no other experience of the mage-born."

"Haval."

He glanced at her again. "She is a child, Hannerle. She is not Ararath, and she is not involved in the things that made Ararath's life so difficult."

"What is she involved in, then?"

"Does it matter? Rath is dead, yes. But it cannot have escaped your notice that Jewel Markess is the *only* person he has ever brought to my store directly; the only one that he has ever walked across my threshold and given into my hands. He did not ask me to do more than teach her what she needed to learn to survive." This was not entirely true; with Jewel Markess had come Duster, and Hannerle had had opinions about *that girl*. But it was for Jewel that Rath had come, besides which, embellishment was some part of Haval's arsenal.

"There is very little that I can now do for Ararath. He was not a man for funerals, and he was not a man for idle gestures of useless respect, that much at least we can agree on. Any grief I might feel or express—" and his wife knew well how little the latter would be "—he would have openly scorned."

Still, she did not speak. Which was either a good sign or a very bad one. "But this, Hannerle, this I *can* do. Let me do it."

"Could I stop you?" was the quiet reply.

He looked up; her expression contained many things: Anger, bitterness, and fear, which he expected. But she was also resigned, and in some part, he saw a glimmer of approval, and the weary affection that she so seldom openly displayed. "With a word."

"And I am to be the heartless villain, then? I'm the one to tell you to turn your back on an ignorant *child*?" She snorted. But after a moment, she said, "It won't bring him back."

"No, of course not. And yes, if you must hear it, it pains me to lose him. He was both amusing and competent, and he was one of the very few friends I had left. I did not expect to outlive him, and at the moment, while I am grateful for my existence, I also resent it. Thus, the contradictions of life.

"But what I cannot now do for Rath, I can do for his Jewel. And I surprise even myself; I want to do it."

"Why?"

Haval shrugged.

Ararath.

He had not lied to his wife. Rath, called Old, had been some years younger than Haval when they had first met, and he had been canny and cautious. Haval took pains not to become attached to things he knew he must lose, and he had taken few such pains with Ararath, a man who knew how to watch out for himself. He had admired Rath's ability to observe what he witnessed; it was, of course, inferior to Haval's own, but not by so much that it could be disregarded.

He had found Rath's life colorful, and Rath's history surprising. That Ararath could be a dangerous man, he had never doubted, and he had witnessed it on occasion, although Rath was cautious. He had some respect for Rath's formidable godfather, and his equally formidable servant, Andrei; Andrei was, or could have been, either domicis or Astari, in Haval's opinion. He had no idea how Hectore had found Andrei, and had always been deeply curious about what he paid the man; he, however, had known better than to ask. To Rath, Andrei was as much a part of House Aravan as the man at its head, and he would have been suspicious of any inquiry. They had met precisely once; Haval had no desire to meet Andrei again.

He moved pins in the light that was slowly fading as he worked.

Ararath was dead.

Damn him, anyway. Haval had escaped Ararath's fate; he had stepped down from the edges and the high places; had given up the excitement, the danger, and the intrigue that all but guaranteed death. He had urged Rath to do the same, and in the end, for selfish reasons. He had become a much more sentimental man as he had aged—something he would have sworn his very valuable life against in his youth.

But so went the plans of the wise and the canny. He sewed; Hannerle, understanding why, had withdrawn, granting him space and a privacy he did not require.

Epilogue

23rd of Scaral, 410 A A
Terafin manse, **Avaralaan Aramarelas**

THE MANSE WAS HUGE. The rooms were huge. Even the so-called bedrooms were large enough to fit their entire den, the kitchen, and the larger room in which they'd eaten meals. Finch knew; she was in one. She was alone in one. This much space, the floors thickly carpeted, seemed almost like sleeping in the open streets at the wrong hour, it was so damn empty.

The windows—filled with real glass, and not warped shutters in constant need of tending—had curtains for miles, and at the moment, they were pulled back and held in place by a tassel wound round the whole of the drape and attached to a hook on the wall. She couldn't actually remember what color they were; it was dark. Dark enough that she had fumbled with those tassels in the shadows, had pulled the curtains back. It was cold, yes—but these windows ignored the chill wind. Or at least the cold it brought; she could hear it as a distant whistle, otherwise.

She had, in this room, more chairs than they'd had in the whole apartment, and it had already come with a bed. The bed was high off the ground, and its thick, sturdy legs didn't even creak when she sat on one edge. It was framed by wood at the top and the bottom, and the wood was carved at the edges with things that looked like either really strange leaves or really fat feathers. The desk, which sat nearest the window's light, was closed and locked. Ellerson had given her the key on a chain, and that chain now encircled her neck because she was afraid of losing it.

I don't have anything to put in a desk, she'd told him gravely.

Not yet, was his equally grave reply. *But it is customary to have one in guest chambers, because a guest might desire to write a diary entry or a letter home.*

She had nodded, smiled, and said nothing. What could she say to a man like Ellerson? He was old, yes, but he was intimidating, so precise in his use of language, and so proper. Even his clothing fit perfectly, and everything—even his socks—matched. He was a special class of servant, she'd been told—by one of the servants—but even so, he was clearly far better educated, fed, and clothed than *any* member of the den had *ever* been. The old people she'd met—Helen, for one— were so unlike him she'd been afraid to talk at all.

Jay had been gone for almost all of the day; Arann was not allowed to join them—although both Carver and Jay said he was "fine." The food that they'd been offered for dinner—and for which they'd been forced into baths—was more than they'd seen all week, and every single one of them had squirreled some away in pockets or sleeves against the next day's hunger.

But . . . morning had brought breakfast. Morning had taken Jay away. Lunch hadn't brought her back either.

Angel fretted. He wanted to be wherever Jay was. So did Carver. Finch and Teller were both accustomed to staying behind unless there was work to do—because there *was* work that needed doing: Laundry. Cleaning. Cooking. Water.

But here? There was *nothing to do*. Nothing at all. There were no books, no slates, no new lessons—or old lessons—to be learned. There was no laundry. Even if they'd wanted to clean up their old clothing—which caused Ellerson to almost pale, the lines on his face deepening into etched, stone grooves—they weren't to do it in the bathing room, where all the *water* was. The manse, apparently, had a cistern somewhere, but if laundry was done, it was *not* done in the West Wing.

Neither was cooking, at least not by the den. Or, apparently, the daily and necessary trip to the Common in order to have something—anything—*to* cook. Even had that been necessary, they had no money with which to do it—and telling Ellerson that they intended to go out to pick pockets and cut purses off the arms of the careless was not anyone's idea of smart or useful.

And so, they waited, in a silence of nothing, restless and worried. Relieved, yes, in part because Arann was still alive.

But Duster was not.

Maybe, Finch thought, as she lay back in bed. She sat up, slid down, and pulled the sheets—and the heavy thick comforter that lay atop them—to one side before she tried to fall asleep again. This time, between the sheets, she stared up at the darkened ceiling. *Maybe Duster's alive. Maybe she made it. Maybe she'll come back to the trough, and we'll find her. Somehow.*

But not even Finch had been able to put this hope into words. It was what they *all* wanted to believe. It was what none of them *could*. Arann had been hit, twice, in the side, twice in the head, by *fists*—and that had almost killed him. They understood that, had Alowan not intervened, it *would* have. Duster had closed with Arann's attacker, pulling him away so that everyone else could make it out.

Duster.

She closed her eyes. She had played the game of maybe before. Three times. For Fisher, whose disappearance was so inexplicable, so unexpected, it seemed—and felt—unreal. It had been easy then. Easy to hope. The confusion had been almost stronger than the dread. But days had passed, and hope had thinned, stretching until its break was inevitable.

She had played the game again, when Lefty disappeared, adding to it the desperation of fear. She had listened for the door, watching Arann and Jay as if they would unravel at any second, and with them, the fabric of the life they'd helped build. She was silent, both times, because there were no words she could add that would have changed the outcome.

But with Lander, she'd played maybe pathetically, because they *knew*. Even without Jay's gift behind them, they knew he would never be coming back. Then? She had worried for Duster. For Duster, who hated worry and loathed fear and spit on signs of concern.

Duster, who had told them to run, wielding the dagger she had sworn she didn't want, and turning her back on anything but the man she had called a demon. Duster, who took risks with her own life when she was in a foul mood.

She hadn't been in a foul mood then. She'd been almost peaceful.

In the silence, Finch lifted her hands over the folds of thick, heavy down, and ran them across the softest sheets she'd ever slept in. Duster would have *crowed* at the size of these rooms and the weight of the silver, the shine of the magestones that were littered throughout the manse. There was *so much here*. Duster who would have told Ellerson to take a hike unless Jewel was standing on her feet, glaring.

No one had mentioned Duster by name. Not when Jay was there. Not after. There was too much guilt, too much shame. She'd told them to run, yes—but she regularly told them to drop dead, and that was on her good days; they never paid attention, then.

This time, they'd run.

They'd run and *because* they'd run, they were here, in the most powerful House on the Isle. They each had beds, and each bed was as tall, as heavy, as finely made as the one Finch now found herself in. They didn't need bedrolls—thank *Kalliaris*, 'cause they didn't have 'em—they had these thick, heavy comforters instead. They didn't need them either; they had real windows made with solid glass, and the wind didn't whistle through the boards. The rooms were warm—there were fire grates here, and the fires were fed heavy wood that burned long and slow.

But the rooms were empty. There was no Teller and no Jay lying on the floor in arm's reach. No *Duster,* her dagger beneath her pillow, or sometimes curled in her sleeping hand. There was no magelight, no steady, soft glow alleviating the worst of night's darkness.

Just Finch, alone.

Oh, she knew the others were safe. But if she got out of bed, if she tripped on the way to a door that seemed impossibly far away and actually opened it, it wouldn't open into Jester's shoulder or arm; she wouldn't have to step over Carver or Angel.

She couldn't sleep, though. It was too strange here, and her throat ached in the silence. So she got up. She made the long walk to the door. She opened it. It probably didn't swell in summer, jamming in the frame; it didn't even creak a warning when she pushed it. It just slid, in unnatural silence, into the hall.

She would have said she had no destination. She would have believed it, while saying it; Finch was never much of a liar, and the only lies she told herself were the ones she believed—or the ones she desperately wanted to believe.

But she wasn't surprised to find herself outside of Jester's door.

Jester was not a person to whom one went for comfort, unless by comfort you mean an awkard joke, or even a good one. She hovered there, her feet sinking into carpet, her hands on the doorknob. The doors here were heavy, but they weren't hard to open. It was the permission she lacked.

Idiot.

She'd never needed permission to wander about her own apartment before. She'd needed caution, of course, because Arann slept in the outer room and you did not want to wake Arann—but she'd often risen, especially on the nights Duster was absent from her spot near Jay on the floor. How was this different?

The answer, of course? *This isn't our home. This isn't our place.*

And on its heels, another answer, one even less pleasant: *We don't have a home anymore.* She took a deep breath to quell panic. It wasn't the first time she'd lost her home, and this second time? No one had sold her.

Duster had saved her the first time. Duster had given her the chance to run, and she'd run to Jay, and to the only home she wanted.

Duster had saved them *all* the second time, because Duster had given them all the same chance. And they'd run to Jay. But this? This wasn't home. This was a place full of people who were so far above the den that even the servants were better dressed, better educated, and better behaved.

They weren't needed here; it was hard to believe that they were even wanted.

She took another breath. Did it matter? In the twenty-fifth, no one had needed them either. They had needed *each other*. She pushed the door open and slid into the room. Like hers, it was huge, and like hers, the walk from the door to anything else made it seem almost empty.

"Hello?"

She froze. After a few seconds of awkward silence, she said, "Jester?"

"Finch?"

She nodded. "You're awake."

"Yeah. Too much food."

She made her way across the room, shuffling her feet; her eyes had mostly accustomed themselves to the darkness, but his room was slightly different. Still, Finch reached the wall and the windows there with only a couple of stubbed toes and no cursing.

His curtains were closed and she struggled with them in the dark, pinning them back to let moonlight, even cold moonlight, add silver and texture to shades of gray. Then she turned to where he sat. He wasn't in bed; he was resting, back against the wall, in the corner of the room farthest from the door. His legs were stretched out before him, his feet turned slightly toward each other; his hands were in his lap.

"I hate rich people," he said, and she almost didn't recognize his voice.

"Why?"

He was silent. She walked across the room, passing the windows one by one, until she was five feet away. There she sat, folding her knees up to her chin and hugging them with both arms as if she were cold.

He didn't answer; she didn't ask again.

Because she suddenly knew what the answer would be, if he could ever put it into words. They had been captives, after all, at the same mansion. Jester had been there longer than Finch, and Jester had had visitors. Not like Lander's. Not like Duster's. But it didn't matter. No one without money had visited that manse. No one.

There was no magelight here, but Jester had never slept in a room with the magelight; he'd slept as far away from Jay's nightmares as he could. He had, she realized, his own.

"It's just us," he said, when the silence had grown too long, too deep. "Just you and me. The others are gone."

She started to tell him that the others were in their rooms, and again, she stopped, wondering why she was so damn tired and so damn thick. Jay had rescued Jester, Duster, Fisher, and Lander from the manse in which they'd been locked in rooms, or chained there. It was the manse to which Finch had been sold, and from which she'd barely managed to break free.

Jester was silent again.

Minutes passed; moonlight continued to shine. There wasn't a cloud in the sky, at least not on this side of the mansion. She glanced up at its bright face; the second moon was almost entirely eclipsed. Hidden. Shadowed.

She had no words to offer him. He had always used words, and when they were absent, physical humor. Where Duster and Jewel raged in the open, others found their own ways to hide. She, like Teller, Lander, and Lefty, had retreated into silence. Jester was the only one who hid behind laughter, when he could force them to dredge it up.

He was silent, now. She wondered if this was like her silence: a way of hiding. A way of avoiding causing—or receiving—either conflict or pain. But when she looked at his face, she saw he hid nothing; the darkness did that, and in the moonlight, now, it wasn't enough of a mask.

She started to rise, aware that for Jester, this silence was akin to what vulnerability would have been for Duster, but even as she gained her feet, he lifted his hands. Not his voice; his lips pursed in brief pain, but he didn't speak.

And yet, he did.

No. Stay. He very seldom signed. They all could, of course—but the den-sign was so basic it was harder to convey humor with the familiar gestures.

She lifted her hands as she once again sat on the carpet. *Stay?*

Stay.

Her hands rested above her lap; Jester's rested just in front of his chest. But they weren't still. They moved, slowly and painstakingly, through the vocabulary created by Lefty and Lander in the corner of their home, in silence. Lander had words for food, water, pain, injury; he had words for silence, for running, for magisterians, for rain. Those were used seldom, and Finch struggled with them herself, remembering them as her fingers shifted, tapping her palm or each other.

There seemed to be no rhyme or reason to Jester's den-sign, not at first. But she realized, as she struggled with gestures, that he was trying to remember the ones they almost never used, because the only two people who would otherwise remember were now gone. So she joined him, and an hour passed, maybe more. When they spoke at all, it was to agree—or disagree—about what different signals meant.

At the end, Jester tilted his face toward the ceiling, took a deep breath, and left his gaze there. His hands spoke.

548   ✦   Michelle West

Fear. Death. Fear. Lost. Den. There was a sign for Jay's den and a sign for everyone else's. He used theirs.

She swallowed. He wasn't looking at her hands, now, but she responded anyway. *Yes. Afraid.*

He continued. *Angry. Lonely.*

She closed her eyes. Opened them. Crept slowly across the carpet, the five-foot separation like miles because of her hesitation. The den did not, as a general rule, touch each other; they pushed, shoved, smacked, but everything was staccato.

But Jester signed. If he heard her, he didn't look down.

Because he didn't, because she didn't have to meet his eyes, because he was still speaking, in silence, his hands moving steadily, she joined him in the corner, and she very carefully put her arms around his neck and the front of his chest.

He didn't startle, didn't look down, and didn't stop, although his hands slowed. *Where. Home.*

She caught both hands in one of hers and he did look down then, but she didn't speak. Instead, she drew back just enough to sign two words. The first: *Home.* The second: *Our den.* She was crying, but she didn't care; she wasn't Duster. She wasn't Jay or Carver or Angel. She wasn't even Jester.

He answered: *Home. Our den.* And then he reached out for her, hugging her as tightly as any of them had ever hugged her.

MICHELLE WEST
The House War

"Fans will be delighted with this return to the vivid and detailed universe of the *Sacred Hunt* and the *Sun Sword* series.... In a richly woven world, and with a cast of characters that range from traumatized street kids to the wealthy heads of highest houses in Averalaan, West pulls no punches as she hooks readers in with her bold and descriptive narrative." —*Quill & Quire*

To Order Call: 1-800-788-6262
www.dawbooks.com

DAW 41

Violette Malan

The Novels of Dhulyn and Parno:

"Believable characters and graceful storytelling."
—*Library Journal*

"Fantasy fans should brace themselves:
the world is about to discover Violette Malan."
—*The Barnes & Noble Review*

THE SLEEPING GOD
978-0-7564-0484-0

THE SOLDIER KING
978-0-7564-0569-4

THE STORM WITCH
978-0-7564-0574-8

and new in trade paperback:

PATH OF THE SUN
978-0-7564-0638-7

To Order Call: 1-800-788-6262
www.dawbooks.com

Sherwood Smith
Inda

"A powerful beginning to a very promising series by a writer who is making her bid to be a major fantasist. By the time I finished, I was so captured by this book that it lingered for days afterward. I had lived inside these characters, inside this world, and I was unwilling to let go of it. That, I think, is the mark of a major work of fiction…you owe it to yourself to read *Inda*." —Orson Scott Card

INDA
978-0-7564-0422-2

THE FOX
978-0-7564-0483-3

KING'S SHIELD
978-0-7564-0500-7

TREASON'S SHORE
978-0-7564-0573-1 (hardcover)
978-0-7564-0634-9
(paperback)

To Order Call: 1-800-788-6262
www.dawbooks.com

DAW 110

Patrick Rothfuss

THE NAME OF THE WIND
The Kingkiller Chronicle: Day One

"It is a rare and great pleasure to come on somebody writing not only with the kind of accuracy of language that seems to me absolutely essential to fantasy-making, but with real music in the words as well.... Oh, joy!" —Ursula K. Le Guin

"Amazon.com's Best of the Year...So Far Pick for 2007: Full of music, magic, love, and loss, Patrick Rothfuss's vivid and engaging debut fantasy knocked our socks off." —Amazon.com

"One of the best stories told in any medium in a decade. Shelve it beside *The Lord of the Rings* ...and look forward to the day when it's mentioned in the same breath, perhaps as first among equals." —*The Onion*

"[Rothfuss is] the great new fantasy writer we've been waiting for, and this is an astonishing book." —Orson Scott Card

ISBN: 978-0-7564-0474-1

To Order Call: 1-800-788-6262
www.dawbooks.com